ADVANCE PRAISE

In *The Last Rancher*, a stunning new novel by Robert Rebein, an emergency forces Leroy and Caroline Wagner's grown children home to the Bar W Ranch. Crises converge on Dodge City: Annie stalls on her PhD, Michael interrupts his law practice, and Jimmy pillages his parents' medicine cabinet. In memory lives the looming specter of Wade, son and brother who died too young. The novel intimately follows a jarring collision of selves—not to mention cars, motorbikes, and a nun. In this ranching community, lives are intertwined like barbed wire, like tree roots that run under fences and buckle the ground, unearthing secrets into the blinding prairie light. I loved this book. A family drama with humor and heart, *The Last Rancher* gives you the prized shotgun seat and guns the gas. You'd be wise to buckle up.

—Sarah Layden, *Imagine Your Life Like This* and *Trip Through Your Wires*

Dodge City, Kansas, has found its bard. His name is Robert Rebein, and his debut novel, *The Last Rancher*, showcases an assured new voice of the contemporary American West. Prepare to be lassoed in an unforgettable and utterly satisfying family saga."

—Will Allison, *What You Have Left* and *A Long Drive Home*

Love and horses, whiskey and weed, land and money: *The Last Rancher* has it all. Robert Rebein has written a big-hearted literary page-turner to rival the family sagas of Richard Russo, Richard Ford, and John Irving.

—Kyle Minor, *Praying Drunk* and *How to Disappear and Why*

With *The Last Rancher*, Robert Rebein has crafted a story as timeless as storytelling itself—a patriarch in decline, a family marked by loss. By rooting these elements firmly in the Dodge City of today, though, Rebein has created a narrative unique to himself and the place. Reading *The Last Rancher*, I came to feel that I know these people in some elemental way and, just as importantly, know what their land means to them.

—Hozy Rossi, *Appointment with Il Duce*

In *The Last Rancher*, Robert Rebein's characters are so real that I would swear I know them. He seamlessly weaves together past and present to cover decades of a Kansas family broken by tragedy. I was hooked from the first page to the last.

—Cheryl Unruh, *Gravedigger's Daughter: Vignettes from a Small Kansas Town* and *Flyover People: Life on the Ground in a Rectangular State*

THE LAST RANCHER

ROBERT REBEIN

Meadowlark Press, LLC
PO BOX 333, Emporia, KS 66801
meadowlarkbookstore.com

The Last Rancher

www.robertrebein.com

Cover photo: Alyssa Chase
Cover image enhancement: Julie Taylor Reed
Cover & Interior Design: TRMS/Meadowlark Press

Ordering Information: Special discounts are available on quantity purchases by corporations, associations, and others. For details, contact the publisher at info@meadowlark-books.com.

FICTION / Westerns (contemporary)
FICTION / Small Town & Rural
FICTION / Family Life

ISBN: Paperback—978-1-956578-59-1
Hardcover—978-1-956578-63-8
Ebook—978-1-956578-60-7
Audio—978-1-956578-61-4

Library of Congress Control Number: 2024937062

To the memory of my parents,
William and Patricia Rebein,

and

to Ria and Jake,

There are two gifts
we should give our children:
One is roots, and the other is wings.
—*Goethe*

Also by Robert Rebein

Headlights on the Prairie: Essays on Home

Dragging Wyatt Earp: A Personal History of Dodge City

Hicks, Tribes, & Dirty Realists:
American Fiction after Postmodernism

THE LAST RANCHER

THE BAR W RANCH

Annie Wagner always felt a certain ambivalence about the Bar W, her family's cattle ranch on Sawlog Creek in far southwestern Kansas. Ambivalence being, for Annie, one of the many five-dollar words she loved and learned to wield as a cowboy wields his rope: words like ubiquitous, juxtaposition, querulous, cacophony. On one hand, the ranch, with its spring-fed creeks and chalky bluffs and beautiful, rolling hills, its slow-grazing cattle and fast horses and hawks circling overhead on banks of invisible air, represented exactly who she was and where she belonged in the world. On the other hand, though, the Bar W could be a dangerous, isolating place, a prison designed to contain and perhaps to kill her, as she had seen it kill her brother Wade and very nearly kill her mother.

She couldn't remember a time when the ranch's cattle brand—a W capped with a short bar—had not figured prominently in her outer and inner worlds. On the ranch itself, of course, the brand was indeed ubiquitous: burned high into the left hip of every cow, calf, and bull on the place; adorning gates and signs of every sort, including the entrances to all the pastures and wheat fields and the doors of all the pickups, tractors, grain trucks, loaders, balers, and livestock trailers; emblazoned alike on saddles and bridles, hats and coffee cups, belt buckles and spurs. A magnetic stencil and a can of spray paint accomplished what welding rod and branding iron could not, each repetition telling the twin tales of ownership and belonging, belonging and ownership.

As a small child, Annie thought the brand looked like a pair of fangs protruding from a thin upper lip, scary but also comforting, the way certain cartoons can be both of those things. As she grew older, the brand came to look like a mountain range blocked by clouds; a pair of "awful hanging breasts" (to quote Elizabeth Bishop, whose work Annie discovered at thirteen, sneaking into her mother's room to steal *The Complete Poems*); a couple of black crutches leaned against a white wall (in those days, her father still ran Charolais cattle rather than the Angus he later came to favor), the juxtaposition of dark against a backdrop of white adding an additional layer of meaning to the symbol. She doodled the brand on napkins, drew it in magic marker across the covers of notebooks and diaries. Once, when she was sixteen and competing in nearby rodeos for the dubious crown of Miss Teen Rodeo, she even considered getting the brand inked into the flesh of her left shoulder, just above her heart, the way she'd seen older contestants do with their families' brands. But then she grew older still, and the utilitarian nature of the symbol stopped her cold. She was nobody's head of livestock; she belonged nowhere and to no one.

All this got worse after Wade died. Hearing her father explain to a stranger the two ways a cattle brand could be read—from left to right, like English, or from top to bottom, like "one of them Oriental languages"—she found herself wondering if her Wagner ancestors hadn't chosen the less apt configuration. After all, when read from left to right rather than top to bottom, a single bar followed by a W was quite clear in saying minus Wade, or the W ranch minus its natural heir, or the Wagner family minus everything that had once made them whole.

One afternoon, only weeks before he was lost to them forever, Annie had asked Wade what the brand looked like to him. But he was in one of his moods, not himself at all, and had answered, querulously, "Hell, *I* don't know. Like half a VW, I guess." Her brother Michael, three years younger than Wade and, like her, in awe of him, had had a good laugh at that. But when Annie pushed Michael, demanding that he provide an interpretation of his own rather than relying on Wade's, all he would offer was, "It means exactly what it says. Jesus! Give it a rest, why don't you." Irritated, Annie had run into the house to put the question to her mother, who sometimes welcomed such queries. But on this day her mother barely looked up from the pie crust she was rolling. "Ask your father when he gets home," she said, distracted. "He knows all about that stuff."

And so, past ten o'clock, when her father and older brothers quit loading hay bales and rolled up to the house amid a cacophony of barking dogs and buzzing cicadas, Annie waited until they'd taken their seats at the dining room table and her mother had put a plate of warmed-over Salisbury steak and mashed potatoes before each of them, then asked her father in the most serious tone she could muster, "Dad, what do *you* think the Bar W brand looks like? What does it *remind* you of?"

Her father paused, turning the question over in his mind, the only person in the family other than herself who had taken it seriously, then said in a voice worn thin by work, "Well, your great grandpa used to say it looked like a two-legged table. Which is kind of stupid, when you think about it." He took a bite of steak, chewing the food a long time before washing it down with a long drink of milk. "On days like today, though, I look at it and see a man condemned to hold up the sky with nothing but his bare hands and the top of his head."

It would be many years before Annie grew to be book smart enough to register the allusion to Atlas, and even then, she couldn't be sure her father had intended it. He'd never been that kind of man.

"You know what I think?" she asked, her eyes moving from one member of her family to the next, challenging them each in turn.

"What's that, dear one?" her mother said.

"I think it looks like somebody *reaching* for the sky. Not holding, *reaching*."

"Is that so?" her mother said, already clearing plates from the table. "Well, honey, you hang onto that idea, you hear? No matter what happens to you in this life, don't you ever let it go."

ONE

Leroy Wagner backed his flatbed Dodge out of the driveway of his house in town and headed for his ranch on Sawlog Creek, fourteen miles away. It was a little after six, a warm morning without clouds, and the wind had begun to pick up out of the southwest, causing the yellowing wheat in the fields north of the hospital to wave at him in the semi-darkness with what felt like insidious intent. The harvest was approaching fast, and Leroy was not close to being ready. The teeth on his aging John Deere 9500 combine were hopelessly dull; the cabover Freightliner he'd rebuilt over the winter lacked a hoist; the PTO shaft on the Kinze needed new U-joints; and so on and so forth, world without end, amen.

Adding to his feeling of impending disaster, Leroy's hired man of five years, DW, had chosen the previous weekend to rekindle his love affair with whiskey. There was no telling what shape the man would be in when Leroy went to roust him from bed, but if the previous two mornings were any indication, vomit and dried blood would surely play a part.

It got worse. Unbeknownst to anyone but himself and his banker—or so he hoped—Leroy found himself smack in the middle of the worst financial crisis he'd suffered in four decades of ranching and dryland wheat farming. Every decision he'd made over the last year and a half—whether to sell calves or hold them, plant wheat or pray for rain, borrow money to buy more land or let another fool beat him to the winning bid—had ended up biting him in the ass. It was still possible, in theory, that a bumper crop of winter wheat, something in the range of, say, fifty or fifty-five bushels to the acre, could prevent his day of reckoning from coming. But that was like holding out hope for a winning ticket in the Kansas Lottery. Wasn't gonna happen. Not in Ford County. Not in that dry, hot summer of cicadas.

As if all this weren't enough, in the wee hours of the morning he'd had the dream again. The men in black were lowering Wade's coffin into the cold, dark prairie, when Leroy, alone among the mourners, realized the boy was still breathing. He tried to yell at the funeral home workers to shut down their infernal lowering machine, but the wind caught his voice and hurled it into the distant trees. He tried to bull his way to the grave the way he'd once bulled his way through a line of scrimmage, but there was something wrong with his legs. He had to stand by helplessly as members of his family shoveled dirt on top of the plain pine box. First Leroy's wife, Caroline, tossed a shovelful, followed by Wade's younger brother, Michael, followed by his baby sister, Annie, who looked hardly bigger than the spade she wielded. Even Leroy's youngest boy, Jimmy, who wasn't even *born* at the time, started in with big, sweeping scoops, black dirt flying cartoonlike through the air in one continuous stream.

"Stop!" Leroy shouted between gusts of wind. "Put that goddamn shovel down!"

But Jimmy just smiled, ignoring him, and the dirt continued to fly.

Ordinarily, at this point in the dream, Leroy would wake in a cold sweat. But somewhere along the line, the dream had acquired an additional gear wherein the funeral home director, a big guy with slicked-back blond hair and wraparound sunglasses, reached into his suit pocket and unscrolled a long sheet of paper with the words PAST DUE stamped across the top in red ink.

"What's that?" Leroy asked.

"The bill for all this. It's time to pay up."

"But I need more time," Leroy said, as the wind gusted powerfully, ripping the graveside tent from its moorings and sending it cartwheeling through the air.

But the worst part came a moment later, when Leroy's eyes flew open in the darkness of his house in town, and he was forced to realize, yet again, that Wade really was dead. Had been for going on twenty years.

"What is it?" Caroline had whispered. "Did you have that nightmare again?"

He nodded and told her about the addition of the funeral home director and his six-foot-long unpaid bill.

"I think I know what that's about," she said.

His pulse quickened. "You do?"

"Yes, it's about Jimmy. Remember? We were arguing about him last night before we went to bed. I tell you, Leroy, I've got this bad feeling in my stomach. Something's going on with him. I just know it."

He let out a breath he didn't know he'd been holding. Jimmy was their youngest, a tattooed, pot-smoking high school dropout Leroy had all but given up trying to understand.

"I don't think that's it," he said, relieved she hadn't guessed his secret.

Turning right on Garnett Road, which part of him still thought of as the Correction Line, because that's what his grandfather had called it, Leroy lowered the truck's visor against the first rays of the rising sun. The Bar W was four thousand acres of grass, alfalfa, and summer-fallow wheat located at the convergence of Duck and Sawlog Creeks, on the western edge of a triangle of fertile land formed by the towns of Dodge City to the south and west, Jetmore to the north, and Spearville to the south and east. Leroy's grandfather, Ludwig Wagner, a welder by trade, had bought the first thousand acres during the worst days of the Dust Bowl, when no one in his right mind was buying land, and in the decades that followed, the Sawlog Wagners earned a reputation for stubbornness and grit, as well as a few less fortunate traits like episodic depression and heavy drinking. In good times, they hoarded money and bought more land. In bad times, they hunkered down and held onto what they had, even if that meant selling equipment or cows or disowning offspring who failed to share in their tightfisted ways. Thus it happened, when Leroy's father died at the age of forty-five of what was politely called liver cancer, Leroy's vagabond older brother Bob, who'd run off to join the hippies in California years before, was summarily passed over, and the Bar W—grass, cows, burden, and all—fell directly to Leroy.

In his early days of running the ranch, he'd often wondered if he was cut out for the life. The operational side of things—feeding, fixing fence, preg-checking mother cows—bored him to tears, and his tendency was to neglect it, focusing instead on big, forward-looking projects like putting up machine sheds or building corrals out of salvaged irrigation pipe. But then God provided a potential answer to these problems in the form of Leroy's firstborn son, Wade. Unlike Leroy, Wade loved to put up hay and fix fence and move irrigation pipe and sort and doctor cattle from the back of a horse. Everything of a physical nature came so easily to Wade, whether it was throwing a tight spiral far downfield or foot-sweeping another wrestler straight to his back. Schoolwork, though, was another matter. From the age of twelve onward, Wade struggled to concentrate and was prone to mysterious headaches, taking hours to complete assignments that would've taken his younger brother, Michael, five or ten minutes, max.

Of course, he and Caroline had taken the boy to doctors, both in Dodge City and three hours away in Wichita. There was talk of "fugue states," even epilepsy, but nothing was ever definitively diagnosed. In spite of this uncertainty, by the time Wade reached high school, a plan of sorts had been put into place, in Leroy's mind if nowhere else. They'd get Wade the help he needed to make it through high school and maybe a year or two at the community college, where he had a standing offer of a football scholarship. After that, he'd partner with Leroy on the ranch, Leroy focusing on the long-range stuff, Wade on all the things he excelled at without ever seeming to try.

It never happened.

A quarter of a mile down Garnett, just when he'd got the diesel pickup out of third gear, Leroy glanced out his driver's side window and caught sight of his nemesis Byron Branch slithering through the grass of his half-acre lawn like the snake he was, pulling a black garden hose behind him. What was the fool *doing* out there, watering tomatoes? Leroy could remember when the entire subdivision, Rolling Hills Estates, had been a bindweed-choked wheat field. Which, though not a pretty sight by any means, was a far better fate than being hacked into one- and two-acre lots by the likes of Byron Branch. What was it about witnessing Branch pull the black hose through the dew-covered grass that so unnerved him?

Then it hit him squarely in the face: the dream. Of course. Why hadn't he realized it before? Byron Branch was the sumbitch in the coal-black suit holding the unpaid bill.

In the eighth of a mile it took him to bring the Dodge to a halt in the middle of the patched blacktop, Leroy considered the wisdom of what he was about to do, the pros and cons of action versus inaction, a potentially costly advance versus a safer retreat. But this was mostly a mental exercise. He couldn't have stopped what happened next if he'd wanted to.

He'd been hearing stories about the blond Texan almost from the day the man arrived in Dodge City and started buying up the place with a ferocity nobody in Ford or Hodgeman Counties had ever witnessed before. First it was the truck wash behind the Flying J on East Wyatt Earp, then the Flying J itself, then the motel across Wyatt Earp (upon which he bestowed the ridiculous name of Branch Inn & Suites), then a commercial trash service headquartered on Trail Street, so that trucks with the words BYRON BRANCH ENTERPRISES emblazoned on their sides could be seen raising dust from Dodge City to Garden City and beyond. In this way, the extent of Branch's holdings spread like an oil spill until it reached the valley of the Sawlog, where he began to buy up one piece of ground after another from their absentee owners without Leroy or anyone else in the neighborhood ever knowing the land had come up for sale. But the final straw, at least in Leroy's eyes, came when the man flat-out *stole* a half section of land, including a quarter of grass Leroy had been renting for going on twenty years, in a deal so wrapped in shadow that Leroy didn't even realize it had happened until a crew out of Oklahoma showed up and started building an eight-foot-high fence on his eastern property line. Shocked, he drove out to ask the crew of men raising the fence what in the hell they thought they were doing.

"We got a contract to fence this whole property," the foreman said.

"That's not possible," Leroy said. "This land belongs to Chester and Fanny Stewart, and I can tell you right now, they don't have the money to build anything like this here."

The foreman dug a clipboard out of the cab of his truck. "All I know is that the job was ordered by someone named Byron Branch, and Mr. Branch paid cash."

Thinking there had to be some kind of mistake, Leroy drove to the Flying J to confront Branch in the office he kept in the back of the truck stop. Branch kept him waiting for twenty minutes before emerging from the office in khaki slacks and a golf shirt, one of those ugly Greg Norman deals with a shark logo on the front.

"What can I do you for?" he asked in his Texas drawl.

"Well, for starters, you can explain why there's an eight-foot-high fence going up next to my ranch," Leroy said.

"So you've seen where I'm putting in my game farm, huh?" Branch said. "What do you think of that fence? Pretty slick, huh?"

"That's one word for it," Leroy said.

In the brief conversation that followed, Branch claimed that his acquisition of the Stewart land had been "done by the book," never mind that it was Branch, and not the Farm Credit or some other reputable outfit, who'd loaned Chester Stewart the money to buy out his sister Alice in Colorado when everyone knew that Chester could barely afford to keep himself and his invalid wife in groceries. But it seemed that stealing the Stewarts' land was just the beginning of what the Texan was capable of in terms of outrage, because as Leroy stood there shaking his head, Branch went a step further and offered—or threatened, rather—to buy Leroy's place, too: land, cattle, equipment, and homeplace. "I heard you've been having some cash flow problems or whatever you want to call it," he said, blue eyes alight in his pudgy face like the eyes of a Siberian Husky. "When you're ready to sell, just give me a call and name your price. That little spread of yours fits my plans like a halter top on a Highland Park divorcée."

"Not interested," Leroy managed to get out through clenched teeth.

He left the Flying J in a rage—*Little spread! Halter top!*—and drove straight to the offices of his longtime attorney, Harold Krebs.

"Get ready, Harold. We're gonna sue Byron Branch so hard he's gonna wish he never heard of Dodge City, Kansas."

"For what?" Krebs asked. "Being an asshole from Texas who wears funny shirts? I don't think there's a law against that."

"Well, there's one against *theft*, ain't there?" Leroy shouted. He went on to explain what he knew about the whole nefarious deal, concluding with an extended riff on how the early residents of Ford County had dealt with men like Byron Branch. "They strung 'em up from a tree in Horse Thief Canyon, Harold. And that's exactly what Branch deserves, too."

"Okay, calm down," Krebs had said with a laugh. "We'll talk to the Stewarts and get their side of the story, maybe file a suit on their behalf. Just promise me there won't be any more talk about hanging people. Good Gawd Almighty!"

Now, weeks later, with the lawsuit about to come to trial, Branch had encroached even further—into Leroy's dreams. PAST DUE? Is that what the paper in the dream had said? Well, Leroy would show the sumbitch PAST DUE.

He backed the Dodge up Garnett Road until he came to Branch's long driveway. By the time he had pulled onto the concrete pad in front of the three-car garage, the Texan was making his way around the side of the house, pulling the black hose behind him. He was barefoot and shirtless, the bottoms of his silk pajamas wet at the ankles. Spotting Leroy, a smile crept into his thick white face.

"Well, if it isn't my good friend Leroy Wagner," Branch said, dropping the hose in the grass and crossing the driveway in his bare feet. "I didn't think I'd see you until our court date. What are we, three weeks out? Or is it four?"

Leroy switched off the Dodge's engine but didn't bother taking his foot off the clutch. "I thought I'd give you one last chance, Byron."

"Ha! At what? Buying your spread? You heard what I said. Name your price."

"No, at giving the Stewarts their land back. Let them sell the sister's half at auction, fair and square, the way it should've been done in the first place."

"Yeah, right," Branch said. "And why would I do that? So *you* can get your filthy hands on it?"

The blood in Leroy's face began to throb. He could feel it from his temples all the way down to his chin. A storm was building inside of him, and it was not just Branch and his thieving ways that was stirring it up. It was everything—the coming wheat harvest upon which so much depended, the hired-man troubles that had started shortly after Wade's death and had never abated in all the years since, the looming financial reckoning that even Branch, apparently, had gotten wind of. He started the pickup and tucked the shifter into reverse.

"Last chance," he said.

"Sheeeee-it," Branch began, bringing his face so far into Leroy's window that he got a whiff of the man's Aqua Velva. "Let me tell you what you can do with your last—"

At this, Leroy popped the clutch and the Ram leapt backward in the driveway, its outsized mirror catching Branch in the side of the face and spinning him backwards into a line of shrubs beside the concrete drive. Leroy watched through the truck's dirty windshield as Branch regained his feet and shook a meaty fist at him.

Well, it's not like I didn't warn the sumbitch, he thought with a low chuckle.

He put the truck in gear and goosed it out of Branch's second driveway onto 112 Road and rolled up to the stop sign at Garnett with his foot riding the clutch. By then, the sun had risen above the trees and was blazing directly out of the east. He looked right and then left, where the road dipped down and out of view, fumbling for the truck's visor as the sun hit the bug-splattered windshield. He didn't even see the landscaping rig bearing down on him from the east until it was too late. His last thought before the truck T-boned him at thirty miles an hour was, *God, no. Not with all the shit I got to get done today.*

Then everything went black.

TWO

The Chef Dan's Bistro at Tulsa International Airport was its own special kind of hell, but Michael Wagner inhabited it with the grace under pressure of someone who'd been flying business class out of minor Midwestern airports two or three times a week for the better part of a decade. Although his early bird flight to Kansas City didn't leave for another hour and he was still waiting for the breakfast special he'd ordered to be delivered to his table, he'd already paid his tab and tipped his server. If he'd suddenly realized that he'd gotten the time wrong, and his flight was boarding now instead of twenty minutes from now, all he'd have to do was close his laptop, grab his to-go Americano and roll the hell out of there.

His work in Tulsa had wrapped up the night before, and he was looking forward to using the flight time to KC to work his way through the files of a dozen cases that were crying out for his attention. For now, though, while he still had access to the airport's Wi-Fi, he focused on the fifty or so unread emails inhabiting his inbox, especially the five or six from Russ Frederick, his mentor at the Kansas City offices of Curtis, Frederick, and Lyles.

On the surface, Russ was a fat, folksy guy from southwestern Missouri, the sort of man who hunted and fished instead of playing golf and who knew precisely in what company (or not) to break out his repertoire of off-color jokes. But beneath the good-old-boy surface beat the heart of a man who cared about one thing and one thing only—money. Which was why, when Michael began making noises about leaving behind their brand of backroom, war-of-attrition litigation to try his hand at actual, go-to-trial cases, Russ had laughed in his face.

"Why you wanna go playing Perry Mason for? We got hired guns for that stuff."

"I know," Michael said. "It's just something I've been itching to do."

"Well, find another itch to scratch. You'll have plenty of money for it after you get them Tulsa boys to come to heel."

"Sure," Michael said. "I get it, Russ."

But he didn't get it. In fact, he'd all but made up his mind to quit the firm and strike out on his own. The only thing holding him back was timing. That and his wife, Vanessa, who, predictably, was not on board with the idea. He'd brought it up most recently the previous Fourth of July, while they were getting ready to go out on a cigar boat at Lake of the Ozarks with some friends from law school, and Vanessa's response had been immediate and negative.

"Quit the firm? *Now*? But there's all the work we're getting done on the house. And we talked about sending Sam to Pembroke Hill next year, remember?"

Vanessa had grown up poor in Hammond, Indiana, the daughter of a Mexican mother and a deadbeat Italian American father; part of her had never recovered from the trauma stemming from her father's high-profile bankruptcy (before drinking and gambling the family into poverty, he'd owned a Cadillac dealership in the suburbs of Chicago) and her parents' subsequent divorce.

"Of course I remember," Michael shot back. "But you've got to listen to me. If I stay at the firm much longer, I'm going to suffocate. I'm not kidding. It's like every time I try to come up for air, Russ or one of the other partners is right there to stuff my mouth and nose with money."

"I can think of worse things!" Vanessa joked.

"I'm serious!"

"I know you are, honey," she said, crossing the carpeted floor in her black two-piece swimsuit and kissing him softly on the mouth. "But there'll be plenty of time to explore your options as an attorney after the boys are out of school, right?"

Undone by the kiss, Michael had taken "out of school" to mean "next summer," when, as the conversation continued, he realized Vanessa had actually meant something more like "out of college." Which would be, what, *fifteen years* from now, when he'd be pushing fifty and any chance of changing up his legal game would be long gone.

"Thanks for being so understanding," he'd said, storming out of the room.

Later that night, they'd had steamy make-up sex, but that didn't mean he'd forgotten about the core of their disagreement. On the contrary, it was all he seemed to think about anymore.

He continued to hack at the forest of emails through the first and second boarding calls before joining the line of stragglers at the gate. He had almost made it to the door of the aircraft when the phone in his left breast pocket—his personal rather than business line—began to buzz. He shouldered his computer bag and fished the phone out. It was his mother calling, which was strange. She never called in the middle of a workday, having been trained not to do so, he supposed, by his workaholic father.

He stepped out of line. "Hello? Mom?"

"Michael! Thank God you picked up!"

"Of course I picked up. What's going on?"

The "wreck," as she called it, had taken place on a busy paved road on his father's way to the ranch. Luckily, the other driver was uninjured (he'd have to confirm that). As for his father, it had required the Jaws of Life just to rescue him from the wreckage.

"Where's he at now?" he asked.

"The hospital. I'm on my way there now."

By then, Michael was the only passenger waiting to board, and the flight attendant was beckoning him with aggressive waves of her hand. He pointed at the phone and started up the gangway in the opposite direction.

"Hey!" the flight attendant called after him. "We're getting ready to close the door!"

He raised his hand above his head and kept on walking. "I'm in Tulsa, but I'll be there as soon as I can. What about Annie and Jimmy? Do they know what's going on?"

"No. You're the first one I called."

"Where are you now?"

"Five minutes from Western Plains."

"Okay. Just get there and see what you can find out. I'll take care of calling them." His mind was clicking now, thinking two and three moves ahead. "What about Dad's hired guy? Have you got his number? Wait a minute. It's DW, right? I've got it right here. I'll call you back as soon as I can book a flight or rent a car. How's that?"

"Thank you," his mother said. "I knew I could count on you."

"Of course. Drive safe and I'll see you soon."

As he expected, there were no direct flights from Tulsa to Dodge City, only ones routed through Denver or Dallas. He started toward the rental car desk at the far end of the terminal. As he walked, he rehearsed the order and content of the half dozen calls he needed to make. The first would have to be to

Russ Frederick. Or, better yet, Russ's secretary. Yes, that was the way to handle Russ. After that? His father's hired guy. The wheat harvest could not be far off, and somebody had to take charge. After that, Vanessa. They had plans for that evening, a fundraiser on the Plaza or something like that. Then Annie and Jimmy.

It was in moments like this, moments that called on him to perform the role of the oldest and most reliable son, that Michael missed his dead brother the most. It was not that Wade would have known what to do or say better than he did, because, let's face it, even by the age of fourteen, Michael had already passed Wade by in that regard. No, it was just the old chain of command, the memory of what it had been like to have someone older and more experienced who paved the way in life, as Wade had done so brilliantly when they were young. But now Michael was the older brother, and poor Wade was forever frozen in time, like a butterfly preserved in amber. Forever young, yes. But also forever dead.

THREE

A dog was barking somewhere in the vicinity of Annie Wagner's second-floor studio in Buffalo, New York. The low, rasping sound of it entered her consciousness slowly, a far-away irritant that shifted the landscape of her dreams without fully waking her.

That's not Lola, Annie thought, rolling over and covering her face with a pillow to block out the late morning sun streaming in through the apartment's batik curtains. Lola, a beagle/blue heeler mix she'd kidnapped from her family's cattle ranch in Kansas and brought to New York in a moment of weakness, had a high-pitched, almost shrill bark, whereas the dog outside sounded more like a Rottweiler or a Lab.

Oh, give me a home where the blue heelers roam and the deer and the rattlesnakes play, where seldom is heard an encouraging word, and the skies are not— Man oh man, did she have to pee. Her bladder, tiny in the best of circumstances, was gonna burst and soak the floor with the darkest yellow pee in the world if she didn't get to the bathroom soon. And yet, she still didn't move or make a sound, but simply licked her dry lips and kept her eyes tightly closed, consciously matching the rhythm of her breathing with the throbbing in her renegade brain. The night before had been . . . how had Joyce put it in the quote that opens *The Lost Weekend*? A festival of riot? No. Not a festival, a *spell*. A spell of riot. *The barometer of her emotional nature had been set for a spell of riot.*

She held out for as long as she could, then lifted the pillow from her face and saw Jeremiah sleeping soundly on the floor beside her, his black hair and beard juxtaposing strongly with the white pillow he'd pulled from the daybed the night before along with its twin mattress and sheets. The sight of him sleeping so peacefully, his handsome face unmarred by the anxious twitching she imagined her own face had displayed in the moment before she woke, made her rush to the studio's tiny bathroom, where she vomited and then dry heaved into the toilet for five minutes before kneeling at the open bowl with her forehead resting on its porcelain rim.

The events of the day before were coming back to her in all their riotous force. The fruitless search for Lola, who'd gone missing amid a terrible clap of thunder thirty-six hours before. The humiliating meeting with Dr. Hilman, the seventy-year-old director of her stalled dissertation on "Thomas Hardy's 'Fallen' Rebel Women," who'd observed with a cruelty she'd not seen from him before that women her age (she'd just turned twenty-nine) really ought to "think long and hard about a different career" if they were "the sort to procrastinate" (she was the queen of procrastination) or experienced long periods of writer's block (ditto). "After all," he'd concluded in his geriatric way, "the clock is ticking, whether you've noticed it or not." Finally, following hard on the heels of this, the fateful decision to join a crowd of her grad school cronies for "a drink or two" (yeah, right) at Founding Fathers, their favorite Allentown watering hole.

Okay, but how did Jeremiah get mixed up in all that? she wondered as her throbbing brain allowed more and more of the previous night's wreckage to float to the surface. It had been after midnight, and she had been, what, four or five tequila shots in? Her phone—long the cause of so many of her problems—began to buzz with texts from a certain handsome man she'd promised herself she'd never, ever see again.

The smoke has cleared unexpectedly
Wanna get a drink? Or something?
I miss our #notorious rapport

Smoke was code for Jeremiah's wife, Emily, a nice if tragically unhip person who had followed Jeremiah to Buffalo to work as a teller at a bank while he pursued his doctorate in UB's ultra-hip poetics program. The two of them were high school sweethearts, their small Idaho town's version of Jack and Diane, married in what amounted to a shotgun wedding toward the end of their senior year after Emily got pregnant with a mini-me Jeremiah, now ten, whom Annie had thankfully never met. Their #notorious rapport, as Jeremiah had styled it in a poem he published in an obscure online literary journal, developed over the course of his first and her third year in the program, after Annie had agreed, at clueless Emily's suggestion, to give Jeremiah rides to and from campus in her beat-to-hell, LS-swapped Porsche 996. This so that Emily could have their Subaru to drop JJ at school on her way to her job in Orchard Park.

Annie had known right away the situation was trouble. First of all, there was the 996 itself, which, in spite of its 198,000 miles and mismatched body panels and fried-egg headlights, possessed a certain raffish charm that was not lost on Jeremiah, who immediately dubbed the car "Frankenporsche"—a name that stuck even as Annie steadfastly refused to let him drive it. Then there was Jeremiah himself, who, with his shoulder-length black hair, lumberjack's beard, and eyes of speckled blue, was without question the most handsome man Annie had ever sat a mere gear shifter away from in all her years on this earth. At stoplights in the city, especially when they drove with the car's top down, women and men alike would openly gawk at him. He just smiled and pretended not to notice. Or maybe he really didn't notice, being too wrapped up in whatever it was they were talking about at the time. Because, like her, Jeremiah could talk for hours and hours, spinning one yarn after another about what it was like to grow up in a family of anti-government loggers in the mountains of western Idaho. (*Remember Y2K? Well, my stepdad stockpiled so many boxes of granola bars, it took us ten years to eat our way through them. To this day, we don't even call them granola bars in my family. We call them Y2Ks.*) But he was just as comfortable listening to and riffing on her tales of growing up in a grief-shattered family on the plains of western Kansas (*Okay, so let me see if I have this straight: your family owns this beautiful cattle ranch in far western Kansas—the Bar W, right?—and, by the way, what a name, right? The metaphorical possibilities and all that—only ever since the heir apparent —what was his name? Clint? Cody? No, Wade, that's right—ever since Wade dropped dead at the tender age of eighteen, your mom insists you live—where was it? On a golf course, that's right! Perfect! Okay, okay, keep going*). The headlong conversation would start up as soon as he'd tossed his book bag into the tiny back seat of the 996 and wouldn't stop until they'd gained the fifth floor of Clemens Hall, where they both had offices. Then, six or seven hours later, when they were done teaching or attending grad seminars, their #notorious rapport would start up all over again right where it had left off, the only awkward moments coming when Annie pulled up in front of Jeremiah's rented house on West Ferry, where the outgoing, handsome, lumberjack-poet would morph into a deeply depressed married person barely able to open his own door to get out. Annie couldn't help it—her heart went out to him. In a big, big way. What was it her pious-to-a-fault, Catholic-convert of a mother had said about an unhappily married neighbor lady, back in the days when they still lived on the Sawlog? "We all make our own beds in this life, but for goodness' sake, nobody should have to live like *that*."

A single thump came from outside the door to the tiny bathroom. Jeremiah waking up? Annie raised her head from the rim of the toilet and listened carefully, the way a horse raises its head and listens for sounds of danger carried on the wind. But no more thumps came, and she lowered her head and closed her eyes again.

Their notorious rapport remained just that and nothing more until the beginning of Jeremiah's second semester in the program, when clueless Emily headed out of town to visit her aging parents in Idaho, taking JJ with her. Up to this point, Annie and Jeremiah had crossed no line more serious than holding hands on the drive out to Amherst or making out a few times in her office in Clemens Hall. But now the full riot was on, and they spent the entire week Emily was out of town in Annie's studio on Park Street, drinking wine and smoking Marlboro Lights (they'd both quit years before but decided they were entitled to a lapse) and screwing their brains out. According to Jeremiah, those seven days represented the happiest he'd felt in at least ten years, maybe ever, and Annie wasn't far behind him in that assessment.

Still, they were both wracked with guilt from their respective religious traditions (his Mennonite, hers German Catholic), and after Emily and JJ returned from Idaho, they agreed to be more vigilant, to keep the riot of their rapport from breaking out once more. They'd manage to be good for a couple of weeks, but then something would happen—she'd get lonely, or he and Emily would have one of their frequent spats—and they'd suffer a collective relapse.

"We've got to be *stronger*, show some commitment to the cause," he said after one particularly riotous night.

"What, you mean like in AA?" she joked.

"Exactly!" He laughed. "Annie Anonymous!"

"And for me, what, Jeremiah Anonymous? JA?"

"Not as poetic, but yes. JA. Why the hell not?"

The night before, at Founding Fathers, when he'd started his campaign of text messages (*The smoke has cleared. Wanna get a drink? Or something?*) she'd been close to earning her one-month medallion in JA. *So much for that*, she thought now, struggling to her feet and splashing her face with cold water from the bathroom's tiny sink.

As the night wore on, and Annie's tequila count rose to six and then to seven, Jeremiah had ramped up his texting campaign (*I have to see you. Don't make me beg. Okay, I'm begging. #nr!*) until finally she powered her phone all the way down, so as not to be tempted. Before the night was over, however, he guessed where she was and made a dramatic appearance at Founding Fathers, walking straight up to the table where she sat and holding out his hand like a dancer at a ball beckoning a lady to stand and take a turn across the floor with him. Instead, she had risen from her chair—this part remained wrapped in fog, but she was pretty sure it had happened—and had taken a swing at his handsome face in front of God and everyone. He'd caught her fist easily in his lumberjack hand and pulled her into a tight hug.

"What's going on?" he'd whispered. "What's wrong?"

"It's Lola," she'd said, sobbing. "She ran off, and it's all my fault, and I'm never, ever going to find her again."

"Don't worry," he whispered. "We'll find her. I'll help."

"Really?"

"Yes. We'll visit every animal shelter in this town. Drive down every street."

"You promise?"

"Yes," he whispered. "I promise."

Now, seven or eight hours later, she stood looking at herself in the mirror above the tiny sink. Her eyes were a little bloodshot, the half-moons of skin beneath them a little gray and puffy. Otherwise, there was no outward sign of the previous night's rioting. She brushed her teeth, ran a comb through her long red hair, and went out to face her fellow rioter.

She found him standing shirtless in the middle of the studio, cell phone in his hand. She could tell by the look on his face that whatever he was about to tell her would not be good.

"What is it?"

"Emily."

"What about her?"

"She's on her way back. She'll be home in, like, twenty minutes."

"What? I thought you said she was in Idaho."

He shook his head and started gathering his clothes. "She went up to Toronto to visit a friend who has a kid JJ's age. I guess last night the kid started running a temperature, and then this morning he threw up, so Emily freaked out and called the whole trip off. They're in line at the Peace Bridge right now."

As he spoke, Annie felt her stomach beginning to twist and tighten.

"You fucking said you were gonna help me find Lola. Remember that? We were gonna, *quote*, search every shelter in town, *unquote*."

"Of course I remember," Jeremiah said, avoiding eye contact. "And I *will* help, too. I just can't do it right now. I've got to get home before—"

"I knew I couldn't count on you," Annie said. "I knew that when push came to shove, you'd leave me standing alone in the fucking rain. Why do we keep doing this shit? Can you tell me that?"

He was dressed now, had his keys and wallet in his hand. "Because we can't help it," he said. "Because we love each other, and there's nothing either one of us can do about that. It just happened, that's all."

"And?" she said. "*And?*"

His shoulders slumped visibly as he looked down at the keys in his hand. "And Emily and JJ are probably pulling up at the house right now. I'm sorry, but I have to go."

"Fine," she said. "Go."

He took a step toward her. "Annie—"

"No," she said, stepping back and away from him. "Just go."

He paused, and for a moment she thought he might change his mind, but then he shrugged his broad shoulders and, turning from her, walked straight out the door.

She wrapped herself in one of the sheets they'd lain in, his smell all over it, and stood before the apartment's wide front windows, watching as he emerged on the street below. The rain she'd been hearing all morning without registering it had begun again. He didn't look up to see her standing there. Instead, he hurried down Park Street, shoulders hunched, in the direction of his unhappy home on West Ferry.

"Yeah, that's right," she said aloud. "Run home to mommy. Just like you always do."

It wasn't until after she'd taken a shower and swallowed a handful of Advil that she remembered her phone, powered down so dramatically the night before. She pulled the thing out of her book bag and powered it back up, expecting to find a string of desperate messages from Jeremiah regarding the state of their doomed love. Instead, the phone blew up with a dozen texts and voicemails from her brother Michael in Kansas.

This can't be good, she thought, touching his name in the list of recent calls and waiting for him to pick up.

FOUR

Jimmy Wagner kicked his vintage Ducati 450 to life and pulled out of the crowded parking lot of the Flying J Truckstop on the east side of Dodge City. He'd just finished another double shift, the first washing trucks by hand in rubber boots and gloves in the truck wash, the second struggling to stay awake behind a cash register in the filling station as the night turned slowly to day. Now he was on his way to his second (or was it his third?) job, a tidy bit of agribusiness that had been a lot of fun at first but had since ballooned out of control, trapping him in a cycle of sleep deprivation that would end only when this third job ran its full course. In the old, carefree days, he'd have done a couple of donuts or at least pulled a wheelie on his way across the Flying J's asphalt parking lot. But those days were long gone. He had to be *careful careful careful* all the time now if he didn't want to fuck up and land in jail.

Usually when he came off a night shift at the Flying J, he headed straight south to his trailer off Lariat Road. Not this morning, though. This morning, he needed to get some food in his belly before facing down job number three, and so he headed west on Wyatt Earp, a vegetarian in a beef-packing town on a heroic quest for a breakfast burrito.

But no sooner had he gotten the Ducati into second gear than the ringtone on his phone, the opening guitar riff of The Eagles'

"Hotel California," began going off in a pocket of his cargo pants. Leaning sideways, he pulled the phone from his pants to see who the hell was calling him so early, in the middle of a burrito emergency, no less. Fucking Michael. He should've known. Leave it to his tight-ass older brother to call first thing in the morning, no text or warning of any kind, just *bam*, here I am.

Well, fuck that, Jimmy thought, declining the call.

Although they were brothers by blood, he and Michael had been born fifteen years apart and had grown up in radically different versions of the Wagner family, Michael during the glory days (to hear him talk) of the Bar W, Jimmy during the later years in town, after Michael and Annie had both flown the coop.

He passed the toxic waste dump that was National Beef LLC and was deep into the East Dodge world of grain elevators and Mexican groceries (a few of which sold decent cheese tamales, not that he was in the mood this morning) when the phone went off again, the second time in less than a minute. He let it go to voicemail, reassured by the fact that his inbox was full and would receive no new messages. Even so, the thought of Bro Michael and what was sure to be some kind of demand-slash-reprimand must have gotten to him, causing him to pull back a little too hard on the Ducati's throttle, because he barely got the brick façade of Tacos Jalisco in view before the carousel of lights atop Officer Charlie Bassett's white Crown Vic began flashing behind him.

"Jesus H. Christ!" Jimmy shouted, downshifting hard.

He blew past *El Rey De Los Taqueros*, as Tacos Jalisco called itself, and hung a left into the parking lot of Central Station, a bar and grill next to the old Santa Fe Depot, where he stood the bike on its kickstand while Bassett, who'd been on Jimmy's ass about one thing or another since at least the seventh grade, ran the Ducati's plates for what had to be the third or fourth time. What did the stupid sumbitch expect to find? That the bike had once belonged to the legendary Wade Wagner? Everybody knew that.

He watched as the cop climbed from his flashing cruiser and waddled with a series of tiny, fat-ass steps to where Jimmy sat straddling the Ducati. If you believed the teen gossip about him, Bassett had served as a prison guard in Arizona before moving to Dodge to follow in the footsteps of the legendary Wyatt Earp, a statue of whom stood maybe fifty yards away, on the other side of the street that bore his name.

"Well, well, what do we have here? James Joseph Wagner on his bright yellow *I*-talian motorbike. Do you know why I pulled you over, Mr. Wagner?"

"No idea," Jimmy said. "Speeding?"

"Yes, sir. Forty-five in a thirty to be precise. Also, you got mud on your license plate."

Jimmy leaned back in the seat to have a look for himself. There was some river mud on the plate, sure, but come on. What license plate in a town like Dodge City *didn't* have a little mud or cowshit on it? He started to argue the point, then caught himself.

"Okay, whatever. Write me up."

"I'm afraid there's more," Bassett said. "I also observed you swerving from left to right in your lane. I'm gonna need you to perform a little sobriety test."

"You've gotta be kidding me," Jimmy said. "Look at my clothes. I just got off work."

"But I'm not kidding, is the thing."

"Fine," Jimmy said, stepping off the bike.

Walk fifteen feet heel-to-toe. Close eyes and locate nose with index finger. Count backwards from one hundred. The whole thing was a joke. It wasn't even nine o'clock in the morning, and as Bassett surely knew by now, Jimmy didn't even *drink* alcohol. Couldn't stand the taste of it. But that hardly mattered. After Jimmy aced the sobriety test, Bassett moved along to the Ducati, checking to see that the lights and turn signals were in working order. Only then did he walk back to the Crown Vic and start writing tickets.

Jimmy took out a vape and hit it hard a couple of times before blowing the white smoke into the cloudless blue sky. In about the only decent conversation he'd ever had with his father, Leroy had said that one of Jimmy's problems (there were many) was that he always had to speak his mind, make the grand statement, tell the world to go fuck itself, and so on. "You get that from me," the old man had said. "It can feel like a strength, but trust me, it's a weakness. It'll reach out of the darkness and bite you in the ass sometime when you least expect it."

He'd vaped himself into something approaching nicotine nirvana by the time Bassett heaved himself out of the Crown Vic. As usual, before handing over the tickets he'd written, the former prison guard stood a moment looking Jimmy up and down.

"You're a real piece of work, you know that, Wagner?"

"I do my best to keep you entertained, officer."

Bassett licked his thin white lips in anticipation of the speech he was about to deliver, one that, unfortunately for him, Jimmy already knew by heart. "One of these days, and it won't be long, you're gonna screw up in a big-boy sort of way, and when that happens, I want you to know that I'm gonna be right there to nail your candy ass to the wall, and no fancy big-brother lawyer out of Kansas City is gonna be able to save you then."

"Consider me officially warned," Jimmy said, bringing his right boot into position to kick the starter. "Are we done?"

Bassett nodded, and Jimmy started the Ducati. His appetite ruined, he waited for Bassett to depart the parking lot, then hung a left on Wyatt Earp and another left on South Second before turning right into Wright Park. He passed the band shell and Hoover Pavilion, where he'd performed many a BMX trick back in the day, hung a left in front of the pathetic excuse for a zoo his mother had taken him to as a child, and accelerated up the side of the levee until he came to an access ramp to the dry Arkansas River, where he caught a little air before landing on the lower part of the ramp and turning east under the graffiti-covered base of the Second Avenue bridge. Once on the bumpy sand road that ran where the water should have been, he pulled the Ducati's throttle all the way back, and yelled at the top of his lungs, "*I gotta get outta this town!*"

The river road ran for miles in both directions, its course roughly parallel to the Santa Fe tracks and Wyatt Earp, providing an alternate, largely hidden way of traversing the length of the town for anyone with a dirt bike or a Jeep (or a horse—the rodeo grounds were a mile in the opposite direction). Jimmy used the road more often than he used Wyatt Earp or Trail Street. Three and a half miles after entering it at Wright Park, he came to the bridge at Highway 56/400, passing under it and up a steep ramp and over a set of railroad tracks before turning left on Lariat Way and left again into a run-down, half-abandoned trailer park that had no name that Jimmy had ever learned. A Mexican bull hauler had told him about the spot, located in a weed-choked, semirural area directly south of the packing plants and the feed yards.

The part of the park closest to Lariat Way was thick with trailers, but as you wound back closer to the river, and the names of the gravel road changed from Green Acres Drive to Lariat Side Road to El Torro Street (these names existing in the world of GPS only; there were no actual street signs that Jimmy had ever seen), the trailers thinned out dramatically, with fewer than half occupied and those that were like mini fortresses, protected from intruders by makeshift iron fences hung with the occasional Mexican flag or Our Lady of Guadalupe banner, hungry guard dogs roaming the perimeter within. The lot where Jimmy's trailer squatted on cement blocks was even farther back from the road than the rest, with three abandoned trailers serving as a buffer between him and his closest neighbor. Rolling up to his fortress-lair, he unlocked the heavy padlock on the gate and pushed the Ducati inside and locked the gate behind him and ran a heavy chain through the bike's front and back wheels, watching with satisfaction as a brother-sister pair of Dobermans named Hammer and Kush emerged from where they'd been sleeping under the trailer and began to bark like the maniacs they were.

"That's right, that's right, you're fucking dying of hunger," he said, reaching down to pet each of the dogs in turn. "Just give me a minute, okay?"

He tossed each dog a hunk of beef jerky, spun the padlock he'd installed on the trailer's front door, and stepped inside. The first plants started midway through the living room. From there, through the kitchen and bathroom to the nether reaches of the back bedroom, pretty much every square foot was given over to the hydroponic cultivation of a strain of high-grade weed out of California known as "Girl Scout Cookies." The plants, three feet high and packed tightly together in a pattern the grow magazines called "sea of green," were nestled beneath rows of HID lamps. Rotating fans circulated the chill air provided by a central air unit Jimmy had bought on eBay. It wasn't as sophisticated a grow room as you'd find in, say, Denver or Colorado Springs, but for a backwater like El Torro it wasn't bad at all, and you better believe that every last plant he harvested was gonna be loaded with THC.

Of course, none of that was gonna matter if Jimmy couldn't get the weed chopped and cured to the specs given to him by his business partner, a California-based trucker named K-Dog. It was just the latest in a series of worries that had multiplied seemingly every day since K-Dog and Jimmy had unloaded the GSC clones from K-Dog's truck two and a half months ago. This morning alone, he needed to trim weak branches, top the plants that were reaching too high, check pH levels in the basins, and clean the filter on both of his pumps so that the river of nutrients on which the whole enterprise depended continued its steady flow.

He fed Hammer and Kush a pound of raw hamburger each—just because he was a vegetarian didn't mean they had to be—put a cheese pizza in the oven and pulled out his phone to cue up his favorite playlist. Michael had called twice more and left a couple of text messages, the most recent of which began, *Goddamn it, Jimmy, call me back right now . . .*

"Bro, just give me a minute," he said aloud.

While the pizza cooked, he put in his earbuds and hit shuffle on a playlist he'd dubbed "Back to Cali." Right away, Guns N' Roses started into the opening riff of "Paradise City." He let the song play for ten seconds, nodding his head the whole time, then skipped forward to "Los Angeles" by the punk band X, then forward again to another punk number, "California Sun" by the Ramones. It was all good stuff but not what Jimmy was looking for after pulling a double at the Flying J followed by a heart-to-heart on Wyatt Earp Boulevard with Officer Charlie Bassett Hound. He hit skip again, and this time he landed on the acoustic opening of John Mayer's "Queen of California." That was more like it. As the opening continued, he sparked a fat joint, picked up a pair of pruning shears, and started trimming weed, singing along to the song as he worked.

Growing up, Jimmy had often heard his father and his father's rancher cronies complain about the "nonstop babysitting" that was the life of a Kansas cattleman. But tending cattle was nothing compared to the care and attention to detail required to grow a crop of Girl Scout Cookies. All the pruning and feeding and fucking around with lights and fans and pumps and spray rigs, all the campaigns against aphids and other pests, the endless testing and logging of pH numbers. And none of that even touched on the real trick, which was to keep the whole enterprise secret for the ninety days required to get from clone to cured, vacuum-packed produce. You had to keep regular hours, plan like a madman, and swear off loud partying and talking back to the police. You had to become a monomaniac—serious about business and nothing but business.

Jimmy had learned all this the hard way, growing weed in closed five-gallon buckets in the rafters of the dorms at Thomas More Prep–Marian, and later in the basement of his parents' house in the days before Leroy kicked him to the curb for good. He'd even tried his hand at an outdoor grow, tending his plants in the dead of night with a flashlight taped to his forehead, only to see the entire crop wiped out when his father's idiot hired man mistook his beautiful ladies for ditch weed and rode over them in a tractor pulling a bush hog mower. But all that was child's play compared to the situation he'd gotten himself into with K-Dog.

It had started out innocently enough, the two of them sitting high in the cab of K-Dog's blue Peterbilt smoking some of Jimmy's bucket-grown weed one sleepy Sunday morning at the Flying J.

"This shit ain't half bad," K-Dog had said. "Where'd you get the genetics?"

"Denver."

"Should've known. Hydroponic?"

"Deep water culture."

"You little alchemist you."

As a rule, Jimmy had little use for truckers, but K-Dog was different. He was younger than the grandpa truckers Jimmy was used to, had grown up in Canada and California and could speak French fluently. He owned his own truck, a $200,000 custom rig with a Jumbo sleeper with the words CALIFORNIA DREAMIN' painted as a series of puffy white clouds across it. K-Dog was cool. He took orders from no man and booked all his own loads, his bread-and-butter being the California-to-Kansas run, hauling produce one way, boxed beef the other.

"I get out east to New York or down by Miami, and I start to get the jitters. Too many people—and too many cops."

"We got cops here, too," Jimmy said.

"Yeah, toy cops," K-Dog said. "There's not a genuine law-enforcement official in this whole county, and I don't care if it is the former stomping grounds of Messieurs Masterson and Earp."

Jimmy had a good laugh at that. *Bassett Hound!*

On the Sunday in question, the conversation had turned naturally enough to a little side hustle of K-Dog's: supplying high-end weed to his fellow truckers. "The guys I sell to are picky, and they buy weight. They won't stand for any garbage in their dope, if you get what I'm saying."

"Connoisseurs," Jimmy said. "Sure, I'm the same way myself."

Here K-Dog fixed Jimmy in an uncomfortable stare.

"Dude, listen," Jimmy began, but K-Dog raised his hand to stop him.

"Look, I know you been dealing this deep-water shit, so don't even try to deny it. The thing is, it's only a matter of time before some stoned trucker out of Nebraska or Oklahoma"—he nodded out the window at the line of trucks stretching from where they were parked all the way out to 113 Road—"accidentally spills the beans in front of your boss, and then what's gonna happen? He's gonna call the cops, that's what."

"What?" Jimmy said, beginning to laugh. "You're telling me to get off your turf?"

"Well, yeah. As a matter of fact, I am. But how about we team up instead? A dude with your mad skills as a grower has got no business peddling weed anyhow. It's a waste of time and talent."

Jimmy couldn't help but feel flattered. When he'd climbed into the cab of K-Dog's truck that morning, he'd been expecting to be recruited as a dealer, not a grower.

"Are we talking indoor or outdoor grow?"

"Indoor, of course."

"How big?"

"I don't know, maybe fifty to a hundred plants to start with. I'm not interested in any penny-ante shit."

"Neither am I," Jimmy said. "And, dude, I've got the perfect place to pull this caper off!"

That same day, he showed K-Dog his fortress on the river, the trucker riding on the back of the Ducati with surprising poise and balance. Two weeks later, in the dead of night, K-Dog delivered a load of clones and nutrients, and they were up and running. But as the plants grew and the work of taking care of them grew along with them, Jimmy began to get antsy. What if someone smelled the skunk-strong aroma wafting out of the ventilation holes he'd drilled into the top of the trailer? What if the electric company began to wonder why a two-bedroom trailer in the Mexican part of town was pulling more juice off the grid than a welding shop? He drove out to the Bar W in the Flying J service truck and "borrowed" a diesel generator, and that helped tamp down his anxiety for a while. But the truth was, he needed the whole caper to be over as soon as possible.

As he moved from the kitchen and living room to the trailer's back bedroom, dispensing love to one lady after another, the playlist moved along with him, slip-sliding from Phantom Planet's "California (the OC theme)" to Hole's "Malibu" to Joe Croker's "LA Dream" to Notorious B.I.G.'s "Going to Cali." The deeper he got into the playlist, the more his mind floated free of the toxic world of feed yards and beef packing plants and slurry lagoons he inhabited like a caped crusader rocketed there from another planet, focusing instead on his glorious, untainted, yet-to-be realized Dream of Escape.

LA, baby. The Golden Coast. The City of Angels. That's where he needed to be. That's where he needed to *go go go*. And he'd get there, too. Just as soon as he got this crop of Girl Scout Cookies harvested, cured, and vacuum-packed to K-Dog's stringent specifications.

But just as Biggie was getting into the incantatory chorus of "Going to Cali," Jimmy's phone blew up yet again, and the lyrics pouring into his earbuds switched abruptly from B.I.G.'s deepthroated flow to the opening riff of "Hotel California."

"Bro, what the fuck?" Jimmy said, finally picking up the call. "I'm trying to ride a wave here!"

"Of course you are," Michael said in a flat, tired voice. "Of course that's what you'd be doing. In a moment like this."

"Dude," Jimmy said, all ears now. "A moment like what?"

FIVE

Caroline Wagner sat in the small waiting area just inside the front doors of Western Plains Regional Hospital, eyes closed, lips moving slowly as she fingered the beads of a wooden rosary her friend Sister Margaret had given her in the middle of her freshman year at St. Mary of the Plains, the small Catholic college she'd attended before dropping out—on a whim, or so it seemed to her now—to marry Leroy and start a family. But try as she might to focus, she kept losing her place in the prayer and forgetting to advance her fingers on the beads. "Oh, hell," she said finally, spooling the rosary into a ball and dropping it into her purse.

She'd been sitting there for three and a half hours and still knew nothing more than she had when she walked through the sliding glass doors to the ER that morning. Leroy was "still in surgery." The doctor would "tell her more when he came out of the OR." That was it. The rest was just sitting and waiting and then waiting some more, over and over, world without end, amen.

She'd known from the first that marriage to a man like Leroy wouldn't be easy. Her mother in Wichita had predicted as much, and so had Sister Margaret, who'd known Leroy since he was a boy in her fifth-grade math class at Sacred Heart Cathedral. But nobody, not even the stubborn man fighting for his life on the other side of the double doors leading to the OR, could tell Caroline what to do once she'd set her mind on something.

She could still vividly recall the day she and Leroy met. It was a blustery Friday afternoon in November, and she was riding in Ted Kramer's red convertible, on their way to pick up a few other kids before heading across the railroad tracks to drink beer in one of the cowboy saloons Ted favored in his tongue-in-cheek way. Halfway to the dorms, they came upon Leroy in the grass parking lot next to Hennessey Hall. He was standing beside a mud-splattered green pickup, its front end jacked high off the ground, spare tire lying in the grass at his booted feet. Seeing him, Ted chuckled under this breath and swung the convertible into the grass beside the old farm vehicle, which even Caroline, with her spotty knowledge of automobiles, recognized as being straight out of the 1950s.

"Old Bull Wagner, working as usual," Ted said, using the nickname a local sportswriter had bestowed on Leroy to describe his bruising style of running the football. "Need any help there, Bull?"

"No," Leroy said, straightening to reveal his full height, which was several inches taller than Ted's five foot ten. He was muscular and dark, with nearly black eyes and wavy black hair, one curly strand of which fell into the middle of his white forehead, Superman-style.

"You sure?" Ted asked.

Leroy just stood there looking at them in his surly way. Looking at *her*, it felt like, his black eyes penetrating her in a way that made her both uncomfortable and vaguely excited.

"We're going to play pool," she said. "Do you want to come with us?" Ted gave her a look out of the corner of his eye, but she just shrugged and said, "How about it?"

"All right," Leroy said, wiping his hands on the front of his denim jacket. "Tell me where you'll be, and I'll meet you there."

"Kate's," Ted said.

Leroy nodded, and Ted put the car into reverse and backed out of the grass lot.

"Why'd you do that for?" he asked as they pulled up before the dorm where a crowd of their friends stood waiting.

"I don't know," Caroline said. "I guess I felt . . . sorry for him."

"Didn't seem like it to me," Ted said, laughing. "Seemed more like you've got a crush on the Bull."

"Oh, Ted," she said. "Don't be ridiculous."

But she did have a crush—a big, headlong crush that only grew the more she realized just how wrong a man like Leroy was for her. Where Ted was lighthearted, sociable, and kind—if, yes, a tad conceited—Leroy was quiet and serious, a lone wolf of a man who worked on his family's ranch north of the college while also playing football and taking eighteen credit hours a semester, compared to the twelve or fifteen she and her friends got by with. Some of this she found out at Kate's, where Leroy showed up, showered and in a clean shirt, an hour after they'd left him changing his truck tire. But most she found out later, after she and Ted broke up and she started spending most of her free time with Leroy, riding with him in feed trucks and tractors, sitting in the middle of the bench seat of his dark green pickup as he steered it with the index finger of his left hand, his right hand resting on her knee and, later, on the inside of her thigh. What Leroy lacked in social skills and thoughtfulness, he more than made up for in other ways. At least at first.

Although they were the same age, he seemed older to her, as if he was already living his real, authentic life while the rest of them, including Ted and her friends on the cheerleading squad, were just playing at life, trying on this or that pose to see how it fit. Leroy's mother had died when he was nine years old, and in the aftermath of the loss, his father retreated into work and booze. The one constant in his life had been his grandfather, of whom Leroy spoke in reverential tones. Caroline's own childhood had been happy, if far from perfect. Her mother married and divorced young, then remarried when Caroline was ten. The second husband was a nice man, younger than her mother, and he treated Caroline better than any of her half-siblings, who came one after the other in the later years of her adolescence, the baby of the family still a toddler on the day Caroline left Wichita for Dodge City and her freshman year at St. Mary's. Growing up, she'd been the only person in the family who'd had her own room. It was something she took for granted, so she was a little shocked when she returned home for Thanksgiving break that first year at St. Mary's to find that her twin bed had been shoved into a corner to make room for a set of bunk beds where two of her younger brothers now slept.

"It's still your room, too," her mother said with a nervous laugh. But Caroline recognized an eviction notice when she saw one. The nest was overfull, and it was time for the oldest of the hatchlings to fly or fall to the ground.

She and Leroy had been dating for four months when her mother began to ask where the relationship was headed.

"I don't know," Caroline said on one call, standing in the stairwell of the women's dorm where the pay phones were located. "I guess I haven't thought much about it."

"Well, what does he say about it?"

"About what?"

"Where the relationship is headed! My God! Did I raise a total ninny?"

Caroline felt her face go red. "He doesn't say anything. I mean, it hasn't come up. We haven't talked about it."

"Well, don't you think you should?" her mother asked, and Caroline could almost see the older woman rolling her eyes.

The way her mother saw it, relations between men and women were part of an elaborate game, and you were a "ninny" if you weren't on top of all the rules and strategies. But Caroline saw things differently. It was 1973, for heaven's sake, not 1953.

Still, for a whole week after their conversation, bits and pieces of it kept running through her head like a song lyric that had gotten stuck there. *Where's the relationship headed? Well, don't you think you should ask him?* By the time she saw Leroy again, late on a Saturday evening, after he'd spent the whole day on a tractor in some lonely field far from the college, she was so worked up she immediately picked a fight with him, complaining that he hadn't called or stopped by her dorm room in days.

He saw right through it. "What's wrong? Are you okay? Caroline?"

"I'm fine," she said. "It's my mother who's not fine. She keeps asking me where this is headed."

"This?" he asked.

She nodded.

"Oh," he said.

She watched him out of the corner of her eye as he turned the question over in his head. It was clear that, like her, he was thinking about it for the first time.

"I don't know," he said finally. "I guess we're gonna get married."

"Get married!" she said. "What on earth gave you that idea?"

He shrugged. "I don't know. It's just the first thing that popped into my head."

She couldn't believe any of it was happening. It was as if her mother had called Leroy on the phone, and together they'd come up with this elaborate, twisted joke to play on her.

Not, "Will you marry me?"

Not even, "Let's get married."

But this crazy, half-cocked, "I guess we're gonna get married."

She started to say something, but the words caught in her throat, and she jumped out of the pickup and started walking fast.

"Come back," he called after her. "Caroline!"

But she kept walking across the asphalt parking lot as he followed her in the ancient pickup, head hanging out the window, pleading softly. "Caroline, come on. Get back in the truck. I'm sorry I upset you."

She kept on walking. When she came to the end of the parking lot, she stepped over the curb and started walking across the playing fields behind the dorms. The dry buffalo grass crunched beneath her feet, dust rising up to coat her socks and shoes. She heard the door of the old pickup creak open, followed by heavy feet running across the crunchy grass. She turned as he came up behind her.

"Leave me alone."

"Why? What the hell's gotten into you?"

"Like you don't know."

"Look, I said I was sorry. I wasn't expecting any of this to come up, and I just said the first thing that came to mind."

He reached for her hand, but she drew back. "Did you mean it? What you said about getting married?"

"Sure, I did," he said without hesitation. "I mean, it's all new to me, but, well, why not?"

They drove to Wright Park in his pickup and spent the rest of the night talking as a yellow moon rose above the banks of the dry Arkansas. He told her more about his mother's death, how in retrospect the event seemed to signal the end of his childhood. She talked about enduring the sad smiles of aunts and uncles and grandparents who pitied her after her biological father ran off to California, stranding her and her mother in a holding pattern that went on for the first half of her childhood.

"Do you want kids?" he asked.

"Sure," she said. "Do you?"

He nodded.

"Kids are a lot of work, though," she said. "I've seen the toll it's taken on my mother, having so many so late in life."

He considered what she'd said. "Well, just because both of our families are messed up," he said finally, "doesn't mean that *our* family has to be that way. We can change all that. Start something new."

He opened his burly arms and she scooted closer to him on the bench seat, resting her head on his shoulder while he held her body tightly against him, the fingers of his square hands flat against her stomach, seeming to claim both it and her. It was like they were already married, had already taken their vows. So the following evening, when they drove to the same spot and he presented her with a diamond engagement ring, her only surprise was that he had managed to get his hands on one so quickly.

"It was my mother's," he said in a voice tight with emotion.

He slipped the ring onto her finger, and she was shocked that it fit her perfectly. "What are the odds of that?" she asked in wonder.

To which he responded, "That's the way it works when something's meant to be. It just fits, that's all. No need to change anything."

She searched his eyes to see if they contained even a hint of irony. They didn't. Apparently, he believed every word he'd said.

"So how about it? Will you marry me?"

"Yes," she said, her heart pounding. "Yes, I will."

At noon, the windowed reception area behind her changed shifts, and the young Hispanic woman who'd given Caroline regular if vague reports on Leroy's surgery was replaced by an older, tight-lipped white woman with a sour expression. Caroline let the woman get settled behind her glass window, then went up and asked how things were going in the OR.

"The doctor will come and see you when your husband's out of surgery," the woman said without looking up.

"So people keep telling me, but it's been almost four hours since they took him back. How much longer do you think it'll be?"

"I can't say," the woman said. "I'm sorry."

She took up her rosary again, but her mind drifted mid-prayer, and she settled for closing her eyes against the florescent glow of the lights and holding the wooden beads in her hand like a talisman. Married life had turned out to be much harder than she expected. She hadn't foreseen the loneliness, all those hours by herself while Leroy worked and worked in some faraway pasture or field, not returning home until well after dark, often in a mood that left him unwilling to talk about his day or ask about hers. Despite these struggles, she'd done her best to be a good wife and mother. Looking back, she had mostly succeeded. There was only one thing that could be held against her, and she had confessed it long ago and supposed she was forgiven.

Give thanks to the Lord for He is good.

His mercy endures forever.

The Lord has freed you from your sins. Go in peace.

Thanks be to God.

Wasn't that how it was supposed to work in the church she had chosen of her own volition at the age of nineteen, a full year before she and Leroy married?

As she sat absorbed in these thoughts, the glass doors at the front of the hospital parted and Michael walked in looking surprisingly fresh for someone who'd spent the better part of a day driving across half of Oklahoma and Kansas. She stood as he walked straight up to her and gave her a hug.

"How's Dad? Any word?"

"Nothing for hours."

"I'll go check."

It irked her to see how the woman behind the window jumped to attention when Michael approached in his blue suit and red tie. That's how things worked in Dodge City, the epitome of a man's world. And yet, when Michael returned and sat down beside her, he had no more information than what she already knew.

She looked at this handsome, fit son of hers. Michael was not her firstborn, nor the daughter she'd always wanted, nor her youngest and most needy child. But in the years since Wade's death, and especially since the onset of Jimmy's troubled adolescence, she had come to rely on his rock-like stability, the fact that if she ever needed him, all she had to do was pick up the phone and call, and he'd be there for her almost instantly, no questions asked.

"Thank you for coming so fast," she said. "I know how busy you are. Were you able to reach your brother and sister?"

"Annie's on her way," he said. "I finally got ahold of Jimmy a little while ago. He's been informed. Let's just leave it at that."

She started to say something in Jimmy's defense, then stopped. Michael had done so much for his younger brother over the years, most of it at her insistence, and she sensed that his patience was wearing thin.

It was nearly four in the afternoon when the surgeon, a short, dark man with wire-rimmed glasses, finally emerged from the OR and started for them across the tile floor. He was still in his scrubs, hair in a little skull cap, face mask hanging from his neck. He looked . . . rattled, somehow.

"Leroy Wagner?" he asked in a thick accent.

"Yes, that's us," Michael said, standing.

"I'm Dr. Reddy," the man said with a slight bow. "I just finished operating on your father."

"How is he?" Caroline asked.

"Well, his vitals are stable, so that's good."

"And?" Caroline prompted.

"And, well, have you seen pictures of the wreck?"

"Yes," Michael said.

"You have?" Caroline asked, surprised.

"I know one of the patrolmen who responded," Michael said. "He messaged them to me."

"Then you know how lucky your father is to be alive," the doctor said.

They sat down in a corner of the waiting room, and the doctor went into a lengthy description of the operation, which included separate procedures on Leroy's left shoulder, arm, hip, and lower leg, all of which had been impacted in the crash. "The leg was probably the worst," the doctor said. "That procedure alone took four hours." He paused. "He's got a possible TBI as well."

"TBI?" Michael asked.

"Traumatic brain injury. We won't know how serious it is until he wakes up, and so far his body's shown no signs it's ready to do that."

"I don't understand," Caroline said. "Are you saying he's in a coma or something?"

"Well, I don't know that I would say it's a coma," the doctor said, smiling weakly. "More like a deep sleep. We'll monitor it for now, make sure there's no additional swelling or bleeding."

"Swelling?" Caroline said. "You mean . . . his *brain*?"

The doctor nodded, and she felt herself take a deep breath. "When can we see him?"

"Give the nurses a little time to get him set up in his room in the ICU, then you can go in. Just prepare yourself. He's unresponsive—and will be at least until the drugs we gave him during surgery begin to wear off."

"Thanks," Michael said.

An hour later, they were shown into a curtained room in the ICU where Leroy lay unconscious, his head wrapped in gauze, his broken body a tangle of elevated casts and monitors producing ominous beeps. Caroline had known about the wreck for almost seven hours by then, but nothing had prepared her for this. What if he was crippled, confined to a wheelchair for the rest of his life? What if a blood clot broke loose and headed for his laboring heart or brain? What if what they were calling a traumatic brain injury turned out to be brain *damage*? It was hitting her now—the full reality of the situation.

"Oh Lord," she said. "This is far worse than I thought."

"Easy," Michael said, putting an arm around her. "We don't know anything yet. For all we know, he's gonna wake up any minute and start ordering everybody around. The doctors, the nurses, you and me."

"You think so?"

"Of course. Don't forget, that's not just anybody lying there. That's Bull Wagner, and he's too damn tough and obstinate to let something like this slow him down for very long."

"I hope you're right," she said, turning and hugging Michael tightly. "Boy, do I hope you're right."

SIX

Annie threw some clothes and a stack of books into a large red duffel bag with the words DODGE CITY RED DEMONS emblazoned on its sides in white letters. Once upon a time, the bag had belonged to her brother Wade. She'd found it in his old closet in the basement of the homeplace and had claimed it as her own, a bag big enough to hold shoulder pads and helmet, but which she'd used to carry notebooks and clothes and a pair of scuffed but beautifully broken-in riding boots all the way from London to Lisbon to Kairouan, Tunisia.

The series of staccato conversations she'd had with her brother Michael over the past couple of hours had left her deeply unsettled. First came the shock of her father's accident, then the realization that she was going to have to drop everything and get to southwest Kansas as soon as possible, then the terrible update from the hospital during which Michael ran down every broken bone in their father's body, ending with the ominous news that he still hadn't regained consciousness.

"What are you saying?" she'd asked. "He's got a concussion or something?"

"No, I'm saying he's got a *brain injury*. He didn't have his seat belt on when the landscaping rig hit him—big surprise there, right?—and apparently his head bounced off the windshield before ricocheting back against the driver's side window, shattering it."

"Now you're scaring me."

"I'm sorry. I don't mean to. When are you leaving?"

"I don't know. As soon as I pack, I guess. I'm teaching a class here, you know."

At this, Michael had sighed audibly and said, "Look, Sis, I don't know how to break this to you, but this isn't going to be some quick in and out. Dad could be in the hospital for weeks, and after that, who knows? In the meantime, we've got a wheat harvest staring us straight in the face, and I'm not at all sure Dad's hired guy is up to the task. I've talked to him twice on the phone, and he sounded drunk both times."

"And?"

"And, well, so *you* might have to do it."

"Me? Have you lost your mind? I can't run the wheat harvest!"

"Why not?"

"Well, to begin with, I've got a dissertation to write!"

He sighed again, even louder this time. "Hey, I'm sorry I brought it up, but somebody in this family has to look reality in the face." He began to say more, then stopped short. "Look, I've got a call coming in that I have to take. Talk later?"

"Sure," she'd said, and just like that, he was gone.

In the aftermath of that conversation, she'd emailed the students in her summer writing class and informed them that the last two weeks of the term would consist of a series of online assignments she'd be grading using a simple rubric. They hadn't exactly revolted at the news. Then she'd locked up her apartment and tossed her duffel and computer bags into the front trunk of Frankenporsche and sat a moment waiting for its transplanted V-8 to warm up. The car, a preposterous choice for a daily driver in a place like Buffalo, was a hand-me-down from Michael, who'd bought it wrecked from a salvage auction in Dallas as part of some as-yet-undisclosed midlife crisis, only to have the car's IMS bearing explode in the middle of I-435, grenading its flat-six engine. Annie could still recall the moment he'd phoned her in disgust from the side of the road to ask if she wanted the damn thing. She was living in London at the time but immediately said *yes yes yes*, of course she wanted it, who the hell was he kidding? Before he could change his mind, she'd had the Porsche trailered to Dodge, where her father and his hired man at the time dropped the ruined flat six and replaced it with an aluminum V-8 out of a wrecked Chevy Silverado. The car rattled and shook on its worn-out suspension; half its gauges failed to work after the transplant; its leaky Cabriolet roof let in both wind and rain. But all of that was a small price to pay for a vehicle that would do a hundred miles an hour in fifth gear, all the while reminding her of Wade, who'd driven a souped-up VW Scirocco back in the day, and hapless Michael, who in giving her the car had demonstrated that whatever quiet desperation was brewing within him had yet to reach its boiling point.

She was desperate to get on the road, but she'd be damned if she didn't make one more last-ditch effort to find Lola. As the rain slowed and then stopped altogether, she drove up and down every street in a five-block radius of Elmwood and Allen, calling and calling out the windows and later out the open roof. She was at a stop sign in a scrappy neighborhood on the far side of the Old Pink when she heard it—a high-pitched, blue heelerish bark. She switched off Frankenporche's big engine and listened. The bark came again—somewhere behind her and to the left. She parked in the first space she came to, left the roof down, and jumped out to investigate.

As nearly as she could tell, the barks were coming from behind a high, wooden fence in the alley behind a dilapidated duplex.

"Lola!" she called, and the dog answered instantly with her shrill bark.

She ran up to the fence and took a quick peek through a knothole in its ragged surface. Sure enough, there was Lola, tied to a stake in the beaten grass with a length of nylon rope.

"Lola girl!"

The dog turned its head in her direction and began a nonstop series of barks, the same way she did when Annie took too long feeding her.

"Don't worry! Mama's coming!"

She ran around to the front of the row house and banged at the tall wooden door. The place was a rental unit, cut into three apartments, their mailboxes nailed haphazardly to the clapboard siding.

"Who is it?" came a gruff voice.

"That's my dog in your backyard!"

The door creaked opened to reveal a big, disheveled man in green sweatpants and a stained work shirt that barely covered his large stomach. He was barefoot and looked her up and down with a sneer.

"Get lost, little bit."

"I'm not going anywhere until I get my dog."

"Oh yeah?" the man said. "How about you get the hell off my porch before I call the police?" Then he slammed the door in her face.

Little bit! she thought. *I'll show that arrogant sumbitch!*

In the alley behind the house, she turned a trash can upside down and used it to climb high enough to reach over the gate and undo the latch. She was halfway across the beaten yard, Lola barking at the top of her lungs, when the man emerged on his crumbling back porch.

"Hey! Whaddya think you're doing?"

She sprinted across the wet grass to where Lola was tied and started pulling as hard as she could on the nylon rope where it was tied to the corkscrew stake. As the man started down the steps in his bare feet, she moved up the rope to where it attached to a leather choke collar and started fumbling with the buckle. She almost had the buckle off when she felt the man's hands on the back of her neck. She ducked out of his grip, but he followed her across the wet grass, grabbing her by both wrists. A struggle began, and she fell back on a trick her brother Wade had shown her long ago—*Never fight the whole hand when you can fight a finger*—and grabbed the man's left pinkie and bent it back as hard as she could.

"*Ouch*! Goddamn you!"

Lola took it from there, biting the man's exposed ankles so that he let go of Annie and began to stumble backward in the direction of the porch. Halfway across the wet lawn, he slipped in the grass and fell, his heavy body making a satisfying thud when it hit the ground. In the chaos that followed, Annie worked the collar free from Lola's neck.

"Let's go!" she yelled, and the two of them ran through the open back gate and down the alley.

A female traffic cop had just put a ticket under Frankenporsche's passenger-side wiper when Annie and Lola ran up to the car and jumped in. It had begun to rain fat single drops. The traffic cop backed onto the curb and stood there, slack-jawed, as Annie started the car and the man from the row house appeared barefoot on the sidewalk, cursing and giving them the finger.

Annie laughed and gave him the finger back. They were outta there.

Somewhere past Ashtabula, with daylight failing and the Mother of All Headaches coming on, she pulled into a truck stop to get gas and coffee and some Alpo for Lola. At the last second, she asked the teenaged clerk for a pack of Marlboro Lights as well.

"I shouldn't, but I'm gonna anyway," she said.

"Why shouldn't you?" the clerk asked, fingering his wispy goatee.

"Because I quit, like, four years ago."

"Fuck that," the clerk said. "Life's too short, right?"

An hour later, when her phone rang on the seat beside her, she was already on her fourth cigarette. She picked the phone up without checking the caller, expecting it to be Michael.

Instead, she heard Jeremiah's deep voice say, "Annie, thank God. I was just at your apartment, and your downstairs neighbor said he'd seen you loading your car."

"That's right," she said, rolling down her window and tossing the cigarette out.

"Where are you right now? I need to see you. We need to talk about last night."

"I don't think so," she said.

"What? Why not? Baby, *please*."

She'd just entered the multi-lane spaghetti northeast of Cleveland, trucks and cars zipping by on both sides. On impulse, she held the phone out the window, dangling it over the rushing highway. Jeremiah's voice was completely gone now. Completely erased. She laughed and yelled, "How do you like it out there, Lover Boy? Kind of windy, huh? Well, it's better than *you* deserve! What you so really deserve is—"

Before she could finish the thought, a semi blew by on her left, causing her to lose her grip on the phone. It flew out of her hand like a released carrier pigeon, bounced twice on the pavement, then disappeared beneath the front tires of a panel truck.

Just like that, the digital tether that had kept her connected to friends and family and national news events, to say nothing of cat memes and wedding pictures and lengthy, impassioned political rants, had been cut. She felt a moment of horror, but a few seconds later, the feeling left her, and she began to feel bizarrely relieved. She'd entered a new period of change and austerity, a period several stages of seriousness beyond Jeremiah Anonymous.

She was unplugged now. Completely off the grid.

SEVEN

Michael arranged to leave his rented Nissan at the Dodge City airport and booked the last seat on a puddle hopper to Kansas City.

The suddenness of the move alarmed his mother, as he knew it would. "What? Now? But you just got here!"

He explained that he had a date in federal court he couldn't miss but would be back as soon as he could shake loose of this and a few other responsibilities. "Anyway, Annie will be here before you know it," he added.

"Okay," his mother said, shrugging heavily. "You know best, Michael. I wouldn't think of doubting you."

Why couldn't Vanessa find the grace to say such things? Michael wondered. Would it be so hard to show a little faith in his judgment instead of treating him like some kind of unconscious repetition of her deadbeat father, somebody who had to be watched constantly lest his weaker impulses lead the family into ruin? As quickly as it had occurred, he shook the thought off. It wasn't Vanessa's fault she was the way she was. In fact, there'd been a time when they first began to date when this side of her had secretly thrilled him. Looking for a lover and protector? I'm your man, baby. The psychic cost, though, had turned out to be a little too high.

Before he left town, there were a few logistical matters that required his and his mother's immediate attention. For example, now that his father was "out of it," as his mother had taken to saying, who was going to pay the bills and otherwise manage the complex finances of the Bar W? Did Caroline want to take this on, or would she prefer to share the online passwords, so that he and Vanessa could pick up the slack?

The question brought a weak smile to his mother's face. "This is your father we're talking about," she said. "There aren't any *online passwords*. There's a pile of bills on his desk in the basement, a line of credit I know nothing about, and a checkbook. That's it."

He left the hospital and drove straight to his parents' house, a midcentury modern with a big backyard where a leaky pool had once been, before Leroy had it filled with dirt shortly after they'd moved in, when Michael was in the middle of his sophomore year of high school. It was his mother's house, really. His father's "office," as she'd so quaintly called it, was a steel desk in the unfinished half of the basement, which had originally been conceived as a Cold War era bomb shelter. As he switched on a light and descended the stairs, the steel desk came into view, smack in the middle of the bunker with its blast-proof steel doors and concrete ceiling and empty shelves for storing food and water in anticipation of Armageddon.

Hell, he thought, examining the desk, piled high with unopened bills. *Armageddon is now.*

Among the bills: Black Hills Energy. Dodge City Cooperative Exchange. Federal Land Bank. Digging deeper, he found another layer of bills, these opened but apparently unpaid, and beneath that, the portfolio checkbook in its green plastic case. He opened the binder. Half the checks were gone, but the attached ledger, which should have contained clues as to the payees of all those missing checks, was a complete blank.

"Well, well, this is gonna be fun," Michael said into the cavernous space.

Sitting at the metal desk, he began to sort the bills by date, with the oldest at the top. As he did so, one category of correspondence stood out from all the rest: a series of unopened letters from Harold Krebs, attorney at law. Ripping open the most recent of the letters, he found an invoice for June, fourteen hours billed at $125 an hour. It was a measly amount compared to what Michael charged, but what really caught his eye was the description, which read, *Billable Hours*, nothing more. What the heck was that all about?

He looked at his Rolex. One envelope in, and already a mystery. He was going to have to take the whole mess home with him and try to sort through it there.

Ascending the stairs to his parents' bedroom, he found a large suitcase and brought it down to the desk and began to load it with bills, undeposited checks, bank statements, and folders from the desk's filing cabinet. When the suitcase was full, he lugged it up the stairs and loaded it into the trunk of the rented Nissan and headed off to see Krebs, whose office was in downtown Dodge City, a mile and a half away.

By the time Michael was a teenager, downtown Dodge had already begun its ignominious slide into flea market irrelevance. Once upon a time, it had been a vibrant, special place, or at least that was his memory of it. His mother had bought him his very first real suit—well, a blue blazer and khakis—at a men's store near the old Carnegie library. He could still remember the instore tailor measuring his arms and legs for the necessary alternations. Now, of course, the whole area was a shadow of its former glory, home to small, mom-and-pop stores selling Mexican groceries and *quinceañera* dresses.

He parked on the red-brick street and entered through the front door of the dated office building, finding Krebs sitting behind a massive wooden desk of the kind you couldn't give away these days, the floor around the desk piled high with white banker boxes in various states of collapse. Was this the sort of second-rate, country law office Michael would've been condemned to if he'd come back to Dodge after law school instead of marrying Vanessa (already pregnant with Sam at the time) and taking the job at Curtis, Frederick, and Lyles?

"How's your father doing?" Krebs asked, taking Michael by surprise.

Back when Michael was first considering law school, he'd paid a visit to the man in this very room, and apparently Krebs had not forgotten it.

"Not great. He still hasn't regained consciousness. Who told you about the accident?"

Krebs waved him into a seat across from the massive desk. "This is a small town, Michael. News travels fast. I mean, the Jaws of freaking Life? Are you kidding me?"

Michael winced. "At least, by all reports, the other guy's okay."

"Yeah, I heard that, too," Krebs said. "If this was Kansas City, we'd already have heard from some ambulance chaser looking for an easy payday."

"I had the same thought. But luckily for us, this isn't Kansas City." He reached into his breast pocket and brought out Krebs's most recent invoice and handed it across the desk. "What's this all about?"

Krebs barely glanced at the invoice. "Does the name Byron Branch ring a bell?"

"No."

"Well, it ought to."

According to Krebs, Branch was a businessman from Dallas who'd recently begun buying up land in the general vicinity of the Bar W. "Long story short," Krebs concluded with a chuckle, "your dad's convinced Byron Branch is out to get him."

"What gave him that idea?"

Krebs sorted through some papers on his desk and handed Michael a file folder with the words *Chester and Fanny Stewart vs. Byron Branch Industries* printed on the outside in permanent marker. "This, to begin with."

Michael began flipping through the file, which contained copies of a couple of motions along with some handwritten notes on yellow legal paper. "This is about the Stewart place? That half section of grass my dad rents on Back Trail Road?"

"Used to rent," Krebs said. "Branch has got his mitts on both of those quarters now, and from what I can tell, there ain't much to be done about it. Actually, it turns out that Chester owned only one of the quarters that make up the place. The other belonged to a sister out of Colorado who decided to sell. There was an auction set up and everything. Leroy and half the other ranchers in the neighborhood were all set to bid on the land. But at the last minute, Chester somehow found the money to buy his sister out, and at that point, your dad and everybody else backed off, out of respect for the family."

"Let me guess," Michael said. "It was this Branch character who loaned Chester the money to buy out his sister."

Krebs nodded. "That's right. And Chester defaulted on the loan before the ink on the new deed was even dry."

"And the collateral Chester put for the loan was—"

"That's right. The quarter the Stewarts did own."

Michael let out a low whistle. "Which means that Branch, what, got a two-for-one deal on the whole place?"

"Not quite," Krebs said. "But you're getting the general idea."

Michael sat there shaking his head. He knew the Stewarts vaguely from the days when he and Wade and the rest of the family still lived on the ranch. There had been a son who was close to Wade's age, but something had happened to him. He'd drowned in a reservoir or gotten killed in the military or something. Even then, almost twenty years ago, the Stewarts had seemed old and broken down, Chester Stewart in bib overalls and mail order boots, Fanny in the sort of cheap, homemade dresses Michael associated with reruns of *The Waltons*. According to Leroy, Chester Stewart had grown up on the land but had spent most of his adult life working in the oil fields near Great Bend. It was only after he'd retired from maintaining oil derricks in his late fifties that Chester and his wife, Fanny, bought a small herd of cows and moved back to the crumbling homestead, which no one had lived on for years, and tried to make a go of it. Leroy, whose history with the family went back to those times, helped them out as much as he could, making sure Chester's beater Ford got fixed when it broke down and checking from time to time to see that they had enough firewood to make it through the winter. It was the sort of knee-jerk good Samaritanism that drove Michael's mother crazy. "Here I can't get your father to do so much as change a light bulb around this house," she'd complain. "It's all ranch, all the time. And yet, he'll split firewood and carry it to the neighbors down the road without them even *asking* him to do it!"

"Okay, here comes another guess," Michael said, leaning back in his chair and looking across the wooden desk at where Krebs sat with his chin in his hand. "You're representing the Stewarts in their suit against Byron Branch."

"Bingo."

"And it's my father who's paying for the whole thing."

Krebs offered a nervous smile. "Well, in a manner of speaking."

"Wait," Michael said, sitting up. "You're telling me you haven't been getting paid either? How long are we talking?"

"Since before all this," Krebs said.

"Jesus. And when does the case go to court?"

"Next month. Although I suppose we could ask the judge for a continuance. Would be a little hard to explain, though, given that, technically, your dad's not a party to the suit."

The whole thing, from the knee-jerk good Samaritanism (if that's, in fact, what it turned out to be), to the calling in of old favors, to the sloppy bookkeeping and tardiness in paying bills—it was all classic Bull Wagner stuff. Michael looked across the desk at Krebs. "So give me your honest opinion. What do you think we should do?"

"Honestly? Cut our losses and drop the whole thing. Get the hell out while the getting's good."

"And why is that?"

"Look," Krebs said, his voice rising higher the longer he spoke. "I don't like Byron Branch any more than your dad does. I can't figure out if the guy's a snake or just a snake oil salesman. But this particular case? It's thin, Michael. Very thin. And that's before we even get to the question of why your dad's sticking his nose into what many people would say is none of his goddamn business."

By then, Michael had heard enough. He looked at his Rolex, then stood, the file folder still in his hand. "What's the damage so far, Harold? How much does my dad owe you?"

"Well, I don't know, exactly," Kerbs said. "I'd have to generate a new invoice."

"You do that," Michael said, pulling a business card from his wallet and handing it to Krebs. "And when you've got it all totaled up, send it here."

A thin smile crept onto Krebs's face. He was finally putting it together. "You're firing me, aren't you?"

"It's nothing personal, Harold," Michael said. "Let's just say that my father can no longer afford your services."

Later, as he waited for his puddle hopper to take off from the Dodge City airport, Michael called an old friend from law school he hadn't spoken to in a couple of years—an ambulance chaser out of Oklahoma City, no less—and replayed the whole exchange.

"How'd it feel?" the friend asked.

"Fantastic," Michael said. "It felt fantastic."

"I'll bet. If I didn't know better, I'd say you're getting ready to jump off that treadmill they've had you on all these years. Am I right?"

"Well, not quite," Michael said. "But you know what? I'm getting closer."

"Hell, yes, you are," the friend said. "And it's about fucking time, too."

EIGHT

Growing up, Annie had often thought of herself as an outcast, someone better suited to life in a big, loud city than a small western town like Dodge City. But then she'd tasted life in London and New York and had come to understand that it wasn't the bustle or size of those places she craved, but the anonymity. In Dodge, especially in the days immediately following Wade's death, such anonymity had been impossible. Everyone in town, adults and children alike, stared at her and exchanged whispers. *That's her. The sister.* Sometimes they even tried to touch her or offer condolences. *I'm so sorry for your loss.* She hated the whole overwrought display and vowed that when she got old enough she was gonna get the hell out of Dodge and never, ever look back.

But lined up opposite of all this was her love of the Bar W and everything it represented. An atom bomb could have dropped on Dodge City, and she wouldn't have cared. Good riddance! But the Bar W with its rolling hills of buffalo grass and meandering creeks and long, lovely shadows that fell across the land as the sun sank every evening, was a different story altogether. Simply put, it was her favorite place in all the world, and she could say that without a trace of irony or second guessing. She couldn't even remember the first time she sat a horse. An entire wall of the homeplace was devoted to framed pictures of the animals, some of them dating back fifty years or more to when her father was a brawny teenager with a crew cut and a just-try-me stare. In one of the more recent pictures, taken in 1986 or '87, she sat perched like a tiny bird on the pommel of Leroy's saddle. Then came the pictures of her riding double behind Wade's worn Billy Cook saddle, arms wrapped around his thin waist, stubby legs dangling free. Even now, she could summon the names of those big-rumped ranch geldings—Traveler, King, Cuba, JR, Slim, Dillon. When she was three or four, her father bought her an Appaloosa/POA mix named Smoky on account of its mottled gray coloring. The little horse was cantankerous, stiff in the neck, and hopelessly barn sour, but none of that mattered to Annie. During fall or spring roundups, she'd ride Smoky alongside Wade and Cuba for hours at a time while Michael helped their father with more earthbound tasks like setting up and taking down corral panels. She'd joke with Wade as they rode through the deep grass, asking who he planned on marrying when he grew up, and Wade would scratch his beardless chin, pretending to consider the question. Then his face would break into an easy smile and he'd wink at her beneath the brim of his sweat-stained Stetson. "Hell, honey," he'd say in an exaggerated drawl, "you know I could never love another girl the way I love you."

No matter how many times the game played out, she never got tired of hearing those words.

Then Wade dropped dead of some kind of brain tumor—she'd come across the exact name when snooping in her mother's desk as a child, but she'd long since blocked it from her memory—and Jimmy was born and the family moved from the Bar W to the house in town with the swimming pool that her father filled with a load of dirt from the ranch and later tore out altogether—in retribution for what, she could not say. But for Annie, the move registered as a triple loss: first Wade, then her father, who often didn't come home from work on the Bar W until ten or even eleven o'clock at night, and finally the ranch itself with its horses and cattle and fast-running creeks.

She didn't ride for a couple of years after the move. Horses were dead to her, same as Wade. In place of the old life, she submitted to a new regimen of dance and piano and swimming lessons—the last of these more than a little ironic, given what her father had done to the pool—all of these activities planned, paid for, and cheered on by her mother, with whom she shared a tight if mostly silent bond in those years. But then, as she entered her preteen years, her mother signed her up for Girl Scouts, and soon after that, the troop she was a part of took a field trip to a stable with trail horses so dead in the side you could've gone after them with a chainsaw and not gotten them above a walk. The horse Annie had been given to ride didn't even have stirrups. To climb on, she had to walk up a set of stairs with rails on either side and wait for the teenager running the concession to position the horse beneath her, a far cry from the way Wade and her father used to boost her onto Smoky's back with the aid of a single hand cupped at knee level. Halfway through that pathetic excuse for a ride, she was sobbing and telling the other girls and their alarmed troop leader to keep the hell away from her. She knew damn well what horseback riding was, and what they were doing wasn't anything close to it.

"Honey, what's wrong?" her mother asked, pulling her away from the other girls. "I thought you loved to ride horses."

"We never should've left the ranch," she said through gritted teeth, snot running down her lips and chin. "It's all your fault. You made Dad do it."

"Honey, it's more complicated than that."

"No, it's not," Annie said. "Why did you do it? *Why?*"

But no answer came, only whispers of *There, there* and an aborted attempt at a hug.

In the middle of that hug, Annie was visited by a memory that would later become a kind of blurred home movie that played over and over again in her mind, especially in times of uncertainty or stress. It was in the days just before Wade died, and Annie was waiting for her mother to pick her up from a dance lesson in a studio across from the First National Bank with its Stan Herd mural of stage coach drivers with rifles pointed high. Her mother was late, which was unusual for her, and when she did appear on the street in front of the bank it was not in her brown Buick Skylark but in a big, blue Cadillac driven by a man who was not Annie's father. That was disturbing enough, but the part Annie could never forget was the look on her mother's face. She was smiling and laughing like a girl—just radiating happiness. Or at least she was until she spotted Annie standing there on the sidewalk, at which point all the happiness disappeared. Had the scene even happened? Or was it some kind of fever dream she'd developed to explain the distance that began to creep into their relationship in the years that followed?

Whatever the case, shortly after the Girl Scouts trail ride debacle, Annie unceremoniously quit dance and piano and even swimming lessons and began bumming rides to the Bar W with her father and Michael every chance she got. She was her father's daughter now. While he and Michael worked on farm equipment or fixed fence, she'd catch the youngest, wildest horse she could find and take off on it bareback like something shot out of a cannon. She loved the jarring feel of the horse against her body, bone on bone, flesh on flesh, the way the heat of the animal rose up through her thighs into her stomach and lower back, burning away any space that remained between them, so that after a while there was no Annie at all and no horse either, only a wild, unthinking creature called *girlonhorse*.

Later, in college at the University of Kansas and while studying abroad in England, she continued to ride as opportunities arose, trading chores at this or that barn for a few hours a week on a lesson horse, understanding all the while that there'd always be a difference and she couldn't expect to feel what she'd felt when riding on the ranch. But that was okay, too. She didn't necessarily want the world of books and ideas that she'd discovered upon leaving Kansas and the Bar W to overlap with her childhood world. They were separate realms, just as her mother's house in town existed in a different universe altogether from that of the homeplace.

It was late afternoon by the time she pulled into the parking lot of Western Plains, the small, regional hospital on the north side of Dodge. She switched off the ignition and sat for a moment with her eyes closed and her head resting on the steering wheel, listening to the gentle *tick tick tick* of the engine as it cooled. She'd come 1,362 miles in a little under twenty hours of driving. Not a record, by any means, but an accomplishment all the same, especially considering how hurt and hungover and tired she'd been when she pulled out of Buffalo. Now that she was here, she had one final gauntlet to run: seeing her father and mother in what Michael had described as the worst shape of their lives.

Before facing that down, she walked Lola in a stretch of grass between the parking lot and Ross Boulevard on the north side of the hospital. The rain of New York and Pennsylvania and the dank humidity of St. Louis had been replaced by wind and dry heat. The grass beneath her feet made a dry, crunching sound as she walked on it, and the wind whispered incessantly in whichever ear was facing it. After Lola had done her business, Annie fed her a can of Alpo and poured a little water into her heavy plastic bowl. The dog lapped it all up and turned her nose into the wind, sniffing. Did she realize she was almost home now? Could she smell it on the High Plains air?

Annie stepped into the wind block provided by a stunted elm and shook her last Marlboro Light from the pack she'd bought outside Erie. As she smoked the cigarette, the sliding glass doors beneath the hospital's EMERGENCY entrance opened and an older, slightly stooped woman emerged and stood looking steadily at her with one hand raised visor-like to her forehead. It took Annie a couple of seconds to realize that the woman, who wore jeans and white tennis shoes and a purple blouse, was her mother. Instantly, as though shocked by a hot wire, she dropped the cigarette into the grass and began stabbing at it with the toe of her shoe. When she was certain it was out, she crossed the asphalt parking lot in a series of long strides, pulling Lola behind her.

"What are you doing out here?" she asked when she reached her mother.

"Getting some air. What are you doing?"

"Letting this pup stretch her legs a bit," Annie said, nodding at Lola. "She's been in the car since yesterday afternoon."

Her mother bent down and began to scratch Lola behind her ears. "I know this one. She's a ranch dog, isn't she?"

"She was. Then I got this bright idea of bringing her with me to Buffalo. That didn't work out quite the way I thought it would."

They hugged awkwardly.

"I'm sorry I didn't call. I lost my phone . . . long story. How's Dad?"

Her mother shrugged, and it was almost as though Annie could see the physical weight of the situation sitting on her shoulders like a bag of mason's sand. "Come see for yourself. That'll be a lot easier than me trying to explain it to you."

"Should I bring Lola or lock her in the car?" Annie asked.

"Bring her. If anyone asks, we'll say she's a whatchamacallit."

"Service dog?"

"That's it. Though I doubt anyone will ask, dear."

Her father's room in the intensive care unit was small and had a curtain for a door. Annie held her breath as she followed her mother across the threshold and then pulled up short a couple of feet from the bed. There he lay, the hero of her childhood, unmoving, white bandage wrapped around his battered head, tubes running into his nose, IV line stabbed into a vein on top of his brown right hand. For some reason, it was the IV line that got her. Why put it there, in the top of his hand? What if he needed that hand to check the oil on Annie's car or bend back the pinkie of an attacker?

While Annie pondered these questions, a plump nurse arrived to check his vital signs, seeming surprised to find Annie and her mother standing in the small space.

"How's he doing?" Annie asked.

"He's stable," the nurse said. "What's the dog's name?"

"Lola."

"She's a cutie."

When the nurse was gone, Annie steeled herself and approached the bed to have a closer look at her father. He was a ghostly white and his black hair, which had flecks of gray in it now, was sweaty and pasted to his forehead. She fought an impulse to turn tail and run down the hallway to where Frankenporche waited in the parking lot.

"They've cut back on the drugs they've been giving him, but he still hasn't woken up," her mother said.

"Is that normal?" Annie asked.

Her mother let out a deep sigh. "Nothing about any of this is normal, dear one."

They sat together in the cramped, dim room, neither of them saying anything. To Annie, everything about her arrival felt anticlimactic. For the better part of twenty hours, she'd been focused on nothing more than getting here. But now that she was here, she couldn't wait to leave, to get the hell out of that dim room and away from her mother and this version of her father that made no sense at all to her.

"You must be exhausted from your drive," her mother said. "Why don't you go home and get some sleep. I'm going to sit here a little longer, then I'll join you."

Annie looked down at her hands, the desire for a cigarette suddenly very strong.

"Wait," her mother said. "You're planning to stay at the house in town, aren't you?"

Annie shook her head. "Michael and I talked about it, and we agreed it would be better if I stayed out at the ranch, so I could keep an eye on how things are going out there."

"I see."

Annie could feel the hurt and disappointment radiating from her mother, but if she was going to make it through this crisis, she needed some privacy and breathing room. Staying at the house in town with her mother simply wasn't an option.

"I'm going to need a phone out there," she said. "Is there one I can borrow? Dad's, maybe?"

Her mother dug through the plastic bag containing her father's wallet and other personal items and came up with an old-fashioned flip phone. "Here. I guess your father won't be needing it anytime soon. I don't know where the charger is. Probably still in that pickup he was driving when he, when he—"

Then her mother was crying—terrible, guttural sounds coming from somewhere deep in her throat—and Annie was holding her, determined not to start crying herself, thinking that if she did, how would she ever be able to stop?

Michael had been right, as usual. This was just the beginning. Things would only get harder from here. Would she be able to rise to whatever it was the occasion was about to demand of her? Would any of them?

This was what prayer was for, she supposed, but she'd long since given up on all that. It had not brought Wade back from the dead, nor uprooted them from the house in town and returned them to their rightful place on the ranch, nor closed the yawning distance she'd often felt between her parents, and she did not suppose it would help here, either. Should she try anyway? Should she struggle to remember the words?

NINE

Jimmy waited until after midnight, then left Hammer and Kush sleeping on the red faux leather couch that was the trailer's only real furniture and rode the riverbed west all the way to the rodeo grounds before taking Fourteenth across town to see his father on what Michael, in his hysterical way, had described as their father's "near-death bed." Jimmy would believe that shit when he saw it. The way he had it figured, Leroy was too stubborn and self-absorbed to die. He had too much of his precious work to get done, and whatever stupid mess he found himself in now would turn out to be temporary, the way it always did.

"Stupid mess" was not a bad description of Jimmy's entire life up to that point, at least the parts he had no control over, like being born too late into a family with this weird, toxic cloud of grief hanging over it. When had he first become aware of the cloud, how it sat parked above his family's house on Country Club Drive in a way that wasn't true of any other house on the block? That was hard to say, but a good guess might've been his very first day at Sacred Heart Cathedral, when Caroline brought him to the wide sloping parking lot behind the school where all the other moms and a few dads were dropping off.

It was the usual first-day drama of kids bawling and clinging to their parents' legs and so forth. Then the teacher, an overweight, overly enthusiastic woman named Miss Rash, appeared before them. "Hello! Welcome to kindergarten! Did your grandma bring you to school today? Lucky you!"

"I'm his mother, actually," Caroline said in a low voice.

"Oh, goodness, I'm sorry!" Miss Rash said, her face turning red.

And there it was in all its glory. *The difference*. The thing that set Jimmy apart and would always set him apart. At tee ball games, summer camp, visits to the doctor. His parents were old enough to be his grandparents, his siblings old enough to be aunts and uncles, and Jimmy himself was, what, an afterthought? Some kind of gruesome mistake?

At dinner that night, without thinking any of it through, he declared that he wanted Annie, who was just entering tenth grade, to drive him to school.

"What? Your mother's not good enough for you anymore?" his father asked.

"I want Annie to do it, that's all," he said, looking down in shame.

"Do I have to?" Annie whined. "I'll be late to first period if I have to drag his little butt around."

"It's okay," Caroline said. "I can drop him down the street from the Chancery, and he can walk the rest of the way on his own." Then she smiled at him in a way that made him feel even worse.

"If you're gonna do that," Leroy said, shaking his head in disgust, "make him walk the whole way. It's only a mile."

The difference. Once you'd noticed it for the first time, you could never stop seeing it. It was everywhere. In the way his parents talked to Michael and Annie compared to the way they talked to him. In the silences that occurred when certain subjects came up, subjects he knew nothing about and never would, because *they* didn't want him to know.

Later that fall, after he'd gotten into hot water with Miss Rash for the tenth or twelfth time, she sent him down the hall to Sister Margaret's office. Sister Margaret was a plainclothes nun, maybe a hundred years old, who was known throughout the school for the stern, sour looks she'd give a kid who stepped even a toe out of line. But that morning she was all smiles, a never-seen-before tactic that made Jimmy trust her even less.

"Do you know who I am?" the nun asked when they were alone.

"Yeah, you're the boss lady."

"I'm the *principal*, yes. But I'm also a special friend of your mother's. She and I have known each other for a long, long time." He said nothing to this. What in the hell was there to say? "And did you know I taught your dad and your older brother when they went to school here?" She paused wistfully. "You remind me of him sometimes. You have the same boundless energy. Oh, those were dark, terrible days. For your mother, especially. But God works in mysterious ways, Jimmy. He gave us *you* to remind us that life goes on."

He had no idea what she was talking about. All he knew was that she was making some weird and mysterious claim on him, and he wanted no part of it. Not even a little bit. Later, on the playground, when he realized she hadn't been talking about Michael, but rather his other brother, the one who was *dead*, things got even weirder. Up to that point, Wade had been little more than a cartoon character, but not now. Now it felt like his dead oldest brother was the key to everything bad that had ever happened to him, every gaping hole in his life where a parent or a sibling should have been.

At the hospital entrance, Jimmy downshifted hard and let the Ducati's engine whine as it absorbed the RPMs. Visiting hours were long over, and the parking lot was nearly empty. Caroline's Camry was nowhere to be seen. He pulled a wheelie the length of the parking lot before sliding the bike to a stop near the doors to the ER and popping the kickstand.

Whenever he thought about his fucked-up childhood, there was one memory that always seemed to float to the top. It was a flashpoint of sorts, a perfect example of *the difference*.

His whole life he'd been hearing about what crazy-good athletes Wade and Michael had been. Football, baseball, wrestling. Especially wrestling. So when he was eight years old and a coach at summer camp talked him into going to some practices at the Y, he figured what the hell. Why not? The coach was this super-intense dude with a six-pack and cauliflower ears, and Jimmy was a little afraid of him. Whatever the coach yelled at him to do, he'd do it, *boom!*—no questions asked. Long story short, he got to be pretty good, pretty fast, and before he knew it, the crazed coach had signed him up to wrestle at the kids' state tournament in Wichita. The plan was for Jimmy to catch a ride with the coach, who had a son Jimmy's age. Later, Leroy and Caroline, or maybe it was just Caroline—this part was never completely clear—would make the two-and-a-half-hour drive, watch him wrestle, and then give him a ride home. Jimmy was so excited he tore through the kids in his side of the bracket like a tornado. Before and after matches, he'd scan the stands, searching for his parents. But the semis came and went, and still they hadn't appeared. Then the finals, which he lost in overtime, and *still* there was no sign of Leroy or Caroline. Nothing. Zilch. Complete no-shows.

Finally, after the tournament was over and people were rolling up mats and sweeping the floor, in walks his mother, looking guilty as hell. "Oh, thank goodness! I was worried you'd be gone. I broke the speed limit the whole way. How'd you do?"

"He wrestled like a champ," the coach said. "Tough bracket, but he beat a lot of really good kids."

"Oh, that's fantastic!" Caroline said. "I'm so proud of you!"

He just looked at her. "You forgot, didn't you?"

"Well, not exactly—"

"Don't even try to lie about it," he said, looking around. "What about Dad? Did he forget, too?"

"It's a busy time. Your father's been in the field all day."

And here they came, all the same excuses. But rather than listen to them, Jimmy walked over to one of the trash cans scattered across the arena floor, dropped his silver medal in amid the coke cans and wads of chewing tobacco and half-eaten hot dogs, and walked straight the fuck out of there.

By the age of ten, he was hanging out with a group of much older kids at a skate park built on some derelict tennis courts a half-mile south of Comanche Street. A "bad" neighborhood, if you believed what certain old people told you. But to Jimmy, there was no better feeling than getting lit on weed and hitting some awesome trick where both tires of his bike came off the ground, and for a second it was like you were floating in outer space and none of the bullshit of Planet Earth could touch you. Before long, he was spending three or four hours a day at the park, more on weekends, just smoking weed and practicing his bag of tricks—bunny hop, manual, bar spin, tail whip. He nagged Caroline into ordering him a twenty-inch Diamondback BMX in candy apple red, putting the thing together himself with some tools Leroy kept in the garage. He worried a little that his father would find the expensive bike in his room and freak the fuck out, but it took Leroy a month just to come to know of its existence, and by then all he said was, "Will you look at the size of those stem bolts. Kind of overkill, wouldn't you say?"

Stem bolts! Typical Leroy.

This was in those final, peaceful days before Jimmy's hair got too long and his clothes began to reek too much of weed and his teachers at Sacred Heart began to find fault with every last thing he did. It was bullshit stuff, mostly. He'd get into an argument with one of the kids in his class, usually an athlete who thought he was better than everybody else, and Jimmy would have to kick the kid's ass just to prove him wrong. Or else he'd space out when one of his teachers was asking him a question, and before he knew it, the teacher would get all up in his face, and Jimmy would "retaliate" and get hauled down to Sister's office.

"Oh, Jimmy, not again," Sister would say. "What are we gonna *do* with you?"

"Dang if I know, Sister Maggie," he'd say, turning on all the charm he could muster. He was the only person in the world who could get away with calling the old nun that; in spite of everything, she still had a soft spot for him.

Eventually, though, Sister had no choice but to give him the boot, and off he went to the public middle school. On the morning Leroy drove him over there, he gave Jimmy a long speech about how he was "embarrassing the Wagner name" and needed to "straighten up before it's too late."

Jimmy just sat there smiling, high as a kite at 8:15 in the morning. "And what's gonna happen if I don't straighten up?" he asked.

"I haven't thought that far ahead." Leroy shrugged. "But whatever it is, you ain't gonna like it, I can promise you that."

Somehow, he made it through the fall semester of his sophomore year of high school before the hammer came down for good. He was already on a "short leash," to quote the vice principal, when a ninth grader got busted for smoking weed in the school parking lot and ratted Jimmy out as the "dealer" who'd sold him the stuff. It was all bullshit. Jimmy was no "dealer." Half the time, he gave the shit away.

Regardless, what happened next was absolutely Jimmy's favorite memory of his father, maybe the only truly good one that came to mind. Jimmy was reclining on a bench outside the principal's office when Leroy appeared in the polished hallways and blew right by him without so much as a fare thee well.

"Sir, you can't go in there," came the halting voice of the school secretary.

"You called me, and I'm here," Leroy said in his loud voice. "Now how about you tell me what the hell this is about?"

Next came the principal's self-important voice. "Sir, if you'll just take a seat—"

"To hell with that," Leroy shot back. "I'm paying the taxes that are paying your salary, and I'm sure as hell not gonna wait around while you shuffle a bunch of papers. Are you kicking the little sumbitch out or not?"

"Well, yes. We have to, you see—"

"Fine, that's all I need to know."

The door to the principal's office swung open violently, and here came Leroy, walking fast as always, the soles of his work boots slapping the floor. "Come on, Jim. We don't have time for this crap."

Jim!

Never in his life had Leroy called him by his given name; it was always "You, this" or "Boy, that." But he'd said it now—and in public, no less.

"So now what?" Jimmy asked as they climbed into the cab of Leroy's mud-splattered Dodge.

"Now we're moving on to Plan B." He started the truck's diesel engine and let it idle a moment before putting it into gear. "I'm gonna let the monks at TMP have a shot at you, and if they fail, well, we're done."

"The monks?"

"The priests at Thomas More Prep in Hays. My brother Bob got sent there back in the day. Didn't do him any good, but hey, got to try something, right?"

"But what if I don't want to go?" Jimmy asked.

Leroy turned and looked him dead in the eye. "This isn't one of them deals where you get to choose. I've been way too lenient with you as it is. I should've taken control of this situation years ago, but out of respect for your mother's wishes, I didn't."

Jimmy had to laugh at that. "Oh my God, what bullshit! Don't go blaming any of this on Mom. You were too damn busy *working* to have anything to do with me, and you know it."

Leroy sighed. "Maybe you're right about that. Maybe this whole deal *is* my fault. But I'll tell you what. What happens from here on out is on you, not me. Are we clear on that?"

"Whatever," Jimmy said.

The glass doors of the ER slid open before him, and Jimmy took a hard left, nearly running into an orderly who was napping in a wheelchair. Jimmy knew the dude in passing, having hooked him up with weed a couple of times. "My old man's in here somewhere," he said. "Any idea which room is his?"

"Sure, follow me," the orderly said, pushing off in the wheelchair and leading Jimmy through a series of turns until they came to the doors to the Intensive Care Unit.

"Gracias, Amigo."

"De nada." He started to roll away, then stopped and looked back over his shoulder. "You, uh, holding anything I might like?"

"Nah, I got out of that biz."

"Too bad," the dude said, wheeling away.

Jimmy pushed through the doors of the ICU and had a peek behind a couple of curtains until he came to his father's room. It was gray-dark in there, with little monitor lights flashing silently like the lights atop a wind turbine. In the red glow of the lights, Jimmy could see Leroy's eyelids fluttering, his head moving side to side as in a dream. Was the old man really in a "coma-like state," as Michael had said, or was he just faking it, trying to twist the situation around to his own advantage in some way that only he understood? He stepped closer and gave his father a little shove on the shoulder. “Hey, dog. You awake? It’s Jimmy. Your favorite son.”

The old man just lay there, his eyes continuing to flutter beneath paper-thin lids. Jimmy pulled a chair up next to the bed and sat back with his hands behind his head. “Dude, I don’t know if you can hear me, but I’m gonna assume you can. How’s that? Will that work for you? Good, because, Dude, I got some shit to say. I know it’ll come as a shock to you, but little Jimmy’s been paying attention all these years. Not keeping score. I wouldn’t say that. Just watching and wondering and storing shit away for future reference. A *lot* of shit, actually. So, where to begin? Oh, yeah, *the difference*.”

And for the next hour, as the maintenance crew mopped the already spotless floors and the nightshift nurses came and went, Jimmy talked and talked. A couple of times, he could’ve sworn he got a reaction out of the old man, a slight raising of an arm or finger, a more intense than usual fluttering of the eyelids. Probably it was nothing, but it felt real to Jimmy. He was getting it all out on the table. The difference, the dream, everything. And boy did it feel *good*.

TEN

Her first night back on the Bar W, Annie slept in a tangle of blankets at the foot of the old stone fireplace. It was where she'd slept on trips home from college, and even before that, on weekend nights during her teen years, when she needed a break from town and everything it represented. She loved the view off the front porch, a panorama of grass, grazing cattle, horses, and sky. She loved the sounds of the place—the bellowing of calves, bull frogs croaking in the mud of the creek, coyotes yipping in the bluffs across the road, and the deep-throated barks of the ranch dogs, answering them.

The homeplace, as the single-story house at the center of the Bar W was called, had stood empty for the past eighteen years, ever since Annie's mother had decreed, for reasons all her own, that life on a southwest Kansas cattle ranch was just too sad and lonely to be endured. It was a brick house, a rarity in rural Kansas, built at no small expense at the height of the booming 1920s by a family that had drifted down from Iowa under the illusion that the southwest Kansas sky would deliver the same sixty inches of annual rainfall they were accustomed to back in tall grass country. That hadn't happened. Instead, starting in 1930, the skies failed to deliver even *ten* inches of rain a year. One wheat crop after another failed. The pastures dried up, then disappeared altogether under an assault of overgrazing. Trucks arrived and took the cattle away. In their place came the terrible dust storms of the mid-1930s, day after day with the skies so full of dirt you couldn't see from the homeplace to the tack barn, three hundred yards away. In April 1935, Dodge City recorded more than a dozen such days. Then came the "great grandaddy" of them all, April 14, 1935, so-called Black Sunday. In her father's telling, which Annie supposed he had gotten from his father or grandfather, the Iowans made it through that terrible day, hunkered in the basement of the homeplace with wet handkerchiefs covering their mouths and noses. But the very next day, Monday, April 15, 1935, they packed up their Model A Ford and headed back to where they'd come from, never to return.

The homeplace sat empty for a couple of years after that, until Annie's great-grandfather bought the house and all the outbuildings, along with the surrounding wheat ground and pastures—which looked more like sand dunes at the time—for half of what the Iowans had paid in 1920. It was a story of tragedy and triumph rolled into one, and sometimes, when things got dicey, as they often did on a ranch in southwest Kansas, her father had been known to speculate openly about the defeated Iowans, imagining them stopping on Back Trail Road in their Model A Ford to have one last look at the yellow brick house they'd built and then been forced to abandon. The subtext, or anyway the underlying question raised by the story, was crystal clear: would the Wagners be next? What sacrifices would be required of them to make sure that the worst thing that could happen to a ranch family never happened to them?

At dawn, the sun came streaming in through the big front windows of the homeplace. Annie rose and set a pot of coffee to brewing in the antiquated kitchen and descended into the basement, switching on lights as she went. Though the temperature outside would be in the nineties by early afternoon, it was still quite cool—cold, almost—in the semi-finished basement. It was easy to imagine the Iowans hunkered down here, dust floating in the air, as it did even now as Annie walked barefoot across the painted concrete floor. When they'd moved to town after Jimmy was born, their mother had insisted on a fresh start where furniture was concerned, and as a result, Michael's and Wade's old room in the basement had remained curiously frozen in time. Opposite the two twin beds was the trophy case her father had built to contain all the hardware that Wade and Michael were forever bringing home from track meets and wrestling tournaments and the like. Opening the dusty glass door of the case, Annie took down a large bronze statue of a wrestler that Wade had won as little kid at the state tournament in Wichita, probably before she was born. The statue, which she'd held many times, felt heavier and colder than she remembered it.

"Jesus, it's like a fucking grave down here," she said, shivering.

She put the statue back in its place in the glass case, careful to make sure that its base sat perfectly within the circle created by the dust that had settled around it, shut the door to the case, and walked back upstairs, shutting off lights as she went. The basement of the house in town, with its crazy 1960s-era bomb shelter, was certainly an upgrade from this, as hard as that was to admit.

She poured herself a cup of black coffee and carried it through the front door and onto the wide porch that looked out on the bluffs she loved so much. Lola, who'd spent the night on the couch in the living room, squeezed through the door behind her and jumped off the porch with a piercing bark. Four ranch dogs boiled up from beneath the porch, one of them, an Aussie/Lab mix, running up to Lola and planting his nose inches from her nose. They stood that way, frozen, both of their bodies tense, until Lola let out another high-pitched bark and the Aussie/Lab began to chase her through the derelict flower beds Caroline had maintained with such care when Annie was a child. The other dogs soon joined in the chase, and just like that, Lola was a member of the pack once more.

Annie drank a second cup of coffee and smoked a Marlboro Light—yes, she'd bought a fresh pack after seeing her father on his near-deathbed; she deserved at least that much after all she'd been through in the past couple of days—then pulled on boots and donned her favorite gimme cap with its Kansas Livestock Association logo splashed across the front. She grabbed a rope halter and scooped up a can full of grain and carried them into the horse pasture across the road from the house.

There were six horses in the pasture, and Annie recognized all of them but one, an athletic mare with big eyes and a dark roan coat the color of smoke. The horse reminded her of her old Appaloosa, who'd died at the age of twenty-five while Annie was off teaching English and finishing her master's thesis in North Africa.

"Well, well, who might you be?" she wondered aloud as she opened the iron gate to the pasture and slipped through.

The five ranch geldings, all of them sorrels or bays, came right up to her, sniffing at the can and rubbing their long noses against her shoulders. "Get back, you," she said, brushing them off and walking toward the little mare. She looked to be three or four years old, and, unlike the ranch horses, was shod. Annie approached the horse slowly, talking to her in a low voice, the rope halter hanging loosely from the crook of her bent elbow. The mare turned away from her at first, pinning her ears and contemplating a kick, but Annie put a stop to that nonsense by scooping some grain from the can and cupping it beneath the mare's black lips. When the horse lowered her head to take a nibble, Annie brought the rope halter up over the mare's nose and tied it off behind her left ear. Then she fed the other horses what remained of the grain and looped the lead rope into a makeshift rein and hopped belly-first onto the mare's back, hanging there a moment to see if she would offer to buck. When she didn't, Annie slid her right leg over the mare's back and came upright with the lead rope in one hand and a hunk of mane in the other. In a single, fluid motion, using more leg than anything, she wheeled the mare away from the other horses and started up the fence line at a fast walk.

The little mare moved with fluidity and grace, head down, no straining at the lead rope or looking back at the other horses. She responded to the lightest of cues and could neck rein some. After fifty yards, Annie squeezed her into a trot and then into a slow, rocking-horse canter. *She's sure got a lot of buttons on her*, she thought. *But what the heck's a show horse, and a mare no less, doing in Leroy Wagner's horse pasture?*

They splashed through Duck Creek at a spot where the water was only a foot or so deep, and would have ridden farther east had they not come to an eight-foot-high game fence Annie had never seen before with a large PRIVATE PROPERTY sign hanging from it. *That sure wasn't here the last time I rode this pasture*, Annie thought. She rode alongside the fence for a mile, then crossed the creek again and headed west and crossed into Owl Rock pasture, so named because of a large outcropping of rock with a hole in the face of it from which she and Wade had once seen an owl take flight, where she paused to look down at a herd of a hundred or so Black Angus that were bedded down in the distance. The cattle looked up in mild alarm as she rode in a broad circle around them. At first sight of the cattle, she had felt the mare's attention quicken beneath her. Only when the cattle had dropped out of sight behind them did she urge the mare into a long lope.

Half an hour later, having ridden both sides of the Sawlog, she circled back through Owl Rock until she came to the bluff closest to the road and rode to the top and sat looking down on a familiar scene that included, in addition to the brick ranch house, shop buildings and corrals: a red tack barn made out of a derelict grain silo; rows of rusty implements, trailers, and baling equipment; stacked fence posts and irrigation pipe; and, farther in the distance, hundreds of large, round bales of alfalfa and Sudan grass. The sight of the bales in their neat rows always reminded Annie of the fun she and Michael had had as kids, racing each other across the tops of the bales, leaping over the gaps between until one of them, usually her, misjudged the takeoff or landing and found themselves wedged into the soft V where the bales met. How they had laughed and laughed. At the time, it had seemed that nothing bad could ever happen to any of them. They were invincible, blessed by God and agriculture. She felt a smile spread across her face as she remembered. But a moment later, she spotted something farther off in the distance, and the smile faded. There in the weeds behind the shop building, visible to her only because she had ridden to the Bar W's highest point, sat what was left of her father's flatbed Dodge. Michael had warned her that he'd directed the towing company to deliver the truck to the Bar W rather than to a salvage yard in South Dodge, but in the whirlwind of meeting her mother at the hospital and seeing her father in his weakened state and then driving out to the ranch on Highway 283 as long shadows began to stretch across the horizon, she'd forgotten.

She rode the mare down from the bluff and past the corrals and tack barn, noting along the way several gates that stood open and at least five cows and calves that had found their way into the uncut alfalfa. But she ignored these troubling signs for now and rode straight to the destroyed pickup with its crumpled cab and bent wheels and roof ripped open like the top of a can of tomatoes, this last clearly the work of the firefighters or EMTs or whoever-the-hell's job it had been to extract her father from the wreckage using—what had Michael called it?—the *Jaws of Life?*

The next thing she knew, she'd wheeled away from the wrecked truck and was running the little mare as fast as she would go down Back Trail Road in the direction of the hired man's peeling white frame house, where a second ranch truck, identical to her father's but still whole, stood in the middle of the sun-scorched yard, windows rolled down, driver's door standing open. Sliding to a stop before the wooden porch, she swung down from the mare's back and wrapped the lead rope around the top rail before ascending the steps and giving the front door a couple of hard knocks.

Nothing.

She knocked again, the skin of her knuckles beginning to fray against the rough wood of the door. Again, nothing. She turned to go back to the homeplace, but the sight of the ranch pickup with its door standing open, and the contrast it made with the image of her father's destroyed pickup one pasture over, stirred something in her. Turning to face the door again, she began to kick the bottom of it in rapid succession with the toe of her boot, as if she were pounding out eighth notes on a keyboard, no gaps in between, just *bang bang bang bang.* "Open up, you sumbitch! I know you're in there!"

Still no answer.

She resumed her kicking. *Bang bang bang bang bang bang bang bang.*

"God Almighty!" came a voice from within. "Will you quit that goddamn racket already?"

"Not until you open this door!" Annie yelled.

She could hear someone stumbling around inside the two-bedroom house, which had stood empty for decades before her father had it moved to its current location. Then a curtain in one of the front windows moved and she caught a glimpse of the hired man's bearded face. A moment later, the door creaked inward and there he stood, shirtless and barefoot, his eyes a blur of red, his long yellow hair flattened against the side of his head. A strong smell of whiskey and cigarettes and dried vomit poured off him.

"What?" he said, rubbing his eyes.

"You know who I am, right?"

His red eyes took in her and the horse tied to the porch behind her. "Yeah. So?"

"So, aren't you supposed to be running this place while my dad's in the hospital? I was just over by the tack barn, and there's gates left open everywhere and the hot wire around the alfalfa is down."

He let go of the door handle and stepped back into the filthy living room with its upended saddles and coiled ropes and dirty clothes strewn across the floor like murder victims in a crime scene. Against one wall was a blue polka-dot couch Annie recognized as a hand-me-down from the homeplace. He collapsed into it and began patting himself down for a cigarette.

In the kitchen, she found a 1.75-liter bottle of Lord Calvert on the counter next to a sink piled high with dirty dishes. She scooped up the half-empty bottle by its handle and upended it in a gap between the dishes.

"What're you doing in there?" came the hired man's scratchy voice.

The bottle empty, she moved on to the refrigerator, where she found a six-pack of Coors with three cans remaining. She'd just pulled the beer from the bottom shelf of the fridge when the hired man stumbled into the room.

"Hey! Put that back!"

He lunged at her, but she pirouetted out of his reach, and he tripped over his own feet and fell face-first to the floor.

"Ain't fair," he said, not even trying to get up.

"You're damn right it isn't," she said. "What *would* be fair is if it was *you* who got T-boned on the Correction Line one of these nights, driving home drunk from the bar in one of my dad's trucks, like the one sitting outside with the door wide open." She stepped over him, cradling the beer in her arm like a football, and headed for the front door, pausing only long enough to say over her shoulder, "I'll be back in an hour, and you'd better be cleaned up and ready to roll. We've got a to-do list as long as my arm."

"Hey," he called out. "Do a guy a favor and leave a couple of them beers."

"Not a chance."

Leaving the door open behind her, she unwrapped the halter rope and stepped off the porch right onto the mare's back, holding the beers by one finger through an empty plastic loop of the six-pack. The little horse looked back at her with wild, curious eyes, as if to say, *Who knew her ladyship could get so worked up?*

"Girl, you have no idea," Annie said, kicking the horse into a lope.

ELEVEN

The Bar W could be a lonely, desolate place for a young wife, particularly one who'd grown up in the city, as Caroline had. Much of the time, in the early years of her marriage, she felt like one of those women in a pioneer novel, the ones who lose their minds listening to the wind rattle the makeshift windows of a sod house while their husbands are off God knows where, working, always working, as if work were the only thing that mattered in the world, and anyone who couldn't see that was weak in body or mind or both. But then lunch time would arrive, and Leroy would roll into the yard in his ranch truck, and they'd laugh and carry on like the newlyweds they were, their bodies homing in on each other even before he'd scarfed down the meatloaf sandwich or mac and cheese she'd made for him. They were both virgins on the day they married, and this new world of lying together on lavender-scented sheets while a breeze blew the curtains back and drifted across their naked bodies was a marvel to them. They could make love two or three times a day and still feel the same passion for each other when they crawled back between the unmade sheets that night. It was a wonder they didn't come apart at the seams.

Then Wade was born, and both her happiness and her misery increased.

"Just look at all that black hair!" a nurse at the hospital raved. "And those fat red cheeks!"

"Looks just like his dad," another nurse added.

Leroy flashed a smile and took Wade from the nurse and held him in his arms. "Does he recognize me, do you think? Does he know who I am?"

"He knows," the nurse said.

It scared Caroline how much she loved Wade—and how much he, in turn, needed her. Growing up, she'd helped her mother take care of each of her younger siblings as they were born, but little in that experience had prepared her for having a baby of her own. Gazing into Wade's face while he nursed, she was overcome with the thought that she would gladly die to save him. But then another thought would occur. If she died, who would take care of him? And that thought, too, was unbearable.

From the first, Leroy was a proud and doting father. He loved to feed Wade and give him his bath. On Sunday afternoons, he'd lie on the old polka-dot couch in the living room of the homeplace, listening to a ball game on the radio while Wade slept on his naked chest. But that was only in the evenings and, if she was lucky, on Sunday. The rest of the time Leroy was off working in some far-flung field or in town chasing parts for a baler or some other ancient piece of ranch machinery that had broken down yet again. Compared with the epic struggle of keeping the ranch solvent and running, her quiet attempt to keep from slipping into what her mother called "the baby blues" seemed small and inconsequential. Who was she to complain about being tired all the time, or crying for hours for seemingly no reason, or losing all interest in sex, when her husband was faced with making sure the bank got paid on time or putting up enough hay to feed the cattle through the coming winter? But then her thoughts, already in turmoil, would swing wildly in the opposite direction: who was *he* to silently play the martyr when she served leftovers two nights in a row or failed to put on makeup in anticipation of his coming home at night?

Then something happened that tested her faith not just in Leroy but in God, too. It was a windy Saturday afternoon in March, and she'd just put Wade into his wheelie walker so she could clean the ashes out of the fireplace in the front room, when she heard the *clack clack clack* of plastic wheels on the basement stairs, followed by a sickening *thud* at the bottom. She dropped the shovel and dustpan and ran to the basement door, which was meant to stay closed all the time but which had been left open. At the very bottom, where the stairs gave way to naked concrete, lay her baby in his upended walker.

She ran down the steps and struggled to get his legs free from the contraption. He was limp, not even crying, and his face was covered with blood from a gash on the top of his head. Holding the child, she ran out into the yard, yelling for Leroy. He emerged from the machine shed, a look of surprise on his dark face. Then he was running toward her across the buffalo grass.

They were fourteen miles on muddy roads from the hospital on the north side of Dodge City. Leroy broke ninety miles an hour at least twice in that distance, a fact almost as terrifying as the unconscious, bloodied baby she held in her arms.

"What in the hell happened?" he asked.

"What do you mean? *Somebody* left the door to the basement open, that's what happened."

"What, you weren't watching him?"

"Please, just get us to the hospital without killing us all."

As soon as a doctor in the ER took Wade from her, she retreated into a near catatonic state. The nurses asked her question after question—how long ago had it happened? had he cried or thrown up?—but all she could think about was the *clack clack clack* of those wheels on the stairs, followed by that sickening *thud*. Why didn't they ask her about *that*?

Then Sister Margaret showed up, and they escaped into the candlelit darkness of the hospital chapel, where they knelt down on the cold tile floor and gave themselves over to prayer. For the next couple of hours they prayed, Caroline making wild promises the whole time. *Please, God, if you'll just let my baby live, I'll be the best wife and mother ever, I'll suffer anything you ask me to suffer, just please please please let my baby live.*

They were still at it when one of the ER nurses flipped on the fluorescent lights of the chapel, startling them out of a deep, trance-like state.

"Oh, *here* you are. We've been looking for you everywhere. Your baby's gonna be okay. He's alert now. Nasty cut on his head, but that seems to be it."

"Thank the Lord!" Sister said, rising from her knees in triumph.

It was a miracle sent directly from God, and as parents, they should have been eternally grateful. But in the days that followed the accident, a sort of chill settled over and between them. It wasn't that Leroy blamed her, exactly, but he didn't find her completely innocent, either, and she felt much the same way about him. Then, barely a week after the accident, Leroy left the door to the basement open *again*, and Caroline barely managed to grab Wade before he went down the stairs on his hands and knees. In the fight that followed, she demanded that they move to town, where they'd at least be closer to the hospital.

"This is our home," Leroy said, shaking his head. "We're just gonna have to be more careful, that's all."

It was the only thing she'd ever asked of him, and he'd denied it to her. Wouldn't hear another word about it. Sure, he carpeted the stairs to the basement and put a deadbolt on the door, but that was the extent of his concern. In the wake of her disappointment, she was careful not to get pregnant again, at least not right away. The accident had shaken her confidence in the benevolence of the universe even as it had confirmed, even hardened, her belief in God.

Then, six or seven months after Wade went down the stairs, she was in town doing the grocery shopping when she happened to run into one of her old college friends, a rail-thin, gossipy woman named Judy who'd dropped out of St. Mary's to get married about the same time Caroline had.

"Say, did you hear about Ted Kramer?" Judy asked.

"No. What about him?"

"He's getting married."

"Really?" Caroline said, feeling a stab of disappointment. "Who is he marrying?"

"Betty Ludlow."

"No way."

Betty Ludlow was a brassy blonde with a loud laugh that sounded like a car horn.

"I was surprised, too," Judy said. "But word is that Betty's 'in the family way,' and apparently Ted's not too upset about it. Her dad's got a nice real estate business up in Great Bend, and you know Ted. He'd be great at that."

She brooded over the conversation for the rest of the afternoon, and that night she made love to Leroy with a passion she'd not felt since before Wade was born. Of course, the guilt started up soon after that, and the following Saturday, she left Wade with Leroy and drove into town to go to confession. But when her turn came and she knelt in the dark confessional, she could come up with nothing to say. She mentioned her tendency to shade the truth and her struggles with pride and her resentment of the long hours Leroy insisted on working, leaving her alone in the house with a small baby when what she craved was adult company, adult conversation.

"Anything else?" the priest said in a bored tone.

He was a visiting priest from another parish and didn't know her from Adam.

"An old boyfriend of mine is getting married," she said.

"And?"

"It makes me feel sad and . . . angry."

"Angry? At whom? The bride?"

"No. At him, I guess."

"Your husband?"

"No, the boyfriend."

A pause followed during which the only sound was the priest's breathing.

"My child," he said finally, "you must resist even the thought of this man. You should take care not to see him, and especially not to be alone with him."

"What are you saying, Father?"

Another pause. "You're being tempted, make no mistake. Worse, you're in danger of becoming a temptation to *him* as well."

She knelt there, stunned into silence by the priest's words, then got up and walked straight out of the church without asking for or receiving absolution. The whole episode made her angry and confused. She had entered the confessional seeking comfort and reconciliation. Instead, she'd been admonished, cast in the role of evil temptress. It wasn't fair at all, and she vowed that from that moment on, she would keep her own counsel when it came to Ted and whatever feelings she might still have for him. It was her business and nobody else's, and she would deal with it alone.

Years passed. Michael was born, and Wade started kindergarten. Then she got pregnant with Annie, and instead of rejoicing at the news, as she had with her first two children, she felt a kind of dread descend upon her. It was not that she was against having more children. She and Leroy had always talked about a large family—four, five, even six kids—and she had always longed for a daughter. It was just that the gulf between her and Leroy had continued to widen after Michael was born, and she worried that the thin string of common feeling that held them together wouldn't be able to withstand the demands of having a newborn in the house along with two rambunctious boys.

Then, another blow. Back in Wichita, her longsuffering mother was diagnosed with breast cancer and died soon afterward. The speed with which she was plucked from this world—and how little she was missed by anyone, including her own children—shocked and appalled Caroline. Was this what the life of a mother amounted to, this business of birthing and raising children, only to have them leave you in the end and not even miss you when you died? When she thought of her mother's life, how dominated it had been by happenstance and poor choices in men, including Caroline's own biological father, she felt sick and confused. Would this end up being the story of her life, too?

One day, while Leroy was working cattle and she was dusting the bookshelves in the living room, she came across a short novel by Anton Chekhov she'd read during the single year she'd spent in college at St. Mary's. On impulse, she picked up the book and, opening it at random, began to read. *What troubled me particularly was the thought that my life had become more complicated, and that I had completely lost all power to set it right, and that, like a balloon, it was bearing me away.*

She was stunned by the words, which a previous version of herself had underlined and then forgotten. Though not completely, it seemed. For years, ever since Wade's birth and possibly before that, she'd been troubled by the exact same dream of a hot air balloon carrying her away into a cloudless blue sky. In the dream, she searched everywhere for a rope, some kind of ballast or shutoff valve, *something* to help her steer the balloon or at least bring it safely to the ground. But there was no rope or ballast, and the balloon went higher and higher, until she woke in a cold sweat beside her husband, who snored lightly on his side of the bed until she elbowed him and he rolled over with a grunt.

When morning arrived, she tried to share her misery with Leroy. But in her own mouth these woes of hers ended up sounding abstract and trite compared to the stark realities of his working life. He listened to her, but it was not with the patient attention he'd shown in the past. Instead, his listening felt impatient and strained, as if he were just waiting for her to finish so he could change the subject. Really, it was not listening at all.

The year Annie started kindergarten was an especially difficult one. She was thirty-six, all three of the children were in school, and she floundered a bit, trying to figure out what to do with herself. Ironically, it was Leroy who came up with the solution, suggesting that she return to school to finish her degree, or at least to take a class or two.

"Why shouldn't you go back to school?" he said. "I'd do it myself in a heartbeat if I could."

His kindness surprised her, but then, as she thought it over, she began to suspect that it wasn't kindness at all that had prompted his suggestion, but a perverse kind of selfishness. With her off in town half the day and doing homework at night, he'd be free to work as long as he wanted to without having to come home and face her disappointment. So long as his needs were met—particularly *that* need—he didn't much care what she did.

She enrolled in an English course at the community college taught by a poet she was pretty sure was gay, though nobody talked about those things in Dodge City in the early nineties. She was the oldest person in the class—even the gay poet was five years her junior—but after a while all of that ceased to matter. While her classmates wrote their papers the night before they were due and groaned at any mention of revision, she gladly performed two, three, even four drafts of the smallest assignment.

"My dear, you're a superstar," the poet said to her during one of their conferences in his tiny office.

"Oh, I don't know about that."

"No, no, you are," he insisted.

By the time Annie entered fourth grade, Caroline had earned her associate degree from the community college and would have returned to St. Mary's to work on her bachelor's were it not for the fact that the college closed suddenly in 1992, a victim of declining enrollment and fiscal mismanagement. This was a blow, to be sure, but now that she had gotten it into her head to finish her degree, nothing could stop her, and she enrolled in a distance education program offered by a Catholic college out of Wichita instead.

Despite all these changes in her life, she felt restless much of the time and was still prone to dark, Chekhovian visions that her life was a hot air balloon carrying her somewhere she had no desire to be. Leaving the public library, where she relied on public computers to do the work in her distance ed classes, she would drive around the wealthier neighborhoods on the north side of Dodge, looking at houses with FOR SALE signs. Before long, a fantasy developed wherein she'd bought a bungalow at the edge of Snob Hill, as people called the neighborhood near the country club. The tiny house would be her secret hideaway, a place she could go to read and write and be entirely alone, without Leroy or the children or anyone else to bother her.

It was while cruising a neighborhood of sprawling brick houses north of the country club golf course that she first spotted a yellow-and-brown realty sign with the name EDWARD KRAMER emblazoned across the bottom. On closer inspection, the sign featured a picture of Ted's smiling face—he'd gained weight and his hairline had retreated a bit, but he was still handsome for all that—along with a cheesy slogan—NEED A PLACE TO LAY YOUR HEAD? CALL TED!—and a phone number.

Of course, she'd heard that Ted's marriage to Betty Ludlow had ended in divorce several years before, and that he'd moved back to Dodge with his second wife, a young, single mother he'd met in Great Bend. Gradually, without meaning to, she began to keep track of his successes in real estate, thrilling each time the word SOLD appeared atop one of his signs along with a magnetic sticker bearing the phrase THAT TED! HE DID IT AGAIN!

Why am I doing this? she wondered. *What on earth is wrong with me?*

Still, she told no one about these secret thoughts of hers—not Monsignor McCarthy, not Sister Margaret, and certainly not Leroy.

Then, one afternoon a week or so before Halloween, she pulled into the driveway of a Frank Lloyd Wright–inspired house directly across from the golf course and was shocked when a powder blue Cadillac convertible pulled into the driveway behind her, blocking her in. The driver of the Cadillac tapped on his horn twice before getting out of his car and ambling up to her window.

"You're early," came a deep voice she recognized from her days at St. Mary's. "I usually like to beat my customers to a showing, but—"

At this point, the voice trailed into silence, and she turned her whole body in her seat to look at him, feeling a smile beginning to creep into the corners of her mouth.

"Caroline? Is that really you?"

"Yes, it is."

"Well, I'll be. What on earth are you doing here?"

"I was just, I don't know, turning around . . ."

She trailed off, and he took a couple of steps back in order to get a better look at her. "You haven't changed a bit! You look exactly the same as when we were kids at St. Mary's!"

She had to laugh. "I've changed a lot, actually. So have you, Ted. We're not kids anymore."

"Speak for yourself!" Ted said, making a show of sucking in his gut, and they both laughed at the joke. My God, how good it felt to actually laugh again!

"Come on," he offered. "I'll show you around this overpriced pile of bricks."

"Are you sure? I don't want to interfere with your work."

"Ha, that's a good one," he said, opening her car door. "Believe it or not, this *is* my work."

He gave her the "grand tour," as he called it, interspersing his observations about the house with questions about her life in the country. "The pool isn't heated, but as you can see, it sits in direct sunlight in the afternoon. So, how far out in the country do you live? Fifteen miles, did you say?"

"Fourteen."

"Ah, well! Big difference."

She laughed again. She couldn't remember the last time she'd laughed like that.

When the grand tour was over, he got them both a glass of sweet tea and they sat together in a pair of padded wicker chairs by the covered pool. It was a warm day for October, and it felt good to sit there. If she closed her eyes she could imagine the pool's glistening blue water, hear the faint gurgle of its underground plumbing.

"You know," Ted began.

"Hush," she said, raising a hand to halt him. "Don't say anything. I just want to sit here in the quiet for another moment or two. Is that okay?"

"Well, sure. Whatever you want, Cal."

"Cal" was his name for her from their days at St. Mary's. No one else, before or since, had ever called her that. It was almost as though he were talking to another person—an alternate version of herself, the person she might have become if she hadn't rushed headlong into her current life as the wife of a workaholic rancher.

Then the doorbell rang at the front of the house, and she was shaken back into reality.

"That's my two o'clock," Ted said. "Do you want to stick around until I'm finished?"

"No, no. I'll just slip out the back, if you don't mind."

"Suit yourself. The keys are in the Caddy. Just leave her in the street when you pull out."

"Thanks, Ted. I'll do that."

She reached out to shake his hand—a ridiculous gesture, but she could think of no other. Bowing his head theatrically, he took her hand in his and gave it a kiss in the manner of a courtier in a costume drama. They both laughed again. "It's so great to see you, Cal. You can't even imagine."

"Maybe I can," she said, her heart beating so hard she thought she might break a rib. Then she turned and ran through an open gate in the side yard and stood peering around at the front of the house, where a young couple stood waiting for Ted to open the door.

"Welcome!" came Ted's booming voice. "I can't wait to show you this house. Boy is it something special!"

When the coast was clear, she ran across the front yard and climbed behind the wheel of Ted's Cadillac. As she backed the boat-like car out of the driveway, she looked up to see Ted standing alone on the front porch, waving to her. She waved back, a little tentatively at first, and then with full theatrical flavor, like a beauty queen on a parade float.

On the seat beside her was a pile of his business cards. After he'd gone back into the house, she folded one of the cards and slid it into a pocket at the back of her purse. She felt more alive and in control of her life than she'd felt in months, maybe years.

TWELVE

On her way back from the John Deere dealership in Dodge, where she'd bought a new set of sickle teeth for the combine, Annie pulled over in a roadside ditch and waded into the waist-high wheat. It was hot for late June, low nineties by noon with a warm wind that blew steadily out of the southwest. Forget about needing a blow dryer after washing your hair, she thought. Just walk outside and it would be dry in two minutes. The wheat scratched against her jeans as she descended a long slope, where she broke off a couple of heads and rolled them between her palms. The grain separated easily from its husk. She popped a couple of kernels into her mouth and chewed them down to a paste before spitting them out on the ground. Harvest was several days off yet, and if the wind would just back off, maybe longer.

At the ranch, her father's hired man, DW, had the sickle blade off the combine's header. Annie and he laid it flat on the long metal bench, and Annie held the blade steady while DW knocked the old teeth off one by one with a hammer and punch. In the days since she'd found him drunk on the floor of his house, they'd settled into a truce of sorts. She bit her tongue every time she felt compelled to tell him how worthless he was, and he refrained, for the most part, from reminding her that she was a woman, which in his view amounted to the same thing. They'd just knocked out the last of the teeth when Annie looked out the open shop door to see a dually Ford coming up Back Trail Road pulling a twenty-four-foot aluminum stock trailer.

Here comes the cavalry to the rescue, she thought. *About time, too.*

The night before, she'd called the number of a hired cowboy Michael had given her and was shocked at how quickly the cowboy, whose name was Jacob Hess, had agreed to help with the harvest. "I figured someone would be calling," Hess said in his twangy southwest Kansas voice. "Last week, I had to pull a couple strays from the pasture behind your homeplace, and rather than make two trips with the trailer, I left my mare in with your dad's geldings."

So I guess that's one mystery solved, Annie thought.

As she stood watching, the pickup made a broad circle across the front lot until it pulled up in a cloud of dust directly in front of the tack barn. As the dust cleared, a short, wiry man in a straw hat and knee-high, buckaroo-style boots hopped down from the truck and began unloading horses, tying them at intervals of six feet along one side of the corrals. The horses were smallish and young, and they were all saddled, with bridles hanging from their saddle horns.

Leaving DW to the sickle blade, Annie walked across the front lot to where the wiry man was moving among the horses, reaching down here and there to slap a belly or lift a foot.

"Looks like you brought some friends," Annie said.

"I did," the cowboy said, offering her a calloused hand to shake. Up close, Jacob Hess was not short but a little over medium height with strawberry blond hair and a thick mustache. Talking to him the night before, Annie had pegged his age at anywhere from thirty-five to fifty, but she could see now that he was on the low end of that estimate, maybe five years older than her brother Michael. "I figure even if I can't ride them, at least they can practice standing at a rail not making a fuss every time a truck or a tractor rolls by. That's half the battle with horses as young as these knuckleheads. Lack of worldly experience."

"So you're a horse trainer?" Annie asked.

"Trying to be."

"What are you training them to do? Ranch work?"

Hess nodded, continuing to lift and put down feet. "Ranch work, reining, 4-H, western pleasure. I ain't real picky, so long as there's a check involved."

"What about that mare across the road?"

He straightened his back and looked at her with a little more interest than he'd shown up to that point. "What about her?"

"Her gaits seem a little refined for a ranch horse."

"Her *gaits*, huh? That sounds like the assessment of someone who's been up on her."

Annie felt herself go a little red in the face. "Well, I did climb up bareback a time or two. I'm sorry. I know I should've asked and all that, but I was at a loss for whose horse she could be. I hope you don't mind."

"Nah, it's okay," he said, moving among the horses once again. "But seeing as you've been on her and all, how about you tell me how she did for you."

"My professional opinion," Annie said in an ironic tone that seemed to go right over the cowboy's head.

"Sure, if you wanna call it that."

She shrugged and thought back on the two times she'd ridden the horse. "I liked how calm she was. I liked the way she walked in a straight line, head down, no rubbernecking around. Oh, and that rocking horse lope of hers. You won't get that out of any of my dad's geldings."

He dropped the hoof he'd been holding and stood up straight again. "You loped her," he said. "Bareback."

"Well, yeah." She laughed. "Was that a mistake?"

He laughed, too, and shook his head. "Well, just speaking for myself, I don't know as I'd ever climb up on a strange young horse, bareback, and just take off loping. Not unless there was gonna be money waiting for me at the pay window."

"You rodeo?"

"Yes, ma'am. Used to. And let me tell you, I got the ex-wives to prove it, too." He smiled again, and a slight twinkle came into his light blue eyes. "Anyway, I'm glad you like that little horse of mine. I set an awful lot of store by her myself."

What was the deal with the "ma'am" business? Annie wondered. Was it a joke? Some kind of aping of old-time westerns?

At length, Hess finished fooling with the horses and began a slow walk to the cab of his truck, where he pulled off his high-topped riding boots with their jangly spurs, exchanging them for a pair of low-heeled ropers. "They say you're studying to be a doctor, is that right?"

"Not exactly. I'm working on a doctorate. Anyway, it's no big deal."

"Sounds like a pretty big deal to me."

"Well, thank you for saying so."

With one offhand compliment, he'd made her feel better about herself than Dr. Hilman had in dozens of margin comments on the first chapter of her stalled dissertation. To say nothing of a certain black-bearded lumberjack. But she cut that thought off as soon as it popped into her mind. She was, after all, back in Jeremiah Anonymous.

When Hess was ready, they walked together across the grass lot to the shop building, where DW sat on a folding chair smoking a cigarette.

"Got those new sickle teeth on?" Annie asked.

The man shrugged.

"I guess I'll take that as a no?"

"Taking a break is all," the man said. She and Hess exchanged glances. It was what it was.

Later, with evening setting in and DW gone home for the day, Hess changed back into his riding boots and spurs, pulled the cinch on the first of the six horses he'd trailered over that morning, and climbed into the saddle. Annie climbed onto the top rail of the corral and sat watching as Hess put the horse through a short warm-up followed by a series of bending exercises, bringing the horse's face around on each side until its nose touched the toe of his boot. After that, he worked the horse along the rail where Annie was sitting, executing a series of elegant rollbacks. After less than five minutes in the saddle, Hess climbed down from the horse, eased the bridle from its mouth, and tied the animal at the front of the stock trailer.

"He sure got off easy," she said.

"He did everything right the first time I asked him. When a horse does that, you learn to leave well enough alone."

The next horse took a bit longer to "do everything right," and the one after that was a forty-five-minute "disaster area," as Hess termed the ride. "Sometimes they're just like that. They have their good and bad days, same as us."

By then, the only light to see by was coming from an iron pole Leroy had put up years ago to illuminate the area around the tack barn. But that appeared to be enough for Hess.

"By God, I love riding horses on this ranch," he said. "Most places you go, there's no room to work a horse in front of the barn. Every square inch is given over to cars and trash dumpsters and whatnot. You're always riding *away* from where the horse wants to be, fighting him the whole time, and before you know it, the whole dang string is barn sour. But here, you got all this room to fool with a horse right outside his own front door. He ain't got no chance to turn barn sour. After a while, all he wants to do is ride off somewhere else."

"It's the same with people," Annie said. "Didn't you want to go off somewhere else when you were young?"

"You got that right." Hess laughed. "I couldn't wait to get off the little ranch where I grew up. It was like the place was radioactive, and I needed to get the hell away from it just to escape the fallout."

By now, she'd moved off the fence where she'd been sitting and had taken over the job of unsaddling and brushing the horses down after Hess had finished riding them.

"How old were you when you left?" she asked.

"Seventeen."

"What about school?"

"They weren't teaching the kind of stuff I wanted to learn."

"Which was?"

"I don't know. How to make a living without hating what you're doing all day long. I wasn't cut out to be no welder, and no accountant either."

"Most folks aren't," Annie said.

It was after ten o'clock when Hess unsaddled the last of the colts.

"So, that's it?" Annie asked. "Are you finally done for the day?"

"No, ma'am. Got a couple more to ride back at the house. But I'll eat some dinner first."

There it was again. That "ma'am" business.

"Since you'll be over here the whole time we're cutting wheat, you might as well leave these horses here. That way you can get in a couple of rides early, while we're waiting for the dew to dry."

"Are you sure?" Hess asked.

"Of course. It'll be fun having them around."

They turned all six of the colts out in the big corral and threw them some alfalfa. The little mare they left in the pasture across the road, because, according to Hess, she was "too darned good to shack up with the likes of those knuckleheads."

Annie had to laugh. "If someone had said that to me eight or nine years ago, who knows, maybe my whole romantic history would be different."

He gave her a blank look.

"Sorry! TMI!"

Another blank look.

"Too much information."

THIRTEEN

Jimmy dropped his duffel on the bunk he'd been assigned in the barracks-like dorm on the top floor of TMP-Marian's single academic building, a Tudor Gothic monstrosity dating from the 1930s, and followed the sound of an acoustic guitar until he came to a corner room where a wiry, Asian-looking kid in flip-flops and a Raiders cap strummed his way through an eerily familiar chord progression while a big blond kid in blue sweats did pushups in the middle of the floor.

"Yo," Jimmy said. "What's shaking?"

"Nothing," the kid with the guitar said. "What's up with you?"

"Not much. I live here now, I guess. What was that song you were playing?"

"'Hotel California.' Fucking barre chords." He waved the fingers of his left hand before his face, as though trying to bring them back to life. "You play?"

Jimmy shook his head. "Is that why you're rocking that Raiders cap? You're from California?"

The blond kid squeezed off a final pushup and rolled onto his back. "Not just Cali, man. We're from *LA*." How beautiful those two letters, *L* followed so closely by *A*, sounded in Jimmy's still-cold ears. Before that moment, he'd never given LA or California much thought, but all of that was about to change.

"You holding?" the blond kid asked.

Jimmy laughed. "Let me guess. A little *dry* around here?"

"Dude," said the kid with the guitar. "It's positively Saharan."

"In that case," Jimmy said, "I'm about to get real popular, real fast."

Although they looked nothing alike, Kaid and Brock were half-brothers, the separate offspring of a movie producer dad, originally from Salina, who hadn't had much to do with them over the years but *had* paid to have them shipped off to Thomas More Prep–Marian, a co-ed Catholic school with a dorm for male boarders, at the first whiff of adolescent trouble.

"A dick with an Amex card," Kaid said.

"Yeah, well, my dad's a dick *without* an Amex." Jimmy laughed.

The day kids at TMP–Marian were all cut from the same Catholic-school cloth. They drank like fish and went to football games and screwed their brains out (or so they claimed) in the back seats of their hand-me-down Cadillacs and Toyotas. When the weekend rolled around, they were out of there, leaving Kaid and Brock and Jimmy to sneak weed and play video games with the other boarders, most of whom hailed from far-off places like Taiwan or South Korea.

Since the debacle at the kids freestyle finals in Wichita when he was eight, Jimmy had not given a shit about sports, especially traditional ones like football, basketball, and baseball. But he soon learned that not playing a sport at TMP meant hours of tedium in chapel or study hall, and so, a few days into his imprisonment, he borrowed a pair of Asics Aggressors from Kaid and went out for wrestling. The practices, held in a decommissioned swimming pool in Billinger Fieldhouse, a.k.a. "the Snake Pit," were two and a half hours of unmitigated hell overseen by a small Japanese dude, Yoshiro Hatta, who'd wrestled under the legendary John Smith at Oklahoma State and knew all kinds of crazy and possibly illegal holds designed to inflict unspeakable pain. Jimmy took to it right away. A month or so into the season, wrestling a ranked kid Coach Hatta had scouted for latent vulnerabilities, Jimmy hit a move called a cement mixer and then *squeeeeeeeeeeeezed* until he got the fall. Everyone in the Snake Pit went bananas, and the next thing Jimmy knew, he'd gotten his picture in the *Hays Daily News* below the headline TMP–MARIAN GRAPPLERS DOWN TOUGH LARNED SQUAD. The Monday after the meet, a couple of cute Marian girls who'd never given him the time of day asked where he was from and why he didn't wear a letter jacket like the other jocks.

"I don't know. Because they're so uncool?"

"Or maybe it's because you don't have any varsity letters yet?" one of the girls said.

"That, too." Jimmy laughed.

A week later, warming up before a tri-dual in Scott City, Jimmy glanced over to the gym entrance and spotted Leroy standing there in his rancher clothes, a tightly rolled program jutting from his meaty fist.

What the fuck is he *doing here?* Jimmy thought. The memory of being forgotten in Wichita on a day when he might have won a state title came back to him in all its gory detail, and part of him considered charging up to where Leroy had taken a seat at the top of the bleachers and telling him to get the hell out. But another part of him knew it wouldn't do any good. The old sumbitch was too stubborn and hardheaded for that. "It's a free country," he'd say, chin jutting out before him. So Jimmy tried something else, losing his first two matches in spectacular fashion. However, that didn't work either. Leroy just bellowed all the louder from his spot atop the bleachers. "Let's go, Jim! Forget the score! Take him to his back and stick him!"

Finally, he could take no more, and in his last match of the day, he hit a cement mixer and pinned the kid he was wrestling in something like ten seconds flat.

"Atta boy!" Leroy yelled, shaking his fist in the air. "Way to take it to him!"

Kaid and Brock were laughing like a pair of hyenas when he came off the mat.

"Who the hell is *that?*" Brock asked.

"Nobody," Jimmy said.

"Sure doesn't sound like nobody."

"Tell me about it," Jimmy said.

It was as embarrassing as hell, and yet, on the long bus ride back to Hays, Jimmy had to admit that at least some of what had gone down in that gym had felt pretty good. The singular focus and attention. The to-hell-with-all-of-you way Leroy had bellowed his encouragement. *Let's go, Jim! Forget the score! Take it to him!* Was this what it had been like for Wade and Michael back in the day when they were throwing touchdown passes and pitching no-hitters? If so, he could almost understand why they'd worked so hard to please the old sumbitch.

However, the glory was short-lived. A few weeks later, after he and Kaid and Brock had qualified for regionals and Jimmy had upset a ranked wrestler to win the Red Cloud Invitational in South Dakota, they got busted sneaking back into the dorm after a night running amuck on the streets of Hays—Jimmy's first offense, but Kaid and Brock's third—and the principal kicked all three of them off the team, ending their season.

"Never in my life have I seen such a waste of talent," Coach Hatta said, shaking his head of porcupine-like black hair.

"It's okay, Coach," Jimmy said. "Brock'll win a state title next year for sure."

"Not talking about Brock," Hatta said. "Talking about *you.*"

In the end, though, getting booted from the wrestling squad turned out to be a good thing. More time for planning capers. Come spring break, the three of them were on a plane to

California, having put the cost of the tickets on Kaid and Brock's dad's Amex card.

Other than the trip to South Dakota to wrestle in the Red Cloud tournament, Jimmy had never been out of the state of Kansas before. The cab ride alone from the airport to the beach house in Malibu was a mindblower, six speeding lanes of the most exotic and expensive cars Jimmy had ever seen, to say nothing of choppers encased in chrome and vintage VW buses straight out of the 1960s. And that was just the beginning. Kaid and Brock's dad was in Almería, Spain, shooting a reboot of a spaghetti western, leaving them with unfettered access to the beach house in Malibu, the dad's resto-mod 1974 Triumph Bonneville, and all the medical marijuana they could smoke.

The first night in Cali set the tone for the rest of the week. They smoked weed until the world began to turn at just the right speed, then wandered down to the beach, where hundreds of kids their age were roaming free. All day long it was song and smoke and one beautiful girl after another wandering up to say hey. One of the girls, a cute Asian chick named Lily, fifteen years old with hair reaching down to her bikinied butt, offered to teach Jimmy how to play guitar. "Hell yeah!" Jimmy said. "Let's doooooooo it!"

He'd messed around with Kaid's acoustic a time or two, but this was different. Sitting across from Lily in the warm sand, he worked his way through the chords to "Free Falling," "Leaving on a Jet Plane," and "Wish You Were Here." She even showed him how to play and sing at the same time, a feat that had seemed impossible only hours before. He'd never felt so free or good in his entire fucked-up life. Halfway through that magical night, he and Lily donned a couple of helmets and sneaked off together on the '74 Bonny. Baked beyond belief, the sun beginning to drop on the Pacific Coast Highway, an absolute babe on the bike behind him with both of her brown arms wrapped around his waist. If life got any better than that, Jimmy thought, just tell him when and where and he'd hack his way through jungles and brave alligator-infested swamps to get there.

When the spring semester ended and summer vacation rolled around, they tried to replicate the days of magic, spending most of July and part of August living in the garage of the Malibu beach house, Kaid and Brock sleeping until two or three in the afternoon while Jimmy vacuumed cars for minimum wage at a Hertz dealership on Sweetwater Canyon Drive to pay his way. But Kade and Brock's dad was back from Spain and around all the time now, killing the vibe, and the Queen of California, beautiful, bikinied Lily, had flat-out disappeared.

Rather than destroying the dream, however, these disappointments only served to stoke it. If you wanted to live the dream for real, if you wanted to escape Kansas forever the way Kaid and Brock's dad had somehow managed to do, you had to find a way to make some serious bank, not this tired business of vacuuming cars at Hertz. The Malibu beach house and the '74 Bonny couldn't belong to your best friends' dad. That shit had to be *yours*, free and clear.

Hence K-Dog and the Girl Scout Cookies.

Was it risky? Hell yeah.

Did it wear his skinny ass down to a frazzle? Absolutely.

But when your dream was so close you could almost reach out your hand and touch the motherfucker, you owed it to yourself to go *big*. Forget the score. Hit a damn cement mixer if you had to. Cali was waiting, and from what Jimmy had seen, that girl had no time for losers.

FOURTEEN

The Pembroke Hill Summer Open House started at 7:00 PM, but Michael's wife Vanessa was determined they arrive no later than 6:15 so they could take part in a special, pre-open house tour she'd arranged with the director of admissions.

"If Sam likes it," she said while Michael dressed for work in the ground-floor suite of their 5,000-square-foot McMansion in Leawood, "and we all agree that it's the perfect school for our family, I want to put down a security deposit right away, so they'll be sure to hold our place."

"They'll hold it," Michael said, knotting his tie.

"This is Pembroke Hill we're talking about," Vanessa said. "It's the best school in the city."

"The most expensive, you mean."

Although he was careful not to complain about it in front of Vanessa or the boys or, God forbid, Vanessa's mother, Rosa, Michael disliked living in Johnson County and missed the early days of his marriage, when Vanessa was still practicing law and they lived in a cozy bungalow near the Plaza in Brookside. When dinner meant going out for sushi or getting takeout from the Thai place. When huge chunks of Sunday morning were reserved for nothing but sex and catching up on *The New York Times* (or so it seemed in Michael's overheated memory of those years). But then Sam came along, followed by Luke, and before long, Vanessa had quit her job to stay home with them.

Vanessa's mom flew in from Chicago to ease the transition, and before the trip was over, the two of them, Vanessa and Rosa, had decided that Brookside was not safe enough, its public schools not good enough, and the only responsible thing for them to do was to escape to the suburbs on the Kansas side. Michael balked, at first. The move would inflate his commute to the firm's offices in downtown KC from a modest fifteen to an outrageous *fifty* minutes or more. But Rosa wore him down with her arched eyebrows and dramatic questioning of why he insisted on denying his wife and children the lifestyle and opportunities they deserved.

"I'm not denying anyone anything," Michael said. "I just think—"

But it didn't matter what he thought. What mattered was making sure there was no tragic repetition of the event that had defined Vanessa's childhood: her father's loss via bankruptcy of the Cadillac dealership he'd inherited from his father, a loss that had catapulted Vanessa and Rosa, post-divorce, from their million-dollar home in Naperville—that's how Rosa always put it, *million-dollar home in Naperville*—back to Rosa's parents' two-bedroom house in Hammond, Indiana. The whole rags-to-riches (and back-to-rags) narrative was too much to be up against when you were simultaneously drowning in kids and work, and so, before long, Michael gave up any attempt to oppose it. Sure, they could buy a house in Leawood, the Kansas suburbs' answer to Naperville, even if it meant he'd spend an extra hour a day stuck in traffic. Only now, less than ten years after the move, it turned out that the only middle school good enough for their oldest son was guess where? *Back* over the line on the Missouri side, five minutes from their old neighborhood in Brookside.

The very thought of Pembroke Hill, with its shiny, secular veneer and progressive affectations, made Michael a little sick to his stomach. If there'd been time, he would've started in yet again on all of the things he didn't like about the place, beginning with the fact that it was too prissy, too expensive, too far from home. What was wrong with Nativity, the Catholic school down the street from their house that Sam had attended up to that point? A school like that had been good enough for Michael and every member of the Wagner clan, even if it did feature, in the case of Sacred Heart in Dodge, taped-together textbooks, no air conditioning, and football helmets from the 1970s with less-than-adequate padding. A school like that toughened a boy up, was part and parcel of what it meant to be a Wagner.

But as usual there was no time for any of this, and besides, Vanessa had heard it all before. So instead of fighting the good fight that morning, Michael finished knotting his tie, kissed Vanessa, and headed out to where his fire-engine-red Dodge Ram pickup waited in the driveway.

"Remember, six-fifteen," Vanessa called after him. "You'll have to leave the office before six to make it there on time."

Michael gave her a thumbs-up and climbed into the pickup's high cab and rolled out of their subdivision, leaving a thick cloud of diesel smoke in his wake. With its twenty-four-valve Cummins engine, the Ram was a ridiculous vehicle for a corporate attorney to drive, but Michael didn't care. He'd bought it on a whim, off the same lot across the tracks from Wyatt Earp where his father and grandfather and great-grandfather had bought their trucks, after his 2011 BMW M3 threw a rod during a pheasant-hunting trip to Dodge City. He'd half expected to sell or trade the truck in as soon as he got back to KC, but in the months since, he'd come to appreciate the puzzled looks the Ram inspired in his fellow attorneys when he pulled into the parking garage of Curtis, Frederick, and Lyles. The truck was a statement of sorts. It said, *I am my own man, and I will go my own way, no matter what the rest of you sheep think.*

Or something like that.

In his corner office south of Crown Center, Michael got caught up on email and then turned his attention to a manila folder bearing the label STEWART V. BRANCH—PRO BONO. It was the second of two folders on his desk related to his father and the ranch. The other, labeled BAR W—FINANCES, contained all the facts and figures he'd managed to assemble in the three consecutive evenings he'd spent trying to make sense of his father's bookkeeping. From what he'd been able to deduce, Leroy was not sloppy or inattentive to detail so much as he was *broke*, or very nearly so.

Sure, there was still some cash in the Bar W checking account—more than $5K, in fact. The problem was the stack of unpaid bills Michael had unearthed and carried back to Kansas City, which added up to more than *twenty times* that amount, half of it owed to a bank holding a note that was more than sixty days past due. This was a shocking discovery, to say the least. For as long as Michael could remember, his father had always played his financial cards close to his chest, cultivating in the process an aura of semi-invulnerability. Now that façade was gone, the aura evaporated, and Michael found himself wondering about all kinds of things he'd never wondered about before, such as how much better the ranch might have fared if he'd played a part in running it all these years instead of being forced to the sidelines in the aftermath of Wade's death. Spinning around in his chair, he opened the Excel spreadsheet he'd created on his office computer and entered the large infusion of cash he'd sent to the bank in Dodge City the day before. No doubt Leroy had been hoping for a big wheat crop to help stem the tide of his recent financial setbacks. That had been Krebs's impression. But from what Michael could see now, not even a bumper crop sold at the top of the market would be enough to pay the bank in full, to say nothing of Leroy's other creditors. What in God's name had the old man been thinking? As recently as a year ago, the records showed, he'd been close to debt-free. But then it seemed that a competition of sorts had sprung up between him and Byron Branch, and in the course of it, Leroy had gone on a buying spree, bidding on four circles of irrigated land north of the ranch whose single irrigation well had turned out to be too salty to use anytime other than after a hard rain. That alone had been a costly error, but there were others like it, including several involving cattle that had since been sold at a loss. Meanwhile the clock on the note from the bank kept right on ticking.

Michael barely slept the night his father's financial troubles first became real for him, but by the next morning, an answer of sorts had occurred to him with the force of a revelation. He, Michael, was just gonna have to suck it up and cover the ranch's most pressing debts out of his own pocket, moving the hefty bonus he'd just earned from the case in Tulsa from his firm checking account into the Bar W account. Later, after his father had recovered and they'd made it through the current crisis, he and Leroy could sit down and come up with some kind of repayment plan. None of it was ideal. For example, he'd have to keep the whole thing secret from Vanessa lest he spike her baseline anxiety regarding financial matters to new and epic levels. But with sharks like Byron Branch swimming so close to the borders of the Bar W, something had to be done, and with Leroy out of commission, no other solution came to mind.

Luckily, the second folder, STEWART V. BRANCH—PRO BONO, contained more positive news. In the past week, Michael had put forty-five or fifty hours into the case, and his team of paralegals had put in fifty more, and together their labors were beginning to bear fruit. Yes, the paperwork recording Branch's loan to Chester and Fanny Stewart had been done "by the book," as Branch claimed, but by digging deeper into Branch's preexisting relationship with Chester Stewart, including the fact that Stewart had worked for Branch at the Flying J at the time the loan was made, Michael had unearthed what he considered to be a clear fiduciary responsibility on Branch's part. It could be argued, in other words, that Branch was legally and morally bound to do what was best for the Stewarts, financially speaking, and that by extending them credit when he knew they had no way of paying off the loan, Branch had crossed the line into territory that was not only highly problematic, but also predatory.

It was a very promising angle; even Michael's boss, Russ Frederick, who resented all the time Michael was spending on the case, agreed. And yet when Michael called Melvin Sparks, Branch's Wichita lawyer, to dangle the possibility of settling the case out of court, Sparks had laughed in his face. "Brother, we'll see your Kansas City ass in court."

"Going once," Michael said.

But Sparks didn't even bother to wait for the count of two, ending the call without another word being spoken.

The whole scene gave Michael goose bumps whenever he thought about it. If Branch and his people wanted a showdown in the Ford County courthouse, well, that was exactly what Michael was ready to give them. The more time he put into it, the more the case had begun to take on the dimensions of an epic struggle. Good versus evil, old versus young, original settlers versus unscrupulous interloper. To say nothing of Biblical parallels Abraham and Isaac, Cain and Abel, Joseph and the coat of many colors.

In the years following his older brother's death, Michael had done everything he could to replace Wade in his father's eyes, including following in Wade's footsteps on the Bar W and as starting quarterback of the Dodge City Red Demons. But in the end, those efforts had come to nothing. He lacked Wade's uncanny speed and rifle of an arm, and anyway, it turned out that Leroy didn't particularly want Wade to be replaced, by Michael or anyone else. The message was delivered in a variety of ways, both subtle and not-so-subtle. For example, Michael would sign up for the same welding or auto mechanics class at the high school that Wade had taken, and his father would hear about it and ask, "Why the hell are you taking that?" Or they'd be eating lunch at Judy's Café in Jetmore, and a neighboring rancher would see them and joke that Michael looked big enough to send Leroy into an early retirement, whereupon Leroy, without looking up from his food, would say something like, "You think I'm dumb enough to let any of my kids follow me into this mess?" or "The day I retire is the day you see me lying in a wooden box with a silk tie around my neck."

Then, over Thanksgiving break of his junior year at KU, after suffering through a semester of homesickness so severe it shocked him into speech, Michael had pushed back on his father's narrative of self-sacrifice by declaring that he was dropping out of school to join him on the Bar W. Michael could remember the scene as if it happened yesterday. They were sitting in Leroy's pickup waiting for a stock tank to fill, a convenient arrangement insofar as they could stare out across the hood without looking at each other.

"Like hell you are," Leroy said.

"Why not? *You* quit college."

"Yeah, but I didn't have a choice. My dad was dead, my grandpa was not far from it, and my brother had run off to join the hippies in California. It's different for you."

"I don't care about any of that," Michael said. "I want to farm and ranch. That's my choice."

Leroy paused, nodding slowly, and for a moment Michael thought his argument had won the old man over. After all, how many southwest Kansas ranchers did *not* want their oldest son to follow them into the business? Instead, Leroy had let out a long breath and said the words Michael would never forget. "Listen up. I don't want to have to say this more than once. I don't want you on this ranch. You're not needed, and I won't have you throwing your life away because you got a little homesick and came home with your tail between your legs." Michael felt his face go red. He kept staring out over the hood of the truck while his father continued. "I know that sounds harsh, but I want you to make something of yourself, Michael. Become a lawyer or go into business or something like that. Those are the folks who run the world, not cattle ranchers and dirt farmers. As for the Bar W, the burden of this place is mine and mine alone. You and your sister and your little brother will inherit the place one day, provided there's anything left *to* inherit. But ain't none of you following me on this ranch so long as I'm walking this earth. That's it. End of story."

Michael just sat there, shaking his head bitterly. "Would you have said that to Wade? Because I don't think you would have, Dad."

"Wade?" Leroy said, jolting forward in his seat as if someone had just shocked him with an electric cattle prod. "What's your dead brother got to do with anything I just said?"

"I don't know, Dad," Michael said. "You tell me."

Instead of answering, Leroy had climbed out of the pickup and trudged across the frozen ground to shut off the water before it overflowed the stock tank. When he returned and threw the truck into reverse, it was like the conversation had never happened. Indeed, they never talked of it again. The Friday after Thanksgiving, against his mother's cries of protest, Michael loaded up his Jeep Wrangler and drove straight back to Lawrence, where he switched his major from business to a prelaw focus. In Michael's mind, however, the conversation by the stock tank had never stopped. It was still going on in his head, even to this day.

Pembroke Hill, as its name implied, sat on a little knoll on the Missouri side of State Line Road. Michael had driven past the school a hundred times on his way to and from work, but until now, he'd never taken the time to visit its five-acre campus, the grounds of which looked more like a small liberal arts college than a combined middle school/high school. When he pulled into the visitors' parking lot at 6:15 on the nose, Vanessa and the boys were there to meet him, Vanessa in a tight-fitting business suit and heels of the kind she used to wear when she was still practicing law. Why had she quit? Michael wondered for the thousandth time.

"Hey, buddy," he said, running a hand through Sam's short black hair. Both boys had inherited their mother's dark hair and olive skin. It was another way in which Michael, with his light hair and pale skin, was an outlier in his own family. "You ready to see this place?"

"I guess so," Sam said without looking up from his phone.

"I am," Luke said, smiling up at him. At nine, he still thought Michael was a superhuman figure who could do no wrong.

"Let's go," Vanessa said. "We don't want to keep Mr. Johnstone waiting."

Johnstone was the admissions officer, a soft-spoken Black man in his early thirties with a gym-chiseled body and a faint aura of the Ivy League about him. He met them on the steps of the main academic building and proceeded to give them a tour of the school's "assets," as he called them. Although the original incarnation of the school, Pembroke Country Day, had been around for over a century, at least half of the buildings on the campus looked new or were under construction—a sure sign that the financial commitment of sending a kid to Pembroke did not end with tuition but extended to what would surely be aggressive and never-ending fundraising appeals. Standing in the impressive main quad, Mr. Johnstone paused to note that sixth-graders began the school year with a three-day camp that was "a great introduction to middle school and a wonderful, comfortable way to meet new friends." Vanessa looked at Michael out of the corner of her eye, smiling knowingly. One of Michael's main objections to Pembroke was that Sam would be leaving behind the friends he'd made at Nativity.

"At Pembroke Hill, we focus on the whole student," Johnstone said. "In addition to our stellar academics and low faculty-to-student ratio, we offer a wide range of organizations and clubs, interscholastic sports, and community service opportunities."

"Do you have a wrestling team?" Michael asked.

"Well, yes," Mr. Johnstone said. "We do for now."

"For now?" Michael said.

The admissions officer smiled; a little cavalierly, Michael thought. "Well, I'm afraid it's not one of our more popular sports. We had only two boys go out for the high school team last year, so naturally there's been some talk of dropping it. We also offer football, soccer, lacrosse, basketball, baseball, and track and field. But basketball is definitely our most popular winter sport."

"What about tennis and golf?" Vanessa asked. "Do you offer those?"

"Those start in high school, along with swimming," Johnstone said. "But rest assured, there are club practices and private coaching available to make sure your son's ready when the time comes, regardless of what varsity sports he chooses to focus on."

Club practices. Private coaching. Leroy had been Michael's private coach, throwing him into action against his older and heavier brother on a 14-by-14-foot Resilite mat in the basement of the homeplace. Michael had spent the majority of those matches with his face planted firmly in the mat, both arms chicken-winged behind his back, but the experience had toughened him up in a way he feared Sam and Luke would never experience, no matter how much money he and Vanessa poured into private coaching and the like.

The school's new performing arts center featured not one but two theaters. Room after room full of easels and drawing tables, expensive camera and computer equipment, a fancy gallery space for displaying student work. On the way to the new athletic center, which featured two gymnasiums (in addition to the 1940s-era gym off the main quad) and a new artificial-turf football field with a synthetic track running around its perimeter, he marveled at how many families at the open house looked like carbon copies of each other: dad in a business suit, mom in a dress or business suit of her own, kids as young as eight carrying phones in their hands like they were extensions of their bodies. What, he wondered, would Caroline and Leroy make of the scene? The whole thing would be as incomprehensible to them as the inner workings of Wall Street or Louisville, Kentucky, on Derby Day.

"What do you think?" Vanessa asked as they joined the other families on a slow walk to the new student center, where the president of the school was scheduled to speak.

"Well, I think we need to talk to Sam. You know, get a feel for what he thinks."

"You're kidding, right?" Vanessa said. "Didn't you see the look on his face when he saw the robotics lab? He's sold."

"Maybe," Michael said. "But this is the only school he's seen. I'm sure he'll want to look at Thomas Aquinas and the other places where his grade-school buddies are gonna end up. And, you know, at least Aquinas hasn't dropped its wrestling program. I saw in the *Star* they had a kid place at Fargo last year."

Vanessa halted in the middle of the sidewalk so that the other families had to step on the grass on either side to get past them. "Sam, why don't you and Luke go on ahead and find us some seats?" she said with a familiar edge to her voice.

"All right," Sam said, and the two boys disappeared into the handsome stone-and-glass building.

"What's the problem?" Vanessa asked. "Is it the money?"

"No, it's not the money," Michael said. "Although, you have to admit, spending 24K on sixth grade is a little ridiculous."

"Well then? What is it?"

He sighed audibly, hating the sound even as he made it. "Vanessa, come on. Just look around us. Do these look like our people?"

"What do you mean, 'our people'?"

"I mean I grew up on a ranch outside of Dodge City, for Christ's sake. I had to scrap and fight. I put myself through college and then law school, working on the ranch every summer and in a liquor store in North Lawrence three or four nights a week."

"Your parents live, literally, on Country Club Drive."

"It's just a name, Vanessa. It means nothing. But forget about me. Let's talk about you—a scholarship kid from East Chicago. Think how hard you had to work. Aren't you afraid we're coddling these boys? Aren't you afraid they're gonna grow up, I don't know, *soft*?"

It felt like one of the biggest speeches of his life, but Vanessa barely acknowledged it before launching into a speech of her own.

"No, Michael, I'm not worried about any of that, because, unlike you, I think we succeeded in *spite* of our childhoods, not because of them." She laughed and shook her head. "I mean, the idea that I would somehow want to *replicate* any of what I had to go through, give the boys *fewer* opportunities instead of *more* and *better* opportunities. Well, I'm sorry, but that's what's ridiculous. Not the tuition at what we both know is the best school in the city."

His shoulders slumped forward. He felt like the last general on the battlefield, the solitary defender of a town everyone else had abandoned. He could feel himself losing not only this skirmish at the city's gates, but the larger battle, too, maybe the war as a whole.

"Look, I don't know what's going to happen with my dad," he said. "At this point, it's anyone's guess. But I've got a trial coming up in Dodge in a couple of weeks, and I really want you and the boys to come out there with me. I want them to see and experience where I grew up, spend some time on the Bar W before the trial starts. What do you say?"

"Oh, Michael," Vanessa said.

"What? You're refusing to go?"

"No, of course not. I just want to, you know, talk about it some more."

"And I want to talk about *this* some more," Michael said, nodding at the heavy front doors of the performing arts center.

She looked down at her feet for a moment, and when she looked back up, it was clear she'd made up her mind about something.

"Okay, sure. Of course we'll go with you to Dodge to see your dad and check in with your mom, make sure she's doing okay." She paused dramatically. "But I also want to put down that deposit. Tonight, before we leave."

"Fine," Michael said.

A moment later, they were walking again in the direction of the student center, side by side, if not hand in hand like many of the other parents.

Had he won or lost?

It was impossible to say. All he knew for certain was that a reckoning of sorts was on the horizon. Something was about to change. He could feel it in every cell of his bone-weary body.

FIFTEEN

The first thing Leroy saw when he woke in his bed at Western Plains was a wooden crucifix standing bolt upright on a little table at his feet with yellowed unlit candles on either side of it. He had seen the hideous thing somewhere before, but he could not say where. A classroom at Sacred Heart? The library at St. Mary of the Plains? The answer kept coming to him, only to slip away in the fog.

"Get it out of here," he tried to say, but he hadn't used his voice in a while, and the words came out all garbled. "*Geeeeeeeeeeheeeeeeeer.*"

"Leroy?" came a familiar voice at his side. "Are you awake?"

He turned to find an older woman sitting in the chair beside his bed. He knew her, but he didn't know her. Like everything else, she was enveloped in fog.

"Leroy, honey, can you hear me?" the fog creature asked.

She was standing now, her face pushed close to his. Her nose and hazel eyes were something like Caroline's, but that was not possible. Caroline was in her twenties, no, wait, her thirties, and this woman was pushing sixty, with worry lines gathering around her mouth.

"Who are you?" he asked, his voice beginning to loosen up in his throat. "What did you do with Caroline?"

"What do you mean? I'm Caroline!" Tears ran down the woman's beautiful face. She wiped at them with a tissue. "Should

I get the doctor? Squeeze my hand if you understand what I'm saying."

He tried to sit up but was waylaid by a sharp pain that seemed to radiate across the whole left side of his body. It was like someone had taken a ball-peen hammer and begun whacking him with it, first in the hip, then in his kneecap, and finally in his arm. His head began to throb, and he closed his eyes against the room's harsh lights. Something had happened to him, but he didn't know what it was. A fog creature had grabbed Caroline and stolen her nose and eyes, and now there was a gun in the shape of a crucifix pointed straight at his head. He'd seen the gun before, but where?

He opened and closed his eyes a couple of times in quick succession, and a flash of memory came to him. He was a boy, eight or nine years old. The windows in his mom and dad's bedroom on the ground floor of the homeplace were cracked wide. A breeze moved through the curtains, bringing a faint smell of lilac from the bush outside the window. On the bed, a faceless figure held a rosary. On a table next to the bed, a crucifix stood upright in a little tray with a candle burning on either side of it.

Mom! Don't leave me here by myself! Please!

"Leroy?" the fog woman said. "Leroy, wake up!"

"Leave me be. She's dead, and I'm on my way to join her."

"No," the woman said, shaking him. "I need you to wake up and talk to me."

After a while, another woman appeared holding a paper cup. She shook some pills from it and tried to get him to swallow them, but he knocked the cup from her hand, scattering the pills across the floor. "Keep them damn things away from me!"

"I'll get an orderly," the woman said.

"No, get the doctor," the fog woman said. "No more pills until he's seen the doctor."

The pill woman hurried from the room, and Leroy grabbed hold of the fog woman's hand and squeezed it as the pain in his hip and leg rocked him once more.

"Does it hurt bad? Leroy? Maybe you should let them give you something for the pain."

"No," he said. "No more of them pills. I don't want them, I tell you."

"Okay," the woman said. "Don't worry. I won't let them give you so much as an aspirin if you don't want it."

"Thank you," he said, allowing his head to fall back on his pillow.

He turned his head to have another look at the woman beside him. It was Caroline, all right. She had found him in the fog, rescuing him, and now everything was going to be all right. In a little while, he'd ask her to get rid of the gun that was pointing at him from the foot of his bed. In the meantime, he'd just keep his eyes averted. The fog had to lift sooner or later. It always did after the sun had risen high enough to burn it away. His job was to wait it out. Wait and grit his teeth and find a way to tolerate the pain. He could do that. He'd *been* doing it ever since he was nine, and maybe long before that. Maybe since the day he was born.

SIXTEEN

The wheat harvest began with a test cut in a high, flat field three miles west of the Bar W. It was a tentative, halting first step, but once the grain elevator in Dodge confirmed that the moisture content was below penalty, the work took on a frenzied, all-in quality. Every morning at six o'clock sharp, Annie would make herself a cup of coffee and call Leroy on his land line to talk about the plan for the day. He'd been released from the hospital a few days before, and every time she spoke with him, he was a little more like his old self.

"When you get done with the Rawlings quarter, move on down the road a half mile and knock out that little eighty-acre piece next to the Jennings pasture. That's a rental deal, and the tickets on it have to be kept separate. Just tell the guy at the elevator when you bring the first load."

Annie took it all down in a ruled composition notebook, the first few pages of which were covered with half-hearted reading notes on *The Mayor of Casterbridge*. When her father ended the call—abruptly, as was his habit—she'd carry a second cup of coffee to the front porch and watch Hess ride colts in the front pasture while the sun rose and the dew steadily dried on the uncut wheat. Then, just before seven, she'd pour the dregs of her coffee over the porch rail and drive over to DW's house to roust him from the polka-dot couch. In the past week or so, he'd made the transition from lights-out drinking to a steadier, more continuous form of intoxication, but he was still a pain in the ass for all that. He had to be reminded to do the smallest things, like keeping the combine's radiator free of chaff, or greasing its moving parts at the end of the day.

"I'll do it in the morning," he'd say.

"What's wrong with right now?" she'd counter. "Your clothes are already dirty. In the morning, they'll be clean. At least, in theory, they will be."

"I don't give a shit about any of that."

"I know you don't, but *I* do."

She'd give him a hard, boss-lady look, and after a minute or two of ignoring her, he'd finally pick up the grease gun and disappear into the bowels of the combine, ever-present cigarette dangling from the corner of his mouth.

They were a small crew tackling a ridiculously large task, and each of them had a specific job to do. DW ran the combine, Hess drove the grain cart, and Annie hauled wheat to the elevator in Dodge in the old Freightliner they'd outfitted with a new hoist the night before the harvest began. When she wasn't hauling grain, she was bringing a load of diesel for the combine and tractor or stopping by the house in town to pick up the packed lunches and dinners that Caroline insisted on making even though in some ways it would've been easier for Annie to hit the drive-thru at Wendy's or Kentucky Fried Chicken and thus escape her mother's lengthy reports on what it was like to have Leroy Wagner cooped up in the house all day.

"I know he's in terrible pain, but all he does is stare out the window and grit his teeth. When I ask if he'd like a book or magazine to read, he just grunts and says, 'What the hell for?' Same thing with the television. 'Ain't nothing worth watching but the weather report, and I already seen that.' If this goes on much longer, there's gonna be a murder in this house. Either that or I'll be driven completely insane."

"Well, Mom," Annie said, the need for a Marlboro Light growing stronger every second she had to sit in the driveway listening to her mother's complaints, "the doctors did say he needed to go to a rehab unit in Wichita, remember?"

"Yeah, right," her mother said. "Like your father would agree to that."

Any guilt Annie might have felt about staying at the ranch instead of the house in town was long gone now, if it had ever existed in the first place.

In the first week of the harvest, with the weather cooperating and few breakdowns to overcome, they cut through nine hundred acres and brought in thirty-seven thousand bushels of wheat, an average of better than forty bushels an acre. It was the kind of progress that made Annie's mind reel with the possibilities. *At this rate*, she'd think, *we'll be finished by* . . . and here she'd pencil in some ludicrously optimistic prediction. It was the same way she'd been when she was writing the first chapter of her dissertation. She'd put together a couple of good days at the computer, and the buzz of progress would soon create an illusion in her mind whereby the entire dissertation, all five chapters, numbering seventy-five or eighty thousand words, would be finished in a matter of months if not weeks.

But then, midway through their second week in the field, DW cut into a thick patch of wheat in a swale south of the ranch, and the old 9500 John Deere, which had been running hot all day, redlined. Annie had just gotten back from the elevator when she saw the combine come to an ominous halt at the far end of the field, white smoke billowing out of its engine compartment. She left the Freightliner on the road and jumped into the service truck and tore out across the stubble. When she reached the combine, Hess had the engine door open and was standing off to one side letting the last of the white smoke escape. For his part, DW sat in the cab of the machine with his elbows on his knees, smoking a cigarette. Just seeing him sit there, cigarette in his mouth, huge Styrofoam cup containing God only knew what mixture of Lord Calvert and Coke between his thighs, otherwise not a care in the world, made Annie want to reach her hands into the cab and throttle him.

"What happened?" she asked through the cab door.

"Got hot."

"I can see that. Did it blow a hose or something?"

He shrugged. "Damned if I know. By rights, this piece-of-shit rig shoulda been replaced years ago, but you know your dad. Too goddamned cheap."

He was right, of course, but that didn't stop a bolt of anger from passing through her. Who the hell was *he* to criticize her ailing father? She imagined herself reaching into the cab and grabbing him by his greasy hair. But instead of acting on the impulse, she drove the service truck to the top of the hill, where the cell reception was better, and called Leroy.

He picked up on the first ring. "What is it? Something break down?"

"Combine overheated."

"How bad?"

"I don't know. We're still waiting for it to cool down."

"Have you been cleaning the chaff off the radiator? You got to watch that real close and blow it out good with an air hose when it starts to build up."

"What do you think I've been nagging your idiot hired guy about every morning and night?"

She heard what may have been a muffled laugh, and then he said, "Well, let her cool all the way down, then fill the radiator and see if she'll run at an idle without getting hot."

"All right," Annie said. "I'll call you back in a bit."

She drove the pickup back down the swale to where the combine sat like a beached whale. Climbing up to the engine compartment, she grabbed the radiator door and gave it a pull. A wall of built-up chaff hit her smack in the face. She might have gone tumbling off the platform had Hess not been there to grab her around the waist. Furious, she pounded on the windshield of the combine until DW looked up, his eyes bloodshot but otherwise unconcerned.

"When was the last time you blew the chaff off the radiator?" she yelled through the glass.

The man shrugged and reached into his shirt pocket for another cigarette.

That was it. Scrambling around to the open door of the cab, she stuck her head in and yelled, "I don't believe this shit! It's your fault we're in this spot in the first place, and you're sitting on your ass smoking a cigarette? Get out here and help!"

"In case you ain't noticed, it's gonna take another half hour for that engine to cool down," DW said. "What you want me to do in the meantime, drop and give you some push-ups?"

"Sure," she shot back. "Let's see some push-ups. I doubt you can do more than two, though, you're so hungover all the time."

"Go to hell," he said.

"No, *you* go to hell!"

She could feel the anger rising within her once more, and this time she did nothing to check it. She reached for DW's shirt, but he slinked back from her like a turtle retreating into its shell. She followed, stepping all the way into the cab and grabbing a handful of the man's hair.

"Out! Get out!"

"Arrrrrghhhhh! *Let go*!"

All at once he came to his feet, and that, together with the force of her pulling, carried them out of the cab and onto the platform, where they continued to fight it out until DW lost his footing and they both went over the rail together, locked in a mid-air dance like cartoon characters chased down a canyon by a falling anvil. They hit the ground with a thud, and she rolled over backward, momentarily dazed. DW howled in pain, grabbing at his left shoulder. By the time they managed to struggle to their feet, Hess was there to step between them.

"Calm down, you," he said, taking DW by the shoulders.

"Me?" DW said. "Tell *her* to calm down!" He made like he would take a step toward her, but Hess shoved him back across the stubble.

"I said calm down."

"Oh, I see," DW said. "That little twat has got you wrapped so tight around her—"

He never finished the thought. Hess punched him hard in the stomach, then stepped back and watched as the man fell forward onto his knees.

After a moment, the hired man rolled over onto his back and covered his eyes with his forearm.

"That's it. I quit!"

Annie glanced nervously at Hess. "Look," she began.

"Fuck that," DW said. "I'm done with this whole deal."

He struggled to his feet, still holding his left shoulder, and began a slow limp in the direction of the service truck.

"You can forget about taking that truck," Annie called after him. "We're going to need it to get the combine going."

"Fine!" DW said without turning around. "I'll walk! I don't give a rat's ass!"

"Think I should try to call him back?" Annie asked Hess as the hired man continued his retreat across the yellow stubble. She felt a twinge of guilt now that the anger was passing.

"Nah, he's done," Hess said, struggling to contain a laugh.

"What's so funny?" Annie asked.

"*You*, that's what."

"What about me?"

"Nothing. I just didn't know you were such a badass, pulling guys out of combines and doing back flips and shit."

"There's lots of things about me you don't know," Annie said.

"Same here," Hess said. "Ain't none of us without our little mysteries. Thing about it is, they all get solved in the end."

"Oh, you think so?" Annie said, eyebrows raised in mock challenge.

"Sure," Hess said. "Out here, anyway, they do."

SEVENTEEN

Leroy watched with growing contempt as a group of grown men on the fairway across the street from his house took turns whacking a tiny white ball at a flag flapping in the wind a couple of hundred yards away. How was it he'd lived on this street for eighteen long years without once noticing the ridiculous cavalcade of carts and wheeled bags that began shortly after dawn each morning and continued until the evening light failed and the golfers had no choice but to go home to their bored wives and gray-muzzled pets? It was a mystery, like so much that had happened to him lately. Like the gun that had turned out to be the crucifix from his mother's death bed. Like the woman he'd been married to for forty years without ever knowing, until now, what she did when he was gone all day.

Now that he'd been laid low, he'd begun to glimpse the extent to which work had been his one great refuge, his escape from mystery and reality alike. Work, at least the way he liked to go about it, was like a powerful drug, erasing everything but itself and leaving the person who took it blissfully unaware of anything else. Without work to focus him and dull his senses, the ghosts of the past rose up from their graves to haunt him. His mother, a tiny, energetic woman with a high, bell-like laugh. His stooped and defeated father. His grandfather, not a ghost himself so much as CEO of the ghosts, organizing them from the wheelchair in which he'd spent his final days. Above all, Wade, snatched away in his prime by an uncaring God, leaving a void that could never be filled by anyone, ever.

Without work, the ghosts overran the dim front room, where Leroy sat up all day in the adjustable hospital bed the insurance company had provided at an exorbitant cost, while outside, retirees and teenagers alike whacked their tiny white balls across the green, rolling hills of the golf course, land that if put to its more natural use would've supported a hundred cow-calf pairs, the calves running together in wild packs until the cows' udders began to hurt and they called out to them, their low, insistent voices echoing through the surrounding hills.

If this was what retirement amounted to, a haunted past spooling out against the backdrop of a meaningless present, well then, the golfers could have it. For his part, Leroy was gonna work until a heart attack took him or he froze to death rounding up stray cattle in a blizzard. Yes. His death would be a clean one uncomplicated by doctors or hospitals or, God forbid, time spent in a nursing home like the one in Spearville where his grandfather had spent his final years. That would not be him. Instead, a norther would blow in unexpectedly, and he'd fail to return home at the end of the day, and the search party wouldn't even find his body until the snow thawed in the spring, at which point they could simply dig a hole where he lay and roll him into it, no need for the fuss of a funeral or eulogy or a fancy wooden box to hold him. Just roll him in the hole and call it a life. He was born, worked the land, borrowed large sums of money, suffered, died, and was buried. If there was an afterlife, he'd see his mother and Wade again. If there wasn't, well, the grass he'd been buried under would come up a little greener the following spring.

In the woozy, dreamlike days since he'd escaped the fog, he'd kept his ears pricked for any sign that the secret of the Bar W's precarious finances had leaked while he was "out of it," as Michael called the time before he'd regained consciousness.

Caroline, at least, had said nothing about it, and after a while he began to breathe a little easier. Maybe, somehow, he'd managed to dodge that bullet. Maybe the bank that held the note on his operating loan, hearing of his accident, had extended his credit to cover the missed payments he owed them. It wasn't likely; he knew that. But then, how much of what had taken place recently, including Byron Branch's theft of the Stewarts' land and his own parallel run of bad luck, was?

Somehow the fantasy survived for almost a week. But then one day, while looking through the mail—a task he suddenly had all the time in the world to perform—he came across a statement from the bank holding the loan in question. He ripped the thing open, expecting to see a bloodbath of red ink . . . and saw instead that his account was up to date, the last two payments made in full. He let the paper fall onto the floor beside him and opened his latest statement from the co-op. It was the same story. Someone, and Leroy was already pretty sure who it was, had been paying his bills and making deposits into his checking account with a focus and regularity that Leroy himself had never been able to muster. A variety of emotions passed through him as he stared at the co-op statement with its neat rows of numbers, each of them countered on the opposite side of the statement with another number, the statement itself summed up with a zero and the words PAID IN FULL in caps across the bottom. As he sat there looking at the piece of paper, it occurred to him that the statement served as kind of a real-life counterpart, a cousin of sorts, to the long sheet of paper with the words PAST DUE stamped across the top that Byron Branch had shaken at him in his dream. He was not at all sure how he felt about that. Sure, the wolves had been pushed back from the door for now and he could breathe a little easier. But it was not as though the statement from the bank—or any of his other outstanding bills—had really been paid in full. At best, the day of reckoning had been postponed, the face of the undertaker changed from nemesis to . . . that of his oldest living son.

Knowing this, one desire animated him, and that was to rise up out of the overpriced hospital bed like Lazarus rising from his tomb after having been dead for four days. But before that could happen, his shattered left hip and thigh, to say nothing of his arm and shoulder, would have to heal enough so that he could make it out to his pickup under his own power and pull himself into the cab. Not that he had a pickup to climb into anymore. He'd have to buy a new one, something lower to the ground with an automatic transmission and a door that opened wide enough so that all you had to do was turn your ass to the bench seat and fall in.

In Leroy's grandfather's final years on the Bar W, including a couple of years when he was ostensibly living in the nursing home in Spearville, he'd made his rounds on the Bar W in a black 1968 Lincoln Town Car with whitewall tires and suicide doors. Leroy remembered the car well. He and his father would be putting up hay or cutting wheat or rounding up cattle in Owl Rock pasture, and down the road would come the long black car, a cloud of dust billowing up behind its coffin-like trunk.

"There's your grandpa, riding out to check on us," his father would say in his raspy, dejected way. "He thinks that if he doesn't put an eyeball on a project, it didn't actually get done. Like if we told him, 'Yeah, we got the Rawlings quarter cut,' and he didn't see the stubble for himself, the wheat would still be sitting out there in the field, vulnerable to wind and fire and rain."

"I like it that he comes out," Leroy had said in answer. "I like that car of his."

"I know you do," his father said. "You know why? Because you're just like the old coot."

Leaving Leroy to wonder, *I am? How? Why?* And then, a little later: *Okay, I guess I'm fine with that, so long as I don't end up like you.*

On the fairway across the street, the group of retirees he'd been watching were replaced by four teenaged boys, high schoolers by the looks of them, with golf bags strapped across their narrow shoulders. Leroy let a long sigh escape his nose and mouth. The sight of the teenagers depressed him even more than that of the retirees wasting their final days. What he wouldn't give to be a teenager himself again, or at least to possess their youthful energy and unshattered bones. He'd trade it all, everything. He'd trade the Bar W itself, knowing that the only thing better than protecting a legacy was building one, the way Ludwig Wagner had done in his day.

"The bones in your femur and hip need time to heal," the surgeon had told him. "After that, you'll need several months of rehab and occupational therapy, maybe a second surgery on your wrist—"

"How long before I can go back to work?" Leroy had asked.

"Work?" The surgeon had sounded confused by the question.

"I got a ranch to run, Doc, and I need to get back to it."

"Ah, well, that's a little hard to say," the surgeon had said.

"A month?"

"*What?* No, no, that's out of the question."

"Two months?"

The surgeon had looked at him over his glasses. "With your injuries? No, I think a year is probably more like it, provided the follow-up surgeries go well and we don't run into any complications."

Leroy had stuck out his chin but said nothing. He'd give it a couple of weeks, a month at the outside, and then, come hell or high water, he was going back to work, and God help the man or ghost who tried to stand in his way.

At noon on the dot, Caroline, who'd been working all morning in the home office she'd set up in a spare bedroom at the back of the house, appeared at the side of his bed with a tuna salad sandwich, a fruit cup, and a small plastic tub of chocolate pudding. He picked up the pudding.

"What have you been doing all morning?" she asked.

"Watching geezers whack golf balls down that hill there. What have you been doing?"

"Editing copy. Same as always."

Back when he was healthy, Leroy had never thought much about the work Caroline had taken on after completing her degree. He knew it existed, of course; knew there was money coming in that they paid quarterly taxes on. But only now that he couldn't work himself did it feel real to him. For the first time in all their years together, he felt jealous of her and the life she lived apart from his life.

"Did you try to read any of those books that Annie brought you?" she asked.

He looked at the stack of books on the end table next to his bed.

"No."

"Why not?"

The four teenagers had reached the green at the bottom of the hill. Their bags lay spread out on the edge of the putting surface like body bags on a tarmac in some faraway war zone. "Too busy watching golf. It's my principal form of entertainment, after the market reports and the weather forecast."

Caroline sighed audibly and took the empty pudding tub from his hand and began wiping at his face with a moistened napkin.

"Leave me be," he said, turning his head away.

"In a minute—"

"I said leave it!"

His voice, raw with anger and frustration, seemed to shake the room. She stopped wiping his face and wadded the napkin in her hand and, turning sharply on her heel, left him alone once more.

A *year,* he thought, shaking his head. *Sweet Jesus.*

He fell asleep for what felt like minutes but really was more than an hour. Then the phone in the kitchen began to ring, and he cocked an ear, waiting for Caroline to answer it. It rang and rang.

"*Caroline!*" his voice boomed across the empty room.

"Hold your horses," she yelled from her office at the back of the house.

A minute later, she appeared at his side with the cordless phone. "Here," she said, shoving it at him. "It's your daughter."

He snatched the phone out of her hand and waited until she'd left the room, then brought the handset to his face. "How are things going? Is the radiator holding water?"

"No such luck," Annie said, her voice barely audible on account of the wind. "As soon as we fire up the engine, it comes gurgling out in spurts. Sort of vomiting out, if you can picture that."

He could picture it exactly. "Head gasket," he said.

"What?"

"Blown head gasket. You need to unhook the tractor from the grain cart and pull the combine back to the shop. Let me talk to DW."

"That's another thing I need to talk to you about," Annie said.

He listened quietly, picturing everything as she ran through it: the hired man blowing up the combine through neglect, or maybe on purpose, then retreating like a child leaving the playground in a huff, taking his ball with him. By now, the man was probably sitting on a barstool at Kate's, the bartender denying him a tab, making him pay in cash for every schooner of red beer or shot she poured, calculating in advance when she'd have to cut him off and call . . . who to come get him? Not Leroy. Not this time.

"Just get the combine back to the shop," he said when she'd finished. "I'll call down to John Deere and see about getting a head gasket kit and some new head bolts."

"What about DW?" Annie asked. "Do you want me to see if I can track him down and get him to come back? I will, if you want me to."

"Nah, don't worry about it. He's been looking for a reason to quit for months. You just saved me the trouble of firing him."

"Good," she said, sounding relieved. "We'll get the combine to the shop and see if we can dig up the service manual, then I'll give you another call."

He got off the phone feeling better than he'd felt in days. "Caroline!"

It took a minute, but she finally appeared in the doorway, pen in hand, reading glasses on the end of her delicate nose.

"I know you're busy, but in a little bit, I'm going to need you to run some parts for me."

She just stood there looking at him, not offering a word of guidance or assurance.

"Look, I'm sorry about before. I didn't mean a word of it."

"Then why'd you say it?" she asked.

"I don't know. I'm an idiot, I guess."

She remained in her spot in the doorway, neither in the room nor fully out of it, for what felt like a full minute before she relented and came to him across the carpeted floor. He reached sideways with his good arm and wrapped it around her waist, pulling her to him until she sat perched on the edge of the hospital bed the same way she used to ride with him in the tractor or his pickup, back in the days before everything got so dark and complicated.

"Without you, none of this works," he said. "You know that, right?"

She nodded, her hazel eyes drifting up to the picture window, where a group of women golfers was getting ready to tee off.

"Oh, I know it, all right," she said. "I've been knowing it for a long, long time."

EIGHTEEN

The affair with Ted Kramer went on for nine months and seventeen days and consumed every ounce of emotional and spiritual energy Caroline possessed. For a week after he'd given her the impromptu house tour, Caroline had tried to banish Ted from her mind and focus instead on Leroy and the life they'd built together. But Leroy had been preoccupied with putting up feed for the winter, and what time he didn't surrender to that he handed over piecemeal to the kids and their sports. It was like she didn't even exist on his list of priorities. One afternoon, when he failed to come home for lunch for the third day in a row, she dug Ted's business card from the zippered pocket at the back of her purse and dialed the number printed beneath his name. She was a little surprised when a woman answered the phone, but she managed to keep her cool long enough to make an appointment for him to show her the same house on Country Club Drive where she'd run into him the week before.

"And whom should I say the meeting's with?" the woman asked.

"Uh, Delores."

"Last name?"

"Jackson."

Delores Jackson! She was shocked at how easily the made-up name came rolling off her forked tongue. Was that what she was now—a liar and a snake? Her hands shook as she returned the phone to its receiver on the kitchen wall.

On the day of the appointment, she parked her car five blocks away from the house on Country Club Drive and entered the backyard through the same gate she'd used to make her escape the last time she'd been there. She could feel her heart pounding as she took a seat beside the covered pool. It was autumn for sure now. A light wind pushed a pile of dry cottonwood leaves around the pool deck. *You silly fool,* she thought. *This isn't your house. Why are you pretending it is?*

She heard the smooth purr of Ted's Cadillac pulling into the driveway. A couple of minutes later, he slid open the glass doors to the patio and stepped outside, a big smile on his face.

"Delores Jackson, I presume?"

She laughed even as tears began to form in her eyes. "Don't make fun of me," she said, looking down at where her hands shook in her lap.

"It's all right," Ted said, dragging a deck chair next to hers and reaching out to take her shaking hands in his. Over the years, she'd grown accustomed to Leroy's swollen, calloused hands, so Ted's soft, manicured fingers came as a revelation. The shaking stopped almost immediately, and she looked at him through a mist of tears.

"You must think I'm an awful liar, calling your office and giving some crazy name."

"I'm just glad to see you again. Are you glad to see me?"

She nodded and took a tissue from her purse and used it to wipe her eyes. "Can we just sit here a minute? I know you're a busy person, but I'd just like to sit here for one minute, if that's all right."

"Me, busy?" Ted said, his eyebrows arched in mock surprise.

Later, when she began to talk inanely about Leroy and the kids, he took her face in his hands and planted a soft thumb on her lips.

"Let's not talk about them, okay? They own a big enough chunk of you already."

"Okay. Yes. You're absolutely right."

It was crazy how easily she accepted the idea. On the one hand, it went without saying that nothing in her life was more important than Leroy and the kids. But on the other, she had long felt that they were separate from her, that her true life consisted of a few privately held memories and dreams that had nothing at all to do with them. Was it wrong to feel this way? She remembered an Alice Munro short story she'd read in one of her English classes. In the story, a woman lived a long and seemingly happy life in a small Canadian town not unlike Dodge City. But that was all on the outside. Inside, she lived a completely different life, a secret life her family knew nothing about that centered on a love affair she'd had many years before. In the end, when the woman in the story grew ill and was facing death, it was not her outward life that filled her mind and heart but rather the old, secret life. Was that what was happening to her?

"You're so beautiful," Ted said. "What a fool I was to let you get away."

"Hush. You're embarrassing me."

"That's good. I want to embarrass you. I want to see you blush and smile and laugh. From now on, I'm declaring that to be my sole purpose in life."

She stood up, shivering in the breeze, and he took her into his arms with such ease that it felt to her like they were not middle-aged people living complicated lives, but rather a pair of carefree kids with their whole lives in front of them.

"Nobody can ever know about this," she heard herself say. "It's got to be our secret. And we've got to be very, very careful."

She felt him nod and raised her tear-streaked face to be kissed.

It's beginning, she thought. *God help us both, but it's beginning.*

They met twice more in the house on Country Club Drive, then moved on to another of Ted's vacant properties, and then another. Two or three times a week, she'd wear a track suit to the public library and leave early to go on one of her "long runs," as the librarians on staff took to calling them. And for the most part, that's exactly what she did—took a long run, a different route through town each time. Once a week or so, however, she'd cut the run short and enter a predetermined property through a predetermined gate or door. Five or ten minutes later, Ted would appear carrying a brown leather satchel containing a blanket, a corkscrew, a bottle of chilled white wine, and two delicate, long-stemmed glasses she could not imagine Leroy holding in a billion years.

"Cal, baby," he'd murmur in his deep voice, kissing her face and neck. "How have you been? I've missed you so much."

This attention alone was worth all the trouble and risk.

As exciting as the affair was, though, it also filled her with worry. She worried that Ted would grow tired of her and break it off. She worried that Leroy would find out or, worse, be publicly labeled a cuckold. She worried that one of her children, Wade or Michael or Annie, would learn of her transgression and judge her harshly for it. Above all, she worried that God would run out of patience with her and send some sort of cataclysm to engulf her world. That was the guilt kicking in. Though she was not a cradle Catholic, over the past twenty years she'd immersed herself in the faith's rituals and habits of thought to such an extent that she feared losing touch with them almost as much as she feared getting discovered or going to hell. In a way, it was already happening. Although she still attended Sunday Mass with Leroy and the children, she no longer took communion, and she had stopped going to confession on Saturday afternoons, explaining this change in her routine with a vague reference to a "rough patch" she was going through spiritually. It shocked her how easily her family accepted this bland explanation. Did they really care so little?

However, there was one person who wasn't buying any of the "rough patch" business: Sister Margaret. One morning, after dropping Annie off at the front entrance of Sacred Heart, Caroline tried to continue up Central Avenue, and there was Sister standing defiantly in the middle of the crosswalk. Caroline had to slam on the Buick's brakes to keep from running her over.

"We need to talk," Sister said through the open window.

"Now? I'm too busy."

"Not for this, you aren't."

"Okay," Caroline said, her hands beginning to shake. "I'll pull around back."

A couple of minutes later, the passenger door of the Buick opened, and Sister Margaret climbed in. They sat looking across the asphalt parking lot that doubled as a playground. "You've stopped taking the Eucharist," Sister said. "Do you want to talk about that?"

"Not really, no."

"And, according to Father, you've stopped going to reconciliation, too."

"You're talking to *Father* about me? What gives you the right?"

Sister ignored her outburst. "This isn't like you, Caroline. Now out with it. What's going on?"

"I can't talk about it," she said.

"Why not?"

"I can't, that's all. We're not all perfect, like you."

"What nonsense!" Sister said. "This isn't about me. It's about you and God . . . and Leroy, I'm guessing."

"Leroy!" Caroline said. "You should've married him yourself. Then you'd know what it's like."

"Oh, please. What's going on? Is it bad?"

"I already told you! I can't talk about it!"

She rested her forehead on the car's steering wheel and allowed herself the first good cry she'd had in weeks, Sister's hand patting her gently on the back the whole time. After a while, the tears slowed and then stopped. Sister handed her a tissue. "Will you at least say a prayer with me?"

"Okay," Caroline said, blowing her nose.

They said the Hail Mary a half dozen times in a row, then Sister switched to the Glory Be, and when they had finished that, they both fell silent.

"Do you want me to talk to him?" Sister asked.

"No," Caroline said. "It's private. Please tell me you'll respect that."

"My dear, I'll do whatever you need me to do. Short of lying, of course. That appears to be your specialty."

The words stung worse than any that had ever been said to her. Sister must have seen this, because she opened her arms, something she rarely did, and Caroline clutched her in a tight hug.

"I'm sorry," Sister said. "I know you're suffering, and I hate it. I only want what's best for you. I hope you know that."

"I do," Caroline said. "Of course I do."

With that, Sister climbed out of the Buick and began a bow-legged walk across the parking lot, one hand raised to her head to keep the prairie wind from blowing her little nun's cap from her head.

"God help me," Caroline whispered as she put the car into gear and backed out of the asphalt parking lot. It was what she always said when what she really wanted was the opposite—for God to mind his own business for just a little while longer.

NINETEEN

She had already made up her mind to end the affair when she walked into Sacred Heart Cathedral on Christmas Eve—this was in the days before the new Cathedral of Our Lady of Guadalupe had been built—and saw Ted sitting four pews from the front with his second wife and the three small children she had brought with her from her first marriage. Seeing him there filled Caroline with jealousy as well as guilt, and she spent the whole first half of the Mass staring at the back of his blond head, as though daring him to turn around and acknowledge her. She'd almost given up hope when, during the sign of peace, he turned in his pew and their eyes came together for the briefest of moments. It was pure agony. She'd been hoping to feel nothing, but instead she felt more tenderness and longing for him than she'd ever felt before.

The affair took on a terrible, reckless quality. One night, while Leroy and the boys were at a wrestling tournament in Oklahoma and Annie was sleeping over at a friend's house, she called Ted on his home phone, something she swore she'd never do. He made up some story and met her in the parking lot of a gas station near Wright, and they ended up spending the night together in a motel room in Kinsley, less than an hour from Dodge.

"Babe, we've got to show a little more self-control," Ted whispered as she lay with her head resting on his massive blond chest. "This business of calling the house has got to stop."

"Believe me, I know," she said.

But the meetings continued, growing more frequent and dangerous as time went on. One afternoon, she dropped Annie at her weekly dance lesson at a studio on Second Avenue, near the First National Bank building. But rather than staying to watch the ninety-minute lesson as she normally did, she decided to take a walk instead. It was a gloriously sunny day in late winter, and the High Plains air was fresh and full of promise. It was only after she'd been walking briskly for five minutes, her long arms swinging at her sides, that she realized she'd somehow contrived to guide herself directly to Ted's office, a couple blocks south of the public library. She stopped on the sidewalk and looked up at the big sign with Ted's name rendered in elegant script. Was he inside? What would happen if she walked in and asked to see him? She had almost made up her mind to do it when she heard a screech of tires and looked over her shoulder to see Ted pulling up next to her in the blue Cadillac. The car's electric windows whirred, and Ted leaned across the long bench seat, a look of panic animating his red face.

"What are you doing here?"

"I don't know. I was out walking and—"

"Get in."

"What?"

"*Get in.* Hurry!"

The car's passenger door swung open, and she slid in and pulled the heavy door closed behind her. Before it had even clicked shut, Ted was gunning the Cadillac up the street, where another car approached.

"Get down!"

She ducked beneath view, her head resting in Ted's lap. She stayed that way, her heart beating fast, as he took one corner after another, seemingly at random. Finally, he slowed to a crawl and she heard the tell-tale sound of a garage door going up. The Cadillac inched forward into the dark garage, and the door closed behind them.

She sat up, her eyes struggling to adjust to the darkness. "Where are we?"

"Does it matter?" Ted asked in a gruff voice.

"Please don't be angry with me," she said. "I'm doing the best I can."

"I know you are," he said, his voice softer now.

But was she doing the best she could? If he had not pulled up when he did, she had no doubt she'd have strolled into his office and asked for him. It was crazy, dangerous beyond words, and yet she regretted none of it. She took his face in her hands, and he kissed her roughly on the mouth. She could feel his desire mounting, her own desire rising to meet it. Groaning, her mouth still on his, she pushed his pants down below his knees, shed her panties, and straddled him. Even as she took her pleasure, rocking back and forth in his lap, she was hyperconscious of everything around her. The darkness of the garage with its dust motes still falling, the squeaking of the car's shock absorbers, the steam gathering on the inside of its raised windows, the way Ted's large, soft hands cupped the half-moons of her bottom, intensifying her pleasure.

"Oh God," she moaned. "Oh God oh God oh God."

When it was over, they lay in a tangled heap on the bench seat. Her left arm, trapped beneath Ted's shoulder, went completely to sleep, and her legs began to grow cold in the dark air. A thought beckoned to her from somewhere beyond the darkness. My God. Annie.

She sat bolt upright in the seat. "What time is it?"

Ted groaned and looked at his watch with its lighted dial. "Three forty-five."

"That can't be! We've got to hurry!"

They scrambled to get dressed, and he backed the big car out of the garage. She caught a glimpse of the outside of the house before Ted's hand urged her head back into his lap. It was the same low-slung house across from the golf course where their affair had begun months before.

"Where should I leave you?" he asked as they made their way back downtown. "Not in front of my office."

"No. Drop me at my car or somewhere close by."

"Where is it?"

"On Second. Right under the mural."

"The bank parking lot?"

"Yes. Please hurry."

With any luck, the dance lesson would run late, as it often did when the teacher got carried away demonstrating something. She tried to think of a safe place for him to drop her, but there was none. Every corner and alley presented a different danger.

She felt him slowing. "I see your car up ahead. What do you want to do?"

"I don't know. Just pull over, I guess."

The car rolled to a stop, and she sat up and checked her hair in the visor mirror. When she flipped the visor back up, there was Annie standing on the sidewalk across the street, looking at her.

"Oh God, no."

"Easy," Ted said. "Just play it off and you'll be fine."

She took a deep breath and climbed out of the car. "Thanks for the ride!" she said in a voice that sounded nothing like her.

"No problem!" Ted sang back before gunning the car down Second and disappearing up a side street.

"Why aren't you inside?" Caroline asked as she approached where eight-year-old Annie stood in her pink ballet clothes and denim ranch coat. "It's cold out here."

"The teacher let us out early," Annie said. "Who was that man?"

"What man?"

"That man in the big car."

"Oh, *him*," Caroline said in that voice that was not hers. "He's nobody, sweetie. Just someone who gave Mommy a ride."

"Why? Where'd you go?"

She looked at this cherished daughter with her flame of red hair and perfectly shaped nose. It was her nose, not Leroy's wider nose, broken in a football game before she'd ever met him. "Can you keep a secret?"

The girl nodded.

"I took a walk. It's something I do sometimes when I'm feeling blue. This time, I walked a little too far, and that nice man saw me rushing down the street and offered to give me a ride."

"You accepted a ride from a *stranger*?"

"No, no, of course not," she said, backpedaling. "He's not a stranger at all. In fact, he goes to our church. He's just not a friend or anything like that." She could see doubt beginning to creep into the girl's green eyes. "Anyway, the important thing, the *secret* I was telling you about, is that I'm feeling a little blue today, and I don't want to worry your father or brothers about it. Can it be our little secret?"

Annie nodded uncertainly, and Caroline thought, *I'm gonna have to do better than that.* So instead of heading home, she made an impromptu stop at Kirby's Western Store, one of Annie's favorite places in the world. That evening at dinner, all the girl could talk about was the pair of pink-and-turquoise chaps she'd tried on that she claimed had fit her perfectly, though in truth they were several sizes too big.

"What were you doing at Kirby's?" Leroy asked. There was no suspicion behind it, just an innocent question.

"Well, I *might* have been doing some early birthday shopping," Caroline said. Leroy's birthday was in February. He shrugged and went back to eating.

The rest of the evening went by with no mention of Ted or his blue Cadillac. A day passed, and then another, and Caroline began to breathe a little easier.

Then, out of the blue, both Michael and Wade failed to qualify for the state wrestling tournament. This was expected of Michael, who was only a freshman, but Wade's loss, to an opponent from Garden City he'd pinned the last two times they'd wrestled, came as a complete shock.

"What's the matter?" Leroy asked when Wade waved off breakfast the next morning. "Are you sick or something?"

"No, it's just these dang migraines," Wade said, pinching his nose directly between his eyes, a gesture that had become habitual with him. "I can't seem to shake them. I get dizzy, and everything smells funny."

"Funny how?" Caroline asked.

"I don't know. Like an electrical fire or something. It's hard to explain."

She and Leroy exchanged glances. Electrical fire? The next day, she dropped everything she was doing and took Wade to see the pediatrician who'd delivered all three of her children, but he was just as stumped about the source of the headaches as the athletic trainer at the high school had been.

"Maybe he banged heads during a match and doesn't remember it," the old man speculated. "For now, we'll treat it with rest and some Extra Strength Tylenol. But if the headaches continue or get worse, let me know and we'll run some tests, maybe get a specialist to look at him."

A month later, at a pre-season baseball tournament in Hutchinson, Wade pitched a shutout with Michael catching, and the whole thing fell off everyone's radar. Leroy went back to his spring plowing and culling of cows and bulls, and Caroline went back to her clandestine meetings with Ted.

Then came that terrible morning in July. The night before, as the light was fading over Owl Rock, Caroline had lain alone in her bed at the front of the homeplace, listening to the cicadas in the tree-lined creek sing their carnal song. Her distance ed program was out of session for the summer. All her usual excuses for meeting Ted had evaporated. She'd handled the deprivation well, she thought, viewing it as penance or perhaps as a chance at redemption. But that night, hearing the cicadas call to one another in the creek below the house, she had felt especially desperate and alone. She fell asleep before Leroy had even come in from the shop, where he was working on some broken-down piece of farm equipment, and when she woke the next morning, he was already gone. She rose, brushed her teeth and hair, and, while making the boys their favorite breakfast of blueberry pancakes, decided that after they left the house to move irrigation pipe, she would drive to town and call Ted from a pay phone.

She made it as far as the hill above the ranch when something, a momentary flash of light in her rearview mirror, made her stop in the middle of the road and look back. Something strange was happening down below. Someone was pulling a trailer across the corrugated field west of the house, aluminum pipe flying from both sides. She could hear the long pieces of pipe echo as they bounced off one another and hit the ground. *What in God's name?*

She did a three-point turn in the road and headed back down the hill. By the time she reached the edge of the field, Leroy had emerged from the shop and was frantically trying to unhook the pipe trailer from the back of the pickup while Michael watched helplessly.

"What's going on?" she yelled. "Where's Wade?"

Michael gave her a stricken look, and she ran around to the passenger side of the pickup and looked inside at where Wade lay unmoving on the bench seat. His eyes were wide open but did not blink or move. She tried to pull open the door to get at him, but Leroy came around from the back of the truck and grabbed her around the waist.

"There's no time for that. Get Annie and follow us in the car."

"Where are you taking him?"

"The hospital!"

With that, he and Michael climbed into the truck with Wade and took off across the grass lot. She stood there in the dry grass, watching the dust rise behind the white pickup, and then ran to the house to get Annie.

The whole way to the hospital, they prayed one Hail Mary after another, only to be informed by a doctor in the ER that her firstborn—beautiful, wonderful Wade—was brain dead.

"You mean he's—?"

"Gone, yes," the doctor said.

She sat down hard. *Gone.* The word echoed and echoed. It was echoing still.

Ted didn't come to the viewing or the funeral, appearing only at the cemetery, where he stood watching at the edge of the large crowd as Wade was lowered into the ground. At one point during the service, her eyes met his across the expanse of grass, and she knew at once that what they'd had together was as dead as the son she was burying. Where she was going, Ted couldn't follow. Nobody could.

A week later, she allowed Sister Margaret to drag her to confession and then to holy communion. "God forgives all and heals all," Sister kept saying as she drove the two of them down the same dirt road Caroline and Annie had taken to the hospital only days before.

"Oh God! It's all my fault! How could I have been such a selfish fool!"

"Hush," Sister said. "You heard what the doctors said. A tumor like that, nobody saw it coming."

"I should have, though. I'm his mother."

"I know, honey. But you have two other children, and you need to remember them. They will need you more now than they ever have, and you've gotta be there for them, no matter how much your heart is breaking."

Sister was right, as usual. In the days following Wade's funeral, Caroline could feel Michael's and Annie's eyes on her at all times. She knew that if she surrendered to her grief, they'd be left alone to deal with theirs. She couldn't let that happen.

As for Leroy, he withdrew into his work, leaving the homeplace before dawn and not returning until eleven o'clock or midnight. Once home, he did little but sit in a chair in the dark basement, staring off into space. "Leroy?" she'd say. "Are you all right? Do you want some dinner?" But he just kept staring, saying nothing. He'd always been brawny and muscular, but in the weeks following Wade's death, he lost all interest in food, and his clothes hung from his body as from a wire hanger. Every Sunday morning, with Michael and Annie waiting for her in the Buick, she went to him where he sat in the dark basement and asked if he would change his mind and go to Mass with them. And every Sunday, he'd shake his head, not even looking at her.

"How long are you going to keep this up?" she asked.

"Keep what up?" he answered, his voice betraying no emotion whatsoever.

"You know."

He didn't answer or even lift his eyes, and once again, she had to drive off to Mass without him.

But at night, with the house quiet and moonlight pouring in through the open windows, he would wake from one of his recurrent nightmares and reach for her in the darkness. What happened then was not sex, exactly. It was more like she was a rock he attempted to beat himself against until he was bloodied and unconscious. The dark violence of it scared her at first, but gradually she began to respond in kind, grabbing him by the hair and pulling his unshaven face close to hers. *Oh God, oh God, oh God!* After they were both spent, she would hold him close to her even as he struggled to break away, the tears he wouldn't let anyone see during the daylight hours pouring out of him.

In her grief, she barely noticed when she missed her period. It had been more than a decade since she'd been pregnant with Annie, and she figured that that part of her life was over. It was only when she woke up feeling sick three days in a row that the idea began to take hold of her. *No*, she thought. *It can't be.* But then she remembered those times in the dead of night when Leroy had crawled out of his black hole of grief long enough to reach for her.

She drove to town, bought an over-the-counter pregnancy test, and peed on the thing in a stall of the ladies' room at the back of the store. She kept her eyes closed for the longest time, listening to the rapid-fire Spanish of the women who had come in after her. Only when the women were gone did she open her eyes to see the double pink lines in the middle of the white tray.

She headed north toward the ranch. In three hours, she'd have to turn around and drive all the way back to pick up Annie from school, but she wasn't thinking about that now. She needed to look Leroy in the face and give him the news.

At the ranch, she spotted Leroy's pickup in front of the shop building, pulled up next to it, and switched off the Buick's motor. Something made her pause at the shop door. An eerie quiet hung over the place, no sound at all of work being done, no engines being tested, no revving of power tools.

"Leroy?" she called.

She stepped through the open doorway and paused again, allowing her eyes to adjust to the semidarkness. In the middle of the shop, a sweep plow was suspended above the floor by a heavy chain. She could hear the chain creak as the plow swayed back and forth on the overhead winch, and her eyes followed it to where Leroy lay on his back beneath the long V-shaped blades of the plow. She felt nauseous, like she might throw up, right there on the floor of the shop. One slip of the chain, and the blades of the plow would come crashing down like a guillotine.

"Leroy!" she said. "What are you doing under there? Answer me!"

"Go away," he said in a strangled voice.

She crept closer, bending at the waist to get a better look at him. He lay on his back on a flat wheelie cart with no tools in his hands that she could see. Alarmed, she kneeled on the concrete and called his name again, and this time he turned to look at her, his face wet with tears.

"Please come out from under there. You're scaring me."

"Go away."

"No. I need to talk to you."

She reached for his arm, but he rolled away from her on the little cart, so that his face and neck were directly beneath the center blade of the plow.

"There's something I need to say. It's important." She imagined the chain slipping, the plow blade cutting him in two. "We're gonna have another baby."

Silence. Every second it continued felt like an accusation. Then the wheels of the cart squeaked on the concrete, and she stepped back to see Leroy emerging sideways from beneath the plow. When he was fully out, he stood up and walked past her to the metal sink, where he picked up a dirty bar of soap and began to lather his hands.

"Did you hear what I said?"

"I heard."

"Well? Aren't you gonna say anything?"

He shook his head, his back to her. She walked over to where he stood and put a hand on his shoulder, forcing him to turn and face her. His tears had been replaced by a stony blankness.

"We got no business having another kid, and you know it."

She let his words hang between them a moment. "What are you suggesting?"

"Nothing. It's just that—"

"Oh, no," she said, backing away from him. "We're not even gonna *talk* about that. Never. Do you hear me?"

He gave her one last stony look, then walked past her and headed out the door. She heard his pickup start, its tires spinning in the gravel before the shop building.

Six months later—and a full six weeks before his due date—Jimmy came kicking and screaming into this world, and the gulf that had opened up between Leroy and her following Wade's death grew wider still.

TWENTY

It was late afternoon by the time Annie and Hess got the combine towed onto the slab of concrete in front of the shop building. The tall, billowy clouds that had dominated the hot day had evaporated, and the sky was a deep blue. Hess flipped the switch on the air compressor, and a pack of ranch dogs emerged from the cool darkness, Lola among them. She was still Annie's dog when it suited her, but for the most part, she'd gone back to her old life.

"Please tell me you know something about motors," Annie said.

Hess shrugged. "I ain't no mechanic, but I've torn into a few. Anyway, your dad knows more about these things than all the mechanics at the dealership combined. At the end of the day, it's gonna be Bull Wagner who fixes this combine, not us."

Annie nodded, thinking of the engine transplant that had given life to the Frankenstein Porsche that Jeremiah loved almost as much as he loved her. If he loved her.

As they worked, relying on an old shop manual and phone calls to Leroy, they traded stories about all of the vehicles that had broken down on them over the years. In Hess's case, the list was long. "I remember this one time, outside of Tucson. The whole driveline came flying off the Ford, taking out a brake line and punching a hole in the gas tank. Of course, I'd just filled the dang thing up. A hundred and fifty bucks of diesel fuel spread up and down Highway 10."

"What were you doing in Tucson?"

"Chasing that long white line. What else?"

"I've got a similar story," Annie said, "but mine involves a blown tire on the BQE."

"BQE?"

"Brooklyn-Queens Expressway."

"What were you doing there?"

She thought back to the previous summer, when her #notorious rapport with Jeremiah had reached a fever pitch neither of them seemed able to control. "There was this guy I was trying to avoid, and a friend of mine from Exeter had access to an apartment on Bleecker Street in the East Village, and I thought if I could just hold out for the summer, the spell he had me under might break. You know, the geographical cure? But the thing was, I kept starting for Buffalo in the middle of the night, then changing my mind and turning back around."

"Sounds like you had it bad."

She thought of the rogues' gallery of men she'd been involved with since getting the hell out of Dodge ten years before. Older guys. Motorcycle dudes. A third baseman for the Rochester AAA club she'd kicked to the curb for smelling like Skoal all the time. "As bad as I've ever had it, I guess."

"What'd you do about the tire? Call a tow truck?"

"Are you kidding me? At two in the morning in a Porshe 911? On the BQE? Noooooooo, I drove on that bad boy all the way back to the Village."

"Just to hell with it? Alloy wheel and all?"

She nodded. "Hey, I'd seen cars *set on fire* on that road."

Since they'd ventured this far into her romantic history, she asked about his and got the short version. Married too young to his high school sweetheart. (Shades of Jeremiah and Emily, not that she wanted that thought in her head.) Add in a little bronc riding, fights about money, some competitive infidelity, and it was welcome to the Big D, and he didn't mean Dallas. After that, more bronc riding, surgery on his right knee, then his left. Then a short, second marriage to a girl from Albuquerque who tried to cure him of bronc riding.

"And did the cure take?"

"Sure. For a while."

Another trip to the Big D, followed by a third knee surgery, this one bad enough that he had to lay up for six months on a buddy's family ranch outside Stephenville, Texas. It was on that ranch he met an old bronc rider named Leo Ginetti, who taught him everything he knew about starting colts.

"Leo was a goddamn genius when it come to horses. If he'd had any people skills at all, he could've made a million dollars as a clinician. But Leo didn't have a real high opinion of human beings. All he gave a damn about was horses and giving them the right start in life. He believed that horses deserved a fair deal, that the only way to train them was to make the right thing easy and the wrong thing hard."

A light bulb went on above Annie's head. "Natural horsemanship."

Hess raised his eyebrows. "You know about that stuff?"

"I read a few books about it when I should have been writing my dissertation. My favorite was Pat Parelli's, the one where he's jumping that black horse bareback."

"I like that one, too," Hess said, shaking his head. "And here I've been spouting off about horses like a damn fool."

"Not at all," Annie said. "You've been speaking from experience, whereas just about everything I know is from books."

"I doubt that very seriously," he said.

By nine-thirty that night, they had the massive six-cylinder head loose from the engine, and there was nothing left for them to do but run it into the machine shop on Trail Street where Leroy had arranged to have it tested first thing the following morning. Annie asked if Hess wanted to come along, but he begged off, saying he still had a half dozen horses to ride.

"A cowboy's work is never done," she said with a touch of irony in her voice, the sort of thing that would have ignited a long back-and-forth with Jeremiah.

Not Hess, though. "What can I say? It's true."

On the porch of the homeplace, at his request, she dug through some of the books she'd brought from Buffalo in her Red Demons duffel and handed him Xenophon's *On Horsemanship*, along with Cormac McCarthy's *All the Pretty Horses*.

"What's this?" he asked, holding up the McCarthy.

"Contemporary western."

"There was a movie, right?"

"Not a very good one. You'll like this better."

He nodded his thanks and then drove off, tail pipe rattling.

Nice guy, Annie thought. *Sort of the strong and silent type, couple of warning signs, but nothing too crazy.*

Then, later, on the drive to town: *Okay now, you'd better watch yourself. You've been known to jump in feet first when caution would've been the better game plan.* She was thinking again of the rogues' gallery, particularly the Rochester third baseman, who had a bad habit of yelling up at her window in the middle of the night—*Yo, red! It's me, Brucie!*—every time the Red Wings were in town. But even as she ticked through these mostly bad memories, she could feel an anticipatory smile spreading across her face. She was who she was who she was. World without end, amen.

The next morning, she ran a few errands in town before swinging by the machine shop to see what the verdict on the head was.

"Heat warped," the guy behind the counter said. He was her father's age, tall with a beard that came halfway down his chest. "We got her all ground down and ready to go for you."

"Wow, that was fast."

"Hey, it's for your dad," he said with a wink. "Plus, it's harvest, and we aim to please."

She was glad somebody did.

The whole time she and Hess were putting the motor back together, he kept yawning and complaining that he'd been up half the night reading *All the Pretty Horses.*

She laughed. "I thought that might happen. Where are you at in it?"

"They just made it down to that big ranch in Mexico."

"*Hacienda de Nuestra Senora de la Purisima Concepcion.*"

"Yeah, and John Grady is fixing to start the rich guy's—"

"The *Hacendado's*—"

"Right. His string of colts."

"Just wait. It's about to get even better."

"God, I hope not. I'm plumb wore out, as it is."

When they had the motor back together, they ran through a checklist her father had dictated over the phone, filled the thing with coolant, fired it up, and sat in the cab watching the temperature gauge stick at 185 degrees.

"By God, I think we got her done," Hess said. "I think she's fixed."

"I'll believe it when we get back into that thick wheat," Annie said.

"Believe whenever you want. That sumbitch is fixed."

When they got back to the field, Hess lowered the arm rests on the combine's seat, and she climbed in beside him. It was another cloudy day with rain threatening, and they had to take it slow to keep the feeder house from jamming up with straw. Still, the temp gauge never rose above 190. To celebrate, Annie made a detour to the Dodge City Public Library during one of her elevator runs and checked out the audiobook version of *All the Pretty Horses*. Hess opened the cardboard box and took the first disk from its sleeve and popped it into the combine's ancient CD player.

"You can just skip ahead to where you are in the book," Annie said.

"Heck, no," Hess said. "I'm starting at the beginning. Chapter one, page one. Whatever happened last night, that's over and done with."

He looked at her, and she wondered if he meant that literally, or if something else was in the works. For all the time they'd spent together, she still found him difficult to read.

When they weren't listening to the McCarthy novel, they talked in that slow, unhurried way of people on long road trips who have the whole day, and maybe part of the night, stretched out before them. He told several more stories about riding broncs, and she told him how, for a brief time in her adolescence, she'd been a queen's candidate at a couple of small, amateur rodeos.

"I should've known," he said, slapping his thigh.

From there she went on to talk at length about what she called her "radical uncertainty" about all things western Kansas.

"I mean, part of me thinks this little valley we're in is the center of the known universe," she said during one of these riffs. "But there's another part of me that feels trapped as hell. Especially when I'm in town, I get this panicky desire to run away, along with a feeling of dread that if I were to stick around for any length of time, it would signal a failure on my part, a turning away from my true fate."

"Which is?"

She laughed. "That's the problem. I don't have any idea."

"Well, John Grady left, too," he said. "Lit out for Mexico with his buddy. But if you think about it, he didn't have much of a choice. His mom sold the ranch right out from under him."

"She had her reasons, of course."

"Well, sure. But if she hadn't done that, don't you think he'd have stayed on that place forever?"

"Maybe," Annie conceded. "But that's a very big if. It's like if I said to you, 'What if you'd been born in, I don't know, Guam?' You'd be like, 'That's not me you're talking about. That's a whole other person.' Well, it's the same with me. What if my brother Wade hadn't dropped dead when I was ten? What if my mother hadn't moved us to town? What if my dad had been around more, instead of going AWOL into his work the way he did?"

"I don't know," Hess said, shaking his head. "The feeling I get, just from the outside looking in, is that no matter where you go, no matter what you end up doing, this place is always gonna have its claws in you. The more you run away, the more you're gonna have this voice inside that says, 'Go back. Go back.' I know, because I had that voice in the back of my head the whole time I was chasing that white line."

"And you have no regrets?" Annie asked. "About coming back to Dodge instead of settling in, I don't know, Dallas or Oklahoma City?"

Hess laughed and shook his head. "If you was trying to tempt me, you should've said Colorado or Montana or someplace like that."

"I guess so," she said, laughing with him.

Late that evening, a bank of purple clouds reared up in the west and a light rain started in. The wheat quickly became too damp to cut, so they unloaded the combine into the Freightliner and ran the tarp over its bed. After that, they jumped into the service truck and headed back to the homeplace, the rain coming down harder and harder on the roof.

"I guess there won't be any horse training happening tonight," Annie said when they reached where his pickup was parked next to the corrals.

"I guess not."

"You want to come in the house for a drink? I might have a bottle of Wellers stashed away in there, and I know I've got ice."

Their eyes met in the semidarkness of the cab, and she felt him hesitate on the seat beside her.

"Thanks for the offer, but I think it'd be better all the way around if I headed home."

"Well, okay," she said. "But if you get halfway home and find yourself changing your mind, don't hesitate to turn that rig around."

"What, like you on the BQE?"

"Sure. Why not?"

"All righty, then."

The door opened and she watched as he climbed into the cab of his dually Ford and turned the headlights and wipers on. She could see him lighting a cigarette, cracking the window so the smoke could escape, and for a moment she thought he might change his mind. Instead, she watched as his taillights blurred in the rain.

Lola met her at the back door of the homeplace, soaked and ready to come inside.

"Where's that boyfriend of yours?" Annie asked. "Don't tell me you got turned down, too."

The dog shook out her coat, hopped onto the couch, and turned around three times before curling herself into a tight ball.

"Oh, I see. Nothing beats a dry bed, even if you're sleeping alone. Hey girl, I get it. You better believe I do."

TWENTY-ONE

Jimmy loved all seventy-five of his hydroponic ladies with a love bordering on madness, but the bitches were killing him. Between washing trucks all day at the truck stop and staying up half the night tending to his Girl Scout Cookies and their endless needs, he was getting next to no sleep. It was only a matter of time before the brutal schedule caught up with him. Sure enough, after sleeping through his alarm for the third morning in a row, he showed up at the Flying J two hours late for the start of his shift and was told by one of the girls in the filling station that the boss man wanted to see him in his office.

Here it comes, he thought. *The big finito.*

Byron Branch kept a small office off the storeroom at the back of the Flying J. Jimmy went into the men's room and hit his vape a couple of times before knocking at the office's open door.

"Have a seat," Branch said without looking up.

Jimmy did as he was told.

"What the hell's going on with you, son? We had three trucks drive off this morning after waiting more than an hour for a hand wash. That's a hundred fifty bucks down the drain."

"I know, and I'm sorry," Jimmy said. "If you want, you can take it out of my next check."

"You're damn right it's coming out of your check," Branch said. His blue eyes held Jimmy's in what seemed like a minute-long stare-down, then he asked in an even voice, "What do you know about this crazy lawsuit your dad's filed against me?"

Jimmy felt a jolt of recognition. He should've known his first-ever visit to Byron Branch's office would involve more than showing up a couple of hours late for a shift at the truck wash.

"Not a thing."

"Are you sure?" Branch asked. "No talk about strategy and such around the dinner table of a Sunday afternoon?"

"I work here on Sundays," Jimmy said.

"Well, sure," Branch said. "But maybe you'd like to take this Sunday off? Have a little family reunion?"

Jimmy couldn't believe this shit. I mean, sure, he'd had his share of disagreements with his asshole father. But none of that meant he was ready to sell the sumbitch down the river. And for what? To keep a job that paid eleven-fifty an hour? He gave a little grunt of disgust and stood.

"Walk out that door, son, and don't you bother coming back," Branch said.

"Dude, please," Jimmy said, and kept right on going.

Free of the Flying J, Jimmy became almost completely nocturnal, sleeping though the day and tending to his ladies by night between electric guitar solos and hits from a water pipe K-Dog had given him as an early Christmas present. Aside from the occasional text from Kaid or Brock, he had no communication at all with the outside world. He'd been by the house to see his folks only once since the old man had been discharged from the hospital, and on the whole, he preferred Leroy-in-a-coma to this version of his dad, who was awake and full of questions, such as what was he planning to do for money now that Byron Branch had fired him? Well, fuck that noise. He preferred the company of his Girl Scout Cookies and the sweet voice of his Stratocaster.

A few days into this topsy-turvy schedule, he was awakened by a loud banging at the gate to his fenced-in yard, followed by some spirited barking by Hammer and Kush. He leapt up from the couch and peeked through a curtain to see Annie standing at the gate to his fortress hideaway in red cowboy boots and a white pearl-button shirt with the sleeves cut off at the shoulder. Behind her in the road, beginning to attract the attention of his closest neighbors, was that red Porsche of hers with its mismatched hood and fenders.

"Damn it, Jimmy!" she yelled. "I know you're in there! Come out here and call off these monsters!"

Jesus Christ, he thought *This is all I need. Emma Stone with a fucking attitude.*

He pulled on pants and combat boots and opened the trailer door just wide enough to call the dogs inside. Then he stepped out, locked the door behind him, and strolled, shirtless, to where Annie stood outside the steel gate.

"Dude, how'd you find this place?"

"I asked the girl behind the register at the truck stop," Annie said. "She was only too happy to rat your little ass out. What's with the Doberman gang?"

He smiled. "Beautiful beasts, aren't they?"

"Sure, if you're into killer guard dogs. Aren't you going to invite me inside?"

"Nah, it's a mess in there. Let's take a ride in that hot rod of yours. I'll drive."

"Like hell you will," she said. "Nobody drives Frankenporsche but yours fucking truly."

"Whatever."

He came through the gate, locked it behind himself, and climbed into the passenger seat of the battered car. "Hang a U out of here, then take a left on Lariat and let's see what this piece of shit can do."

She started to say something back, then seemed to think better of it and put her foot through the floor instead. The car took off like a rocket, pinning his head against the bucket seat. Once on Lariat, she really opened it up, climbing from 60 to 100 to 125 before taking her foot of the gas and letting the car coast back down to 85.

"Dude, that was awesome. On the way back, it's my turn." He pulled a joint from a pocket of his cargo pants and held it up for her to see. "Wanna smoke?"

"I'll pass. This is more of a business call."

He shrugged, sparked the lighter, and took a long toke. "So what's up?"

"Dad's hired guy quit."

"Really? Why the hell for?"

"Does it matter? We're a man short now, and I could really use your help."

He took another toke from the joint. "I gotta say, sis, I'm failing to see what any of this has to do with me."

"Are you kidding me?" she said, looking at him out of the corner of those piercing green eyes of hers. "I mean, last I checked, you were still part of this family."

He had to laugh at that. "Yeah, when you *need* me to be, I am. The rest of the time, I'm just pain-in-the-ass Jimmy." A thought occurred to him. "Did Mom put you up to this?"

"No," she said, shaking her head. "This is me asking, Jimmy. Your big sister, remember? The one who babysat you and carried your little ass around the neighborhood and changed your dirty diapers?"

"That's real sweet, Sis. But did I *ask* you to change my diapers?"

She downshifted, sending the RPMs climbing above 7,000, then hung a left toward Wilroads Gardens. "You're really something, you know that? To hear you talk, a person would think it was *your* childhood that got canceled halfway through, not mine and Michael's."

He took another hit from the joint. "Oh, yeah, I forgot. The untimely death of Prince Wade. Well, I wish I could believe the dude was real, but to me he always felt like some kind of cartoon character that you and Michael and Mom made up to explain why Dad was such an asshole."

"Whatever," Annie said. "I can tell you this: if I was ever in trouble or needed help, *Wade* would've been there for me in a heartbeat."

"Yeah, well, I'm not him. Besides, I've got shit to do this week. Important shit."

She pulled a U in front of Wilroads Christian Church, tires spinning in the loose gravel, and started back up the road they'd come in on. "Oh, I'm sure. You probably have a whole bag of weed to smoke, am I right?"

He took a last hit and flicked what remained of the joint out the window. "Look, don't get all mad about it."

"I'm not mad, Jimmy," she said. "I'm *disappointed*. There's a difference."

"Bullshit," he said. "You're mad. Believe me, I can tell."

"You know what? To hell with you, Jimmy. If you can find time in your busy fucking schedule to come help with the harvest, then do it. If you can't, who the fuck cares. I'm done, that's all. Finished!"

She goosed the old Porsche, covering the last mile to the trailer park in something like thirty seconds flat. But rather than turning into the entrance to the park when she came to it, she pulled over on the side of the road and waited for him to get out.

"Seriously? You've not gonna let me drive this thing?"

She shook her head, not even looking at him.

He got out of the car and swung the door shut, and two seconds later she was gone, leaving him standing there on the side of the road. Just him and his family baggage and a buzz that was fading fast.

Forty-five minutes later, as he lay on the couch with his eyes closed, his phone began to buzz with texts. He looked at the screen, expecting it to be Annie calling to apologize. Instead, it was K-Dog.

Guess where I am?

Dunno, Jimmy texted back.

Flying J, waiting to get my truck washed. Dude, you shoulda told me you got your ass FIRED. Now what's your cover gonna be?

He started texting back, but K-Dog cut him off.

Fuck all that. When's that batch of cookies gonna be ready to come out of the oven?

Idk, he texted back. *3 weeks?*

Make it 2. And don't disappoint me again. You got that?

Dude, I got it.

It was a typical text exchange with K-Dog of late—all business, no joking around, no fun at all. Whatever. He could be all business, too. That same night, he flushed the plants' grow medium with a heavy dose of water.

"No more food for you, my ladies."

He repeated the process with fresh water, then took a close-up of one of his favorite ladies and texted it to Kaid in California. Almost at once, his phone exploded with the badass solo from "Hotel California."

"Dude, that is some serious bud!"

"Yeah it is. Hey, what have you and Brock got going on for the next week or so?"

"Nada. Just chilling and getting on the old man's nerves. He's, like, this close to kicking out asses out."

"Dude, welcome to the club." He paused as though at a stop sign, wondering if he should really say what he was about to say.

"Speaking of which, how about you hop on a train and roll on out here? I've got my back against the wall with these bitches, and I could really use your help."

"The train?" Kaid said, laughing. "You mean, like, Amtrak and shit?"

"Hell yeah, dude. I checked, and it runs from LA right into Dodge. It'll be like being in a movie or something. Cheaper, too."

Kaid paused, considering it. "How many plants are we talking about?"

"Hop on that train," Jimmy said. "You'll see."

He got off the phone feeling better than he'd felt in days, but fifteen minutes later, the bad feeling was back. Could he really trust Kaid and Brock? What would K-Dog say if he knew that Jimmy had just brought two relative strangers into their high-stakes biz? And what about Annie? Was she really "finished" with him? He doubted it, but only time would tell.

In the meantime, trimming out seventy-five Girl Scout Cookies was a shit ton of work, and Jimmy had no intention of missing the new deadline K-Dog had just laid down for him.

It was endgame, baby. California or bust.

TWENTY-TWO

Annie and Jacob Hess sat on the front porch of the homeplace, a twelve pack of Coors Light tallboys at their feet, watching the red ball of the sun drop over the corrals. They'd had another shower of rain that evening, but then the skies had cleared of clouds and the wind had picked up, promising at least the hope that they'd be able to get back into the field the next day.

"Don't you love the way them bluffs block that wind out of the southwest?" Hess said, nodding across Back Trail Road at where the land rose sharply before leveling off on the way to town. "Hell, if a guy was to take pencil and paper and draw up a place to train horses, he couldn't do no better than this little piece of ground right here in front of the house."

"That's what you said about the space in front of the tack barn," Annie said. "If I didn't know better, I'd think you were after this place—corrals, horses, scenery, and all."

"Who says I'm not?" Hess laughed. "But seriously. Wouldn't you take the whole shebang if it was offered to you?"

It was not the first time Annie had been asked this question. Whenever someone back East found out her family owned a cattle ranch in southwest Kansas, the first thing they wanted to know was how big it was and how much she stood to inherit. They didn't understand the stark realities of cattle ranch economics, whereby a spread worth six or seven million dollars spun off less than sixty grand in rental income a year. Farm ground did better, of course, but not by much.

"Didn't we already have this conversation?" Annie asked.

"Did we?" Hess said. "Well, okay, maybe we did. But still. You can't tell me you wouldn't be tempted."

"By what?"

"By *taking it over* one of these days. I mean, I don't see anyone else in your family stepping up."

Now it was her turn to laugh. "You're kidding, right? Me? Run the Bar W?"

"I don't see why not. You're doing a hell of a job with the wheat harvest, and that's probably the trickiest part of the whole operation. The rest can be hired out or done from the back of a horse. And from what I've seen, the back of a horse is somewhere Annie Wagner loves to be."

"Oh, I love it, all right. But I also love prowling around bookstores and going to Lucinda Williams concerts and taking a day off more than once or twice a year." She took a sip of her beer. "The thing is, I've spent the whole last decade of my life putting all of this in the rearview mirror. And now I'm supposed to act like none of that happened? I mean, what the hell would I *tell* people?"

"What people?" Hess asked, looking around in mock confusion. "I don't see nobody here but you and me and those horses grazing across the road."

She sat taking in his creased Wranglers, Ostrich-skin Lucchese ropers, and 30X white Stetson. Was he trying to impress her, or was this just the way you had to dress if you wanted to look the part of a horse trainer whose clients ran the gamut from Flint Hills ranch hands to Houston oil men to Denver orthodontists? Was he maybe a little more upwardly mobile than she'd given him credit for?

They split another tallboy, then she went into the house and came back with a marked-up copy of Gretel Ehrlich's *The Solace of Open Spaces* and a cleaner copy of William Kittredge's *The Next Rodeo* and dropped the books into his lap.

"What's this?" he asked.

"Well, since you finished *All the Pretty Horses*, I thought you might like to switch things up and read some creative non-fiction."

"Creative *what?*"

She started to explain, but then she caught the mischievous look in his blue eyes and kicked him playfully on the thigh. He caught the heel of her boot in his cupped hand and sat there holding it like he had no intention of ever letting it go.

"Nice move," she said. "You got any more in you?"

He rested the heel of the boot on his thigh. "Sure. Not tonight, though."

She slid the boot off his thigh, letting it fall to the wooden deck of the porch. "I'm beginning to think you don't like me."

"It's just the opposite. I'm starting to favor you a little too much."

"Well then, why don't you do something about it?"

He took a pack of Marlboro Reds from his shirt pocket and offered her one. She took the cigarette, leaning forward so that he could light hers and then his from the same match.

"You saw what happened to John Grady when he went behind the *hacendado*'s back and started fooling around with his daughter. Didn't end too good for him."

"Aren't you being a little dramatic?" she said. "Last I checked, my dad was laid up in his living room in town, his leg and arm wrapped in plaster of paris. I don't think you're in any danger of being hunted down and thrown into a Mexican prison."

He took a drag from his cigarette and exhaled the smoke in a thin stream. "Maybe not. Maybe I'm just getting a little old-fashioned in my middle age."

Middle age? she thought. Didn't you have to be, like, *forty* or something, to refer to yourself as middle-aged?

"Fine," she said, standing. "Have it your way. Only I wouldn't wait too long. I'm not close to being middle-aged myself, and the only 'Old-Fashioned' I care about has got bourbon and a cherry in it."

Hess laughed but said nothing.

Later, as she lay alone in her childhood bed in the back bedroom of the homeplace, she thought of Jeremiah and what he would've said in response to her "Old-Fashioned" joke. Probably something about forgetting to mention the sugar and the bitters. "What's life without a little sugar to even out the *bitters?*" To which she would've replied, groaning, "That's what the bourbon's for, isn't it?" And so on and so forth, world without end.

Yeah, but to hell with Jeremiah, she thought.

TWENTY-THREE

Early the next morning, they rode all of the horses in Hess's string and turned them loose in the pasture with the ranch geldings, a gesture meant to announce to themselves and to the world, *It's pedal-to-the-metal time. No more riding or anything else until all the wheat is in.*

By nine, a hot wind had blown up out of the southwest, drying the grain where it swayed atop delicate towers of straw. Annie ran a test cut into the elevator in Dodge, then called her father and told him they were good to go. "It's gonna be slow going with just the two of us, but we'll get her done," she heard herself say. Her western Kansas accent was making a strong comeback. By midmorning, they were back in the field, riding side by side in the combine until the hopper was full, at which point Annie would jump down and run through the stubble to fetch the grain cart.

She was rolling the tarp on the Freightliner, getting ready to make her first run to town, when she saw a plume of dust rising in the distance. She watched as a purple dump truck with the words BYRON BRANCH EXCAVATION painted on the side came into view. Sitting behind the wheel of the truck in wraparound shades, long hair blown back in a manner that suggested the lion in *The Wizard of Oz*, was Jimmy.

"What's this?" she asked as he climbed down from the truck.

"A second truck and driver. You wanna finish this job or screw around and get rained out again?"

"Finish it," she said. "But where'd you get the truck?"

He let out one of his crazy laughs. "At the getting place."

He tossed a string bag into the cab of the truck she'd just tarped, climbed into it, and took off down the road to Dodge at a rate of speed she wouldn't have thought possible if she hadn't seen it with her own eyes.

Hail yes, she thought. *Now we're in business.*

They cut past midnight, fueled the combine by the headlights of the service truck, and were back at it before eight the following morning. With two trucks running loads to town instead of just one, the combine stopped cutting only to take on fuel. To speed things up even further, Caroline began bringing lunch and dinner directly to the field, saving Annie a trip to the house to fetch it.

"It does my heart good to see you and your brother working side by side like this," Caroline said with a smile. "He really looks up to you, you know."

"If you say so," Annie said. "I'm just happy we're finally making some progress."

They entered their last quarter section at four o'clock in the afternoon on a still, muggy day threatening rain. Why was it that, in western Kansas, rain hardly ever came when you needed it to; and then, when you did happen to want some dry heat and blue skies, you could be sure to look off to the west and see a line of dark clouds rolling in? There was a poem in that, Annie mused, not that she had time to write it. Since Jimmy had joined the effort, she'd lost all track of time. She couldn't have said if it was a Sunday, a Monday, or a Friday, nor did she care. All she wanted was to close out the last field they had to cut before the sky let loose or they suffered another breakdown.

By ten o'clock that night, the finish line came into view. Jimmy ran a final load to the elevator in the purple dump truck and then took over in the grain cart while Annie moved into the combine beside Jacob Hess.

"Can you believe it?" she said. "We're almost finished."

"You've done a hell of a job," he said, patting her thigh with his left hand while raising and lowering the header with his right. "Getting Jimmy out here with that second truck was a goddamn stroke of genius."

"Thanks," she said. "If there's one thing eight years of Catholic school taught me, it's how to lay down a good guilt trip."

He gave her thigh a squeeze. "I gotta say, I'll be a little sad when it's over. What am I gonna do for reading material?"

"Mister, that's gonna be the least of your problems," she said, winking at him.

They finished cutting at two in the morning, just before a storm they'd been tracking on Jimmy's phone let loose with a torrent of rain. They rolled the tarps on both trucks and the grain cart and took off across the field in the service truck, arriving at the homeplace as wet as if they'd floated there in the swollen Sawlog.

"There's a six-pack of Coors in the fridge," Annie said. "You guys help yourselves while I grab some towels."

In a dresser in Wade's old room, she found a couple of Red Demon sweatshirts with the sleeves cut off and laughed as she tossed them to Hess and Jimmy, who were busy building a fire in the old stone fireplace. In no time at all, they drank their way through the beer, and Jimmy pulled out a bag of weed and began rolling a joint.

"None of that for me, thanks," Hess said. "I got some Crown in the truck I'll fetch here in a minute."

"Fetch it now," Jimmy said.

"All right, I will," Hess said.

She took his place on the couch, and Jimmy sparked the joint he'd rolled and passed it to her. "My God," she said after taking a hit. "Where'd you get this stuff?"

"I grew it," Jimmy said with a wide grin.

"Bullshit."

"No, no, I did. This dude I know from California . . ."

But by then she was barely listening. She was back to thinking about the sky in western Kansas. How people had been looking to it for answers as far back as Fray Padilla and Francisco Vázquez de Coronado—farther, even—and how the sky, perverse to the end, had steadfastly refused to cooperate or give up its secrets. Maybe the idea wasn't a poem at all. Maybe it was an essay or, better yet, a song, something along the lines of "Snowin' on Raton." She took another hit from the perfectly rolled joint and held it deep in her lungs.

"Whoa, be careful with that," she heard Jimmy say. "It's got a way of sneaking up on you."

Then Hess returned with a big bottle of Crown Royal and three highball glasses of questionable cleanliness. And by the way, what was the deal with cowboys and Canadian whiskey? What on earth did they have against the state of Kentucky? Some age-old rivalry having to do with horses or horse racing? Her mind drifted. Ah, but what a strong, handsome son of a gun Jacob Hess was. He looked even better without a cowboy hat than he did with one on, and that was saying something, especially for a man—she'd done a little online snooping—zeroing in on his twentieth high school reunion. She passed the joint back to Jimmy and got up to turn on the radio her father kept in the house for weather reports, twisting the dial until she came to a classic country station playing Keith Whitley's "When You Say Nothing at All."

"Get up," she said, kicking Hess's outstretched boot. "It's time to dance."

"I don't dance, as a rule."

"Tonight you do."

He knocked back what remained of his neat Crown Royal and joined her in the center of the hardwood floor. As they danced, Jimmy sat smoking the joint she'd passed him, a strange, luminous smile on his face.

"You two make a helluva nice couple," he said. "Very western Kansas."

"Stop it," Annie said.

"Ha, you stop it. You think you're all big city and shit, but when it comes right down to it, you're just as big a hick as George Strait here. Yee haw!"

"Hey, I'm an ex-rodeo queen," Annie said, feeling the full effect of the weed. "Well, ex-rodeo queen *contestant*. But I'm also ABD. Don't forget that. A person can be many things at once."

"ABD?" Jimmy said.

"All but dissertation."

They danced some more, Annie's legs growing a little more wobbly with each tune that came on the radio, and then Jimmy got up and looked out the front window at the driveway and the road beyond. "Rain's slowing up," he said. "I'm outa here."

"No way," Annie said. "You're in no condition to be riding a motorcycle on wet sand roads."

"What," Jimmy said. "You're gonna let me drive your Porsche?"

"Uh, no," Annie said.

"That's what I thought. Anyhow, it's no biggie. I ride in worse than this shit all the time."

They followed him outside, where the clouds were rolling back to reveal a full moon.

"Thanks for everything, little bro," Annie said, leaning over the motorcycle's handlebars to give him a kiss on the cheek. "I always knew you'd come through in the end."

"Liar," he said. "I didn't know that myself until it happened."

Annie laughed. "What about that purple dump truck?"

Jimmy started the bike, revved the engine a few times, and let it fall to an idle. "Just leave it with the tire dudes at the Co-op. They'll know what to do with it. Adios!"

"Adios, little brother."

After his taillights had disappeared over the bluffs on 114 Road, Annie turned and walked back up the steps to the porch and into the homeplace without checking to see if Hess followed. Instead, she went straight into the ground-floor bathroom, turned on the shower above the iron tub, and stepped out of her clothes. The hot water felt good on her shoulders and neck as the little room slowly filled with steam.

A few minutes later, the bathroom door opened, sucking steam from the room before closing again with a satisfying thud. She pulled the shower curtain back, and there Hess stood in the steamy air with two glasses of Crown-and-ice in his hands. Annie reached through the steam to take one of them.

"Are you gonna stand out there all night, or are you coming in?"

He drained his glass and set it on the pedestal sink. "I'm coming in."

"Good," she said, and turned her back while he shed his boots and jeans and the rest of his clothes and stepped in behind her.

TWENTY-FOUR

At 11:41 PM, the Amtrak from Los Angeles screeched to a halt beside the old Santa Fe Depot, directly across Wyatt Earp from where a statue of the man himself was frozen in the act of pulling his long-nose Colt from its holster. Jimmy stood watching as an elderly couple and three college kids in ROTC uniforms stepped down from the train. Another minute passed, and he began to worry that Kaid and Brock had gotten themselves kicked off the train somewhere between Albuquerque and Dodge. But then two backpacks came flying out the door, landing in a heap at his feet, and soon after Kaid and another passenger carried Brock down the steps of the train and laid him on his back on the concrete of the platform.

"Dude, we made it!" Kaid said, his voice too loud for that hour.

They stood together over Brock while the train regained its motion and disappeared down the tracks in the direction of Kansas City.

"What the hell?" Jimmy said. "We're supposed to cut down those you-know-what tonight, remember?"

"Dude, we're exhausted," Kaid whined. "The conductor kept hassling us over the bottle of vodka Brock was holding, and we got, like, no sleep at all."

"So we're supposed to lose a whole night because Brock got wasted?"

"Dude, taking the train was *your* idea, not ours. Just let us catch a few Z's and get some food in us, and we'll be good to go."

"Yeah, right," Jimmy said. "You don't cut that shit down during the daylight hours. The smoke gets all starchy and harsh."

"Whatever," Kaid said.

Together, they lifted Brock by the arms and dragged him across the train platform to where the cab Jimmy had taken there stood waiting by the curb.

"Where's the van?" Kaid asked.

Jimmy rolled his eyes. In the days before tending to his ladies and their needs became such an all-consuming task, they had talked about buying a used van to serve as a tour bus for their as-yet-unnamed band. Kaid had wanted to buy the van in Cali and drive it out, but Jimmy had convinced him they could pick one up a lot cheaper in Kansas.

"We'll start looking as soon as we get all that bud trimmed," he said now.

Kaid opened his mouth to complain, but just then, Brock groaned, rolled over onto his side, and began to vomit into the street.

"Holy shit!" Kaid laughed. "What a trip!"

The following evening, after Kaid and Brock had caught up on their beauty sleep, the three of them cut down Jimmy's Girl Scout Cookies one by one and began the process of hanging them upside down to dry. The week before, Jimmy had texted Kaid a list of trimming supplies to pick up from a hydro store in LA, but Kaid had left the box containing the supplies on the train, and so now they had to make do with crappy scissors and rubber gloves scavenged from the aisles of Walmart. Nevertheless, after ten hours of sustained labor, they had the Girl Scout Cookies hanging from the ceiling in the whole back half of the trailer. A dude couldn't even walk around in there without stooping over like some explorer negotiating stalactites in a cave.

"Is that a beautiful sight or what?" Jimmy said, nodding at the upside-down plants as the three of them shared a celebratory smoke.

"Dude, my hands are killing me," Brock said.

"Well, take another hit," Jimmy said.

"I will, but I need something stronger."

"Yeah, yeah, yeah," Jimmy said.

Since hitting town the night before, Brock had done little but bitch and moan. The whole time they were trimming and hanging weed, he kept pestering Jimmy to give him something to ease the pain shooting through his shoulders and back as a result of some vague injury he had gotten lifting weights on the beach. Or was it vacuuming cars at Hertz? The story kept changing. What on earth had happened to the strong, happy-go-lucky dude Jimmy had known at TMP-Marian? Vanished, man. Call out the Missing Persons Unit.

"What's all this bud worth, do you think?" Kaid asked.

"Dude, who knows," Jimmy said. "If I had to guess, though, I'd say we're talking six figures, easy." After another hit, he added, "That's retail, of course."

"Of course. What's our end?"

Jimmy had to laugh. "What do you mean *our end*? I've been sweating over these bitches for three months, and you've been here, what, a day and a half?"

"So? We still deserve a cut."

Jimmy shrugged. "You'll get paid. Just as soon as I do."

He could see now that calling in reinforcements had been a big mistake. But it was a mistake he was just gonna have to live with, so he resolved to relax and go with the flow. After a long nap, they carried guitars and a bottle of Jack Daniels down to

Jimmy's favorite hideaway under the 56/400 bridge, where some-one had dragged a vinyl couch and chairs.

It had been almost two years since they'd jammed together. At the time, Jimmy was just learning guitar, strumming cowboy chords in the background while Kaid took the lead. But in the years since, as they traded tracks online and bullshitted about forming a band, Jimmy's chops as a guitar player had steadily improved, and he couldn't wait to show Kaid and Brock.

"Let's play 'Hotel California.' I've been working on a simplified version of the solo riff."

"Don't know it," Kaid said.

"Yes you do. You were playing it the first time we met." He played through the basic chord progression—Bm to F# to A to E to G to D to Em to F# and back to Bm. "Remember?"

"Yeah, fucking *barre chords*," Kaid said. "Gimme a capo."

"Capo?" Jimmy laughed. "Who uses a fucking capo?"

"Well then, let's play something different," Kaid said. "How about 'Knockin' on Heaven's Door'?"

"Right on. Go for it."

They'd played the song a gazillion times in the dorms at TMP, and Jimmy had often been impressed by Kaid's reggae-inspired approach to the song. But everything was different now. Kaid's voice sounded weak and off-key in the open air of the dry riverbed. He kept messing up the lyrics even though they were super easy to remember. Worst of all, his guitar playing now sounded amateurish to Jimmy's ears. The dude didn't even know how to mix up his strumming patterns. He just kept playing the same one over and over again. Jimmy felt a similar letdown when they played "Hallelujah" and "Girl from the North Country" and "California Stars." After that one, Jimmy yawned and put his Gibson back in its case.

"What's wrong?" Kaid said. "Don't tell me you're finished playing already."

"Nah, just tired," Jimmy lied. "I'll feel a hell of a lot better after all that weed is cured and out the door."

Kaid nodded, his eyes at half-mast from all the dope they'd smoked.

As for Brock, he just lay on his back on the vinyl couch, the half-empty bottle of Jack balanced on his chest.

Missing fucking person, Jimmy thought.

TWENTY-FIVE

Michael pushed the button on the overhead garage door and stepped over several thousand dollars' worth of unused sports equipment—soccer nets, in-line skates, tennis racquets, junior golf clubs—to peer through the window glass of his wife Vanessa's Land Rover LR4. It was just as he'd feared: the entire back half of the luxury SUV was loaded with boxes having to do with some fundraiser Vanessa had been roped into by her country club friends. Rather than packing for the weekend trip to Dodge, which he'd pitched as a necessary prelude, a kind of gathering of his forces in advance of Monday morning's showdown with Byron Branch, she'd been busy with another cause, one that had nothing to do with him or their family but some social-climbing charity.

That was not how things had worked when he was growing up on the Bar W. Far from it. There, the high stakes and the regularity of crises had caused everyone to pull together. He could still recall the March blizzard when he was ten or eleven years old, when he and Wade and Annie, who must have been in kindergarten at the time, were held out of school to venture out into the driving snow to rescue a herd of two hundred yearlings that had walked over a downed electric fence and promptly disappeared. Even Caroline, who rarely took part in ranch work, contributed to the effort by driving a flatbed loaded with hay that Annie periodically forked to the exhausted cattle while Leroy and

Michael and Wade rounded up strays and urged them forward on horseback. It was terrible, grinding work, and by the end of the day, Michael was convinced he'd suffered frostbite in at least three toes and the tips of all ten of his fingers and thumbs. But finally they got the cattle back to the ranch. Leroy built a roaring fire in the fireplace, and they all gathered around it to thaw out and drink hot chocolate out of antique mugs.

"I remember drinking out of these same mugs when I was no bigger than Annie," Leroy said with a tired smile. The relief of getting the cattle back where they belonged had made him chatty. "Same deal as today. Cattle out, cold as hell." He paused to take a sip of his hot chocolate. "We got her done, though, didn't we?"

"Yes, we did," Michael said now, his voice echoing in the cavernous Johnson County garage.

A couple of days before, Leroy had called Michael at work to ask about a couple of the financial moves Michael had been forced to make while Leroy was flat on his back in the hospital.

"What's all this money that's been showing up in the Bar W checking account?" he asked.

"Call it a loan," Michael said.

"What? You're a banker now? You had no right—"

"Sure I did. *Somebody* had to do something, given the mess things were in."

"Mess? You don't even know what you're talking about!"

"I know more than you think. I know about that section of so-called irrigated ground you paid way too much money—"

"Now wait just a goddamn—"

But he didn't wait. Instead, he listed every outstanding debt, down to the penny, his father had hanging over his head, contrasting this with the income from the recently completed wheat harvest, copies of the elevator tickets for which he had spread out on the desk before him. "It doesn't take a math whiz to see there's a huge deficit here," he said in summation. Then, as a kind of prosecutorial final blow, he asked, "Does Mom know?"

Close to a minute of silence followed, and then his father said in a low, dry voice, "No, she doesn't. At least not yet."

"Don't you think you ought to tell her?"

"Why? What good would that do?"

"I don't know. If nothing else, it'd give you someone to talk to about it."

More silence followed, then his father spoke the words that gave Michael chills every time he thought about them. "Well, now I got *you* for that, don't I?"

It was a small thing. Just a few words spoken under duress. But to Michael, it felt like a benediction. He'd been waiting a long time—almost twenty years—to hear his father say that he needed him. That was all he'd ever wanted, Michael realized. To be needed by his father.

And yet, the magic of the moment did not stop there. Because, as it turned out, receiving Leroy's benediction was not an ending but a beginning. The two of them, father and son, had talked on the phone every day after that, and with each conversation—about the ranch, and especially about the case against Byron Branch, which was rapidly approaching—Michael could feel them growing closer, his father trusting him and relying on him more and more. It was scary, almost. What would happen if Michael lost the case, or if, somehow, God forbid, they ended up losing the Bar W? Then what?

He stopped in his house's spacious kitchen, which gave way to an even larger great room, and unburdened himself of wallet, keys, and both of his cell phones, then continued through the formal dining room to the base of the central staircase.

"Vanessa! Sam and Luke! Where are you guys?"

He started up the carpeted stairway but stopped short when he began to hear the telltale explosions of a video game in progress.

He could already picture the scene in Sam's room: both boys sprawled across the plush carpeting, controllers in hand, the wall-mounted wide-screen TV alive with cartoonish warfare. If he had to face that scene right now, in the mood he was in, he'd be in danger of starting a bloodbath of his own. Instead, he turned and descended the stairs to the ground floor and then to the finished basement, where Vanessa, still in the yoga gear she'd donned that morning, sat before a laptop in the home office she kept next to the laundry room.

"I know, I know," she said, holding up a hand as though to fend off an attack. "I've got one more email to send about this fundraiser, then I'll be finished."

"If it's just an email, you can send it from the road."

"Yeah, but there's a ton of attachments. I just want to get it finished so I can focus on other things. Can you just start loading the car?"

"You mean the LR? It's full of—"

"Oh, shit. I forgot about that stuff. Just give me a minute, and I'll move it, I promise."

He stood there looking at her large brown eyes and flawless olive skin. Even without makeup and in workout clothes—especially without makeup and in workout clothes—she was a stunner. "Eva Longoria," the wife of one of his law partners had remarked after meeting Vanessa for the first time. "That's who she looks like! Eva freaking Longoria!"

"What?" she said now. "Why are you looking at me like that?"

"You knew I wanted to get an early start," he said. "We talked about it at breakfast. We've got a five-hour drive ahead of us. And yet, it's past four now, and you've done nothing to get ready. It's like you're working against me, actively trying to sabotage the whole trip."

"Sweetie, I'm not trying to sabotage anything," Vanessa said. "I'm just trying to finish a few things before we go."

Michael shook his head. "Why don't you just admit it? You don't want to go. You hate Dodge City and the ranch, and the thought of spending even a *day* there makes you want to turn and run as fast as you can in the opposite direction."

"I do *not* hate Dodge City," Vanessa said, clicking the laptop shut. "Do I love it the way you do? No. Am I from there? No. But then, that's part of the problem, isn't it?"

"What do you mean by that?"

"Forget it," she said, rising from her chair.

"No, I want to hear this," he said, following her into the laundry room. "What's part of the problem?"

She picked up a basket of folded clothes and stood with it balanced on her hip. "Your family, Michael. It's like the Mafia or something. If you weren't born into it, if you're not from Dodge and didn't grow up on the Bar whatever—"

"Bar W—"

"—you can forget about being accepted. The most you'll be allowed is a tiny little spot on the sidelines to watch the endless drama play out."

"Oh, sure," he said. "Like your family's any different. If I have to hear *one more time* about the long-lost, million-dollar home in Naperville—"

At the mere mention of the word "Naperville," which conjured up hardships occasioned by the loss of her childhood home, Vanessa's eyes began to well with tears, and Michael felt immediate remorse. "Honey, I'm sorry. I didn't mean it."

But the damage was done. She forced her way past him and up the stairs. And later, when he tried the door to their bedroom, he found it locked.

"Vanessa!" he said through the door. "I said I was sorry!"

A moment passed, and then the door cracked open enough to reveal Vanessa's made-up face. "I'm getting packed. Since presumably you're already packed and ready to go, why don't you take those boxes out of the LR and get the boys to load their stuff?"

The door closed again.

"Okay, but we're not taking the Land Rover," he said. "There's no time to move all that stuff. We'll just take the Ram instead."

"Whatever," she called from the other side of the door.

Forty-five minutes later, hair and face perfectly done, wearing a pair of tight-fitting white jeans and an elegant sleeveless blouse, Vanessa finally emerged from the house and climbed into the passenger seat of the Ram. In the back seat, Sam and Luke were watching the first of what would end up being three or four movies. Ordinarily Vanessa would've asked what they were watching and what its rating was, but she let all that go now.

"If we're going to make it through this weekend," she announced, "we're going to have to agree to be more careful about what we say to each other."

By "we," she meant him, of course.

They headed down Metcalf Avenue toward I-435. "Look, I said I was sorry. I'm a little on edge, that's all. I feel like I've got a lot riding on this trip, and I want everything to go well."

"What are you talking about?" Vanessa said, thumbing through some pictures on her phone. "You mean the trial? I thought that was just a squabble over some land deal that your dad got himself mixed up in."

"It is," Michael said. "But it feels bigger than that, too. You remember that case I had down by Branson last year? The one Russ Frederick didn't want me to take because it was going to involve a lot of time in court, and the firm had other lawyers who specialized in that?"

She nodded but continued to thumb photos, her eyes never leaving her phone.

"Well, I feel like this case is a chance at a do-over," he said. "If I can prove, to him and the other senior guys in the firm, that I'm capable of—"

As he was saying this, a fight broke out in the back seat—Luke wanted to start a different movie, and Sam insisted they stick with the one they were watching—and by the time Vanessa had succeeded at adjudicating the situation, the moment was ruined.

"I'm sorry, honey. What were you saying?"

"Nothing," Michael said. "We can talk about it later."

"Are you sure?"

"Yeah, let's just put on some music or something."

Still looking at her phone, she turned the dial on the radio until it came to a classical station. "How's this?"

"Fine," he said, even though he'd always hated classical music, a fact she should've known but somehow didn't.

It was after 10:30, bedtime for Sam and Luke, when they made it to the Best Western Plus on West Wyatt Earp Boulevard. But although Michael had booked two rooms so that he and Vanessa wouldn't have to share one with the boys, that didn't mean she'd forgiven him for his remark about her lost childhood home in Naperville.

"I'm tired, and tomorrow's a long day," she said, turning her back to him in the king bed.

He lay there a long time, listening to the rise and fall of her breathing and thinking about the turn he could feel their lives taking. It was like they'd been sitting in a becalmed boat for the past twelve years, only to have a storm blow up out of nowhere, pushing them toward a rocky coastline. Would they survive the sudden storm? How? What would they do when they reached the shore? *Would* they reach the shore?

Questions, always questions.

TWENTY-SIX

The brittle, hardback copy of Ivan Doig's *This House of Sky* lay open on Leroy's lap, his cast-bound left arm holding it in place while his eyes behind their thick, drugstore glasses moved over the beautiful, confounding words.

Past those first hard-edged months after my mother's death, then, and on into my father's wise instinct of treating me as though I was grown and raised, my sixth-seventh-eighth years of boyhood became lit with the lives we found in the Stockman and the Maverick and the others. The widower and his son had begun to steady . . .

Annie had dropped the book off for him along with a dozen others that had failed to capture his attention. But this one was different. It seemed to tell the story of his own childhood, but through a strange, inverse lens. Montana instead of western Kansas. Sheep instead of cattle. A father who steadied and then weakened over time rather than one who clung to grief so tightly it carried him down a hole so dark he could never claw his way back out. Had Annie guessed the similarities between his childhood and Doig's, or was this simply an accident, the result of throwing darts at a target until one of them finally found the bull's eye?

He'd never been much of a reader beyond the *Daily Globe* and industry publications like the *High Plains Journal* and *Kansas Stockman*. He'd never had the time or the interest, to say nothing of the patience required by a book like Doig's, which mixed together detailed descriptions of things Leroy knew well with startling flights into a kind of . . . well, he didn't know what to call it. Just now, for example, he'd read, *The ranch buildings stood out from behind the lofty line of cottonwoods on the west bank of Camas Creek, just at the base of the grassed ridges stairstepping up into the Big Belts.* He could picture the whole thing clearly, could compare it effortlessly to the Bar W, where the ranch buildings stood out in a similar fashion from the cottonwoods and elms and cedar trees lining the south bank of the Sawlog, but what to make of "grassed ridges stairstepping up into the Big Belts"? Where had Doig gotten these words from, and why were they so right when part of Leroy wanted to stand up from the bed where he was imprisoned and declare how *wrong wrong wrong* they were; there were rules to be followed, in writing as in life, and "stairstepping" had to be in violation of at least one. But then he'd be drawn into the next sentence, and the next, and he'd forget all about grammar and punctuation and be lost once again in the story of Ivan and Charlie and Ivan's grandma, Bessie Ringer.

The book was half as old as Leroy himself; the glue holding its pages in place had dried to the point where they came loose from the binding as he turned them. He tried to hold them in place with the fingers of his left hand as he read, but every once in a while one would elude his grasp and fall to the floor beside his adjustable bed. Just now, for example, he could see the top half of page 68 peeking out from under a chair. When Caroline took a break from her own reading, or whatever it was she did in her office at the back of the house, he would ask her to put the page back into its rightful place between pages 66 and 69.

Two rooms away, the kitchen door creaked open on its dry hinges, and Leroy looked up from his book, listening intently.

"Mom? Dad?" came Michael's voice.

"Back here!" Leroy bellowed, the loudness of his own voice surprising him.

"Coming," Michael called.

But then he didn't come. At least not immediately, the way he would've done when he was a boy and Leroy would bellow from beneath a piece of machinery the precise tool he needed. *Three-quarters box-end. Hurry! Nine-sixteenth socket. Get to going!* Then the sound of the boy's tennis shoes as he ran across the shop floor and back again with all the urgency of a batboy retrieving a bat at Kauffman Stadium. Just now, Leroy could hear him having a one-sided phone conversation with what sounded like a secretary. Quick questions asked and answered, instructions given. "Okay, call me as soon as you hear anything." It was yet another forced exercise in patience, a quality Leroy hadn't even known he lacked until recently, when he'd been called upon to exercise it a hundred times a day.

While he waited, he considered what he'd say to Michael about all the money Michael had been pumping into the Bar W checking account without Leroy asking or even authorizing him to do it. The whole situation was shameful, and yet, like the accident that had precipitated the situation, there was nothing Leroy could do about it. He'd been hoping to pay Michael back in a single, grand gesture once all the wheat was in and he'd sold the spring calves that were still on their mothers over in the Adams pasture. But as Michael had pointed out so succinctly the last time they spoke, the numbers didn't come close to adding up.

Finally, Michael finished his call and breezed into the room carrying a briefcase and a large cup of coffee in a white to-go cup. Instead of a suit and tie, he was dressed in the jeans and cowboy boots he always wore when he visited Dodge.

"Pick up that loose page off the ground," Leroy said.

Michael bent at the waist and scooped it up.

"Put it on that coffee table with the others. Here, take this, too," he said, nodding at the book in his lap.

Again, Michael did as he was told, no hesitation, no questions asked, just like the old days. It was a far cry from Jimmy, who, the few times he'd worked for Leroy, was always asking questions and cracking jokes and calling him by his first name instead of "Dad."

Michael glanced at the cover of the Doig book as he lay it on the coffee table. Then he took a sip of coffee, pulled a wingback chair across the carpet, positioning it so he and Leroy were facing each other, and opened the briefcase.

"About that money," Leroy began.

"We can talk about all that later," Michael said.

"You're right. But I want to talk about it now."

"Okay," Michael said, sitting back in the chair. "I'm all ears."

Leroy pushed his one good elbow against the hard mattress, lifting himself into something closer to a sitting position. "I figure if I sell the herd on Adams, and then somehow find a way to—"

"Sell the herd?" Michael said. "You mean cows and calves both? That's a terrible idea, and you know it."

"You got a better one?" Leroy asked.

"Absolutely."

"Let's hear it."

Michael smiled and took another long sip of coffee. "Sell the cows to me. That way, if you do find a way to dig out of this mess, you can buy them right back."

Before he could respond to this ridiculous idea, Caroline came barging into the room with a glass of water and the handful of pills—blood thinner, blood-pressure meds, another one for something called "pre-diabetes"—the doctors had put him on before releasing him from the hospital.

"Michael!" she said as he rose from his chair to give her a hug. "When did you get here? Did you bring Vanessa and the boys? Where are they?"

"Back at the hotel," Michael said. "It's a little early for them."

"You know how I feel about that hotel," Caroline said with a deep frown. "I don't understand why you can't stay here with us. Will we at least get to see you tonight?"

"Of course."

"Oh good," Caroline said.

While this was going on, Leroy allowed his mind to get used to the idea of Michael becoming his silent, or maybe not-so-silent, partner. There were a number of things he didn't like about the idea, foremost among them the loss of power and control it would entail, but he had to admit it beat having Byron Branch or some other vulture pick his bones clean. Beyond this, it kept the secret of his recent losses in the family, where it belonged. By the time Caroline had fed him the last of the pills and left the room again, he'd done a complete 180 on the matter.

"About those cattle. Maybe we sell the steers and hold back a few of the heifers as replacement cows? We've had a lot of rain this month, and there ought to be plenty of grass in that pasture heading into the fall."

"Are you asking or telling?" Michael said, a satisfied smile creeping into the corners of his mouth.

"Asking, I guess."

"Well, good," Michael said. "But I'll take you one further. How about we hold back *all* the heifers? Or, better yet, sell them as pairs after they have their first or second calf. I mean, have you seen what pairs are bringing?"

"I have," Leroy said, nodding. Now it was his turn to smile.

For the next two hours, they pored over every aspect of the upcoming court case, everything from the "false auction" (Michael's words) at which Leroy and other neighboring ranchers had agreed to hold their bids, to the "illegal mortgage"

that Byron Branch had extended to the Stewarts, to the "clear fiduciary responsibility" on Branch's part that, in Michael's interpretation, made the sale null and void. It was brilliant stuff, way more imaginative and outside-the-box than anything Harold Krebs could've come up with, even on his best day.

"Give it to me straight," Leroy said. "Where are we the weakest?"

"That's easy." Michael laughed. "You."

"Me? Hell, I'm just an innocent bystander in this whole deal."

"Sure, you are," Michael said. "All the same, if I was Branch's lawyer, my whole strategy would be to get you on the stand and make you look every bit as greedy and plotting as Branch himself. They're gonna want to turn this case into Byron Branch v. Bull Wagner, because that's gonna be a hell of a lot easier to win than Chester and Fanny Stewart v. Byron Branch."

"Well, good luck with that," Leroy said. "Byron Branch is a Texas rattlesnake, and everybody in this town knows it, including Judge Stevens."

"Whereas Leroy Wagner's been an absolute angel his whole life," Michael said, holding back a laugh. "Never gotten sideways with anybody. Never pissed anybody off or knocked anybody over with his pickup mirror."

"You heard about that?"

"You better believe I did. The judge did, too."

He let this sink in a moment. "Well, so that's their strategy. What's ours?"

Michael shrugged and leaned back in his chair. "We don't need a strategy. We've got the Stewarts. Their mere presence in that courtroom, Fanny in her wheelchair, Chester in his bib overalls, looking like a relic from the Dust Bowl. I mean, my God, isn't that better than any 'strategy' you or I could sit here and dream up?"

Leroy nodded in appreciation. And to think that once upon a time Michael had wanted to drop out of college and follow him into the quicksand of farming and ranching. What a waste that would've been.

"There's only one part of this whole thing I don't get," Michael continued.

"Oh yeah? What's that?"

Michael's expression gradually changed from a kind of playful mirth to something more serious than that. "What's all this to you? I mean, even if the Stewarts are given a second chance at an auction, they're still gonna have to sell, right?"

"Sure. So?"

"So, is that what this is all about? You get the land, instead of Byron Branch?"

A month ago, having the question raised in this way, by his own son no less, would've pitched Leroy into a fit of angry denials. But something was happening to him. The more time he spent alone in that dim room, accompanied only by books and the daily cavalcade of golfers, the more measured and contemplative he became. If it went on much longer, he'd become like one of those monks in rural France Sister Margaret had told him about, who prayed four or five times a day and made cheese and brewed beer without drinking any of it themselves.

"It's not about the land," he said. "Although, if it does come down to a loose ball between us and Byron Branch, and by some miracle we're able to come up with the cash to buy the south quarter, well then, sure, I'd be interested. Who wouldn't?"

Michael shrugged.

"But really, it's simpler than that. You don't go kicking a guy when he's down. You don't steal his land out from under him just because he's lost the ability to read and understand a loan agreement. And if you see someone else doing it, you don't stand there and watch it happen. You *do* something, by God."

He looked at where Michael sat nodding slowly.

"Are you with me?"

"You better believe it. I mean, I can't wait to see the look on Branch's face when that verdict is read. Can you?"

"No, I can't," Leroy said.

He sat watching as Michael began to gather up his papers and other things. "When's the next time you're gonna be out to the ranch?"

"This afternoon," Michael said.

"Do me a favor, then. Stop by Tractor Supply and pick up one of those big bags of dog food. Chester calls about it every morning, and I keep forgetting to tell Annie."

"You got it," Michael said. "Anything else?"

"Yeah," Leroy said. "Next time you get coffee, bring a cup for me, too."

"Shit, I'm sorry. I just thought—"

"I know what you thought," Leroy said. "But I ain't dead yet. Not even close."

TWENTY-SEVEN

The scene at the Best Western Plus was even more discouraging than Michael had imagined on the drive over from his parents' house. Not only were Vanessa and the boys watching a movie on Vanessa's laptop, but they were doing it in his and Vanessa's bed. Why had he even bothered getting two rooms instead of one? It was as if a gigantic message board had been mounted on the wall above the headboard: NO SEX FOR YOU, MICHAEL WAGNER!

"Time for lunch," he said with forced cheerfulness. "Who's getting hungry?"

"I am!" Luke answered.

Vanessa and Sam barely looked up from the movie.

"It's just getting good," Vanessa said. "Anyway, I was on the phone with your mother. You know those neighbors of theirs? The ones who let us swim as their guests at the country club the last time we were here?"

"I guess," Michael said, not liking where this was headed. "What about them?"

She paused the movie and handed the laptop to Sam, who disappeared with it into the adjoining room, Luke following closely behind.

"Well, I asked your mother if we could swim there today, and she called the neighbor, and it's no problem at all. We just have to sign the neighbor's last name at the gate."

Michael let out a sigh. "I thought we were gonna grab some Mexican and take it out to the ranch. That's what we talked about on the drive here."

"I know," Vanessa said. "But can we do it tomorrow instead? I just checked the forecast, and it's going to be really hot, like one hundred degrees, today. Windy, too, by the look of it."

"Baby, it's western Kansas. It's always hot and windy in the summer."

She got out of the bed, still in her pajamas, and walked to the bathroom sink, where she picked up her toothbrush. "All I'm saying is, it would be really nice to avoid all that heat and wind. Besides, you're going to be busy with work stuff anyway. Isn't this the day you're gonna talk to that old couple, the Stewarts? We'd just be along for the ride."

"Well, maybe I *want* you along for the ride," he said. "Maybe I *need* that from you right now."

"Baby, you know I support you," Vanessa said. "I just don't see what driving around a dusty ranch on a hundred-degree day has to do with that."

She began to brush her teeth, her eyes never leaving his. Everything about her excited and exasperated him. It was for her he had rented two rooms at the Best Western instead of staying with his parents in their house with its ridiculous bomb shelter. It was for her he had all but agreed to Pembroke Hill for Sam and, by extension, for Luke, too. It was for her he was killing himself in a job he'd begun to hate. And what did he get for all this? Backsliding on everything they'd agreed to. Yes, and one roadblock after another when it came to sex.

"What about you, Sam?" he called into the adjoining room. "Do you really want to go to the pool instead of the ranch?"

The boy appeared in the doorway, a sheepish look on his face. "I don't know. Maybe. I mean, what's there to do out there anyway? Mom says you're just going to talk to some old people, and we're going to sit in the truck and wait for you."

"For the record, I did *not* say that," Vanessa put in.

"No, it's fine," Michael said, throwing up his hands. "It's pretty clear where all of this is headed. I'll just go by myself."

"I'll go with you, Dad," Luke said, emerging from behind his older brother and crossing the carpeted floor to stand before Michael like a soldier at inspection. This was all Michael had been asking for, all he wanted. A show of belief. A small vote of confidence in his ability to pull off a simple plan.

"You don't have to do that," he said.

"But I want to. Can we get McDonalds on the way?"

"I don't know, maybe. For now, just go and get dressed. You can wear shorts, but no flip-flops. Tennis shoes."

At this, Luke bolted into the adjoining room, and Michael locked eyes with his unsmiling wife.

"I don't like this," she said. "You're going to get distracted and forget to watch him."

"No, I won't," Michael said.

It was a relief, half an hour later, to drop Vanessa and Sam at the gate to the country club pool.

"Are you sure you don't want to go to the pool with us, Lukie?" Vanessa said in a naked attempt to win the boy to her side. "It's going to be awfully hot at the ranch."

"So I'll get him some Gatorade on the way out of town," Michael said.

"At McDonalds?" Luke asked.

"Wherever you want."

Vanessa rolled her eyes and stepped out into the melting parking lot. Watching her tiptoe across the hot expanse did little to alleviate his mixed emotions. Sure, he was annoyed and frustrated. But the sight of his wife in a bikini, beach towel wrapped around her exquisite body, brought to mind certain days on

Hilton Head when the boys were still young enough to take afternoon naps, and the world was ripe with potential for amorous adventure. Where had those days gone? Were they ever coming back?

"Bye, Mom," Luke called after her.

"Bye-bye, honey," Vanessa called over her shoulder. "Have fun with Daddy, and be sure to drink plenty of water."

TWENTY-EIGHT

With the Girl Scout Cookies hung to dry, Jimmy turned his attention to the promise he'd made Kaid, the two of them riding double on the Ducati all the way out to a derelict farmstead south of Cedar Bluff State Park to see a purple-on-white 2005 Chevy Express that Kaid had spotted on Craigslist. The conversion van had 343,000 miles on it and was beginning to rust out below the picture window, but Kaid was completely taken in by the seller's tale of how much money he'd poured into the vehicle's interior and stereo system.

"It's cherry, man," the guy kept saying. "You won't find another like it. Just look at that carpet. It's practically brand new."

He was one of those old, pony-tailed dudes with a gray beard and Jerry Garcia glasses. Total boomer. "Cherry," Jimmy said, shaking his head. "By the looks of the hitch, I'm guessing you hauled a boat with this thing?"

"Well, yeah, a little bit," the guy said.

Jimmy popped the van's hood to look at the motor. It had the dinky 4.3L V6 instead of the 6.0L V8 he'd been hoping for. He pulled the dipstick, and the thing was at least two quarts low on oil. "What's the story? Is it leaking oil, or burning it?"

"Good question," the guy said.

Jimmy was getting ready to crawl under the van to have a look at where all the oil was going when Kaid grabbed him by the elbow and led him out of earshot of the seller. "Dude, what's up *your* butt?"

"What are you talking about? He's asking five grand for that piece of shit!"

"So? Make him an offer. Meet him halfway or something."

"Yeah, right," Jimmy said. "I told you before we rode over here, I'm tapped out until this deal we've been working on goes through."

"Yeah, well, what about your old man? You're always talking about all the land and cattle and shit he owns."

Jimmy shook his head. "Ain't happening. Not in a million years."

"Why? You could at least call him and ask."

"You're right. I could. But I'm not going to."

"Why the fuck not?"

"Because I'm done with all that shit, even if you're not."

"Done with *what?*"

"With running to mommy and daddy every time I want or need something. If I can't get it on my own, then guess what? I don't want it, man. I'm out."

He left Kaid where he was standing and walked back to where the yellow Ducati waited in the shade of a cottonwood. It killed him to have to piss on Kaid's dreams, but the dude was spoiled rotten, conditioned to having his parents buy him whatever he wanted because of how guilty they felt about the divorce they'd put him through when he was a little kid. But that wasn't Jimmy's story at all, and he wasn't about to start acting like it was.

Kaid spent another ten or fifteen minutes talking to the boomer. Then, without speaking another word to each other, they climbed back onto the Ducati and rode back to Dodge, where it turned out they had bigger problems to deal with than an overpriced conversion van. Brock was nowhere to be found.

The dude had vanished, leaving the gate wide open and the door to the trailer unlocked. Worse, Jimmy's Gibson J-45 was gone from its place under his bed in the front bedroom.

"What the hell," Jimmy said. "Does he need a bottle of Jack that bad?"

"Dude, it ain't that," Kaid said.

"What then?"

"Percocets, man. He ran out yesterday."

"What? Why didn't you tell me?"

"I don't know. Maybe because you've been such a dick the whole time we've been here?"

"*I've* been a dick!" Jimmy said. "Are you kidding me? Man, I'm so through with this shit I can't even tell you!"

"You're not the only one," Kaid said.

Leaving Kaid to guard the Girl Scout Cookies—a dubious proposition, but what choice did he have?—Jimmy rode the Ducati west through the sand of the river road, the wheels in his mind turning and turning. The only pawnshop he could think of was on Matt Down Road, across from the cemetery. Jimmy doubted Brock could've gotten that far, but he rode over there anyway, finding the place closed. Next, he tried the Santa Fe Depot and the 66 station that doubled as a Greyhound stop.

Nada.

Where would I go if I was from somewhere like LA and I needed to score some Percs in a hurry? he asked himself.

No sooner had he formed the question, than the answer came to him, clear as day. The Flying J, baby. Pharmacopeia to the trucker class, open 24 hours a day.

It had been less than two weeks since he'd walked out of Byron Branch's office, but it felt more like months as Jimmy pulled into the truck stop's broken asphalt parking lot. Branch's black Silverado was nowhere to be seen, so Jimmy headed straight for the driver's lounge at the back of the filling station, where he found Brock in the middle of a heated conversation with an Oklahoma City bull hauler named Earl Pickens.

"Dude, I got the money right here!" Brock was saying, holding out a wad of cash.

"How's it hanging, Earl?" Jimmy broke in.

"Hanging fine," Earl said. "You know this kid?"

"Yeah. He's a friend of mine."

"Can you please tell him I don't have any of the shit he's looking for? I keep trying, but he don't listen real good."

A retired guy who usually worked nights sat behind the counter of the filling station, watching it all go down. An hour from now, Jimmy knew, every detail of the conversation would be known to every trucker and Flying J employee on the premises.

"I got him now," Jimmy said, taking Brock by the shoulders and steering him toward the exit. "Come on. We need to get you out of here."

"To hell with that!" Brock yelled, shaking him off. "I'm not leaving here until I get a fix, man!"

"Tell him to try the hospital," Earl said.

"That's all right," Jimmy said. "I think I got what he needs."

"You do?" Brock asked.

"Sure," Jimmy said. "Head on outside and I'll tell you all about it."

Brock nodded and went out the front door to stand in the shade of the islands.

"Did he have a guitar with him?" Jimmy asked. "Sunburst Gibson J45 in a black case?"

"Sold it an hour ago to a bull hauler headed to Liberal," Earl said.

"How much did he get?"

"I don't know. Fifty bucks? Couldn't have been much more than that."

Jimmy winced. He'd paid almost fifteen hundred for the Gibson when he'd bought it on Reverb.

They stopped at a liquor store on East Wyatt Earp, where Jimmy bought a half gallon of Jack Daniels and a carton of Camel Lights.

"That's great," Brock said. "But it's not—"

"I know, I know," Jimmy said. "That's just to tide you over until I can put my hands on something stronger."

Pulling away from the trailer for the third time since noon, this time on a quest for Percs, Jimmy was visited by a memory of accompanying his father on a mission to bail one of his hired guys out of the Ford County Jail. Jimmy could see now that the whole thing had been meant as a life lesson: *This is what'll happen to you if you don't straighten up.* It was a crude message, and Jimmy hadn't thought much about it at the time. But now, riding the river road in search of painkillers for Brock, he was visited by a realization that the bane of his father's existence—the impossibility of "finding good help these days"—had somehow become the bane of *his* existence, too.

How fucking crazy was that?

TWENTY-NINE

Michael and Luke were stopped at a light across from Tractor Supply when Michael remembered the dog food his father had asked him to buy for the Stewarts. He wheeled the Ram into the parking lot, which adjoined a newly remodeled Wendy's. The sunlit part of the lot was a frying pan, and he and Luke moved quickly across it toward the shade near the front door.

"Why are we stopping here?" Luke asked. "I don't like Wendy's."

"We're running an errand for Grandpa," Michael said. "Come on."

"But—"

"No buts."

The air-conditioned interior of the store was a hodgepodge of the practical and impractical: fencing supplies and stacked animal feed next to a rack of overpriced ball caps with silly slogans like SKI KANSAS! or BACON, THE CEREAL KILLER. The place smelled strongly of horse feed and gear oil, and the dog food came in only two sizes—too big and bigger. Michael wrestled a too-big bag onto his shoulder and headed to the checkout.

Back in the steaming parking lot, an old guy in a red Tractor Supply Company vest limped toward them pushing a shopping cart. "Whoa, there! Put that bag in here before you herniate a disc or something."

Michael let the guy help, and after they'd loaded the bag into the back of the Ram, they stood a moment before a row of chained-up go-karts and riding lawn mowers. One of the few clouds in the sky drifted across the sun, blocking it so that the temperature seemed to drop by twenty degrees in just a few seconds.

"Did you have one of these things as a kid?" the man asked, kicking the knobby front tire of a two-seater go-kart with a padded roll cage.

"Yeah, but nothing this fancy," Michael said, wiping sweat from his brow. "The ones we had were made out of old lawnmower parts."

"Ain't that the truth. Who's this you brought with you? Your son?"

"That's right. This is Luke."

"Hi, Luke. How old are you?"

"Eight," Luke answered. Turning to Michael, he asked in a tone Michael was all too familiar with, "Dad, are we gonna *buy* one of these?"

"No, son, we're not." Michael turned to the guy in the red vest. "His mother would have a heart attack if she knew we were so much as looking at this thing."

The guy shrugged, as if to say, "What are you gonna do?"

"Can I sit in it?" Luke asked.

"Okay," Michael said. "But let me put a towel down or something first. I'm sure that seat is blazing hot about now."

He grabbed an old T-shirt from the Ram and covered the seat, then stood watching as Luke got behind the wheel and strapped himself in.

"This is so cool! Where do I put my feet?"

"Down there on the pedals. But your legs are a little too short to reach."

"The seat adjusts forward," the old guy said. "You just got to grab hold of this lever." With Michael holding one side steady, they slid the seat forward until Luke's feet reached the pedals.

"Could I have it for Christmas?" Luke asked. "Or my birthday? It would be the only thing I'd ask for, I promise."

"Your birthday's not until March," Michael said, winking at the old guy. "Now scoot over and let me drive."

The boy took off his seat belt, and Michael slid the seat back as far as it would go and climbed in behind the wheel. With his feet on the pedals, his bent knees nearly touched the steering wheel.

"Tight fit, but you could sure drive her," the old guy said.

"Can we take it for a spin?"

The man laughed and shook his head. "If we allowed that, the rednecks would be holding the Indy 500 right out here in the parking lot. I say that as a proud redneck myself, of course."

Michael barely heard the man. He was thinking about when he and Wade used to race a pair of homemade go-karts on a track they built next to the alfalfa bales on the Bar W. He could almost hear the whine of the karts' Briggs & Stratton engines as Wade chased him around the track, pretending to lack the space and speed he needed to pass, only to close the distance between them at the very end of the race and snatch away victory in classic, big-brother style.

"I should check inside," the old guy was saying. "If I'm not mistaken, these things go on sale in a day or two."

By then, the sun had popped out from behind the bank of clouds, and the heat was back. Michael climbed out of the go-kart and reached for his wallet.

"Don't worry about it," he said. "So long as you take American Express, we're good."

Half an hour later, the go-kart secured in the back of the Ram with nylon straps, he and Luke topped the last hill before the ranch, and the Bar W spread out before them in all its complicated, highly leveraged glory. In the corrals behind the tack barn, two riders were at work amid a dust cloud of cows and calves. Both riders wore long-sleeved shirts and straw cowboy hats, but even from a half mile away, Michael could easily pick out his sister by how she sat on her horse, back ramrod straight, right arm hanging loosely at her side. It was a carbon copy of the way Wade had sat a horse.

He parked the Ram in front of the pipe corrals and watched as Annie and the other rider, whom Michael guessed to be Jacob Hess, finished cutting the last of the calves and trailing them into a large pen at the back of the corrals.

"Who's that?" Luke asked.

"Aunt Annie."

"Aunt Annie's a *cowboy*?"

Michael laughed. "Does that surprise you?"

"Well, *yeah!*"

A few minutes later, as they were unloading the go-kart in the grass in front of the tack barn, Annie rode up on a gray mare Michael didn't recognize and tipped her hat at them.

"Hey, Lukie."

"Hi, Aunt Annie. See what my dad bought me for Christmas?"

"I already told you," Michael said. "It's mine, not yours." Turning to Annie, he added, "Thanks for sending me the tickets from the wheat harvest. Nice work."

"Thanks," she said, smiling. "Let me tell you, I'm feeling some big-time relief now that it's over."

"I'll bet." He watched Hess work his colt along the pipe fence, executing one beautiful turn-back after another. He was a good hand. Maybe too good. He'd have to check with Leroy to see what they were paying him. "Anyway, Mom's having everyone to dinner tonight. Will we see you there?"

"I forgot all about that," Annie said. "I don't know. Maybe not. We've got a lot going on out here."

Michael nodded at where Hess worked the colt. "I can see that."

"Shut up," Annie said.

He laughed and gave her a wink. "Anyway, you'd better come, or Mom will be bent out of shape. Vanessa, too."

"Me, too," Luke said. "Don't forget about me."

"See?" Michael said.

"Okay, okay," Annie said. "But only because I don't want to upset Mr. Luke here."

She started back to the corrals at a low trot, pausing only to open and close the gate from horseback in one fluid motion, the way they did it at the feed yard. Michael could ride. He could rope if the situation required it. But he'd never pretended to be the rider Annie was. Like Wade, she was a natural, practically born in the saddle.

They set up a mini road course in the dirt between the tack barn and the alfalfa, where he and Wade had built their course thirty years before. After making Luke drink for a full minute from the hose behind the tack barn, Michael found a dusty riding helmet and adjusted it to fit the boy's head. He wished he'd thought to buy a real helmet and some goggles and gloves, but that was okay. Part of what he loved about the Bar W was the way it challenged you to make do with what you had. There was a lesson in that, one that it would be good for the boys to learn before their prissy world in Kansas City obliterated the possibility.

The banked corners and hairpin turns of the old track were gone now, but the basic outline was still intact, and before long, Michael was sliding the kart's rear tires through the corners and gunning it hard into the straightaways. He'd almost forgotten Luke was strapped into the seat beside him when the boy began to pull on his arm.

He stopped on the front straightaway and let the motor fall to an idle. "What?"

"My turn!"

The boy's eyes had dirt pocketed at the corners, and there was dirt lining his nose and the corners of his mouth as well. Michael felt a wave of emotion pass through him, love mixed with nostalgia mixed with a fledgling hope. This was indeed his son of whom he was most proud. Maybe if he found a way to keep bringing Sam and Luke to the ranch, they wouldn't grow up to be pampered city kids, after all, but could acquire something like dual citizenship, their lives shaped as much by the Bar W as by the world of Pembroke Hill.

"Listen," he said, climbing out of the kart and pushing the seat forward until it locked into place. "I can't ride with you, so you're gonna have to be extra careful."

"I will!" Luke said, punching the gas so hard that Michael had to jump back to keep his feet from being run over.

In spite of his quick start off the line, Luke took the first couple of laps around the course so slowly it was almost comical to watch. The stick-like arms reaching forward to grip the steering wheel. The helmeted head so far out of proportion with the rest of his body. As he got the hang of it, though, the boy gradually increased his speed on the straightaways and stopped braking so hard in the corners. Michael stood watching for a couple of laps, a smile on his sweaty face, then sat on the wooden bench in the shade of the tack barn's metal awning. As he sat there, listening to the waxing and waning of the kart's engine, a distant memory came to him, slowly at first, then all at once.

A pre-dawn summer morning. The forecast calling for temperatures crossing into the hundreds by early afternoon. The night before, he and Wade had agreed to rise early and move irrigation pipe before the sun got too high. Michael was up first, drawn to the smell of coffee and blueberry pancakes coming from the kitchen upstairs. He finished a plate of the cakes with bacon and a second cup of coffee, and still Wade wasn't up.

"You probably ought to go wake him," Caroline said.

Michael descended the steps to the dark, cool basement in his bare feet. As a baby, Wade had taken a ride down these steps in his walker, cracking his head on the concrete floor below. The episode had long since passed into Wagner family legend, one of the many things that set Wade apart and made him special. Michael knocked at the closed door to his brother's room.

"Wade? You up?"

"I'm up," came Wade's voice. "Just keeping my eyes closed another minute or two."

"Are you having a migraine?"

His brother's headaches, another part of the legend, were closely monitored by everyone in the family, and lately it seemed that both their frequency and their duration had increased.

"Yeah, but I'm okay," Wade said through the door. "Hook up the trailer and come back for me. I'll be ready."

"Okay," Michael said. "Mom made pancakes. Blueberry."

"Good," Wade said.

In the cool, fragrant alfalfa, they quickly fell into the rhythms of moving irrigation pipe, Michael driving the truck forward in twenty-yard increments before throwing it into neutral and running back to help Wade lift each piece of gated aluminum onto the waiting trailer. Had Leroy not been such a cheapskate, Wade sometimes joked, he'd have bought enough pipe to cover the entire length of the field, rather than relying on them to drag the same twenty lengths of pipe from one end of the muddy field to the other and back again throughout the irrigating season.

But there had been no joking that morning. Instead, they worked at the slow, quiet pace Wade always set when he was having one of his headaches—no radio, no talking, no extraneous movements of any kind. The sun was still on the rise, the sky still a dull blue, Wade's body visible in the rearview mirror only when Michael pressed on the brakes and the red of the brake lights found him. In this dull, bluish-red light, the eeriness of it refracted through the pickup's door-mounted rearview mirror, Michael saw Wade collapse in the field behind him like someone shot by a sniper. That's how quickly it happened. One second, Wade was walking in the red glow of pickup's taillights, red-tinged dust rising from his feet and ankles, the next he was face down in the dirt. No warning at all. Not a sound.

Michael threw the truck into neutral and ran back to find Wade writhing on the ground, tongue stuck out, eyes rolled into the back of his head.

"*Wade! Wade!*"

Holding his brother in the dusty road, Michael could feel the exact moment when the seizure released him. There was a final tensing up, followed by a long, slow relaxing of all his muscles, his jaw slack, eyes open but unblinking.

"*Wade! Wake up, damn it! Wade!*"

Wailing, his voice alien in his ears, he dragged Wade's limp body back to the cab of the truck and somehow managed to lift him inside. Then he was driving the pickup across the corrugated field, the trailer bouncing crazily behind him, spilling pipe off both sides. By the time he pulled up in front of the shop, where his father waited with the red ball of the sun rising behind him like some terrible omen, there was not a single pipe left on the trailer.

The deep, urgent sound of the go-kart throttled down, then disappeared altogether. Michael stood up from the bench where he'd been sitting and looked north. There was no sign of Luke or the kart. He came out of the shade of the metal awning and started walking toward the vanished sound, slowly at first, and then more briskly, until finally he was running.

"Luke! Luke!"

He was on the verge of panic when he rounded a corner created by the stacked hay bales and Luke and the go-kart came suddenly into view, the kart wedged between two bales, the boy behind it, tugging at the roll cage where it encircled the motor.

Seeing this, Michael released the breath he'd been holding and dropped down to a walk.

"Are you all right?" he called out.

"It's stuck," Luke shouted back. "Can you help me to get it going again?"

"Sure," Michael called. "Just give me a minute."

Bringing a hand to his face, he was surprised to find it wet with tears.

THIRTY

Chester and Fanny Stewart lived a mile east of the homeplace in a green-sided farmhouse hidden behind rows of half-dead elm and pine trees, the fallen branches of which had not been cleared from the yard in at least twenty years. Abandoned cars and pickups and ranch equipment, some of it from the 1940s and 50s, littered a weed-choked lot beside a pole barn whose tin siding was in the process of being peeled away by the wind. As Michael and Luke pulled up beside the house, a young dog, black with a white eye patch, what looked to be a Lab/border collie mix, came bounding from a gaping hole in what had once been a garage or shop building and stood barking at them with its tail wagging.

"Whose dog is that?" Luke asked.

"I don't know," Michael said. "Chester's, probably."

"Can I play with him?"

"Sure, just stay in the yard where I can see you. I don't want you climbing on any of this old junk. You're liable to step on a rusty nail or something."

"Dad, I got this," the boy said, rolling his eyes, still crusted with dirt.

As soon as Luke stepped down from the pickup, the dog was all over him, pawing at his chest and licking his face. Luke yelled with delight and took off running across the overgrown yard, the dog following close behind. It was strange to think of stove-up

Chester having a dog so young and full of energy, but people from Dodge and Jetmore and Spearville dumped puppies on this road at all times of the year, and sooner or later most of them turned up hungry at the doors of the scattered ranches. That's how half the dogs on the Bar W had come to be there. Volunteers, Leroy called them. Michael watched as Luke and the puppy began a game of fetch amid the fallen branches of the front yard. He then shouldered the bag of dog food and carried it into the dilapidated shop building, where he set it down atop a workbench littered with antique tools.

It's like a damn time capsule in here—and not in a good way, he mused.

Coming out of the shop, a smell of woodsmoke came to him, and he looked up at where a pair of chimneys, one square and brick, the other little more than a tin pipe, protruded from the patched roof of the farmhouse. Lord only knew what that could be about. He knocked a long time at a screen door at the back of the house before an old man in coveralls and a ratty, threadbare sweater shuffled into view.

"What do you want?" Chester Stewart asked through the broken screen.

"I'm Michael Wagner. Leroy Wagner's son. We were gonna talk about your case?"

"Oh, right," the old man said. "What's your name again?"

"Michael."

"That's right. Come on in."

A wall of heat hit him as soon as he stepped through the door. My God, it had to be 120 degrees in there. He followed Chester through the kitchen into the main part of the house, where a fire roared in the blackened fireplace and a more recently installed wood-burning stove ticked against an interior wall.

"Jesus, Chester," Michael said. "What are you trying to do, burn the place down?"

"Gotta keep Fanny warm. The doctor said so."

"Maybe in the winter," Michael said, feeling the plaster-and-lath wall behind the stove and finding it hot to the touch. "It's like an oven in here. Where's Fanny? Is she okay?"

"In bed. I just brought her some lunch."

"Can you show me?"

He followed the old man through a narrow hallway littered with stacks of old magazines and newspapers—tinder for the fire that would burn them both to death, he thought—until they came to the front bedroom, where a woman with thin arms and white hair lay beneath a faded quilt.

"Are you all right?" Michael asked. "What's with the stove and the fireplace?"

"I keep telling him it's burning up in here, but he won't listen," Fanny said, shaking her white head. "He thinks it's wintertime or something. Some people from town came out last week and took away all the firewood he had stacked on the back porch, but he's got a chain saw hidden in the shop, and he keeps cutting more."

Michael turned to Chester. "Is that true? You've got a chain saw?"

Chester nodded, sweat rolling down his creased face and collecting at the neck of his ratty sweater. "My son gave it to me."

"He's talking about Mr. Branch," Fanny said. "Our son's been dead for going on twenty years."

"Ronnie, right?"

"That's right." Fanny smiled. "Do you remember him?"

"A little bit. He was closer to my brother's age."

The table next to the bed was covered with orange prescription bottles. From reading her case file, Michael knew that Fanny suffered from a heart condition among other ailments that kept her bedridden. Rather than putting her and Chester in assisted living, the county paid a social worker to deliver groceries and meds twice a month, the idea being that Chester, who was deemed to be too active for assisted living, would take care of her. It was a sensible enough plan, Michael thought, so long as Chester didn't burn the place down with both of them in it.

"We need to talk about the trial, but first I'm going to quiet down those fires and get some air in this place."

"Trial?" Chester asked.

"You've got a court date first thing Monday morning, remember?"

"A court date," Chester repeated, his eyes full of confusion and fear.

With Chester shadowing his every move, Michael used a poker to spread out the wood in the fireplace and stove, shoveled ash over the embers, and propped open the doors at the front and back of the house to let in some air. He tried to open some windows, too, but they'd all been painted shut long ago. Then he and Chester pulled a couple of chairs into Fanny's room, and he went over what they could expect on Monday.

"I'll call you up to the witness stand, one at a time, and ask you some questions. All you have to do is answer the questions honestly and to the best of your ability. Then Mr. Branch's lawyer will ask some questions, and maybe the judge, too."

"The judge?" Chester asked.

"Jack Stevens. Do you know him?"

Chester shook his head.

"If you have any questions about any of this, we should go over them now," Michael said. "Once you're on the stand, I won't be able to help you. Do you have any questions?"

Chester looked at him as if he'd never seen him before and asked, "Are you from the sheriff's office?"

"No, Chester, I'm not," Michael said. "I'm Michael Wagner, your lawyer. I'm Leroy's son."

"Oh, okay," Chester said, sounding none too sure.

Michael turned to Fanny. "What about you? Any questions?"

"No," she said, shaking her head from side to side. "We're both just so grateful to you and your father. I hope you know that."

By the time they finished talking, Michael had sweated all the way through his shirt and jeans. He was certain that as soon as he left, Chester would try to restart the fires, so he searched the shop building until he found the chainsaw hidden beneath a tarp and loaded it into the back of the Ram. He stood calling for Luke for a good five minutes before boy and dog came bounding up the south bank of the Sawlog, both of them wet, their feet and lower legs black with mud.

"Can we keep him, Dad?" Luke said, falling to his knees in the grass next to the driveway and allowing the dog to lick his face. "Please? I promise I'll take good care of him."

"Sorry, bud," Michael said. "That's Chester and Fanny's dog. Come on. Let's get you back to the homeplace and get you cleaned up before your mother kills us both."

In spite of the strangeness he'd witnessed at the Stewarts'—those fires raging in the middle of a summer day—Michael felt upbeat about the case and the time he and Luke had spent together at the ranch. There was dirt beneath his fingernails from where he'd handled the go-kart and Chester's filthy chainsaw, and Luke was so covered in creek mud that Michael had him take a shower in the basement of the homeplace while he washed his jeans and T-shirt in the kitchen sink and laid them out to dry in the sun on the front porch. But it was all worth it, somehow. A story they'd tell—or not tell, as the case might be—for a long time to come.

THIRTY-ONE

Annie sat in the passenger seat of Jacob Hess's Ford F-250, looking out the window at the pastures rolling by on either side of Highway 283.

"You're awful quiet tonight," Hess said. "Usually when we drive to town, I can't get a word in edgewise."

"Yeah, well, usually we aren't going to dinner at my mother's house," Annie said.

"What's the deal with you and your mom?" Hess said. "She seems pretty harmless to me."

Annie turned and looked at him with narrowed eyes. "Don't do that."

"Do what?"

"Take my family's side like that. If I want to complain about my mother, I need you to let me do it. Maybe even commiserate a little bit."

"Com-*mis*-er-ate," Hess said, drawing the word out. "Okay, sure. I got it."

Ever since the harvest ended, there'd been an awkwardness between them that only went away when they were riding horses or making love. She wanted things to be fun and easy, the way they'd been before they started sleeping together. Instead, they'd taken a more serious turn, especially for Hess, who'd said to her, the morning after their first night together, with her head still foggy from all the weed she'd smoked, "No pressure or anything, but you just tell me when you're ready, and I'll put all my cards on the table."

"Okaaaaaay," Annie said, thinking, *Oh my God, what kind of monster have I created?*

Unlike Hess, Annie didn't claim to be certain about anything. On the contrary, she was haunted by doubts. Doubts about Kansas, Dodge City, and the Bar W. Doubts about Hess and his phantom deck of cards. But also, since she was an equal opportunity doubter: doubts about Buffalo and grad school and Thomas Hardy's fallen, rebel women—to say nothing of the long-term prospects for happiness of anyone who committed too early or too completely to the rigors of Jeremiah Anonymous. In a couple of weeks, she was supposed to order books for the fall classes she was scheduled to teach, which included not only her usual section of English composition, but also a British literature survey course that included works by the likes of Joseph Conrad, Virginia Woolf, T.S. Eliot, and James Joyce. It was the sort of big, juicy opportunity that rarely fell to a mere grad student, and Dr. Hilman had gone out of his way to make sure it fell to her. Was she really going to walk away from that just to keep knocking around with a twice-divorced ex-rodeo cowboy? But then she'd look out across the front porch of the homeplace in the early morning light and see Hess loping a two-year-old cutting-horse prospect, and she'd sigh and forget about everything else.

"What did you make of that Gretel Ehrlich book I gave you?" she asked in an attempt to clear the air between them.

"*The Solace of Open Spaces?*" Hess said. "Not too shabby. But what I really liked was the other one you gave me."

"*The Next Rodeo?*"

"That's the one."

"What did you like?"

He drew himself up into a mock-oratorical pose. "*When people ask where I'm from, I still say southeastern Oregon, expecting them to understand my obvious pride.*" He laughed. "Just change 'southeastern Oregon' to 'southwestern Kansas,' and that kinda says it all, don't you think?"

"I do," she said, laughing.

Instead of taking the highway all the way into town as she'd been expecting, he turned right on Garnett, and soon they were rolling past the entrance to the mud hole that was Ford County Lake. Hess nodded at the sign. "Got any special memories of that place?"

"Sure," she said. "Bad ones."

"Such as?"

"You know, stale Coors out of a pony keg, drunk people tripping over the bonfire at midnight, biker dudes sticking their ZZ Top beards into my car window at two o'clock in the morning. Was that the scene back when you were in school?"

He gave her a look out of the corner of his eyes. "Back in the Stone Age, you mean?"

"I didn't say that."

He laughed. "I know you didn't. But it sure felt like you might be thinking it."

They drove on, getting ever closer to the spot where her father had driven blindly into the path of a westbound landscaping rig. The skid marks from where the driver had locked up his brakes were still visible in the asphalt of Garnett Road. She steeled herself for seeing them again.

"Here's a story from back in the Stone Age," Hess said. "I've never told it to you, although I got close a couple of times." He paused, continuing to look straight ahead. "It involves your brother."

"Michael?"

"No. Wade."

Something about the way he said the name made her stomach drop. "What about him?"

He took a deep breath and let it out slowly. "I don't know if you know this, but Wade was just a year ahead of me in school. He went to Dodge, of course, whereas I was up at Jetmore. But the crowds we ran with overlapped a bit. Especially at those lakeside keggers. Anyway, we were all out there one night after Dodge got knocked out of the football playoffs. This would've been Wade's senior year, and he was letting loose pretty good, knocking back whiskey straight from the bottle, taking hits from whatever got passed his way. By the time everyone started to leave, he was drunk off his ass, way too far gone to drive home. I told him to sleep it off in the back seat of that fancy car of his—"

"The '88 Scirocco?"

"I think so. It was red, I know that."

"Tornado red."

"Whatever. Looked like a goddamn spaceship, especially to a poor ranch kid like me. Anyway, Wade kept going on and on about how he had to make it home *that night*. Your dad would be up waiting for him, wanting to talk about the big game. So, long story short, since I was going in that direction anyway, I gave him a ride in my dad's rattletrap F-150. The heater core was bad, and we had to keep the windows rolled down so the inside of the cab wouldn't fog over, and the whole way out to the ranch, your brother kept saying the craziest shit. Yelling it out the open windows of that truck like he wanted the whole world to hear."

"What kind of crazy shit?" Annie said, a feeling of dread coming over her.

Hess leaned forward with his elbows on the steering wheel and lit a cigarette, passing it to her. "I'm sure you remember what a big deal your brother was in those days, name all over the Dodge and Hutch sports pages, guys on the radio talking about him like he was the second coming of Joe Montana. So anyway, just trying to make conversation, I asked him where he saw himself playing football in college. Well, let me tell you, he wasn't having none of it that night. He was like, *Fuck college! You wanna know how much I care about playing football in college? Zero! Fuck that shit!* Then, after a while, it was, *Fuck this town, too! I can't wait to put this whole place in the rearview mirror!* I remember I said something like, *But what about the ranch? What about your family?* And off he goes again. *Fuck the ranch! You think I'm gonna waste what I got left of my life sitting around out there? Noooooooo! I'm outta here!*"

"Bullshit," Annie said. "I don't believe any of this. Not a word."

She passed him the cigarette and he took a drag. "Hey, I didn't believe it, either. Are you kidding me? Wade Wagner talking about hating football? But the thing is, I heard it with my own ears, Annie."

They came to the site of Leroy's wreck, and Annie stared at the water tower on the horizon to stop herself from searching out the skid marks in the asphalt or the bright new telephone pole the county had to put up next to the ditch to replace the one the landscaping truck had taken out after T-boning her father and running off the road.

"Okay, let's say it did happen, just like you said. It was probably just disappointment talking. They'd just lost a huge game, and it's true my dad could get pretty intense about that stuff. Wade was probably feeling like he let everyone down. He needed to blow off some steam."

"Maybe," Hess said. "But the feeling I got was that it was more than that. The feeling I got was that he was fed up with the whole shebang. The whole Wade Wagner show. Football. Wrestling. Bar W. Volkswagen Scirocco. All of it."

They turned off Garnett and headed south, the site of Leroy's wreck behind them now. Was it really possible her heroic older brother had been plagued by the same doubts, the same "radical uncertainty" she suffered from? It was crazy to think so. Blasphemy, in fact.

"Why are you telling me all this?" she asked.

"I don't know," Hess said. "Got tired of not telling you, I guess."

They entered her parents' house through the kitchen door and were immediately set upon by Michael's wife, Vanessa, a knockout with a gorgeous complexion who managed to ruin the effect by wearing enough makeup to do the morning show on Fox. As usual, she was dressed to the nines in a white designer dress and heels. "Annie, hello," she said. "I was just pouring your mother a glass of chardonnay. Would you like one?"

"Yes, I would. A big one."

"A big one it is."

Annie took the full glass Vanessa offered. "This is my friend, Jacob Hess."

"Pleased to meet you," Hess said, touching the brim of his white Stetson.

"Michael says you're a horse trainer," Vanessa said. "What is it you train them to do?"

"Well, ma'am," Hess said with a low chuckle, a practiced part of his cowboy repertoire, "if I could train the sumbucks to *write checks*, I'd do that." Vanessa burst out laughing, exactly the response he was looking for. "But, failing that, I just try to get them to do the kinds of things that will provoke their *owners* to write checks."

"Oh yeah?" Vanessa said. "Like what?"

"Ever heard of a flying lead change?"

"A flying *what*?"

That was enough for Annie. She could fill in the blanks of Hess's answer without having to hear it rolled out in his aw-shucks-ma'am cowboy drawl, and she'd be damned if she'd stand there and watch Vanessa bat her big brown eyes at him. Instead, she picked up the glass of wine Vanessa had poured for her mother and carried it into the living room, where Caroline sat on the couch looking at a photo album with Sam and Luke.

"Where's Dad?" Annie asked.

"On the patio with your brother. Come give me a hug."

Annie complied, setting her mother's wine glass on the table before her. There was something about Caroline's little demands for affection that always made Annie feel like someone had cut off her oxygen. Over her mother's shoulder, she saw that the photo album was open to a picture of Michael and Wade in their Red Demon football uniforms, Michael looking small and unsure of himself—he would have been a freshman then—Wade smiling steadily into the camera, no indication at all that somewhere in his handsome head of black curls the tumor that would kill him was growing like the iceberg in Thomas Hardy's "Convergence of the Twain." She thought of the strange conversation with Hess on the way to town. *You wanna know how much I care about football? I fucking hate it!* Well, you wouldn't know it from that picture.

"Is that Jacob Hess talking to Vanessa?" Caroline asked.

"Yeah, do you know him?"

She took a sip of wine and put the glass back on the table. "He's helped your father on the ranch a few times. Seems like a nice young man."

A nice young man, Annie thought. *What the hell did she mean by that?* That was the thing with her mother. It was so hard to tell. Was she trying to communicate approval of Hess as boyfriend or even husband material, or did she mean to imply the opposite, subtly calling into question everything from his age (not *young* at all) to his status as a hired man ("helped your father on the ranch a few times")? Like so much else having to do with her mother, it was all a mystery, one that Annie was not at all sure she wanted to solve.

As if on cue, here came the nice young man himself, strolling into the room with Vanessa as if the two of them had just come off the dance floor at Billy Bob's in Fort Worth.

"Jacob was just telling me how cutting horses are trained," Vanessa said.

"Is that right?" Caroline said.

Vanessa nodded. "They use buffalo instead of cattle. Do you know why?"

"Why?" Caroline said.

Instead of answering, Vanessa turned and nodded at Hess.

"Well, it's pretty simple," he said. "A calf will wise up to the whole game after a time or two. Fetch up along the fence and just stand there, no try at all. But a buffalo, he's a different breed altogether. He'll keep on trying to get back to that herd whether you've cut him five times or five hundred times."

"Isn't that crazy?" Vanessa said. "They're just too dumb or primitive or whatever to figure it out."

"Maybe," Annie said. "Or maybe they've just got less quit in them than a cow does. Maybe they're the real thing, and a cow's just a pale imitation."

"Maybe," Vanessa said. "Who's ready for another glass of wine?"

"I am," Annie said, handing her empty glass to her sister-in-law, who disappeared back into the kitchen with it.

"The men are on the patio," Caroline said to Hess. "Why don't you grab yourself a beer out of the refrigerator and join them?"

"Thanks, ma'am," Hess said. "I think I will."

"Grab one for Leroy while you're at it. I'm sure he's ready."

When Hess had gone, Annie turned to her mother and said, "Why are you always doing that?"

"Doing what?"

"Enforcing this ridiculous code where the men all congregate in one place, the women in another."

"I didn't know I was enforcing a code," Caroline said, sounding surprised and a little irritated. "I just thought your father might enjoy talking to Jacob about cattle and horses and such. He's been terribly depressed of late, and I'm sure *I* can't talk to him about that stuff."

"Well, maybe that's part of the problem."

As soon as the words were out of Annie's mouth, she regretted them. Why couldn't she just keep her mouth shut and act nice like everybody else? Why did she always have to revert to her bitchy and rebellious teenage self every time she was in her mother's house? An argument they'd had in this very room when she was twelve or thirteen came back to her. It was about condoms of all things. Annie's position, which she'd honed doing research for a social studies paper, was that condoms should be free and widely distributed, especially in schools and poor neighborhoods. Caroline hadn't offered a position, only a question. "Why are you talking about condoms all of the sudden? You're not having sex, are you?"

"No, Mom, I'm not having sex," Annie had said, rolling her eyes. But then, just to get her mother's goat, she'd added a single, dagger-like word. "Yet."

And here she was, fifteen years later, still playing the same old game.

When Vanessa returned from the kitchen with her glass of wine, Annie escaped onto the patio, where her father sat in a rented wheelchair (Bull Wagner in a wheelchair!) expounding on the recent craze for Angus cattle, which he claimed had to do with their uniform carcass size. "You get these long breeds like Simmental and Charolais, sure they throw a nice big calf, but they got to stop the line at the beef plant and adjust the chain for a different size animal. And if there's one thing they don't like to do at the beef plant, it's stop the line."

"You got that right," Hess said.

Annie sipped her wine. She'd been around such talk her whole life. On one level, it was comforting, like the smell of freshly cut alfalfa. But on another, it bored her to tears. Who cared about the chain at the beef plant? What she cared about—cringed at the very sight of—was the wheelchair her father sat in and the big cast on his left leg and the other one on his left arm. They conjured in her mind the skid marks on Garnett Road she couldn't bear to look at, the sound of yawning metal, emergency workers in yellow vests opening up the top of her father's flatbed Dodge with the Jaws of Life. How long would he remain in that chair? Would he ever get out of it?

"Where's Jimmy?" she asked. "Isn't he coming?"

"Who knows?" Michael said, lifting the lid on what looked to be a new gas grill to check the steaks. "I called him and sent a couple of texts, but he stopped picking up my calls a long time ago."

"Sounds like Jimmy, all right," Leroy said, lifting his can of Coors with his good hand and taking a drink. Annie imagined Leroy sitting up in the living room of the homeplace, waiting for Wade to come home from his playoff loss and the drunken night at Ford County Lake that followed it. Had there been a scene? Had Wade said the same things to Leroy that he'd supposedly said to Hess? *Fat chance of that*, she thought.

"How's that red car of yours running?" her father asked.

"Fine," she said.

"Oil pressure good?"

"Yep."

"Well, good."

When the steaks were done, Michael wheeled Leroy's chair to his customary place at the head of the dining room table while

Vanessa poured everyone more wine and Caroline doled out baked potatoes wrapped in tinfoil. Annie served the salad of iceberg lettuce, sliced tomatoes, and red onions, then sat down next to Jacob Hess, thinking, *Okay, that's three glasses now. You'd better button up. Not another word out of you. Not. One. Word.*

But five minutes later, when conversation ground to a halt after the rote Catholic prayer, and the only sound was Leroy's jaw popping as he chewed his ribeye, she broke her vow of silence and turned to the younger of her two nephews. "So, Lukie, did you have fun driving that go-kart at the ranch today? Pretty fast, huh?"

"I sure did," Luke said, beaming. "I went about a hundred miles an hour."

"Go-kart?" Vanessa said, looking straight past Annie at Michael, who concentrated on cutting his steak into very tiny pieces. "What go-kart?"

"Dad bought it for me," Luke said.

"You bought him a go-kart!" Sam said. "That's not fair. I'm older than he is—"

"I did *not* buy him a go-kart," Michael said. "I bought one for the ranch. There's a difference."

Vanessa's delicate jaw hardened as she stared Michael down. If she'd been in a cartoon, Annie thought, there'd have been steam coming out of both of her ears. "And did you think, even once, of calling me to ask what I thought about the idea?"

Michael sighed, put his fork down beside his plate. "No, I guess I didn't. I'm sorry, I just—"

"Excuse me," Vanessa said, pushing her chair back from the table and disappearing into the house's formal living room. A few seconds later, Michael rose and followed her, and the sounds of a muffled argument drifted into the dining room. Only Luke was oblivious to it.

"What you got for dessert, Grandma?" he asked.

"Ice cream," Caroline said. "Chocolate chip. All you can eat."

"I'll have some of that," Leroy said. "When we're done eating."

"Me, too," Sam said.

"Jacob?"

"I wouldn't say no," Hess said.

"What about you?" Caroline asked, a slight edge in her voice telling Annie that she'd not forgotten about her "maybe that's part of the problem" comment from earlier in the evening.

"None for me, thanks," Annie said. Turning to her father, she asked, "Whatever happened to that red Scirocco Wade used to drive in high school?"

Her father looked up from his steak in surprise. "Michael and I drove it to Wichita and sold it. Why do you ask?"

"No reason," she said. She could feel Hess's eyes on her, but she refused to look his way. "Why Wichita, though?"

"Because I never wanted to see the goddamn thing again, that's why," Leroy said in a loud voice. "Any other questions?"

"Leroy," Caroline whispered, nodding at where Sam and Luke sat with wide eyes.

"No," Annie said, reaching across the table for the half-empty bottle of chardonnay. "I think that's it for now."

THIRTY-TWO

Jimmy came out of the river road at Wright Park and headed north on Second Avenue, keeping the throttle on the Ducati low, the engine no louder than a light hum. He'd spent the better part of a day scoring Oxy in whatever quantities he could find, a pill here, a pill there, keeping one step ahead of Brock's furious need, admitting to himself finally that the town was dry, and he was gonna have to come up with another idea. When it hit him, he was shocked he hadn't thought of it before. His father, Big Bull Wagner, was a goddamn martyr when it came to pain. With each new ailment or ranch-related mishap—and there'd been at least a half dozen in the past couple of years alone—Caroline dutifully filled whatever scripts the doctors wrote, only to have Leroy bellow his refusal to swallow any of it. "I don't need that shit," he'd say. "Give me an aspirin and a couple Tylenol, and I'll be fine." Of course, swallowing all that aspirin had done wonders for the ulcers eating away at his stomach, but hey, that was fine with Bull Wagner. Drugs were for pussies.

Well, if Leroy didn't want or need the stash of narcotics Caroline had stockpiled in a plastic bin on a shelf in her laundry room, Jimmy sure as hell did. At the top of the hill above the house, he killed the Ducati's motor and coasted into the driveway of his childhood home like the pilot of a stealth bomber. It was after eleven, and the house was dark. Caroline went to bed at

8:30 or 8:45 to read, and Leroy usually wasn't far behind her, dozing off in his La-Z-Boy or, more recently, his wheelchair or rented hospital bed, while a TV droned in the background.

The knob to the kitchen door turned easily in his hand. Despite twenty years of living in town, Leroy and Caroline still acted like an old farm couple, leaving all their doors unlocked, windows open to the night air, keys in the ignitions of their cars. Closing the door behind him, Jimmy stepped into the dark house. Its interior, which usually smelled of old people, betrayed an aroma of red onions and seared meat. The light of the moon streamed in through the windows. God forbid someone should leave a light on and cause the electric bill to go up twenty-five or thirty cents. Lined up neatly on the countertop were four or five empty wine bottles. He picked up one of the bottles and inspected the label in the moonlight. Chateau something or other; which was strange, given his mother's penchant for box-o-wine. Then, dimly, he remembered. Some kind of "family dinner." Michael had sent him a couple of texts, trying to guilt him into making an appearance.

He put the bottle back where he'd found it. One of these days, the world would wise up and throw out all the booze and oxy and meth and discover the simple joy of Girl Scout Cookies, but Jimmy wasn't gonna hold his breath. Leroy, for example, hated the smell of weed even more than Jimmy hated the smell of booze and old people. It outraged his sense of propriety and control. On what had turned out to be Jimmy's last day in the house, Leroy had come home from work on the Bar W and found Jimmy playing guitar in the finished part of the basement.

"What's that smell?" Leroy called out as he came down the stairs. "Is that pot?"

Sure, Jimmy had partaken of a hit or two, but that was like an hour before, and he'd stepped into the garage to do it. "*Pot!*" he said with a laugh. "Dude, you sound like you're about a hundred and fifty years old!"

Bull Wagner was having none of that kind of talk. He came barreling across the carpeted floor and yanked Jimmy to his feet by his shirt.

"Dude, be careful of the guitar!" Jimmy said, holding his J-45 at arm's length by its fragile neck.

Caroline's head appeared at the top of the stairs. "What's going on down there?"

"Nothing," Leroy said. He waited for her to retreat back into the kitchen, then leaned in close and said in an even voice that was nonetheless full of menace, "I warned you what would happen if you smoked that shit in my house."

"Technically, it wasn't *in* the house—"

Leroy drove him backward into the wood paneling, his fists tightening their grip on Jimmy's sweatshirt. "I warned you, but you didn't listen. You never do."

"Well, maybe if you started saying stuff that made sense—"

"Get your shit and get out of my house."

Jimmy laughed. "Dude, are you serious?"

"You heard me," Leroy said, letting go of his shirt.

That was six months ago, but in some ways, it felt like yesterday. Standing in the dark kitchen, Jimmy could feel the old grievances rising within him. Would Leroy have been so quick to give Michael or Annie the boot for smoking a little weed in the house? What about his highness, Prince Wade? Would he have consigned *him* to living in a trailer home within smelling distance of two beef packing plants and three or four feedyards with lagoons full of shit water and manure stacked twenty feet high inside the pens? Not a chance.

At the doorway to the formal living room, he stopped and listened. Sure enough, the labored sounds of Leroy's breathing where he lay in shadows on the rented hospital bed came to him on the stale air. Backing out the doorway, he headed for the laundry room behind the kitchen. On a shelf above the sink was the clear plastic tub. He brought it down to the counter, removed the lid, and trained his phone's flashlight on its contents. Bingo, baby. The very first bottle he picked up was a full-to-the-brim prescription for hydrocodone.

"What the hell are you doing here?" came a voice from behind him.

He turned, pill bottle in hand, and saw his father standing in the doorway on one leg like a sandhill crane—no wheelchair, no crutch that Jimmy could see. The old man was completely naked except for his baggy Fruit of the Looms, his hairless body amazingly white where the moonlight struck it. How had the sumbitch managed to traverse the space between the living room and the kitchen so quickly on just one leg, and why hadn't Jimmy heard him? It was like he'd flown there, ghost-like, his feet never touching the tile floor.

"Oh, I get it," Leroy continued. "You're a thief now, in addition to being a dopehead. Breaking into your parents' house to steal drugs—"

"It's not for me," Jimmy said. "It's for a friend of—"

"Oh, right. A friend. I've been wondering what you've been doing for money ever since Branch fired you, but I think I see now."

"You've got it all wrong. Branch didn't fire my ass. I fucking quit when the sumbitch wanted me to spy on you. Find out everything I could about some stupid lawsuit you filed against him."

To Jimmy's surprise, his father said nothing, so he turned back to the tub of pills and scooped up two more bottles of hydro and another of oxy. Then he closed the lid on the tub and put it back on the shelf. "I'd hang around here and explain the whole thing to you, but I don't have time."

"I bet. Robbing houses in the middle of the night keeps a guy busy, I'm guessing." And with that, he pivoted on his good leg and hopped from view.

Is this even happening? Jimmy wondered. *Or is it some kind of demented dream? Bull Wagner morphs into the Easter Bunny.*

Stuffing the bottles into the leg pockets of his cargo pants, Jimmy followed his father into the kitchen, where Leroy had resumed his sandhill-crane pose, this time before the open refrigerator door.

"I knew you'd sunk pretty low, but I gotta say, this is a new one, even for you."

"Look, I'll buy the pills off you, if that's what you want," Jimmy said.

"Right. And make me a drug dealer, too? No, thank you."

"Well? What the hell do you want from me then?"

Reaching into the fridge, Leroy extracted a quart bottle of milk and took a long swig before wiping his mouth with his forearm and returning the milk to its place in the door. "It don't matter what I want. The only question worth asking right now is what do *you* want? What's the *code* you're gonna live by? Because from what I can see, the one you're living by right now ain't gonna get you anywhere but the county jail."

Jimmy could hardly believe what he was hearing. "Code, huh? Man, that's some deep, philosophical shit you're putting down. But the thing is, I don't have time for it right now. I got shit to do."

He took a roll of bills from his front pocket, peeled off five twenties, and dropped them onto the granite countertop. Then he started for the door.

"If you walk out now," Leroy said to his back, "you might as well keep going, because I'm about finished with you as it is."

Jimmy had to laugh. It was almost word-for-word what Byron Branch had said to him. "Dude, you *been* finished with me," he said over his shoulder.

Crossing the driveway to where the Ducati sat waiting in the darkness, he was surprised to hear the thud of a deadbolt being thrown behind him.

THIRTY-THREE

Michael dropped Vanessa and the boys at the towering front doors of Our Lady of Guadalupe, the sprawling Spanish-style cathedral that had replaced Sacred Heart in the years after Michael left Dodge for Lawrence and then Kansas City. They were ten minutes late, and he still had to find a place in the crowded parking lot. His mother, he knew, had been inside for a half hour already, holding down seats for them in her preferred spot in the front row. It went without saying that Leroy wouldn't be joining them. So far as Michael knew, his father hadn't set foot in a church since Wade's funeral, or maybe it was Jimmy's baptism. His official reason was his inability to kneel without pain, but there was more to it than that. *He hasn't forgiven God for allowing Wade to die,* Michael mused as he hurried across the expansive parking lot.

Caroline smiled at him as he stole into the pew she had saved, her waiting now at an end. From the surrounding pews, he could feel the eyes of the parish on him. When Wade was alive, Michael had avoided this level of scrutiny, hiding in the long shadow cast by his older brother. After Wade's death, all that changed. *There he is, the younger one. A little small for a quarterback, don't you think?* He'd held up okay, he thought. He wasn't Wade and never would be, but he'd subbed for him as best he could everywhere but in the affections of his wounded, still-grieving father, and who knew, maybe there was still time for that to change.

The priest was a visitor from another parish, a small, soft-spoken man in his sixties. Michael could hardly make out what the guy was saying, but he recognized the gospel reading immediately. It was from Luke, the story of the prodigal son. Most times he'd heard it, Michael had identified strongly with the *non*-prodigal son, the one who'd stayed home and worked in his father's fields without expectation or complaint, while his brother was off blowing his inheritance on wine and loose women. In his mind, there was a direct parallel between the situation described in the story and the separate roles he and Wade had played in life. Only instead of running off to the wicked city while Michael stayed behind and worked, Wade had run off to death while Michael, through no fault of his own, had lived. And like the father in the story, who was also a rancher of sorts, Leroy had ignored his living son and focused all his love on the one who was dead, killing the fatted calf, placing a gold ring on his cold finger, throwing a decades-long party of grief on his behalf. Only now, for reasons Michael could not quite grasp, the story had turned, and he found himself moved almost to tears when the priest, his voice rising, read the part that went, *And while he was still a long ways off, his father caught sight of him, and was filled with compassion. He ran to his son, embraced him and kissed him.*

What had changed? Why did he suddenly feel that it was he, and not Wade, their father was welcoming home? After all, the outcome of the court case was still unknown. There was at least a fifty percent chance the judge would rule in favor of Byron Branch. In which case, the Stewarts would get nothing, and Michael's standing in his father's eyes might suffer a terrible, maybe even a permanent, blow.

"Such a beautiful story, but what does it mean?" the priest asked. "It's quite simple. The story is a picture of God's love for us, his children. God's love does not depend on our faithfulness. No. His love is unconditional."

Michael turned his head so that his family would not see the tears welling in his eyes. When the time for the sign of peace came, he pulled Vanessa into his arms and hugged her tightly.

"What is it?" she whispered in his ear.

"Nothing. I love you, that's all."

"I love you, too," she said, confused by the strength of his emotion.

Craning around her, he kissed his mother on the cheek and shook both of his boys' hands, first Samuel's, then Luke's.

"The peace of the Lord be with you," he said.

They giggled in response, but he didn't care.

After Mass, as they were filing out the back of the cathedral, Michael sought out the visiting priest and shook his hand, too. "It was very moving the way you read the gospel passage, Father," he said.

"The word of God is always moving to him who is ready to hear it," the priest said.

In the windblown parking lot, Caroline asked about their plans for the rest of the day.

"We're going to change clothes and then head out to the ranch to give Sam his turn driving the go-kart," Michael said. This had been decided the night before, during a long conversation at the Best Western Plus that at times had felt more like a negotiated truce.

"Will you stop by the house after?" Caroline asked.

He looked at Vanessa, and she nodded.

"Sure," he said. "I'll give you a call when we're on our way over."

"Now if I could only get your brother to show up," Caroline said. "I'm worried about him. There's something going on with him, I just know it."

"Did you try calling him?"

She shook her head. "He doesn't like me to. Says I'm trying to smother him, and he'll come to me if he needs anything. Annie's the same way. What did I do wrong?"

"Absolutely nothing," Vanessa said, her hand on Caroline's shoulder. "You were the perfect mother. Michael always says so."

Did he say that? He couldn't recall.

"I'll tell you what, Mom. If he doesn't make an appearance tonight, I'll run by that trailer of his and kidnap him. How's that?"

"Thank you," Caroline said, beaming. "If there's anyone in this world I know I can count on, it's you, Michael."

THIRTY-FOUR

From her bedroom window in the homeplace, Annie watched Hess ride the smoke-colored mare in broad circles around one of the telephone poles whose lines stretched across the front yard. Watching Hess ride—especially this horse, which she'd come to think of as her own, bestowing upon her the half-ironic moniker of "Miss Kitty"—always filled Annie with a mixture of jealousy and admiration. Who else rose before dawn without the aid of an alarm clock each and every morning, itching to get back to the same work he'd been hard at until nine or ten o'clock the night before? Her father? In his prime, maybe. She couldn't name another. And even with Leroy, it had often felt like the engine propelling him forward day after day was running on duty and fear, not love. Hess was different. Like the clouds floating above the chalk bluffs behind him, he fit perfectly into the landscape. It was nearly impossible to imagine him anywhere else.

And her? She was more like one of those migratory birds who ranged from the Gulf of Mexico to Canada and back every year. Part of the landscape, sure, but not a steady or permanent part. Nothing like a coyote or prairie dog or even a horse. And now Hess, in his own words, was getting ready to lay all his cards on the table. The thought of it filled her with alarm. What was he expecting her to do or say? Was she supposed to show her hand, too? She didn't know what cards she was holding. Didn't even know what game they were playing, how the game was won or lost.

She brewed a pot of coffee and carried a cup into the bathroom, where she stood for a long time in the shower, the water so hot it turned her pale skin red. She was drying her hair with a towel when she heard the screen door slam at the front of the house. A moment later, Hess stuck his unshaven face into the room. "I was wondering when you were gonna wake up. You wanna ride this morning?"

"You better believe I do."

"Good. I'll make you a bowl of oatmeal. We're about out of food in this house, you know."

"I know," she said. "I'll make a trip into town later."

She was running a brush through her hair when she heard the ring tone on her father's phone sound in the living room. "That's probably my mom calling to give me grief about last night," she called out. "Will you get it?"

"All righty," Hess called back.

She heard him move from the kitchen to the living room, the spurs on his stovepipe riding boots jingling across the hardwood floors. Then silence.

"Jacob? Who called? Is it my mom?"

He didn't answer, but a moment later he appeared in the doorway of the tiny bathroom, a stony look on his face.

"Who is it?" she mouthed.

He handed her the phone and walked in his jingle-jangle way back into the living room.

"Hello?" she said into the phone.

"Finally! Baby, I've been trying to reach you for weeks!"

"*Jeremiah?*" She felt something stir within her. "What are you doing calling me on my dad's phone?"

"Long story. I found an old phone book at the truck stop and called every Wagner in there until your mom picked up. Damn, it's good to hear your voice!"

It was good to hear his voice, too. But her mind was spinning. "My *mom?* Wait. Where are you?"

"Guess."

"Not in Dodge—"

"Yes! I rode all the way here on my CB750. My back is fucking killing me. Where are you right now? Can I see you?"

She heard the jingle of Hess's spurs outside the bathroom door. "Can I call you back in a minute?" she said in a low voice.

"Sure, but be quick, okay? It's been a long time, and I've got a lot to tell you."

"I've got a lot to tell you, too," she said before pressing the button on the flip phone, ending the call.

Jeremiah King in Dodge City, Kansas. In what kind of upside-down world was a thing like that possible?

Wrapping herself in a dry towel, she walked into the living room, where Hess stood with his back to the old stone fireplace.

"Who was that?"

"Nobody."

"It sure didn't sound like nobody."

"All right, it was a friend of mine from Buffalo."

"That married guy from Idaho? What did he want?"

It startled her that Hess knew who Jeremiah was, right down to his marital status and the state he hailed from. Sure, she'd talked about him from time to time while they were working or riding together, but after the first couple of times, Hess had offered nothing in response, and she'd supposed he wasn't paying attention. Clearly, she'd been wrong about that.

"He's in town," she said, retrieving the brush from the bathroom and continuing to comb her hair. "I'm going to have to go in and meet him."

"Oh, really," Hess said. "And why is that? I thought you said it was over between the two of you."

"It is."

"Then why see him?"

The words rankled her. Who the hell was *he* to say who she could and could not see? Did he really think he'd earned the right to make that kind of claim on her?

"Because he's my friend, and he rode halfway across the country on a twenty-year-old motorcycle to see me."

"Oh, so he's your *friend* now."

"He's always been my friend . . ." She trailed off. "Wait a minute. You're not *jealous*, are you? Jacob?"

He turned his back to her and stood looking out the picture window where the bluffs across Back Trail Road rose to meet the scuttling clouds.

"Oh my God, you *are!*"

"So what if I am?" he said, his back still to her.

"It's just silly, that's all."

He turned to face her, and his blue eyes had an iciness in them she'd not seen before. "Is it? I don't think it is."

She gave a laugh that sounded fake in her ears, found her cigarettes on the dining room table, and fumbled to light a match. "Look, it's true I had a thing with the guy. But it's over. There's nothing between us, believe me."

"I wish I could."

She tried to hold the match to the end of her cigarette and was shocked to see that her hands were shaking. Finally, she managed to get the thing lit and took a deep drag. She started a couple of sentences beginning with the word "I," but each one came to feel like an attempt to justify something that in her mind needed no justification. Meanwhile, Hess frowned and shook his head ruefully, as if he should've known all along that something like this would happen. Maybe he *had* known all along, because a moment later, he stomped out the front door, spurs jingling behind him, mounted Miss Kitty, and rode off at a lope like a cowboy in a B western.

Why in the *hell* had she told him to pick up the phone? Everything would be so much easier if Jeremiah's call had gone to voicemail. Even if he hadn't left a message, she would've recognized his Idaho area code and known something was up. At least then she wouldn't have all this cowboy jealousy to deal with on top of the buried emotions Jeremiah's unexpected arrival had dredged up.

She walked onto the wide front porch that had echoed with Hess's spurs only moments before and hit the redial button. Jeremiah picked up right away. "Thank God, Annie. I was beginning to worry you weren't gonna call back."

"Well, here I am. So tell me, what in God's name are you doing in Dodge City?"

"What do you mean? I came to see *you*, of course. I'm about beat to death, too, but that's okay—I finally found you! I've got something kind of big I need to tell you."

"What is it?"

"Can't you meet me somewhere? Or I'll ride out to where you are. I don't want to do this over the phone, Annie. I want to *see* you."

The sound of his lumberjack voice triggered something deep within her. The leg may have been amputated, but the body went on feeling the toes. "Where are you, exactly?"

"In the parking lot of this Boot Hill place."

Boot Hill. Jeremiah King in the parking lot of Boot Hill. "Okay, just sit tight. I won't be there for another half hour at the earliest."

"My God, I've missed you so much," he said. "You can't imagine."

"I think I can," she said, ending the call before any further words betrayed her.

Still in a daze from the call—*Jeremiah King in Boot Hill parking lot*—she wandered into the bathroom and looked at herself in the mirror. The Kansas sun had caused a riot of freckles to appear on her nose and arms. The brittle ends of her red hair were long overdue for a trim. Putting the brush down on the pedestal sink, she picked up her makeup bag and began to rummage through it for eyeliner.

My God, am I really getting dolled up to go and see Jeremiah King in Boot Hill parking lot? she thought. *I guess so. I guess that's exactly what I'm doing.*

Her only clean pair of jeans was low cut and tight across the ass, and it was the same story with her shirts that had not been ruined by ranch work: they were all sleeveless and tight across the boobs. *Ah, well, let the poor fool suffer,* she thought, pulling on her favorite pair of red boots. *Let them* both *suffer.*

At the corrals, she found Hess loading horses into his aluminum trailer.

"You don't have to do that," she said.

"No? You said I could keep 'em here until the harvest was over. Well, it's over."

"Jesus Christ, Jacob! Can't this wait until I get back?"

"I don't think so."

"Why the hell not?"

"I don't know. I'm not built that way, I guess."

Not built that way? What a bunch of cowboy horseshit that was!

"Look, I'm not gonna fall into bed with the guy, if that's what you're worried about."

He tied the last colt into the back of the trailer and stepped down beside her. "Then don't go. Stay here with me instead."

"That's not fair and you know it."

"What's not fair?"

"Forcing me into this false dichotomy between going into town to see my friend and staying here with you. It's bullshit, and you know it."

"*Di*-chot-*omy*," he said, drawing the word out. "Why not call it what it is? A fucking *choice*." He slammed the aluminum trailer door, dropped the pin to secure it, and climbed into the cab of his pickup. "I'll be back for my mare."

Then he was gone down Back Trail Road.

THIRTY-FIVE

Topping the last hill before the ranch, Michael's Dodge Ram crossed paths on the sand road with a Guards Red Porsche 996 doing at least eighty miles an hour, a cloud of dust and sand rising angrily behind it.

"My God! What's that idiot think he's doing?" Vanessa said as the cloud swept across their windshield.

"She," Michael said, checking his rearview. "I'm pretty sure that was Annie. And I know for a fact that's my old car."

"Annie? What on earth?"

"Who knows," Michael said, thinking, not for the first time, that he never should've given away that car—not to his little sister or anyone else. What the hell had he been thinking?

The warm glow of family feeling he'd experienced at Mass had continued when they'd stopped for lunch at El Rodeo, a Mexican place on Wyatt Earp directly across from the Santa Fe Depot. There Vanessa had struck up an animated conversation in Spanish with the high school girl who took their order. Her fluency in this language unfamiliar to them absolutely floored the boys.

"Mom!" Sam said after the girl left.

"What?" Vanessa said, clearly enjoying the moment.

"Where'd you learn to do that?"

"I grew up speaking Spanish, silly. Didn't you know that?"

"I knew it," Luke said.

"No, you didn't," Sam said.

While the boys bickered playfully, Michael had reached across the table and took Vanessa's hand in his. They sat that way a long time, until the high school girl came back with their tacos and enchiladas and they'd needed their hands back to eat. And even then, they'd shared the cold bottle of Modelo he'd ordered, passing it back and forth between them.

When they arrived on the Bar W, he and the boys pushed the go-kart out of the shed where he'd stored it. On the way to the ranch, Michael had insisted they stop at Walmart to pick up two helmets, and now he made a big show of checking to see that the helmets fit each boy's head properly. He was the Minister of Ranch Safety, the Dad of Doing Everything Right. As he filled the gas tank, he patiently explained how to start, stop, and turn the kart, and rather than yawning or looking at her phone, Vanessa listened just as intently as the boys did.

"Aren't you going with me?" Sam asked.

Michael shook his head. "No, you got this. Just go slow on your first couple of laps."

They stood in the shade of the hay bales watching Sam make lap after lap around the makeshift track, his speed increasing as his confidence grew. After ten laps or so, Sam pulled up beside them and let the kart's motor drop to an idle.

"Get in, Luke!" he shouted.

"Okay," Luke shouted back. "Then it's my turn."

Michael strapped Luke in the kart beside his brother, and off they went. It was wonderful to see the two of them sitting side by side, their oversized, helmeted heads leaning one way and then the other as they made their way around the dusty circuit. He hadn't seen them this engaged by something since Sam got his first Xbox for Christmas four or five years before.

After watching a few more laps, he and Vanessa retreated to the air-conditioned cab of the Ram. "Just look at them," Michael said. "They're taking right to it like a couple of farm kids."

"They're good kids," Vanessa said.

"Are you kidding me? They're *great* kids. The best."

"Is that all we have in common, do you think?" Vanessa said. "Great kids?"

He turned to look at her. She'd held up well during Mass and their lunch at El Rodeo, but now that they were alone, the rawness of their spat at his parents' house came rushing back. They'd gone over it and over it in their room at the Best Western the night before, but clearly some of the hurt remained. "God, I hope not," he said, opening his arms.

She scooted across the seat and into his arms, and they sat listening to the far-off whine of the kart.

"You're the best thing that ever happened to me," he said.

"Really?" she said without looking up. "It doesn't always feel like it."

"Well, it's true. Remember that scare we had in law school? When you missed your period that time?"

"How could I forget that?"

"I was thinking about it last night as we were lying in bed. The whole thing came back to me clear as day. I remembered thinking at the time, *If Vanessa wasn't the one, this would be terrible, a real disaster. But she is the one, so everything's gonna be okay.*"

"You're making this up."

"No, no, I'm not. That's the way it was. That's the way it *is*."

She hugged him, then reached into the glove box for a tissue to blow her nose. When she'd finished, she sat up straight in the seat and said, "Tell me about the case. I want to know everything."

"Are you sure?" he said. "We don't have to talk about that if you don't want to."

"I do, though. Start at the beginning and tell me everything."

He did just that, covering every motion and piece of evidence, every line of argument he was planning to use, every counter-argument he was anticipating from the other side. "Wow," she said when he'd finished. "You've put a lot of time into this, haven't you?"

He laughed. "If anybody at the firm knew the full amount, there'd be hell to pay, let me tell you." He let a pause fall, then asked, "What do you think? Do we have a chance in this case?"

"I think you've got a great chance," she said.

"Really?"

"Absolutely."

He listened as she gave him her take on the case, how the whole thing was shaping up to be a "testosterone fest" between Leroy and Byron Branch and Branch's lawyer. But how that created an opportunity for Michael to "cut through the testosterone" and remind the judge that, at the end of the day, the case wasn't about either one of these powerful, warring factions. "Instead, it's all about Chester and Fanny. This is *their* story. Theirs is the only 'side' in the dispute that matters."

He could feel himself nodding the whole time she was talking. Could feel a smile breaking out and then spreading across his face. "This is what I've been trying to tell you. This is what I've been *needing* this whole time. You. Right there with me. Every step of the way."

"What?" she said, sounding surprised. "Like your *partner* or something?"

"I don't know. Yes! Why the hell not?"

"Well, I don't know about that."

He laughed and gave her a kiss. "You don't have to. Not yet, anyway. For now, I'm just grateful to you for listening and offering your take. I think you're dead on about the whole thing. I wish I could give my closing argument right now!"

He tried to pull her in for another kiss, but she held him off. There was something else she wanted to say.

"Do you remember our first date?" she asked. "How it ended?"

He thought back. They'd gone for a drive in the country outside Lawrence and had ended up at Lake Perry. On the way back, they'd gotten ice cream, and at the end of the date, he'd kissed her on the doorstep of her apartment in West Lawrence. Was that what she was talking about, the kiss?

She shook her head. "Before that. There was that car with the flat tire, remember? A woman sitting there on the side of the road, head on her steering wheel, back seat full of kids? You pulled over right away. Didn't say a word. Just got out and started changing her tire."

"I did?"

"Yes. You didn't even ask if she needed help. Just jumped out and started in like it was your job or something. I've never forgotten it." She reached out and took his hand. "This case reminds me of that. It's like the Stewarts are that woman with the back seat full of kids, and you're that same guy rolling up with his farm-kid skills."

He held his head back and laughed. "I guess so. I guess I haven't changed that much, have I?"

After a while, the boys grew tired of karting and came to ask if they could play on the line of round bales that ran between the tack barn and the alfalfa.

"Sure," Michael said. "But get a drink of water first, so you don't get dehydrated."

"And Sam," Vanessa added. "Keep an eye on your little brother, okay?"

"Okay," Sam said.

As the boys took turns drinking from the hose behind the tack barn, Michael put the Ram into gear and began to pull away.

"Where are we going?" Vanessa asked.

"The homeplace. There's something I want to show you."

"But what about the boys?"

"They'll be fine. They're farm kids now, remember?"

He drove across the parched grass to the back door of the old brick house, where he parked the truck and led her inside. "Luke and I were over here yesterday, and I got to thinking," he said, standing in the middle of the dated living room. "Imagine if we gutted this whole floor and started over from scratch. New windows, central air. Maybe get rid of a wall or two, really open the place up. Wouldn't that be something?" He walked to the front windows and pointed at the bluffs across Back Trail Road. "I mean, look at that view. It's spectacular."

"What do you mean?" Vanessa asked nervously. "As a place to *live?*"

"No, more like a family retreat. Somewhere to stay besides the Best Western when we're out here visiting. Get some decent Internet out here. Maybe a game room in the basement."

She looked around the place as if seeing it for the first time. "Well, I agree it could be cute, especially if we did something with a Southwestern theme. Spanish tile. Navajo rugs on the walls. Remember that condo we rented in Vail?"

"I do," he said, putting his arms around her from behind.

"But what about Annie? Isn't she staying out here? And what would your folks have to say about any of it?"

"Who knows?" Michael said. "It's just an idea. But it would be good one, don't you think? Kind of romantic?"

"Wouldn't be cheap, I can tell you that. Not to do it right."

"Who cares? It would be for *us*—and don't we deserve a place to escape to?"

He drew her close and buried his nose in her dark hair. This was what he'd been wanting and waiting for from the moment he'd left work on Friday afternoon. Maybe this was all he'd ever wanted. To get back to the way things had been when they were a couple of kids getting ice cream after a drive to the lake, and all he had to do to impress her was change a tire, something he'd been doing since he was ten years old.

"Oh, no," she said, beginning to pull away. "I know what you've got on your mind, Michael Wagner, but we can't. Not here."

"Why not?" he asked, pulling her back.

"Because the boys are right outside!"

"No, they're not," he whispered into her ear. "They're half a mile from here, playing on those hay bales."

He kissed along her shoulders, all the secret places at the nape of her neck. She turned and put her arms around him in that lovely way she had. Lawrence. Brookside. Hilton Head.

"Okay, but you'd better be quick," she said in a throaty voice.

"Don't worry. I will be."

"But not too quick. Remember, ladies first."

"Yes," he said. "Absolutely. Ladies first."

THIRTY-SIX

On her way home from the cathedral, Caroline stopped at the Dillons on Fourteenth and Comanche to buy a few things for when Michael and Vanessa and the boys stopped by later. The store was nearly empty, and she relished the cool quietness of it. What a wonderful homily the priest from Kinsley had delivered! At one point, she'd sneaked a look at Michael where he stood so tall in the pew beside her, and she could tell he'd been moved by it, too. Had he been thinking about Jimmy, as she had? He must have been—otherwise why had he joked about kidnapping Jimmy and bringing him to the house? In a sudden flight of fancy, she imagined Leroy in a flowing Biblical robe, telling one of his hired men, "Take the fatted calf and slaughter it. Then let us celebrate with a feast, because this son of mine was dead and has come to life again. He was lost and has been found." The thought of it gave her chills.

But when she got back to the house, she found Leroy sitting at the dining room table with his reading glasses on and a sheaf of papers before him.

She put the groceries on the counter. "What's all that?"

"Just some stuff I've been meaning to go through."

She walked over to where he sat in his wheelchair. For days, he'd been wavering between using the chair and loudly insisting that he didn't need it. Today, apparently, he needed it. "What stuff is that?" she asked.

Instead of answering, he handed her a page he'd been marking up with a pencil he'd sharpened with his pocketknife, the shavings sitting in a little mound on the white tablecloth. She recognized the page immediately. It was from the living trust Harold Krebs had drawn up for them five years before, when Leroy had landed in the hospital with what turned out to be a bleeding ulcer. She took her glasses from her purse and put them on. The changes started near the middle of the page, where Leroy had added a penciled-in clause stating, *If JJW chooses to liquidate his share in TRUST before the age of ~~twenty-five thirty~~ thirty-five, he will receive as payment a price no higher than ~~eighty~~ ~~seventy-five~~ fifty percent of one third of the appraised value of land only, no buildings or cattle or equipment to be included.*

"JJW," she realized with a shock, stood for James Joseph Wagner.

"My God, why don't you just cut him out of his inheritance altogether?" she said.

"I'm trying to protect the little sumbitch from himself," he said.

"Oh, please," she said, dropping the paper. "You're trying to *punish* him, that's what you're doing. You're trying to make it like he was never *born*."

"Quit being to so dramatic. Who says either one of us will even *be* dead, sixteen years from now? Hell, at the rate that little sumbitch is going, we'll both outlive him by a decade or two."

"See! You're wishing him dead even as we speak!"

Leroy rolled his wheelchair back from the table and started for the room at the front of the house, propelling himself along with his one good arm. "Well, maybe if you hadn't spoiled him rotten, we wouldn't have to have this conversation. Did you ever think of that?"

She followed him, resisting the urge to give the chair a good push. "Oh, that's rich, coming from you, Leroy Wagner. Maybe if *you* had been the father you should've been, I wouldn't have *had* to spoil him!" She was wound up now. All those years of holding back, of silently accepting Leroy's absences and moodiness and overall lack of thoughtfulness—well, she was through with all of it. "And not just that. Maybe if you'd been the *husband* you should've been, I wouldn't have had to—"

She stopped short, the admission she'd contemplated so many times over the years on the tip of her tongue. Leroy stopped pushing himself along and turned to look at her over his shoulder. "Wouldn't have had to what? Go ahead, say it. I can take it."

"Like hell you can," she said.

She left the groceries where they sat on the counter and walked out the kitchen door and climbed back into her car in a blind rage. She had no idea where she was going and didn't slow down to think about it until she found herself passing through the familiar gates of Maple Grove Cemetery. She rolled past the flat, sundrenched part of the cemetery where all of the Wagners, Wade included, were buried, parked in the older, tree-lined part, and got out to walk. As always, it took her a few minutes to find the tall granite marker she hadn't even acknowledged to herself she was looking for.

Edward M. Kramer
Beloved Husband and Father
Ray of Sunshine on a Cloudy Day
September 1, 1954
March 18, 2001

The stone, which sat in the shade of one of the cemetery's rare cottonwoods, looked out across rolling hills to where a neighborhood of new houses was going up a quarter mile away. Leave it to Ted to find one of the few beautiful spots in an otherwise dreary place.

After Wade died, they'd had no contact at all other than seeing each other from afar around town. Then, a year to the day after Jimmy was born, the telephone in the kitchen of the homeplace rang, and as soon as she picked it up, she knew by the intensity of the silence who was on the other end of the line.

"What?" she asked, speaking in a whisper even though she was alone in the house.

"I'm sorry to call you this way. I told myself I wouldn't, but there's something I have to ask you."

"What is it?"

"Is he mine?"

"Is who yours?"

"*Him.* The baby."

She stood there as seconds ticked by, still not getting it. Then all at once she understood. Jimmy. He was talking about Jimmy, born six weeks premature to a father who struggled to love him as he deserved to be loved.

"No," she said. "He's Leroy's."

"Are you sure?"

"Unfortunately, yes. I'm sure."

"Sorry," he said after a long pause. "I had to ask. I've been up every night thinking about it. I guess I'm a little disappointed." She said nothing to this, and a second later, he added, "I have something I want to give you."

"Give me? What is it?"

"Do you remember that house with the pool over by the country club?"

She thought of autumn leaves on a warm, sunny day. "What about it?"

"I bought it after the funeral and had some work done inside. I want you to have it."

Again, it took several seconds for the words to sink in. "Ted, have you lost your mind? I can't accept a *house* from you! What would Leroy say?"

"Frankly, I don't give a shit what he says. This has got nothing to do with him. It never had anything to do with him." His voice cracked, and he put his hand over the phone, muffling it for several seconds. Then he was back, his voice loud in her ears after the muffled silence. "I left a key to the back door on one of the deck chairs by the pool. Go have a look, then have Leroy call about the asking price. I guarantee he won't be disappointed."

"Oh, Ted."

"I know it's over between us, Cal. But I want to do this. Just go and have a look. Please. For me."

And with that, the phone went dead in her hands.

She got Annie to watch Jimmy so she could make the drive into town. What she saw there moved her more deeply than she would have ever thought possible. The entire first floor of the house had been redone. The darkly paneled kitchen and turquoise-colored bathrooms were no more. Everything was new and fresh, and yet still in keeping with the Frank Lloyd Wright-style of the place. It was as if no one had ever lived or suffered within those walls before.

She sat on the plush carpeting of the living room floor and cried as hard as she'd ever cried in her life. Afterward, she wiped her eyes, drove straight to the Bar W, found Leroy where he was feeding cattle in the big corral, and announced that she'd found her dream house and was done driving back and forth to town twice a day.

He said nothing. It was like he'd been expecting all along that this day would come, and he'd already made up his mind that there was no use fighting it.

"And another thing," she said. "I'm buying all new furniture. I don't want anything from our old lives to get in the way of this fresh start."

"Where's the money for all this coming from, if you don't mind my asking?" he said finally.

"I'm sure you'll figure something out," she said, turning to walk back to where her car sat idling. "You always do."

Six months later, after she and Leroy had made the move from the Bar W to the house in town, Ted dropped dead while hiking up Longs Peak in Colorado. Leroy heard about it at morning coffee and came home to tell her. "Okay, so the guy put on some weight the last few years," he said. "He sure as hell didn't look like he was getting ready to keel over."

She stood in the middle of her new kitchen, trying to hide the fact that her heart was breaking inside of her.

Five years later, when Jimmy started school at Sacred Heart, she finished her degree and took a job editing manuscripts for a small Catholic press in Charlotte, North Carolina. On the first Monday of every month, she drove to Wichita and took a plane to North Carolina to meet in person with the publisher, a warm, brilliant man in his sixties who told her several times that the monthly meetings weren't necessary. The job was meant to be done remotely, and they could conference by phone, if that worked better for her.

"Thanks," she said, forcing a smile. "But I need these meetings, even if you don't."

"Well, then, my dear, you're more than welcome to them," he said, returning her smile.

For the first time in her life, she had work of her own to attend to. Important work. Work she could pour her heart and soul into without the slightest regret.

Of course, there was a limit to the comfort a person could get from work—or from the dead, for that matter. Wade had taught her that, and Ted, dear Ted, had confirmed it.

It was early afternoon by the time she made her way back from the cemetery. She felt a little sheepish, having stayed away so long, but as she parked her car in the driveway, the anger and determination she'd felt before came streaming back. Leroy wasn't the only person who could revise a trust or consult a lawyer, and he'd find that out soon enough if he pushed her too far.

She looked for him in the kitchen, noting that the groceries she'd left there had been put away, then in the dining room and the living room where his hospital bed was. Finally, passing by the tall windows that looked out on the patio, she saw him sitting there in his wheelchair. She parted the sliding glass door and walked across the concrete patio that had once looked out on a pool until she came to where he sat.

"There's something I need to tell you," she said, her voice quavering. "It's about—"

He raised a hand, stopping her. "There's something I want to say first."

"Okay," she said, glad for the momentary reprieve. "What is it?"

He looked at her, and even in the afternoon sunlight she could feel the dark intensity of his gaze. "You were right about the trust. I tore all that up."

"Okay."

"You were right about a lot of things."

She began to say something, then stopped herself. She was through bailing him out. Let him finish what he started.

"What you said about me not being the husband I should've been. Well, that's right, too. I've known it for a long time, but these last few weeks, cooped up in this house, unable to get out and go to work, I've had to face it head-on. Then, when *you* got up and walked out of here, leaving me alone the same way I left you a thousand times, well, it was like I was getting a dose of my own medicine."

"A *thousand* times? Try *seven* thousand times. More, even."

"I know it," he said, continuing to look straight at her. "I know, and I'm sorry."

She could feel herself beginning to give way. "What about Jimmy?"

"I'll try harder."

She gave him a look.

"No, I will. I promise. Even if the little sumbitch drives me crazy, I won't quit on him. After all, you never quit on me."

She sat down in one of the cushioned patio chairs and took a deep breath and let it out slowly. "Okay," she said. "I accept your apology."

"What was it you wanted to tell me?" he asked.

She looked into his dark, searching eyes. "It doesn't matter."

"Are you sure?"

"Yes," she said. "I'm sure."

THIRTY-SEVEN

They were lying side by side in the front bedroom of the homeplace, Michael flat on his back and breathing heavily, when they heard the screen door on the back porch slam, followed by Sam's voice calling to them. "Mom? Dad? Where are you guys?"

Vanessa scrambled to find her clothes while Michael leapt up to bar the door.

"Mom?" came the boy's voice again, closer now. "Dad?"

"Hurry up!" Michael whispered.

"I am!"

Finally dressed, she squeezed past him and out the door.

"What is it?" he heard her ask.

"Nothing," Sam said. "I just wondered where you guys were."

"Well, you found us. Where's your brother?"

"Outside somewhere. When are we going to eat? I'm getting hungry."

The two voices faded as they walked toward the back of the house. Michael finished dressing and followed them out the back door.

"Can we go get something to eat?" Sam asked as soon as Michael appeared.

"In a while. Where's your brother?"

"Playing with a couple of dogs by the creek."

"By the creek," Michael repeated. "I thought your mother told you to watch out for your brother."

"I was," Sam said. "But then the dogs showed up, and—"

Michael didn't wait to hear the rest but started walking along the Sawlog in the direction of the hay bales. Vanessa followed close behind. "Michael? Do you think he's all right?"

"I'm sure he's fine," Michael said. "We just need to find him, that's all."

They walked along the south side of the creek, calling the boy's name over and over again—"Luke! Lukie! Luke!"—and stopping every few yards to listen for an answer. No answer came. Soon they arrived at where the hay bales were stacked in long lines next to the alfalfa.

"Where is he?" Vanessa asked, sounding panicked, her face flushed and sweaty.

"He didn't take the go-kart," Michael said, pointing to where it stood next to the open door of the tack barn. He turned to Sam, who was near tears now. "Sam, listen. I need you to tell me exactly where you last saw your brother."

"We were playing on the hay bales," the boy said, choking on the words, "and then these dogs showed up—"

"What kind of dogs? What did they look like?"

"There was a black one and another smaller one."

"Okay. Go on."

"They were playing fetch, and the black dog ran into the creek. Luke ran after it."

"Which direction did they go?"

At this, Sam broke down and began to cry, tears rolling down his dusty cheeks. "I don't know. I-I-I can't remember."

"It's important," Michael said, taking a knee in front of him. "Try to remember."

Sam gathered himself as best he could and looked up and down the tree-lined creek. "I-I-I'm not sure. It might have been that way, toward the house."

"Okay," Michael said, exchanging looks with Vanessa. "We'll split up and look in both directions."

"If anything's happened to my baby—"

"Listen," Michael said, taking her by the shoulders. "He's fine. We just have to stay calm and find him. Okay?"

She nodded, holding back tears. "Okay."

They split up, Vanessa and Sam looking upstream in a westerly direction, Michael crossing the creek behind the house and heading east along the north bank. Soon the sound of their voices faded, and all Michael could hear was his own voice, calling and calling.

"Luke! Lukie! Luke!"

He followed the tree-lined creek as it meandered through the pasture in the direction of the Stewart place. Soon sweat was running down his face and into his eyes, making it hard to see. That part of the Sawlog was only a few feet wide, but the ravine it ran through was twenty feet deep in places and lined with cedar trees with sharp needles. He passed the fallen-down buildings and wooden corrals of an old homestead where he and Wade had played cowboys and Indians, Wade always insisting on the role of Indian, delegating to Michael the less attractive role of cowboy.

"Luke!" he called. "Luke!"

His voice was getting hoarse, his shadow growing longer. It was late afternoon, headed toward early evening.

"Lukie! Luke! Can you hear me?"

He stood a moment on the bank of the creek, calling and then stopping to listen. A far-off yipping sound came to his ears.

"Luke!" he yelled. Again, a high-pitched yip came in response.

He continued along the creek, the back of Chester and Fanny Stewart's place coming into view a hundred yards downstream. He crossed a barbed wire fence and kept going, pausing every fifty yards or so to yell the boy's name. Then a black dog with a white eye patch popped into view at the top of the creek, barking at him. He recognized the dog immediately as the puppy Luke had played fetch with when they'd stopped at Chester's to talk about the case. A moment later, a second dog, a blue heeler mix he recognized as the one Annie had taken back to Buffalo against his advice, appeared on the bank, barking its head off. What was the dog's name? Lola?

He took off running toward the dogs, and they disappeared back into the creek.

"Luke! Lola!"

At the edge of the ravine where he'd seen the dogs, he paused to listen, his heart pounding.

"Luke! Lola!"

"Dad," came a weak voice.

He slid down the creek bank and splashed into the muddy water at the bottom. Luke lay on his back at the water's edge, Lola and the black dog with the white eye patch sitting beside him.

"Are you all right?" Michael asked.

"My ankle," the boy said, sitting up just far enough to touch his left shin. His clothes were covered in creek mud, and there were lines on his face where his tears had streamed down. "I twisted it."

"I've got you now, buddy. Can you stand up?"

"I don't think so. Dad, it really hurts!" And the tears he'd been holding in since Michael arrived began to pour down the boy's face once again.

"Don't worry, buddy. I'll carry you. But first I need to call your mom and brother."

Vanessa picked up on the first ring.

"I found him. He's okay."

"Thank God! Where are you?"

"At the Stewart place. Just past the bridge on the way to 283. Can you bring the truck?"

"We're on our way."

Michael lifted Luke in his arms and carried him, splashing through the shallow water until they reached a spot where the bank was less steep and he could find footing to gain the top. They were waiting in the shade of the Stewarts' destroyed front yard when Vanessa and Sam rolled up in the Ram.

"Lukie, are you okay?" Vanessa said, running to where they waited.

"I hurt my ankle, but Lola saved me. She went and found Dad."

"Lola?" Vanessa said, stroking the boy's hair.

Michael nodded at the little heeler mix Sam had knelt down to pet along with the Stewarts' bigger dog.

"I don't think anything's broken, but we should get some X-rays, just to be safe."

He was holding his breath, waiting for Vanessa to let loose with a string of accusations. How the ranch was a bad place, a dangerous place, and she'd known all along that something like this would happen. It never came. Instead, looking Michael in the eye, she said, "I'm just glad you found him. I knew you would."

"It was Lola who found me," Luke said. "Dad just showed up later."

"Well, *thanks*, buddy," Michael said to Luke, and soon all four of them were laughing.

They lifted Luke, creek mud and all, into the front seat of the Ram, the boy insisting loudly that Lola be allowed to accompany them to the hospital. To Michael's surprise, Vanessa agreed, watching without complaint as the dog jumped into Sam's lap in the back seat. When they were on their way, Michael turned and looked at her where she sat with Luke's head in her lap, stroking his dark brown hair. Their eyes met, and she gave him a little nod, and he knew then that they were going to be okay.

THIRTY-EIGHT

Jeremiah's 1986 Honda CB750 stood on its kickstand in front of the Applebee's in the northeast corner of Boot Hill parking lot. That there *was* an Applebee's anywhere near Boot Hill felt to Annie like an affront both to the town's storied past (imagine Wyatt Earp or Bat Masterson strolling in there) and to certain memories from her misspent youth, more than a few of which—like making out with town boys in the cramped back seats of their fourth-gen Mustangs and catfish Camaros—had occurred in this very corner of the parking lot. The CB750 was the same bike Jeremiah had bought and ridden back and forth to campus in the days after they'd quit commuting together as part of their respective Annie Anonymous and Jeremiah Anonymous programs, only now the bike featured a cheap bullet fairing and a pair of mismatched fiberglass saddlebags. Neither modification, in Annie's view, came close to making the bike highway worthy.

She paused inside the restaurant's front doors to let her eyes adjust to the semi-darkness. It didn't take long to spot the lumberjack-poet seated at the bar with his back to her. She'd suggested they meet here, rather than somewhere more intimate and authentic like Kate's or El Rodeo or even Central Station Bar & Grill, because she wasn't sure she wanted to be intimate or authentic just yet. Then, as she stood taking in his thin back and shoulders, he turned around in his chair and his blue eyes lit up, and all the caution she'd been careful to manufacture on the ride into town was cast to the wind.

"Hey there," he said, standing to give her a hug. "It's been a while."

"Yes, it has."

It felt like she might disappear into that hug, but she caught herself and pulled back. The full black beard she'd known and loved was gone, replaced by a three-day stubble.

"You shaved your beard! Why? I loved that beard."

"It grows back," he said with a laugh.

She slid into the seat next to him at the bar. "When did you leave Buffalo?"

"Nine o'clock yesterday morning."

"You rode all night on that thing?"

He reached behind himself and rubbed his lower back. "More or less. And I've got the herniated discs to prove it. Ouch!"

"Poor baby."

"Come on. You can do better than that."

"Poor *poor* baby."

"That's better."

Something had happened. He was in some kind of crisis that had caused him to lose weight and shave his beard and ride across seven states on the back of antique motorcycle with zero rider comforts such as you'd find on a Gold Wing or even a bagger BMW. In the meantime, she was trying to get a grip on her side of things. She'd been so angry with him when she left Buffalo. She'd cursed his name the whole way down I-90 and I-70 and on long runs to the elevator and while trying to fall asleep in her childhood bed at the homeplace. She'd repeated, aloud and under her breath, certain talismanic phrases like *He's fucking married* and *He's not a serious person* and *He's not for you, Annie, and he never will be.* All this to stoke the anger, keep it from dying down. But it had all been for nothing. The lumberjack-poet had rolled into town on his vintage Honda, easily found her family name in the white pages, and poof, that was it. Anger gone almost instantly, like dew in the late-morning sun.

The bartender came over with a couple of menus, and although she'd reminded herself several times that *Jeremiah + Annie + Alcohol = Trouble with a capital T*, she joined him in ordering a pint of hefeweizen with a slice of orange. When their beers arrived, they carried them to a corner booth above which hung a blown-up photo of cast members from *Gunsmoke*. Actor James Arness, in full Marshal Matt Dillon regalia, stood on one end, and Amanda Blake, also in character-correct attire as Miss Kitty, stood on the other.

"What's going on with you?" she asked. "I can tell something's happened."

"You go first," he said, groaning as he lowered himself into the booth. "Why'd you run off without saying goodbye, and how come you haven't answered any of my calls or emails?"

As their beers beaded sweat on the table before them, she told him about Leroy's accident, finding Lola chained up in a fat man's backyard, "losing" her phone in traffic outside Cleveland, the high drama of DW quitting on her in the middle of the harvest after they tumbled off the combine—everything, in short, except for the part played in it all by Jacob Hess.

"I'm sorry about your dad," Jeremiah said. "How's he doing?"

"Better. He's out of the hospital, at least. But, he's still covered in casts like a mummy and still can't walk or leave the house. It's so strange, Jer. Kind of terrifying, actually."

"What is? Seeing him that way?"

She took a sip of her hefeweizen. "Yeah. The wheelchair, especially, freaks me out. Here's this guy I've spent my whole life believing was indestructible, maybe even superhuman. And he's sitting there in a fucking *wheelchair*? How does any of that compute?"

"It doesn't. Not at all."

"And Wade! Oh my God, you won't believe the stories I've been subjected to recently. This whole revisionist history has emerged whereby he wasn't heroic or even tragic, but just another lost soul like the rest of us."

"Don't believe a word of it."

"I'm not going to."

"Not a word. Certain myths are necessary. It doesn't even matter if they're true or not."

"I agree."

"It could be something terrifying and lowly, like the myth of Sisyphus. Doesn't matter."

"Yes, or Atlas."

"Absolutely. Or the so-called Inferior Deities. Pan, for example."

"Ah, yes. Or Echo."

"No question." He raised his hefeweizen to the light, as though checking to see if it was sufficiently cloudy. "But to return to the more familiar territory of comic-book superheroes. Which one would your father be, if you had to pick one?"

"Superman, of course."

"Oh, that's right; the whole Kansas thing. And Wade?"

"Captain America."

"Not the Lone Ranger?"

She shook her head. "What about your dad?"

"Are you ready for this? The Incredible Hulk."

"Whoa," Annie said. "I mean, I knew the guy had a temper."

He lowered his beer and took a drink. "Oh yeah. Imagine Bruce Banner transforming into something terrifyingly huge and green right before your eyes."

Just like that, they'd slipped back into the notorious rapport they'd known in Buffalo. They rode the wave of it for another ten minutes, then Jeremiah shifted into a lower, more serious gear and began to talk about the days immediately following her "disappearance," as he called it.

How he'd gone by her apartment on Allen Street and pounded on the door until he thought the bones in his hand would separate from their joints. "Hulk would've just torn the door off its hinges and stepped through the debris, but that's not me, I guess."

How he'd called and texted her every couple of hours until she finally picked up, only to have her hang up on him less than minute later. Or so he'd supposed, never imagining that she'd be capable of losing her phone and not even bothering to replace it. "Although that would explain a lot," he said. "For example, no more Instagram posts about Lola. No more retweets of obscure threads about Hardy's rebel women."

Finally, the terrible silence that had descended upon him like a black cloud in her absence; how he'd descended along with it, growing more irritable and depressed by the day. Of course, Emily guessed the source of his depression. "It's her, isn't it? That girl from Kansas. Annie." He'd denied it over and over, the way Peter denied ever knowing or loving Christ. But in the end things got to the point where he could deny it no longer.

"So what happened? You just up and left?"

"No, she did. Emily. She said she was sick of 'living a lie.' She couldn't imagine another year as awful as the one we'd just lived through. So she packed up the Subaru and preemptively moved back to Idaho before another school year could start, trapping her and JJ in Buffalo."

"Is that where you're headed now?" she asked. "Idaho?"

He leveled his blue eyes on her. "I came here to see you, Annie. That's as far as I've thought any of this through."

She sat turning this over in her mind, then said, "I don't want to be the reason you left your wife. Or even the reason she left you. I've never wanted that."

He reached for her hand and sat there holding it under the stolid gaze of Marshal Dillon. "Look, Emily and I did the best we could—for each other and for JJ. It's not like we didn't try. We did, for years. But we're very different people, and grad school doesn't help with any that, as you know. It just exacerbates an already untenable situation."

"It makes me sad to think of Emily leaving," she said. "That couldn't have been easy."

"It wasn't," he said. "But you know what is?"

"What?"

"Looking at you. Seeing you again, finally. You can't imagine how much I've missed you."

The hand he sat holding wanted a cigarette, bad. "I've missed you, too," she said. "I didn't realize how much until I walked in the door and saw you sitting at the bar, all skinny and beardless and road weary . . ." She trailed off.

"But?" he asked.

"But my life is really complicated and fucked up right now." She looked him squarely in the eye. "And yours is even worse."

He let go of her hand and drank down what remained of his beer, simultaneously holding up two fingers for the bartender across the way to see. "Have you been seeing someone?" he asked.

"Yes, but that's not it."

"Well? What is it, then?"

She didn't want to hurt him, especially not in the bedraggled state he was in now. But she needed to be honest. Completely up front, both with him and with herself. Until that happened, nothing in her vagabond life would ever change.

"I've got some shit to figure out," she said. "Big shit like where I'm going and what I'm gonna do with my life. The whole time I've been here, I've felt like everything was up in the air. Not just my dad, but everything. The dissertation. Buffalo. The whole grad school thing. At the same time, I'm not sure about Kansas or the Bar W, either. I mean, I love it and everything. But is that enough? Couldn't I love it, you know, from afar, or something?" Again, she trailed off.

"Hey, I get it," he said. "I feel the same way about Idaho."

"You do?"

"Sure I do."

The bartender brought two more of the tall, cloudy beers.

"You're not seriously thinking about dropping out of school, are you?" Jeremiah asked when they were alone again.

"I don't know. Maybe. At the very least, I'm gonna have to change the topic of my dissertation. Because, man, let me tell you, Thomas Hardy and I are *finished.* I haven't read a word of the great man's works the whole time I've been out here, and you know what? I don't miss it at all. Not even a little bit."

"Good for you," Jeremiah said.

"You think so?"

"Absolutely. It's high time you ended things with that gloomy bastard." He raised his glass. "To new topics. New beginnings."

"To new beginnings," she said, clinking her glass against his.

They drank and sat looking at each other across the booth. He looked a little sad, she thought. As if he'd been expecting a little more from her than what she'd been able to give him. But that was okay. She was determined to go slow and get things right this time. As if reading her mind, he winced.

"What is it?" she asked. "Are you okay?"

"It's just my back," he said, leaning forward in the booth to give it a rub. "You don't have any Motrin or anything on you, do you?"

"Poor baby," she said in a teasing voice. "Of course I do."

THIRTY-NINE

In a perfect world, Jimmy liked to cure weed in quart Mason jars over a period of weeks, maybe even months. But there was no time for that now, so he stopped by Walmart and picked up a portable vacuum sealer and a roll of heavy-duty food storage bags. Among other benefits, vacuum packing would cut the curing process way down—precisely what he needed if he was gonna hit K-Dog's aggressive new deadline.

Kaid and Brock shared a bowl of Girl Scout Cookies while Jimmy demonstrated the process of fine-trimming the bud and sealing it up in the vacuum bags. Each bag could hold a couple of pounds of weed, and because the vacuum seal created an oxygen-free environment, there'd be zero odor and zero chance of mold forming.

"We still have to burp it once a day, though," Jimmy said.

"Burp it?" Kaid said.

"Let the bud out of the bag for five or ten minutes, then reseal it. It helps control humidity and speeds up the curing process."

"Dude, you're like a mad scientist about this shit," Brock said, lacing his fingers together and cracking his knuckles. He'd chilled considerably since Jimmy had returned from his parents' house with his pockets full of hydrocodone.

"Guess what?" Kaid said after they were good and stoned. "I called my old man in LA He's sending the money to buy the van as we speak."

"Ha, that's bullshit and you know it," Brock said. "You called your *mom* and started whining about it, and *she* called Dad."

"Whatever, dude."

"We still gotta trim and bag all of this bud," Jimmy said. "It's not a small job."

"So? You stay here and get started, and Brock and I'll make a quick run to the dude's place on that dirt bike of yours. Right, Brock?"

"Yeah, man. We already talked the whole thing through."

"I bet you have," Jimmy said.

He was thinking maybe he'd get lucky and they'd buy the van and then just take off for California in it. But luck of that kind had been nonexistent of late, and anyway, Brock still owed him for selling his vintage Gibson. You better believe Jimmy hadn't forgotten.

Like most things having to do with growing a crop of GSC, fine-trimming and curing bud was a tedious process requiring minute attention to detail. About the only way to get through it with your sanity intact was to get good and toasted and play the Dream of Escape playlist at high volume. Each time he sealed a bag, he put it on the scale and calculated the per-plant yield in his head. As nearly he could tell, he was averaging five and a half ounces of smokeable weed per plant. Not bad at all.

He was sealing up the last bag when Kaid and Brock came rolling in all jazzed up from their van-buying errand.

"Dude, you gotta come take a ride in this beauty," Kaid said. "We took her to the car wash, and doesn't she look sweet! Get your phone and take some pictures of Brock and me standing in front of it."

"In a minute," Jimmy said. "I gotta clean these shears and sweep up all these twigs and shit."

"I'm serious!" Kaid said. "Let's get some pics of me and Brock posing like a pair of LA gangsters. The background of this shitty trailer park is fucking perfect!"

"Oh, all right," Jimmy said.

When they came back in from taking the pictures, Brock picked up one of the vacuum-sealed bags and tossed it in the air a couple of times. "Dude, this is some *weight*. What's one of these bags worth?"

Rather than answering, Jimmy lifted the bag out of Brock's hands and put it back with the others.

"You know what we ought to do, don't you?" Kaid said.

"What's that?" Jimmy said.

"Come on, man, it's obvious."

"Maybe to you it is."

"Tell him, Brock."

"Nah, man, you tell him."

"Fine," Kaid said, smiling in a particularly devious way he had when he'd been smoking weed. "We ought to load up all twenty-five pounds of this shit and hit the road back to Cali. I mean, can you imagine how popular we'd be once word spread about how much weed we were holding?"

"I can," Jimmy said, beginning to laugh. The sheer audacity of the idea stunned him.

"What the fuck's so funny?" Kaid said.

"*You*," Jimmy said. "Where do you think you are, Compton?"

"I'm just saying."

"I know what you're saying, and you're out of your mind. In case you've forgotten, I've got a business partner in this deal, and it's not even a fifty-fifty split. More like seventy-thirty. No way I'm running off with K-Dog's weed, and if you think I'm gonna let *you* do it, well, you've lost it, that's all."

Kaid winced and shook his head. "Man, I don't know what's happened to you lately. You used to be cool, but now you're all uptight and shit all the time. Brock and I were just talking about it, weren't we, Brock?"

"Yeah, man. Super uptight. Like you're holding a grenade between the cheeks of your ass, and if you relax for one second, it'll drop down between your legs and blow your dick off."

"Very funny," Jimmy said.

He couldn't believe these idiots. It was like they were still in high school or something. Couldn't keep their minds on business for more than five minutes at a time. The whole thing was pathetic. How pathetic? Not a half hour later, as they were burping the last of the cookies, Brock slinked up to Jimmy with a familiar, hangdog look on his face.

"Dude, my hands are killing me. I need more of them pills."

"What are you talking about?" Jimmy said. "I gave you half a bottle of that shit last night."

"That was last night," Brock said.

Jimmy glanced over at where Kaid sat on the couch, idly strumming his red Stratocaster. Now that they were in the final stages of curing the weed, the trailer, which had seemed cramped only a few days before, felt cavernous and full of echoes.

"Just give him the shit," Kaid said.

"Easy for you to say. You didn't have to rob your childhood home to get it."

Even so, Jimmy pulled an orange prescription bottle from his pants pocket, shook out five pills, and held them out for Brock to take.

"To hell with that," Brock said. "Give me the whole bottle."

"Man, I'm so finished with this shit," Jimmy said. "I can't even *begin* to tell you."

"Oh, really," Kaid said. "What shit is that?"

"You! Both of you!"

"That's pretty funny, man," Kaid said. He set the Strat aside and stood. "Because we're pretty much finished with you, too.

Why don't you just give us our share of the weed right now, so we can blow this fucking town."

"*Your share!*" Jimmy laughed. "I'm not giving you shit!"

A tense moment followed, and then Brock chopped at Jimmy's hand, causing the pills he was holding to scatter across the dirty floor of the trailer. Jimmy just stood there, shaking his head, while Brock dropped to his hands and knees, scooping up the errant pills one by one and popping them into his mouth.

"Dude, don't you think it's about time you kicked that shit? I mean, just look at you. You used to be a badass, scoring touchdowns and shit. But now you're nothing but a junkie stealing from your friends."

"I can still kick *your* ass," Brock said, coming to his feet.

"I'm standing right here," Jimmy said. "Go ahead and try."

Brock dropped his level and took a shot at Jimmy's legs, no different from what he would've done when shooting a double-leg on the padded floor of the TMP wrestling room. But Jimmy saw the shot coming and blocked it with his forearm, catching Brock in a nasty front headlock. They'd been in this position a hundred times before, and mostly Brock had won, or at least stalled the position out. But things were different now. Jimmy was bigger and stronger than he'd been at TMP, while Brock was the opposite, a shadow of his former self. Jimmy thought of his Sunburst Gibson, sold for a fraction of what it was worth to some asshole bull hauler, and tightened the grip around Brock's windpipe until he could feel the air going out of him.

"Say uncle, or I'll choke you out."

"N-n-never," Brock wheezed.

"I mean it. I'll turn out the lights on your ass."

But even as Jimmy said the words, he could see a red blur coming at him out of the corner of his eye. *No, dude, not the Strat—*

Then *smack!*—everything went black.

FORTY

Jeremiah started to fade after his fourth hefeweizen, and Annie couldn't say she blamed him. After all, he'd clung beetle-like to the back of an antique motorcycle across six states—seven if you counted the sliver of Pennsylvania near Erie—the wind assaulting him from all sides. Still, although he complained endlessly that his back was killing him, he wouldn't hear of leaving his precious CB750 in Boot Hill parking lot.

"Fine," Annie said, climbing into Frankenporsche. "You can follow me to my parents' house, and for once I'll try to stay below the speed limit."

An hour before, near the end of a long, back-and-forth riff about their favorite places in the world, Jeremiah had asked about paying a visit to the Bar W, the "postage stamp of native soil" about which he'd heard so much. *Yeah, right,* Annie thought. She could just imagine the scene of testosterone-fueled competition, cowboy versus lumberjack-poet, that would play out if Jacob and Jeremiah were to cross paths even for a second. No, thank you. Having Jeremiah in her parents' house wasn't much better, but what the hell was she supposed to do? Check him into some shitty motel on Wyatt Earp in the middle of the afternoon, after he'd ridden thirteen hundred miles through heat and wind and poured his heart out to her?

She had him park the Honda in the front part of the garage and tried to sneak him from there straight into the finished portion of the basement, where he could take a nap on the overstuffed couch. But the garage was a mess, and he tripped over a wagon loaded with half-dead shrubs, and of course Caroline heard the racket and appeared in the doorway to greet them.

"Is this the young man who called earlier? I'm always so glad to meet a friend of Annie's. She's brought so few of them home to meet us over the years."

"That's not even close to being true," Annie said, rolling the wagon out of the way. "Whose shrubs are these, anyway?"

"Sister Margaret gave those to me as a birthday present," Caroline said. "Things have been so crazy around here, I haven't had a chance to plant them. Maybe you could help me, later?"

"I was just taking Jeremiah downstairs so he could take a nap," Annie said, ignoring the suggestion. "He's been on the road for a day and half straight."

"I hope it's no trouble," Jeremiah said, reaching out to shake Caroline's hand. "I've got a tent in my saddlebags, and I could always crash in that for a couple of hours."

"In this heat?" Caroline said. "Come inside where it's cool, and I'll get you both a glass of iced tea."

Then Leroy made an appearance, not in his wheelchair, as she'd expected, but with the aid of a single aluminum crutch. Standing on his good leg, he shook Jeremiah's hand and asked the same question he always asked. "Where are you from?" Jeremiah answered him with a single word, and Superman nodded knowingly, as if he'd spent half his life in Idaho. Then he pogo-sticked away before Caroline could drop any more hints about tea, allowing Annie the opportunity she needed to get Jeremiah settled in the guest room at the back of the house without anything too embarrassing happening.

"Your dad's doing better than I expected," Jeremiah said.

She sat on the edge of the bed, holding out two Motrin and a glass of water. "He's a fighter, all right, but don't let that fool you. He's also a stoic and a world-class actor. He could be in the most excruciating pain, and you'd never know it."

He downed the Motrin and put the glass on the bedside table. "Sisyphus of the Plains."

"Something like that."

She began to rise from the edge of the bed, but he pulled her back and kissed her on the mouth. It was the old kiss, all right. The one that had exiled her to the East Village and then months of JA. "This isn't happening," she said. "Not here. Not now."

"I know, I know," he said. "Just one more kiss?"

She kissed him until she could feel the urgency rising in him, then broke away and stood.

"God, I missed you," he said, closing his eyes.

"You already said that. Now get some rest. I'll wake you in an hour and you can help my mother plant those little trees before they die."

"Okay," he said in a fading voice.

Before the light was off, he was asleep.

She found her mother waiting for her on the patio with a pitcher of iced tea and two glasses. "Come and sit. Your father's watching Fox News on high volume, but we can escape all that nonsense out here."

She took a seat in a cushioned chair across from her mother and poured them both a glass of tea. It was unsweetened, the way her mother always drank it. Annie preferred a little sugar stirred in, but she couldn't be bothered to get up and find any.

"I like Jeremiah," Caroline said.

"I knew you would. He's exactly your type."

"Oh, really? And what type is that?"

"I don't know. Darkly handsome, polite, just a whiff of the altar boy about him."

"Like your father, in other words."

The comparison surprised her. "Jeremiah's a poet and a world-class talker. A great listener, too. None of that strikes me as being true of Dad."

"Well, maybe not the poetry part," Caroline said. "But your father was a very good listener when we first met."

"What happened?"

"A lot of things."

They sat awhile in silence, neither of them saying a word about the smell of blood and methane gas wafting up from the packing plants and feed yards a few miles away.

"There's one thing you wouldn't like about Jeremiah," Annie said.

"Oh? What's that?"

"He's married."

Her mother nodded slowly. "I wondered about that."

"You did? Why?"

"The thin band of sunburn on his ring finger. It's not so long ago he took the thing off. Are you in love with him?"

Another surprise. Apparently, her mother was full of them today. "I guess I am. I couldn't admit it until about an hour ago, but it's true. I don't know what good that's gonna do me, though."

"What do you mean?"

"I mean the whole thing is doomed, Mom, and I feel doomed being a part of it."

A moment passed. The only sound was the buzzing of cars going past on Country Club Drive.

"I know the feeling," her mother said. "I was in love with a married man once."

It took a moment for the words to sink in. "What did you just say?"

"I was in love with a married man once. In my case, the situation was complicated by the fact that I was married, too. The whole thing felt doomed, as you say. But now I wonder—was it really?"

Annie looked through the patio doors at where her father sat watching TV with his broken leg propped up on the footrest of a La-Z-Boy recliner Michael had had delivered the previous afternoon from a furniture store in Hutchinson. She couldn't believe what she was hearing. It was the most bizarre and out-of-character thing her mother had ever said. Until, a moment later, it wasn't.

"Wait a minute. Did the man drive a Cadillac? A blue Cadillac with a white top?"

Her mother nodded. "His name was Ted Kramer, and he was a classmate of your father's and mine at St. Mary of the Plains. He's been dead for many years now, God rest his soul."

Without further prompting, while Annie's jaw hung open in astonishment, her mother told her the entire story from start to finish. How she'd dated Ted Kramer for six months before breaking up with him to marry Leroy. How hard life had been in the early days of her marriage, when Leroy was gone all the time, and she was forced to deal with what she knew now was a major depression, without meds or support of any kind outside of what she could eke out of Mass and her daily prayers. How, years later, Ted Kramer had reappeared in her life. How they'd saved each other—that's how she put it, *saved*. Finally, how, in the wake of Wade's death and Jimmy's birth, she'd decided that having Ted in her life, while not a mistake, exactly, was something she could no longer afford. Not in the grief-stricken world she inhabited at the time.

Ted, Annie thought. *Ted who is dead. Ted who is dead but who'd once made her sad mother smile in a secret way. That Ted.*

"So I gave him up," her mother said, warming to her tale. "But don't ask me to say I'm sorry, because I'm not sorry, and probably I never will be. Probably it's selfish of me. I'm sure it is. But I've prayed a lot about it over the years, and not once has the Lord put shame or regret on my heart. Guilt, yes. But not shame. And certainly not regret." The whole time she talked, her mother looked straight at her, an intimacy so powerful that Annie had to force herself not to turn away from it. "Your father has been the love of my life, dear. He will always be the love of my life. But Ted, he was . . . I don't know, my soulmate, I guess."

Annie cringed inwardly at the hackneyed phrase, so beneath a woman like her mother, who consumed serious books, fiction, nonfiction, poetry, even theology, the way lesser people consumed tabloids and TV shows, to say nothing of Facebook and Instagram and the like.

"Why are you telling me all this?"

"Two reasons," Caroline said. "First, because I came *this* close to telling your father earlier today, so it's become clear to me that someone other than me needs to know about it, and I guess that someone is you, dear. Second—and this is the important part—I don't want to be the reason you turn Jeremiah away if there's even the slightest chance he might turn out to be *your* soulmate."

Annie looked down at her hands holding the glass of unsweetened tea. They were shaking slightly, the brown liquid in the glass registering the disturbance. Now that it had been applied to her own life rather than her mother's, the word *soulmate* didn't seem so trite anymore. "Wow," she said. "This is going to take some getting used to."

"I know it is," her mother said. "For me, too."

Annie let it sink in a little more. "Whatever you do, please don't tell Dad. It was a long time ago, and the news would kill him."

"Do you think so?" her mother said. "I'm not so sure that's true. All the same, I agree with you. There's no reason tell him now. This can be our secret."

Wow, Annie thought. *Just wow.*

FORTY-ONE

Jimmy woke to water raining down on his face and a dull pain at the base of his skull. Standing over him with a black bucket in his hand was K-Dog.

"What the hell, Dude—"

"My sentiments exactly," K-Dog said.

As Jimmy rolled onto his knees and tried to stand, K-Dog tossed the bucket into a corner of the room and took a seat on the faux leather couch.

"What are you even doing here?" Jimmy said, fingering the golf-ball-sized lump that was rising on the back of his head. "And where the hell are my dogs?"

"Those sweethearts?" K-Dog said. "They're taking a nap outside. Turns out dogs love Klonopin almost as much as truck drivers do."

Jimmy glanced around the room, his eyes falling on his broken-at-the-neck Strat, which lay in pieces next to the front door.

"Yeah, I saw that," K-Dog said. "Looks like you've been having all kinds of fun down here on the farm."

In a pile on the couch next to K-Dog's elbow were the Girl Scout Cookies in their vacuum-sealed bags. K-Dog picked one up and hefted it in his hands. "In a minute, we're going to weigh these sumbitches, and then you're going to explain to me why you're so short."

"Short? What are you talking about, *short*?"

"I count eight bags here. Two four six eight. At two pounds per bag, on average, that's, what, sixteen, seventeen pounds max? Either you're the worst hydroponic grower in the state of Kansas—which, now that I think about it, is entirely possible—or you've got some explaining to do."

"Dude, there were *ten* bags. And they were more like two-and-a half, two-and-three-quarter pounds each."

"So what happened? And don't even think about lying to me. You're no good at that shit, and you know it."

Jimmy sighed and ran down the whole miserable story without embellishment. How he'd called Kaid and Brock to help with the harvest. How they'd turned out to be way more trouble than they were worth. How Kaid had cracked him over the head with his own guitar, and how the two of them—he could only guess here—had run off with what they supposed to be their share of the Girl Scout Cookies.

"Your share, more like it," K-Dog said, shaking his head. "I thought you were smarter than this, a grown man ready to do business. Then I stumble onto this mess, and I begin to have some serious, serious doubts."

"Dude, I'm sorry," Jimmy said.

"*Dude, I'm sorry*," K-Dog repeated in a mock-whiny voice. "You seem to think we're friends or something. Is that what you think? Because there are no friends in this business, just deals. And the guy in Atlanta who bankrolled *this* deal wants *all* his weed, not what's left over after you allowed your grow house to be robbed in broad fucking daylight."

"What guy in Atlanta? You never said anything about a guy in Atlanta."

"Oh, didn't I? Gee, sorry about that. I guess that information was on a need-to-know basis. And let me tell you something: you need to know it now."

Jimmy had never seen this side of K-Dog. It was like something out of a Quentin Tarantino movie, and it scared him.

"I'm guessing those little friends of yours have a phone?"

"Of course."

"Okay then. Let's give them a call."

Jimmy dug his phone out of the pocket of his cargo shorts. It was beginning to dawn on him that this wasn't one of those high school scrapes, where you get caught smoking in the boy's restroom and they kick you out of school for a couple of weeks or a month and everything's forgiven.

Brock picked up on the third or fourth ring. "Dude, I'm sorry, but you had that shit coming."

"Put Kaid on," Jimmy said.

"But dude—"

"Brock, I'm serious. Put him on."

"Okay, just a sec."

Jimmy put the phone on speaker as soon as Kaid picked up, and they listened to his high-pitched voice going on and on about how bad he and Brock had been treated since they arrived in Dodge City. K-Dog let him run on for thirty seconds or so, then said, in calm voice that sent chills down Jimmy's spine, "Sorry, little dude, but this ain't Jimmy. Jimmy's a little bitch who likes to play games. But I'm nobody's bitch, and I don't play. You got something that belongs to me, and I want it back."

"Uh, okay," Kaid said. "Well, see, the thing is—"

Rather than listen to Kaid's rambling, K-Dog opened the photos on Jimmy's phone and thumbed through the last ten or so, shaking his head and laughing under his breath the whole time. "Which one are you?" he asked, cutting Kaid off, "the pill head or the skinny Filipino?"

"Uh, the skinny one?" Kaid said.

"Right. Now look, don't take this the wrong way, *Kaid*, but that Chevy van you're driving is a real piece of shit. I'm sitting here looking at it right now. And here's another picture of you and your pill-head buddy—what's his name? *Brock?*" The trucker gave Jimmy a sidelong smile before continuing. "So. I'm just getting started, and already I know your *name*, what you *look* like, who you're *with*, the piece of shit you're *driving*, and where *the fuck* you're headed. Give me another five minutes, and I'll know all your *friends'* names and where they live, the names and addresses of your *parents*, and, oh yeah, the best place near the beach in Malibu to buy a pack of heavy-duty zip ties and one of those old-school aluminum baseball bats I love so much. Are you getting the picture?"

"Yeah," Kaid said. "I'm getting it."

"Okay, then. Here's what you're gonna do. First, you're gonna share your location, so I know you mean business. Then you're gonna turn that ugly van around and get your ass back here to the scene of the crime, you got that?"

"Yeah," Kaid said. "We got it."

"Good," K-Dog said. "Now get to going. I'm watching."

Afterward, he just sat there, staring at Jimmy and shaking his head.

"What?" Jimmy said.

"Kids and their phones," K-Dog said. "Will you motherfuckers ever learn?"

"Probably not," Jimmy said, rubbing the painful knot on the back of his head.

While they waited for Kaid and Brock to return, Jimmy got his "Back to Cali" playlist up and running on the Bluetooth speaker. As always, K-Dog started bitching that there was only one decent tune on the whole fucking list, "California Love," featuring Tupac and Dr. Dre.

"What about my man Biggie?" Jimmy said. "What about "Going Back to Cali"?

"Point taken. Put that shit on."

Jimmy jumped to it, and soon Biggie's voice filled the trailer. Head bopping, K-Dog took a scale down from the kitchen cabinets and started weighing bags of Girl Scout Cookies one by one, carrying the total in his head. "Okay, so 21.75 pounds for the eight bags. Do the math, that's just under ten kilos. 9.8 to be precise. With the two bags you let your idiot friends run off with, we're looking at twelve, twelve and a half keys for the crop. Not bad."

"Not bad?" Jimmy said. "Who the fuck are you kidding? My old man's like an OG farmer, and he couldn't get yields like that."

"Yeah, but what's the shit *taste* like? That's the true test."

"Too early to tell. This weed's gotta cure for at least another three or four days."

K-Dog rolled his eyes at that idea. "Dude, get me a bong."

Jimmy went into a kitchen cabinet and brought down a clean water pipe and filled it with bottled water. Choosing one of the drier buds from the bottom of the first bag they opened, Jimmy pinched off the top end, loaded it into the bowl, and handed the bong to K-Dog along with a plastic Bic lighter. K-Dog brought the bong to his bearded mouth and bubbled it until the bud was toast. Then he held the smoke for another twenty seconds or so before letting it out in a slow stream. "A little green, maybe, but the taste is very, very good."

Jimmy sat back on the couch, a satisfied smile spreading across his face. "Dude, just wait. Another month, and that shit's gonna top out at 23 or 24 percent THC, easy."

"Maybe," K-Dog said. He chose a second bud from the top of the bag, loaded the bong, and passed it to Jimmy. "But why would we sit around and wait for that to happen? By then, we'll be well on our way to a whole new crop. A bigger one. A hundred, two hundred clones."

Jimmy put fire to the bong and took a nice, long hit. Somehow, he hadn't given much thought to what would happen after the current crop of Girl Scout Cookies was sold. He'd been too focused on his Dream of Escape. But now he was beginning to see that quitting K-Dog wouldn't be as easy as walking out on Byron Branch. No, not by a long shot.

He couldn't have said when he first began to hear the sirens. It was one of those sounds that starts out as background noise and then grows in urgency until finally it commands the attention even of those who've been smoking Girl Scout Cookies.

"What's that?" K-Dog asked.

Jimmy tuned down the volume on the playlist and they stood a moment, listening. The sirens got closer and closer, making their way off Highway 283 onto Lariat Way. They watched in horror from the open door of the trailer as the conversion van carrying Kaid and Brock and five-and-a-half pounds of Girl Scout Cookies appeared at the top of El Torro Street. Trailing them closely were a couple of cop cars, one of them Officer Charlie Bassett's white Crown Vic.

"Idiots," Jimmy said. "I told Kaid he needed to get a temporary plate for that thing, but do you think he listened?"

"Come on," K-Dog said, backing away from the door. "Let's grab the weed and book."

"What about *them?*" Jimmy asked. "They got two bags of our shit!"

"They're on their own, Dude. Come on, let's go."

Jimmy grabbed his old wrestling backpack from the hall closet and held it open while K-Dog stuffed in the remaining eight bags of Girl Scout Cookies. Opening the flimsy back door of the trailer, they hopped down into the grass like a couple of paratroopers heading into combat. A second later, they were running in a low crouch along the river road, headed for the grassy field where K-Dog had parked his rig. But as soon as the blue Peterbilt came into view, Jimmy pulled up and whistled to K-Dog. "You go ahead," he called out, breathing hard.

"What the fuck?" K-Dog said, eyes bugging out.

"I'm going back for my bike. I'll catch up with you later."

"Don't be a fucking idiot. We need to get out of here while the getting's good."

"Maybe, but I'm going back anyhow." Jimmy nodded over his shoulder at the backpack he was carrying. "You wanna take this, or should I keep it with me?"

"Dude, I got priors," K-Dog said. "Just keep it for now, and I'll meet up with you behind the Flying J in an hour."

Jimmy nodded, and K-Dog shape-shifted one last time.

"You try to fuck me on this, and you're a dead man. If I don't get to you, Atlanta will. You got that?"

"I got it," Jimmy said.

FORTY-TWO

The Ducati was chained to the fence at the back the trailer, out of sight of the scene playing out on El Torro, where Officer Bassett's cruiser and another squad car sat with their lights flashing. Jimmy unlocked the padlock and pulled the heavy chains through the wheels. Hammer and Kush appeared on wobbly legs from beneath the trailer. He dropped their collars in the grass and opened the back gate. "Sorry—you dudes have been righteous, but you're on your own now. *Scat!*"

He was thinking about what K-Dog had said about the two stolen bags of Girl Scout Cookies being his cut of their little caper. If that was the case, he sure as hell wasn't gonna let Officer Bassett Hound stumble across them. Working quietly, like the stealth superhero he sometimes imagined himself to be, he tightened the shoulder straps on the backpack and rolled the Ducati up to the tall front gate and cast his eyes up El Torro. He was expecting the worst: Kaid and Brock sitting on the curb with their hands cuffed behind them; Bassett Hound holding the two bags of confiscated cookies in his hands as though weighing them, a big smile on his dough-like face; maybe another cop snapping pictures with his phone. Instead, he saw what he could only call the latest example of DCPD at its finest: Basset Hound busily writing tickets in his air-conditioned cruiser while Kaid and Brock sat waiting in the tagless conversion van, their windows rolled all the way down, Kaid's hand beating time to some song on his rearview mirror. The second cop car had already left.

"Fucking idiots," Jimmy said under his breath. He took maybe three seconds to formulate a plan, such as it was; then he kicked the starter on the Ducati and popped the clutch.

Bassett Hound barely looked up as he rolled past him to the driver's side of the conversion van, startling his friends.

"Hand over those two bags you stole," he said.

"What?" Kaid said, eyes wide. "Are you crazy? The fucking cop is right back there, watching us."

"I don't care. Hand them over."

They heard Bassett Hound's door open and shut behind them. "Hold it right there, you little sumbitch."

"Go fuck yourself," Jimmy called over his shoulder.

Then to Kaid, his voice full of urgency, "Give me the fucking bags and scram. Now!"

Out of the window came the bags, one and then the other. Jimmy added them to the others in the backpack and revved the Ducati's engine.

"Okay, now scram! I'll see you in LA."

The van's tires spun in the loose gravel, raising a great cloud of dust. Jimmy turned to look behind him. Bassett Hound was out of his cruiser and running straight at him with fat little steps, one hand on his holster. Jimmy pulled a long wheelie and hung a left on Armantrout, a route he'd never taken before. It came to a dead end, and he had to brake hard and do a donut in the middle of the road. Coming out of the dead end, what did Jimmy see standing in the middle of the road but Officer Charlie Bassett, pistol all the way out of the holster now, pointed straight at him.

It was a showdown. High noon on Front Street. By now, Jimmy's fellow residents, some of whom he'd never seen before, had emerged from their trailers to cheer him on. He gave them a little wave with his left hand, his right hand still revving the Ducati's engine. Then he popped the clutch on the bike, hunched low over its gas tank, and took off like a rocket straight at the peace officer.

"*Hey!*" Bassett yelled, scrambling to get out of the way.

Jimmy blew by him, headed for the entrance to the trailer park.

He hung a right onto Lariat Way and another right on 283 before the tail end of a freight train slowed him. Turning in his seat, he saw Bassett coming fast in his Crown Vic, siren blaring. Then the last of the train snaked by, and Jimmy gunned it for the steep drop-off that led to the dry riverbed a hundred yards away. He hit the south embankment of the river doing fifty miles an hour and went airborne for a good three seconds. At the very top of his air, just for the hell of it, he hit an epic whip, letting the bike's rear tire fly up behind him before hauling it back down with his right leg.

Landing in the sand next to the riverbed proper, he checked over his shoulder just in time to see Bassett go airborne off the ramp to 283, all four tires of the squad car leaving the ground before landing hard in the sloping dirt road.

Damn, Jimmy thought. *That crazy sumbitch means business.*

He hauled ass under the bridge where he and Kaid had played their guitars only a few nights before, heading west along the roughest part of the river road. If Jimmy was gonna lose Bassett Hound anywhere along the river road, it would be here, he thought. And yet when he came out of the rough stretch and slowed enough to look over his shoulder, the Hound was still behind him in his careening Crown Vic.

Laughing, Jimmy opened the Ducati all the way up. If he couldn't out-motocross the cop, he'd outrun him. By the time he went under the Second Avenue bridge with its Spanish graffiti, he was doing eighty-five miles an hour. He considered continuing up the river to the ramp at the rodeo grounds a mile away, then changed his mind and took his usual exit at Wright Park, pulling off another beautiful whip before landing in the parking lot in front of the zoo. Bassett Hound had dropped out of sight by then, but evidently he'd called in reinforcements, because by the time Jimmy exited the park, heading north on Second Avenue, two more patrol cars had fallen in behind him. The chase was really on now.

He crossed the railroad tracks and ran the red light at Wyatt Earp, veering across four lanes to hang a left at Central, where he ran into road construction and had to make a detour around the Ford County Courthouse. Then he was back on Central, gunning it past his old stomping grounds at Sacred Heart, wondering idly if Sister Maggie was in there, prepping for another school year. With the school behind him, he started zigzagging down alleys and one-way streets until he crossed Comanche and came to the south side of the country club golf course, which he entered through a gap in the fence right in front of the pro shop. Once on the course, he gave the Ducati all the throttle it would take, flying across fairways and greens with nothing to slow him down but the occasional sand trap and meandering golf carts driven by senior citizens with looks of alarm on their faces. Meanwhile, Bassett and his posse of patrol cars, which had grown to four by now, had to detour all the way around the swimming pool and tennis courts.

He came off the golf course just below his childhood home, hopped two curbs, and headed up Country Club Drive. Caroline and Annie were standing in the front yard, Annie with a shovel in her hand, as he flew past. Jimmy blasted the Ducati's horn in a brief salute to them before braking hard and heading up the alley behind the house, where he slid to a stop long enough to unshoulder the backpack and sling all twelve kilos of Girl Scout Cookies through the air and over the six-foot-high fence. When he emerged from the alley, Bassett and company had made it past the pool and tennis courts and came flying down Country Club Drive at sixty or seventy miles an hour. By the time they spotted him and began to put on their brakes, he'd already headed off in the direction they'd just come from.

Here we go, he thought. *Time to lose these fools once and for all.*

In the chase that followed, a map of which would be published alongside a front-page article in the *Daily Globe*, Jimmy passed by every school he'd ever been kicked out of and every Kwik Shop he'd ever entered in the dead of night in search of rolling papers and a veggie burrito. But then he felt a skip in the Ducati's engine and looked down to see that the bike's fuel gauge was on *E*. Reaching below the seat, he switched to the Ducati's tiny reserve tank. By then, every available police and deputy sheriff's car in Ford County had been deployed, and roadblocks began to pop up. He had just turned off Sixth Avenue and started down the long slope of Morgan Boulevard when he spotted a line of squad cars parked bumper to bumper near the north entrance to Memorial Stadium. To his left, on the other side of the middle school, was an expanse of grass that might have allowed him to keep the chase going, had he had more fuel. To his right was the high chain-link fence surrounding the closed stadium.

Then he saw it. A truckload of fill dirt a maintenance crew had dumped in a driveway on the right side of the road, five feet from the stadium fence.

What was it the old man always said? No guts, no glory?

If he hit the mound of dirt just right, the air he caught would carry him over the fence and onto a sidewalk leading to the field where, if legend could be believed, Wade and Michael and, who knew, maybe even Bull Wagner himself, had scored many a touchdown back in the day.

That would be the guts part. As for the glory, well, he'd just have to wait and see about that. He twisted in his seat one last time to give Bassett Hound the finger, then turned and accelerated into the makeshift ramp.

Which, story of his life, turned out to be more like *fifteen* feet from the fence, rather than five.

At the very top of his air, he revved the Ducati's engine and hit an absolutely gargantuan whip, maybe the single best motocross trick he'd ever pulled off. But on his way down, the Ducati's back tire caught the top of the chain-link fence, sending him sailing over the bike's handlebars.

His last thought, as he swam through the air above the naked concrete, was, *My God, what a whip! I bet old Wade never pulled off anything like it!*

FORTY-THREE

The worst of the day's heat had burned off by the time Caroline and Annie pulled the wagon containing Sister Margaret's unplanted boxwoods from the garage into the house's expansive front yard. Mid-July was not an ideal time to plant anything in western Kansas, but Caroline was beyond caring about that. Annie had surprised her by agreeing to help, and this was Caroline's chance to spend some time with her, a rare treat, while also knocking something important off her never-ending to-do list. What could be better than that?

She was watching Annie hack away at a hole for the first shrub when Jimmy rode by on that motorcycle of his, horn blasting. She twisted her torso to watch as he performed a sliding turn and shot into the alley behind the house. *Oh Jimmy*, she thought. *What kind of trouble have you gotten yourself into this time?*

The sirens, which she now realized she'd been hearing for a long time, grew closer as a line of white police cars appeared at the top of the street. Then Jimmy came screaming out of the alley once again. As he passed them for the second time, something caught her eye. She waited for the last police car to disappear after him and turned to Annie.

"Did you see what I just saw?"

"You mean Jimmy getting his ass chased by the cops? Yeah, I—"

"No," Caroline said. "The *backpack*. He had one on when he headed into the alley, but not when he came back out."

Annie dropped her shovel in the grass, and together they passed through the garage into the fenced-in backyard. There, in the middle of her herb garden, lay the backpack with its blue TMP Wrestling logo. Just as she'd suspected, Jimmy had tossed the bag over the alley fence. She stood watching with bated breath as Annie dragged the bag into the sunlight and pulled back the top zipper.

"Holy shit, Mom."

"What is it?"

The girl held up a large, shrink-wrapped package of what might have been basil or dill but was not.

"Don't tell me—"

Annie nodded, sweat beading on her sun-freckled face. "We need to hide this somewhere, and I mean right now."

"Hide it?"

"*Yes.*"

Caroline's mind spun a moment before coming to an answer. "Come on. We'll bury it in that hole you were digging."

"Wait. *What?*"

"Would you rather we take it inside and ask your father what he thinks we should do?"

"Okay, okay, let's go."

Annie zipped the backpack and followed Caroline back through the garage to the front yard, where they took turns hacking at the hole in the flower bed until it was big enough to accept the bag. But just as Annie began to shovel dirt on top of it, the sound of a guitar solo Caroline knew but could not name began to drift up from the hole.

"What the hell?" Annie said.

"It's the ringtone from Jimmy's phone. I've heard it a hundred times."

"What do we do?"

"See who's calling. Hurry."

Sighing, Annie pulled the backpack from its premature grave, found the phone in the front pocket, and handed it to Caroline. She took the phone with trembling hands and hit the speaker button.

"Hello?"

"Jimmy?"

The voice was male and urgent.

"He's not here," Caroline said, waving off Annie's attempts to grab the phone away from her.

"Where is he?" the voice asked.

"I don't know exactly. May I ask who's calling?"

"Who are *you*?" the voice shot back. "More importantly, *where* are—"

She ended the call and handed the phone to Annie, who powered the thing down with a deftness Caroline never would've been able to muster. "Who was that?" Annie asked.

"I don't know. Right now, we need to focus on getting this bag buried."

"Okay, okay."

Handing the dead phone to Caroline, Annie stuffed the backpack back into the hole and covered it with dirt. Even before she was finished, Caroline knew there wouldn't be room to plant a boxwood above it. In a flash of inspiration, she uprooted a statue of the Virgin Mary from another part of the garden, planted it smack on top of the buried bag, and stood back to admire her handiwork. The statue was a tad off kilter, it was true, but who would suspect the *Mother of God* of concealing such a secret?

"What do you think?" she asked Annie.

"It's fine, but we should plant the rest of this stuff while we're at it. It's obvious someone's been digging."

Working together, they dug four more holes, two on each side of Mary, planted the boxwoods, and spread a couple of bags of cypress mulch to cover their tracks. Then they put the wagon and shovel back in their places in the garage, closed the garage door behind them, and went inside.

Annie's friend Jeremiah stood in the middle of the kitchen in his bare feet, stifling a yawn. "What were all those sirens about?" he asked.

A moment later, as if on cue, Leroy hobbled in from the living room. But before Caroline or Annie could say anything, the cordless phone in the kitchen began to ring, and they turned as one to look at it.

"Who do you suppose that is?" Annie asked.

"Only one way to find out," Leroy said, picking it up and holding the receiver to his ear. The look on his face told Caroline all she needed to know.

FORTY-FOUR

Annie retrieved her father's aluminum crutch from the trunk of her mother's Camry and stood watching as Jeremiah struggled to help Bull Wagner reach a standing position beside the passenger front door.

"This is ridiculous," she said to her mother. "Why didn't you let me pull into one of the handicapped spaces like I wanted to? It's a heck of a lot closer."

"Your father says he's not handicapped."

She shot a look at Jeremiah. Sisyphus of the Plains.

"Will you at least let me get a wheelchair? They've got a bunch of them just inside the front doors."

"No more wheelchairs," Leroy said, grabbing the crutch out of her hands. "Go on ahead, if you're in such a hurry."

"Maybe I will," Annie said.

"Go ahead," Jeremiah said. "You, too, Mrs. Wagner. Mr. Wagner and I will follow at our own pace."

"You heard him," Leroy said. "Get to going."

They found Michael waiting for them just inside the sliding glass doors to the ER. It was Michael who'd called the house to give them the news of Jimmy's accident. By some crazy coincidence, he'd been at the front desk filling out Luke's insurance paperwork when an ambulance pulled up and a couple of EMTs wheeled a gurney with Jimmy on it into the farther regions of the ER. Just to be sure it was Jimmy, he'd asked the woman at the check-in window, who'd said, "It's that crazy kid the police were chasing. The one on the motorbike. It's been all over the police scanner."

"Are they saying how bad he's hurt?" Michael had asked.

"No," the woman said. "But he wasn't wearing no helmet, so you tell me."

That was almost thirty minutes ago. It had taken that long for the family to gather their things and get Leroy loaded into the passenger seat of the Camry to make the short drive to the hospital. Even so, Michael had nothing new to report when they arrived. "He's still in with the doctors," he said. "We won't know more until they come out and tell us."

"Oh, Michael," Caroline said, her lower lip trembling.

"Mom, he's gonna be fine," he answered. "Let's find a place to sit by Vanessa and the boys."

"They're here, too?" Caroline asked.

"Yeah," Michael said with a short laugh. "A Wagner in the Dodge City emergency room. Imagine that."

It was the sort of joke, funny but with a dark underside, that Annie felt herself incapable of pulling off, especially in the presence of someone like her mother. Had Annie uttered the exact same words, they would've come out sounding like a complaint or, worse, an accusation. Whereas coming from Michael, they took on an almost philosophical character. Shit happens, you know? Especially if your last name is Wagner.

She left him to get Caroline settled in the cramped waiting area and headed back outside, where she ran into Jeremiah and her father making their shuffling progress.

"Everyone's just inside those doors," she said. "Michael, too."

Her father lumbered forward through the glass doors, clearly in pain, hyperfocused, as usual, on his goal.

"Where are you going?" Jeremiah asked.

She brought two fingers to her mouth. He nodded and the two continued past her looking like contestants in a gunny-sack race. When they were gone, she reached into her purse and brought out a crumpled pack of Marlboro Lights. There were only two cigarettes left in the pack, and one of them was broken in half. She brought her lighter to what remained of the broken one and inhaled deeply, barely managing to hold back tears. Now that she was alone, the thoughts she'd been avoiding ever since she pulled the zipper back on Jimmy's weed-laden backpack came flooding back. Why hadn't she noticed that he was up to something? All the signs had been there, from the cagey manner in which he'd received her at his derelict trailer court, to the trailer court itself, to the conversation she'd started, but then selfishly failed to pursue, the night they'd finished cutting wheat.

Where'd you get this stuff?

I grew it.

Bullshit.

No, no, I did. This dude I know from California . . .

Why hadn't she followed up on any of these blatant clues? Was she that oblivious? That crappy of a big sister? That self-absorbed?

As she raked herself across these familiar coals, the sliding doors opened behind her and Jeremiah appeared.

"I hope you saved one of those for me."

"I did." She handed him the pack and the lighter.

"There's only one left."

"Take it. I'm quitting."

"For real?"

"Yes."

"In that case, we can share it. Then we'll both quit. Together."

He put the cigarette in his mouth and made a big show of crumpling the package and tossing it toward the trash can by the door. Then he lit the cigarette and tossed the plastic lighter in the trash, too.

"I'm sorry you had to witness all this," she said, wiping at her eyes. She was officially crying now. "We must seem like the Addams Family or something. Charles Bon riding up to Sutpen's Hundred in *Absalom, Absalom!*"

He took a drag from the cigarette and tried to hand it to her. She declined, holding up what was left of her broken one.

"Wait until you meet *my* family," he said, pretending not to have noticed her tears. "Wait until you meet my *dad*. He makes Leroy look like the dude on *Leave It to Beaver*."

"Leave it to what?"

"See what I mean? You'd have to have grown up in my family to know. We didn't have cable. We didn't have TV, period. We had VHS tapes of *The Waltons* and *Leave It to Beaver*."

"And *The Incredible Hulk*."

"No, I discovered that much later, when I was in college at Boise State. Are you okay?"

"Yes," Annie said. "I am now. Thank you for asking."

She waited for him to smoke the cigarette almost to its end, then they had a mock ceremony in which they each took a final puff.

"Okay, that's it," she said. "I'm done. And I mean it this time."

"If you do, I do."

"I do," she said.

They went inside and joined in the longstanding Wagner family tradition of stoicism in the face of crisis. After a while, Jeremiah fired up a video game on his phone, and Sam and Luke joined him in playing it with the volume turned down. They waited and waited. A half hour crept by. Then another. Then Caroline stood abruptly and picked up her purse.

"I'm going to the Cathedral," she said, starting for the door. "Call me if there's any news."

Annie looked at Michael and her father, but they only shrugged.

"Mom, wait," she called, getting up to follow. "For God's sake, wait a minute."

She caught up with her just outside the sliding glass doors, where a uniformed policeman with a chirping walkie-talkie stared off into the distance and a goateed man in snakeskin boots was thumbing through his phone, cigarette in hand.

"Mom, will you *please* hold on a second?"

Caroline took a few more steps, then stopped and turned around.

"Do you really have to go?" Annie asked.

Her mother nodded. "If I stay here another second, I'm gonna scream."

"Do you want me to go with you?"

"No," Caroline said. "Thank you, though. Thank you for offering."

Annie looked down at the ground and then up into her mother's hazel eyes, which, she saw now, had also been holding back tears. "I feel so bad about all this. I was around Jimmy for days. I should've noticed something was going on."

"How do you think I feel?" Caroline said. "I'm his mother. I *knew* something was happening with him. I could *feel* it. And yet I did nothing."

They walked to her mother's Camry, and Annie held the door while she climbed inside and put on her seat belt.

"How about we both cut ourselves a little slack?" Annie said. "You go pray, and I'll hold down the fort here, and we'll just assume that everything's gonna be okay. What do you think?"

Her mother smiled and started the car. "Deal," she said. "Just be sure to call the minute you learn of any change in your brother's condition, okay?" Annie nodded. "And another thing. If Sister comes to the hospital, will you tell her where I am?"

"Of course."

Annie tried to say more, but there was no holding Caroline Wagner back once she'd decided on a course of action. All Annie could do was stand by and watch as her mother gunned the maroon car out of the parking lot and headed west on Ross Boulevard toward Our Lady of Guadalupe, a mile away.

At the door to the ER, Annie crossed paths once more with the goateed man in the snakeskin boots. The cop had gone back inside, it appeared, to wait for her brother to regain consciousness.

"Smoke?" the man asked, holding out a pack of Marlboro Reds. He was maybe ten years older than she was, and for all his politeness, gave off a creepy vibe.

"I quit," she said.

"Really?" the man said. "Well, good for you."

What was it about the man's voice? she wondered as she joined the others in the waiting room. She'd heard it somewhere before, and not long ago, either. But for the life of her, she could not remember when or where.

FORTY-FIVE

Somewhere in the middle of praying the Fourth Glorious Mystery, Caroline fell into a waking sleep in which the only realities were her aching knees and the slow repetition of words that seemed to come not from her but from the air around her. This often happened when she said the rosary. She'd learned long ago not to fight it but to "go with the flow," as Sister Margaret had advised back when Caroline was an overly enthusiastic catechumen and Sister was her equally enthusiastic sponsor. Whenever Caroline said the rosary, whether in the cathedral or in her car on a long drive, or in her office during breaks from the work she'd come to love, Sister Margaret was always there in her mind, leading the prayer, calling out the shifts from the Apostles' Creed to the Our Father to the Hail Mary to the Glory Be.

And then, the dream shifting to reality, Sister Margaret really was there, standing beside Caroline where she knelt in the shadow-laced cathedral.

"What is it?" Caroline whispered. "Is it Jimmy?"

"No," Sister whispered back. "There's still no news. Would you like me to pray with you?"

"Would you?"

"Of course. But let's walk a little first. These old knees can't kneel forever like they used to."

It always took Caroline by surprise whenever Sister mentioned her age. Yes, she'd grayed, put on some weight, and complained from time to time about the trouble she was having with an arthritic hip, which needed replacement surgery. But to Caroline, Sister was still the same inspiring if somewhat intimidating friend she'd always been.

They began a slow circle, hugging the inner wall of the cathedral. "Do you remember how hard we prayed when Wade went down the stairs at the ranch?" Caroline asked.

"Yes, of course. How could I forget that?"

"Do you think God answers the same prayer twice?"

"Absolutely. Remember what he tells us in John. *If you abide in me, and my words abide in you, ask whatever you wish, and it will be done for you.*"

"I've asked for so much over the years, though. Sometimes I worry He'll grow tired of me and stop listening."

"Nonsense. He never grows tired. He never stops listening. Now, where were you in your rosary?"

"The Assumption into Heaven."

"In the name of the Father, the Son, and the Holy Spirit . . ."

They made three trips around the circumference of the cathedral, walking in the opposite direction of the Stations of the Cross, so that the events leading up to Christ's passion were reversed, and Jesus met Mary and the women of Jerusalem *after* he'd been stripped and scourged, rather than before.

When Sister began to tire, they chose a pew near the front of the church, and Caroline kneeled while Sister sat beside her with a hand resting on her shoulder. The touch calmed her and filled her with hope. All her life, she had needed to be touched. She needed to feel connected to the people around her. One of the things she had loved about Leroy in the early days of their courtship was the way he rested his hand on her thigh when they rode around in his battered pickup. With the notable exception of

Jimmy, who arrived later in her life, she had breastfed each of her children for a full eighteen months after they were born. People gave her funny looks about it. Even close friends found ways to ask how long she planned to keep it up. "Until they don't want or need it anymore," she'd say, a note of defiance in her voice. Even with Jimmy, she'd held out past the six months her pediatrician recommended, stopping only when the tension in the house made producing enough milk almost impossible. Something died in her the day she switched him over to formula. It was the end of an era. In the years since, she'd often wondered if at least some of the troubles Jimmy had experienced in life were caused by the decision. She blamed herself for that. She should have tried harder, held out longer. Not only for his sake, but for hers, too.

She was lost in a mixture of memory and prayer when she first began to feel it. A subtle shift. A rearranging of the molecules that made up the air of the cathedral. She opened her eyes and looked over her shoulder at Sister, whose dry lips moved slowly over the words of the Our Father.

"Sister," Caroline whispered.

The white, paper-thin eyelids opened, blinked twice. "Yes? What is it?"

"I feel as though something's happened. I'm going outside to call Annie."

"Do you want me to come with you?"

"No, keep praying. I'll be right back."

She genuflected beside the pew, then turned and walked to the back of the cavernous church, passing along the way a young, bearded man who sat by himself in one of the middle pews. Their eyes met as she walked past, and she was struck by the feeling that she had seen him somewhere before. She pushed through the heavy doors to the outer lobby of the cathedral and reached into her purse for her phone. She was scrolling through her recent calls, looking for Leroy's number, when the heavy doors behind her opened and the young, bearded man stepped through. He was wearing a pair of snakeskin boots, and as soon as she saw the boots, she remembered where she'd seen him. At the hospital. He'd been standing outside smoking a cigarette when she and Annie came out.

"Put the phone away," the man said in an even voice.

"Why? Who are you?"

"A friend of your son's."

For one crazy instant, she thought he was talking about Wade. He looked about the age she imagined Wade would've been, had he lived.

"Which son?"

"Jimmy," the man said, smiling darkly. And, in that moment, she understood that he was her enemy and that he meant to do her harm.

"What's your name?" she asked.

"Kevin."

"How come I've never heard of you, Kevin?"

"You tell me. We talked briefly, remember? When I called Jimmy's phone, and you picked up?"

She looked over his shoulder at the tall wooden door on the other side of which Sister sat praying the rosary. How long would it take before Sister felt the same sinister presence she'd felt and came looking for her?

"What is it you want, Kevin?" she asked. "I know it's not to tell me you're worried about my son."

"Oh, but you're wrong about that. I'm very worried. There's a cop standing outside the ER right now, waiting for him to wake up. By now, the District Attorney is probably there, too, asking everyone questions."

"My son's fighting for his life, and you're worried about what he might say to some policeman?"

The smile fell away from the man's face. He was through with the "Jimmy's friend" business. "Where's the backpack?" he asked.

"What backpack? I don't know what you're talking about."

He laughed, showing a single gold tooth toward the back of his mouth. "You're a better liar than your son, I'll give you that."

Just then the door behind them creaked open, and Sister Margaret appeared, a look of concern in her eyes. "Caroline? Is everything all right?"

"Everything's fine, Sister," the man named Kevin said. "We're just talking. Isn't that right, Mrs. Wagner?"

She fumbled to open her phone, but Kevin reached out and took it from her hands. It was scary how easily he disarmed her.

"You don't want to do that. Now, let's try this one more time. Where's the backpack? You know, the one that had the *phone* in it that *you* answered?"

"It's at the hospital," she said. She had no idea where the words came from. They just popped out of her mouth.

"The hospital," the man repeated doubtfully.

"Yes. I was afraid the police would find it, and so I brought it to the hospital. I didn't know what else to do. It's there now. In the trunk of my daughter's car."

The man shook his head and offered a hollow laugh. "Lady, I've got to hand it to you. The lies flow out of you like water from a tap."

"But I'm not lying."

"No? Then why don't you tell me what *the hell* a package that belongs to *me*—and that ought to be on its way to *Atlanta* right now—is doing in the trunk of a car in a hospital parking lot?"

He was agitated. She could see it in the way his breathing had picked up, the way the slits of his snake-like eyes had narrowed.

"I was going to bring it inside, but then I saw that policeman, and I changed my mind."

"So you put it in the trunk of your daughter's car. Why there? Why not in the trunk of *your* car?"

"She'd just pulled into the parking lot. I can't explain it. It was easier than going back to where my car was parked, I guess."

She shut up, sensing that if she said much more, she'd dig herself a hole she'd never be able to climb out of. Even now, he only half believed her.

"What kind of car does this daughter of yours drive?" he asked.

"I don't know what kind, but it's white, four doors, has a rosary hanging from the rearview mirror." She'd seen just such a car parked at the front of the visitor's parking lot when she'd pulled out of there an hour earlier.

"A rosary, huh?" All at once, his whole demeanor changed. He believed her; at least partly so. Why? Had he noticed the white car, too, while he was out there smoking his cigarette? "Well then," he continued, "I guess we're gonna have to take a little ride over to the hospital, aren't we?"

He took her by the arm and motioned for Sister Margaret to walk out in front of them. "You're driving, Sister."

"What?" Caroline said. "She's not a part of this."

"She is now," Kevin said.

FORTY-SIX

Annie's phone—which in reality was Leroy's phone, a fact he had not forgotten—started buzzing as soon as she had walked away from it to use the ladies' room down the hall.

Leroy paused, wondering if he should answer it. But then he looked down at the little screen and saw that it was Caroline calling.

"Hello?"

"Leroy?"

"Yeah. What's going on?"

"I am outside in the parking lot," Caroline said in a voice that sounded nothing like her. "I need Annie to bring me her car keys."

"Her car keys," Leroy said. "Why? She came with us, remember?"

"Yes, that's right," Caroline said. "I need to get something out of the trunk of her car. It's right outside the door. The *white* one with the rosary."

Her words confounded him. As he ought to know, having spent four days in the shop swapping its blown flat six for a V8, Annie drove a loud, fifteen-year-old Porsche convertible with mismatched fenders. The car was not white but a weird mix of two different reds. True, since his accident, she'd also been driving one of his white ranch trucks. Was that what Caroline was talking about? He looked inside the open shoulder bag

Annie had left on her chair and found two sets of keys: the Porsche key on its long blue University at Buffalo lanyard, and the key to the ranch truck on its Kansas Livestock Association key chain.

"She's in the bathroom," he said. "Do you want me to come out there? I can bring you all the keys I'm finding, which ain't many."

"Yes," Caroline said. "Come right away. And Leroy—" Then the phone went dead in his hands.

None of it, not the sound of her voice, nor the talk about Annie's car being in the parking lot, nor the fact that she'd asked *him* to bring the keys, instead of coming in to get them herself, made a lick of sense. Still, he'd been given a job to do, so he stuffed the keys into his pocket and hauled himself to his feet beside the chair.

"Who was that?" Michael asked, looking up from the laptop balanced on his knees.

"Your mother. She's back from church and needs me in the parking lot."

"You want me to go with you?"

"No, I can handle it."

"I'll go," said the kid from Idaho, Annie's friend.

"I don't need you."

"No, I want to help," the kid said, coming out of his chair and retrieving Leroy's crutch from where it stood against the wall.

Leroy took the crutch and balanced himself on his good leg. "All right. Let's get to going."

Halfway down the hall, they ran into Annie coming back from the bathroom. "Where are you two going?" she asked.

"To help your mother. She's back from the cathedral."

"Help her how?"

"Never mind that," he said, irritated by the delay. "Just leave me be and I'll handle it."

"But—"

"But nothing. Now leave me be."

He shook free from the kid's grip and began to hop on his good leg, using the crutch to balance himself. He heard Annie say something in a whisper behind his back. That's what people did now, whispered about him behind his back as if he were a five-year-old. *To hell with them*, he thought, concentrating on his hopping.

Swearing off use of a wheelchair so early in his rehab had been a big mistake; he could see that now. But now that the mistake had been made, he felt he had no choice but to stick with it the same way he'd stuck by so many past mistakes, like working seven days a week for months at a time or denying Michael the opportunity to succeed him on the ranch or abdicating his responsibilities as a father and making Caroline raise Jimmy almost completely by herself. Admitting these mistakes soon after he made them would have been the smarter move in the long run. But there was something shameful about changing your mind once you'd started down a certain road. It was akin to cheating or welching on a bet.

Only now another thought had begun to eat at him. It first occurred to him while he was waiting for Caroline to come home after she'd stormed away following their fight about Jimmy. What if the *real mistake*, the one he'd repeated over and over in his life, was not in any single decision or public pronouncement he'd made over the years, but rather in his unwillingness to admit he'd been wrong and start over? Pulling back from his plan to limit Jimmy's ability to cash out his inheritance was a step in this new direction, as was his admission to Caroline that he'd not been the husband she deserved. What was next? Rethinking the twisted familial calculus that had rendered him, almost against his will (or so it seemed to him now), the last rancher of the Sawlog Wagner clan?

Well, okay, he thought. If it came to that, he could do it. He *would* rethink it, by God. He had no idea how or when or why, but he would.

The automatic doors at the front of the hospital gave way before him. He hopped painstakingly through them, the muscles in his good leg crying out in protest, and stood a moment in the dying light, scanning the parking lot. Caroline's maroon Camry stood fifty yards to his left, pulled over on the side of the driveway the ambulances used to deliver the sick and wounded. Sister Margaret sat behind the wheel of the car, Caroline beside her in the passenger seat. Everything about that picture was *wrong wrong wrong*. Sister hated to drive, always had.

As he stood pondering this, the headlights of the car flashed at him. Once. Twice. What the hell was that supposed to mean? Not knowing what else to do, he reached into the pocket of his jeans and took out the key to the white Dodge, dangling it before him like a talisman. In response, Caroline leaned over from the passenger seat and laid on the horn.

A dark figure, a man by the looks of it, popped up from the back seat of the car, shoved Sister against the driver's-side door, and slid, serpent-like, over the bench seat to take her place. A second later, the driver's door swung open, Sister spilled out onto the pavement, and the man tried to back the car down the long driveway, only to be blocked in by an ambulance that had just turned off Ross Boulevard.

Next, the man tried to turn left into the parking lot, but he was met there by a line of cars coming from the opposite direction. He laid on the Camry's shrill horn, but the woman in the car blocking him was blocked in, too. He tried backing up again, but the ambulance was still there, red lights silently flashing.

It was then that the man turned and looked right at Leroy where he stood on the curb of the hospital entrance. The man had no way out but the tight narrow driveway at Leroy's feet where the EMTs met incoming ambulances. Leroy returned the man's stare, chin jutted out before him, and took his first, tentative hop from the curb into the thin driveway. The man's eyes grew wide with surprise, then narrowed darkly. If it was a game of chicken Leroy wanted, he was up for that. He threw the Camry into drive and floored it. The car's front tires screamed on the asphalt.

From here on, everything seemed to happen in slow motion: the maroon Camry barreling toward him where he stood on one leg; Caroline fighting the man, clawing at his arms and face, until finally he took one hand off the wheel and knocked her against the passenger-side door with a single, vicious blow.

The evil sumbitch's trying to make off with her, Leroy thought.

He couldn't let that happen.

Gathering himself, he took one last hop into the narrow channel and pivoted so that he was facing the oncoming car, crutch raised before him like a tommy gun. The image of the crucifix pointing at him from the foot of his hospital bed flashed before him. Last rites. They'd given him last rites. If he died, he'd go straight to heaven.

As the car continued to bear down on him, Caroline grabbed at the wheel. The man wrenched it back, and for a moment, the Camry was on two wheels instead of four. It jumped a small median, missing Leroy by no more than a foot, and slammed into the first of four brick pillars holding up the roof over the entrance to the ER. The sound of the crash was terrible, a great mash-up of metal and shattering glass. In its aftermath, smoke hung in the air along with the piercing sound of the car's horn.

As onlookers rushed out, Leroy hopped on one foot to the side of the steaming wreck. He dropped his crutch on the asphalt of the driveway and pulled hard at the crinkled passenger door. It groaned and came open far enough for him to see Caroline lying in a ball beneath the deployed passenger-side airbag, eyelids fluttering wildly in the cascading white of the airbag dust.

"Are you okay?"

She nodded, and he knew then that the complicated love they'd shared through the years had not been a mistake after all. On the contrary, it was bigger than either one of them. Bigger than the Bar W. Bigger than Wade and his memory. Bigger even than the secrets they'd kept from each other.

As for the man in the snakeskin boots, he'd taken the car's steering-wheel column straight through the chest, the top half of the wheel crushing his windpipe. When the car's horn finally failed, Leroy could hear the labored rasp of his breathing.

"What about Sister?" Caroline asked. "Is she okay?"

"She's fine," Leroy said. "It takes more than a shove to the ground to hurt that gal."

He turned back to the man, whose eyes were open and pleading, his breath coming only fitfully now.

"The driver's-side airbag on this old heap deployed a couple of years ago," Leroy said. "Unfortunately for you, I never did get around to replacing it."

The man seemed to nod in recognition. A moment later, what light there was left in the man's eyes went out altogether, and Leroy knew, even before the EMTs arrived, that he was dead.

FORTY-SEVEN

The doc working in the ER that night had pulled two tours in Afghanistan, one of them in Helmand Province during the worst of the fighting there, but he'd never seen a case as strange as Jimmy's. All signs pointed to massive head trauma, maybe even permanent brain damage, and yet, while his team was busy discussing what to do next, an orderly happened to walk into the room with a barely audible beat spilling out of earbuds he had hanging around his neck, and Jimmy opened his eyes and said in a loud, clear voice, "'LA Woman'! Turn that shit up!"

The doc, a Doors fan going way back, recounted the scene in detail two hours after the fact. Jimmy himself had no memory of hearing the song—or of anything else, for that matter, after looking down to see the Ducati's fuel gauge tipping toward *E*.

"What are you saying?" he asked.

"I'm saying you've got the hardest head I've ever witnessed. Like a coconut inside a coconut. Either that, or you're just lucky, I don't know. Both, maybe."

"Cool," Jimmy said. "Can I go?"

He tried to sit up, but even this small movement made his head throb as if there were a monkey sitting on his shoulder wielding a ball-peen hammer, tapping away with purpose.

"You're kidding, right?" the doc said with a laugh. "There's a cop right outside the door. The only reason he's not in here right now, grilling you, is because I've been holding him off. Then there's your lawyer—he's your brother, right?—and the woman from the Hutch paper, and the TV crew from Wichita that choppered in here like they were on a special-ops mission to trigger my PTSD."

Jimmy lowered his head carefully until it found its place on the lumpy hospital pillow. Sunset on Malibu Beach. Orange ball kissing the ocean goodnight. Beautiful, bikinied girl singing "It's a Longer Road to California Than I Thought." Gone, man. Just gone.

"Then there's your family," the doc was saying. "There's got to be ten of them out there, including this older lady, a nun by the look of her—"

"Sister Maggie."

"Sister Maggie, okay. Anyway, I tell them the whole 'LA Woman' story, how crazy it is that you can even *talk* after the crack to the melon you took, and Sister Maggie pipes up with, *It's a miracle, doctor. That's what it is. A miracle.* And I'm like, *You know what? I don't have a better answer, so we'll just go with that. A miracle. Sure.* And you know what she says to me?'"

"What?"

"She says, and I quote, *He was, after all, a gift from God.* And right there at her elbow, kind of leaning in to hear, was the woman from the Hutch paper and the TV newswoman who'd just climbed down off that chopper. I wouldn't be at all surprised if the headline in tomorrow's *Hutch News* reads something like, 'GIFT FROM GOD' CRASHES MOTORCYCLE AFTER HIGH-SPEED CHASE. SURVIVAL DEEMED 'MIRACLE' BY LOCAL RELIGIOUS AUTHORITY."

I'll never get out of here, Jimmy thought. *I'll be, like, forty years old, driving some beater car with the muffler falling off, pulling into Leroy and Caroline's driveway.* But then another memory, this one from well before the Ducati's fuel gauge tipped toward *E*, came back to him. The backpack, baby. He could still see it floating over the redwood fence, the sky a brilliant blue; could hear it (or so he imagined) landing in his mother's garden with a satisfying thud. *Well, okay*, he thought. *Maybe the dream isn't DOA after all.*

The doc took a little penlight out of the breast pocket of his lab coat and shone it into one eyeball, then the other. "Anyway, we're gonna run a few more tests, you know, follow all the appropriate protocols and such, and only when I'm satisfied the *miracle* has taken am I gonna let any of them through that door."

"Thank you," Jimmy said.

"Not a problem. It isn't every night we get this kind of excitement around here. Most of the time, it's just car wrecks and beef-plant workers with self-inflicted knife wounds and the like. But you, man. You're a different kind of animal altogether."

"So I've been told."

After the doc was gone, Jimmy lay with his eyes half-closed, watching the light fade behind the room's thin curtains. It was good, in a fucked-up sort of way, to think of his family gathered out in the hall or the waiting room or wherever they were. He pictured them one by one, Leroy, Caroline, Michael and his family, Annie, and the old boss lady herself, Sister Maggie. He pictured them coming together in the middle of the waiting area in some kind of corny-as-hell group hug, Sister Maggie leading them in prayer. *Lord, we offer you our thanks for the miracle you have performed this evening. We thank you also for the gift of Jimmy. What would we do without him, Lord? Oh, what would we ever do?*

He smiled, his eyes beginning to well with tears. All that was missing from the picture was him.

FORTY-EIGHT

Annie woke, fully dressed, on the overstuffed couch in the basement of her parents' house in town, her body forming an S that fit perfectly within the larger S formed by Jeremiah's body. They had lain like this for hours, drifting in and out of talk and sleep, neither of them willing to break the position or the spell of certainty it seemed to create around them. Before drifting off the last time, they'd agreed that Jeremiah would stay another day or two in Dodge before heading up to Idaho to see JJ and settle matters between him and Emily. Annie had surprised them both by suggesting he take her car instead of the CB750.

"Frankenporche?" Jeremiah had said. "Are you serious?"

"Yeah, I don't think I can stand any more whining about your back," Annie said. "Just bring her back in one piece, okay?"

"Oh, I will," Jeremiah said with a chuckle. "But you can quit acting so tough. I know you're sweet on me."

"You wish," she said.

At six, the alarm on her phone went off, and she went upstairs to brew a pot of coffee. Her father was already up, sitting in one of the kitchen chairs with his aluminum crutch standing before him like a ladder he was about to climb.

"The trial starts at nine," he said. "Are you coming?"

"I'll be there. But first I've got to run out to the ranch and feed the horses and dogs."

She poured two cups of black coffee and set one in front of her father. He nodded his thanks. "You surprised me the other night when you asked about that red Scirocco your brother used to drive. What made you remember that?"

"Something Jacob said to me. Did you know he and Wade ran together a little bit, back when they were both in high school?"

He took a sip of the coffee. "Pass me that sugar."

She passed the sugar bowl across the table and he stirred a teaspoon into his cup and took another sip. "I'm guessing you mean that night they showed up drunk at the homeplace? Yeah, I remember that."

"What do you remember? Jacob says Wade was out of it."

"Hess was the drunker of the two, I know that. Your brother came through the back door with him thrown over his shoulder like a sack of horse feed. Hess was just a little guy in those days, could've wrestled 103 easy if he'd been so inclined, which I don't believe he was. Anyway, I asked your brother what in God's name he thought he was doing hauling a drunk kid down the basement stairs at two in the morning, and he said it was because Hess couldn't go home like that. If he did, his dad would beat him to within an inch of his life. I knew Hess's dad a little bit. If the way he treated horses was any indication, I could see that. But to me the bigger issue was the shape they were in. Neither one had any business driving up to Jetmore or anywhere else that night."

"Interesting," Annie said. "Was this the night Dodge lost in the playoffs? Wade's last high school football game?"

He nodded slowly, remembering. "Your brother played a hell of a game that night, but it wasn't close to being enough. Our O-line that year was like Swiss cheese. Holes everywhere."

Annie got up to pour a cup of coffee for Jeremiah. "According to Jacob," she said, "Wade saying all kinds of crazy stuff like how he hated football and wrestling and wanted to get the hell out of

Dodge just as soon as he could. To hell with college and the ranch, too. He was done with all of it."

Her father laughed. "You knew your brother. Does that sound like him?"

"No," she said. "But, I mean, it's possible, right?"

He sat there, considering it. "Well, sure. I guess anything's possible. But tell me this. If everything Hess remembers is true, then why did your brother roust Michael out of bed at eight o'clock the next morning so they could drive fourteen miles into town and get in a couple of hours of drilling in the wrestling room? Does that sound like somebody who was 'done with everything'?"

She stood and put her hand on his shoulder. The physical therapy he'd begun to do on the exercise table Michael had ordered out of Wichita was beginning to pay off. She could feel muscle where only weeks before there had been only bone. "I don't know, Dad. I'll see you later this morning, okay?"

"Okay," he said.

She carried the cup of coffee she'd fixed to where Jeremiah sat on the couch with his eyes half open.

"My dad's upstairs. You should go up and keep him company."

He took the coffee, his eyes searching hers in the dim light of the room. "What about you? Where are you going?"

"I've got something I have to do. When I'm finished, I'll swing by and pick you up. Don't let my parents or Michael guilt you into going to the courthouse with them. They're gonna want to get there crazy early."

He nodded, a smile breaking out across his pale face, where the black of his beard was coming in nicely. "I still can't believe you're letting me take Frankenporsche to Idaho. Are you sure you trust me that much?"

"I don't know," Annie said. "I guess we're getting ready to find out, aren't we?"

She was throwing hay to the horses in the big corral when she looked up and saw Hess's F-250 coming up Back Trail Road, saving her a trip to the small farmstead he rented on Eagle Road a couple of miles east of Hains Lake. It seemed like weeks had passed since she'd announced she was going into town to see Jeremiah and Hess had responded by saying he'd be "back to get his mare." In reality, though, the scene had played out only the previous morning. She stood watching as he opened the gate to the pasture across the road, caught Miss Kitty (no coffee can of grain for him), and loaded her into the trailer.

Well, that's that, Annie thought.

She began to walk out to the road to meet him, but he saved her that trip, too, driving right up to the corrals and switching off the truck's ignition so that it rumbled to a halt. As the dust of his arrival rolled past them, he held out from the cab a short stack of books which included *All the Pretty Horses, The Next Rodeo*, and a couple of others.

"I was hoping you'd keep those," Annie said.

"Nah, you take 'em," he said. "I was only half pretending to like 'em, anyway."

She took the books and held them close against her chest. "Really? You could've fooled me."

"All right, I did like the McCarthy one."

"And were you only pretending to like me, too?"

"No, that was real enough, I'm sorry to say."

"*Sorry*? Really, Jacob?"

He took a pack of cigarettes from the dash and offered her one. She declined, and he lit one for himself and sat smoking it a moment, his tan forearm resting on the base of the window frame. "The feeling I got, almost out of the gate, was that one way or another the whole deal was gonna end up being above my pay grade. I think I was proved right about that, too. Mr. Idaho rolling into town just speeded up the process." He rolled the tip of the cigarette against the rim of a Mountain Dew can, clearing it of ash. "Or would you disagree with that?"

"I didn't run to town and jump into bed with him, if that's what you're asking."

Seeing him smoke made her want a cigarette, too, but a promise was a promise, even if she'd only made it to herself. "Before driving out this morning, I asked my dad about the night you gave Wade a ride home from the lake. His memory of that night is quite a bit different from yours."

"Different how?"

"Well, to begin with, he says *you* were the one who was too drunk to go home that night. He paints this picture of Wade coming up the steps of the house with you slung over his shoulder like a sack of horse feed."

"Really," Hess said.

She nodded. "He seems to think your whole memory of that night is just you projecting your own anxieties and fears onto Wade."

"Leroy said that. He used the words 'projecting anxieties.'"

"Well, no. But that's what he meant. That's what he thinks."

"And what do you think?" Hess asked.

She had given the question some thought while driving out from town that morning, purposely taking the longer way on Highway 283 so she could get the Porsche above a hundred and ten, the speed at which her synapses really started firing.

"I think he's right, Jacob. I think that's what all of us have been doing for a long time." She worried that he'd grow impatient and look away, but he didn't, so she continued. "I mean, who knows who Wade *really* was? Who knows what he would've done, who he would've become, had he lived? Nobody, that's who. Not me, not you, not my father or brother or anyone else. I used to think Wade was frozen in time, you know? 'Forever young,' like the dead athlete in the Housman poem. But now I see it's not true. He changes all the time along with our memories of him. He's constantly changing, constantly becoming who we need him to be. For you, maybe that's a guy you don't have to worry about measuring up to, because as it turns out, *you* were the one who stuck it out around here, or anyway returned, while he was the quitter—"

He started to say something, but she held up a hand, stopping him.

"And for me, maybe he's the opposite. This impossible ideal that none of the men I've known over the years ever had a *prayer* of measuring up to. Which has been convenient, in a way, because it's allowed me to do whatever I wanted to do, whenever I wanted to do it, with no regrets or second guesses to get in the way."

"Okay," he said, allowing her the point. "But what's any of this got to do with us? With you and me. Right here. Right now."

"Isn't it obvious? We're doing the same thing with each other! Take you, for instance. There's this girl you need me to be, this smart, feisty girl on a horse who loves Kansas unconditionally and just *might* be in line to inherit her father's four-thousand-acre ranch. Only it turns out that's not who I am. Not really."

Again, he started to say something, and again she stopped him.

"Just wait. I'm almost finished. I haven't told you what I've needed *you* to be, which is this handsome, stoic cowboy, in his own way forever young, who loves to spend time with me on *my* terms, not his, and who by definition will never ask *anything* in return, let alone insist on 'putting all his cards on the table,' as you've recently been threatening to do like this was some kind of high-stakes poker game."

He took a final drag from the cigarette and dropped it into the Mountain Dew can, where it made a faint hiss before going out. "Can I say something now?"

"Sure," she said. "Go right ahead."

"Wouldn't it have been a whole lot easier just to look me in the eye and say, 'Sorry, bud. You lost, and the other guy won. I like him more than I like you.'"

She looked him in the eye. "It's not that simple, but okay. If you want to make this about 'all-in' or 'all-out,' then I'm sorry, but I'm afraid it's gonna have to be 'out' for me."

"Alrighty, then. That's all I needed to hear."

He swung open the driver's door and brushed by her as he walked around to the back of the trailer and opened it.

"I got something else that belongs to you, though."

"Jacob, no—"

"Yes." He stepped into the trailer and untied Miss Kitty and led her out. "She's your horse, not mine. It's been that way since you first climbed on her, but I didn't realize it until I was riding her yesterday, and she kept looking back toward the house, wishing it was you who was on her and not me. That don't happen to me very often. Ever, in fact." He held out the lead rope. "Go on, take it. Before I do something uncowboy-like and start crying or something."

She reached for the rope, and he dropped it into her hand. Then, as she stood balancing the stack of books in one hand and holding the halter rope in the other, he dropped the pin on the trailer door, climbed into the cab of the truck, and started it in a cloud of diesel smoke.

"Jacob, I don't know what to say."

"Then don't say anything." He brought his hand to the brim of his Stetson. "Ma'am. We'll be seeing you."

And in this way she succeeded in giving him the last word, even though that word, perhaps inevitably, was her.

FORTY-NINE

Michael sat behind the narrow table on the third floor of the Ford County Courthouse, waiting for Judge John R. Stevens to appear. Beside him at the table, lower lip trembling, eyes darting here and there as though in search of hidden dangers, sat Chester Stewart in his bib overalls and mail-order boots. Next to him, in a wheelchair, a quilt smelling strongly of woodsmoke thrown over her legs, sat Fanny Stewart. Michael exhaled through his nose and looked at the blue watch face of the Rolex Submariner he'd received upon making partner at Curtis, Frederick, and Lyles five years before. "Down payment on a gold one," Russ Frederick had said, slapping him on the back. Well, they'd see about that.

He was as prepared for a case as he'd ever been in his life, and yet he still felt antsy and lightheaded, his stomach in knots. It was the same way he'd felt before big football games and wrestling matches, and, as he'd done then, he turned and made a quick tally of his people. In the first row, their heads tipped toward each other in whispered conversation, sat Vanessa and his mother. The two women looked up as he saw them, and Vanessa nodded slowly, her eyes betraying a spark of competitive fire. Now that they'd compared notes on the case, she was almost as all-in as his father, who sat with Sam and Luke at the end of the same row, his chin jutting out before him in classic Bull Wagner fashion. "No matter how this thing turns out," he'd said to Michael as they stood in front of the elevator in the outer hall, "there ain't another man, dead or alive, I'd rather go into battle with than you." Michael had been too nervous and preoccupied to register the full weight of these words, but as he recalled them now, he felt a catch in his throat.

In the row behind Leroy sat the expert medical witness out of Tulsa his friend Skip had recommended. The guy was a gun-for-hire if Michael had ever seen one, but he knew his stuff. The report he'd written after examining the Stewarts was a masterpiece of detail and implication, and Michael didn't doubt he'd be even more persuasive when he took the stand. He stole another glance at the Submariner. The sweep hand was just gliding past 8:57. As he did so, the door at the back of the courtroom swung open, and in strode Annie dressed in jeans and her trademark red boots, her friend from Buffalo following closely behind. She must have been in a hurry, Michael thought, because she hadn't bothered to remove the spurs from the heels of the boots. The sound of them trailed after her like tinkling bells with every step she took. Just like that, all the people he needed to be there were present and accounted for. He could feel the knot in his stomach begin to relax.

At nine o'clock sharp, Judge Stevens, a former Marine a few years younger than Leroy, emerged through a door behind the bench and took his seat. "Is the plaintiff ready to proceed?"

"Ready, Your Honor," Michael said.

"The defense?"

"Ready," said Branch's lawyer, a tall, silver-haired man named Melvin Sparks.

"Mr. Wagner, call your first witness."

Michael turned and looked at where Byron Branch sat with a confident, almost smug look on his tanned face. He had on a gray business suit and a pair of wirerimmed reading glasses Michael suspected were a prop.

"We call Byron J. Branch, Your Honor."

Branch turned to his lawyer in surprise and the two men put their heads together briefly. Calling Branch right out of the gate had been Vanessa's idea. Better to get his version of the story on the record first, so that Chester's later testimony could have its maximum effect. Michael didn't look at his notes once the whole time Branch was being sworn in. Instead, he kept his eyes fixed on Branch's eyes, challenging him to what amounted to a stare-down.

"Mr. Branch, how do you know Chester Stewart and Fanny Stewart?"

"They're neighbors of mine," Branch answered, returning Michael's stare.

"Neighbors?"

"Well, more like tenants, I guess."

"Is that all?"

"Chester used to work for me at the Flying J."

"Doing what?"

"He washed trucks."

Michael picked up a paper from one of the stacks before him on the table. "And how much was Mr. Stewart paid?"

"I don't see what difference—"

"I'm not asking what difference you see or don't see," Michael said in a stern voice. "I asked how much Mr. Stewart was paid to work at the truck wash. Simple question."

Branch's eyes narrowed briefly behind the fake glasses. He stole a glance at Sparks, who nodded.

"I don't know. Minimum wage, I would guess."

"That would be a very good guess," Michael said, getting up to hand Judge Stevens the photocopied pay stub he'd been holding. "Seven dollars and twenty-five cents an hour is exactly what Mr. Stewart made washing trucks for you at the Flying J. That would amount to, what, a little under three hundred dollars a week, call it twelve hundred a month, before taxes. Of course, that's only if Mr. Stewart worked forty hours, and most weeks, he didn't come close to that. Fifteen or twenty would be more like it."

Branch shrugged.

"In spite of the low pay, you cared quite a bit about Chester Stewart, didn't you, Mr. Branch?"

"Cared?" Branch asked. "What do you mean?"

"You looked after his interests. Especially his financial interests."

"I don't know about that."

Branch's lawyer stood to object, but Judge Stevens waved him off. Michael picked up a manilla file folder from the table and held it up. "Isn't it true that your accountant filed a tax return on behalf of Mr. and Mrs. Stewart in each of the last two years he worked for you?"

Branch shifted in his seat. "You know it's true, or you wouldn't have asked me."

Michael glanced at Judge Stevens.

"Just answer the question, Mr. Branch."

"Okay," he said, shifting back in his chair. "Yes, the bookkeeper at the Flying J filed a couple of back returns for Chester."

"At your suggestion?"

"I suppose that's right."

"You *suppose*?"

"I asked him to, okay?"

"Why, though?" Michael asked. "I mean, you have a lot of employees across your different businesses, Mr. Branch. More than twenty, if I'm recalling the number correctly. I'm guessing you don't have your accountant file back returns for any of *them*."

Again, Branch shrugged.

"Then why the special treatment for Mr. Stewart?"

"I don't know that it was special. I was talking to him one day, and out of the blue he told me he hadn't filed a tax return in years. When I heard that, I figured the government probably owed him a big refund. That turned out not to be the case, but it was worth a try, I thought."

"I see," Michael said. "You were trying to help Mr. Stewart. You were looking after his interests, especially his financial interests."

"I didn't say that."

"Well, what are you saying? That you *weren't* trying to help Mr. Stewart?"

"It was a small thing," Branch said, taking off the fake glasses, so that for the first time Michael could feel the full intensity of his icy blue eyes.

"Well, let's see then. If you weren't trying to help Mr. Stewart, then I guess you must have had some other reason for filing a tax return on his behalf. Maybe you knew good and well that Mr. Stewart was in no condition to file a return, that he lacked the wherewithal even to know what he was signing—"

"Now wait one minute—" Branch said.

"—and by filing it for him, not only would you know virtually everything about Mr. Stewart's financial situation, you'd also have gotten Mr. Stewart to trust you."

"Objection!" Sparks said, coming out of his seat.

"Sit down, Mr. Sparks," Judge Stevens said. "I'm going to allow this."

"Well?" Michael asked. "Wasn't that it, Mr. Branch?"

Branch sat forward in his seat, his hands on his thighs, blue eyes burning into Michael's eyes. "No, that wasn't it. I was doing the guy a favor, that's all."

"You were trying to help him."

"Sure."

"With his finances?"

"With his taxes, yes."

"Because, in your opinion, he wasn't capable of doing it himself?"

"I didn't say that."

"No. But you knew it, didn't you, Mr. Branch? You knew everything there was to know about Chester Stewart and his financial situation, including whether or not he could afford, or even *understand*, the terms of the loan you made to him."

"Objection," Sparks said.

"Withdrawn," Michael said. "I'm through with this witness."

His blood was really pumping now, but on another level, he felt calm. He was in a zone, the same zone he'd achieved once or twice on the football field or the wrestling mat, when everything his opponent did felt like it was happening in slow motion, and he could see two or three moves ahead. It was this feeling he'd been chasing when he told Russ Frederick he wanted to take more cases to court rather than settling for their backroom brand of litigation. Squeezing the clip on the Submariner's stainless steel wrist band, he slid the watch from his wrist and laid it face down on the table before him.

On cross-examination, Melvin Sparks did his best to paint a picture of his client as a disinterested third party in a land deal that was really between Chester Stewart and his sister in Colorado. But it was a tough sell given the way Michael had framed the matter. Either Branch was trying to help, or he was trying to do harm, and either way he was culpable. Suddenly the idea that Judge Stevens might rule that Branch had a legally binding "fiduciary duty" to Chester seemed not so far-fetched after all.

After Sparks had finished his cross-examination, Michael called his expert witness from Tulsa, who testified that Chester suffered from dementia and was in no condition to understand the terms of the loan he'd signed. In his cross, Sparks raised the question of why, if all this was true, the folks at the Southwest Kansas Area Agency on Aging would allow Chester Stewart to act as his invalid wife's sole caretaker.

"Money, of course," the expert said. "I've seen it happen a lot, if you want to know."

Sparks rolled his eyes dramatically. "Well, I guess it's a good thing we've got someone like you, from someplace bigger and more sophisticated than southwest Kansas, to explain all this stuff to us. I don't know if we'd be able to get along otherwise."

"Objection," Michael said.

"No need, no need," Sparks said, raising his hands in mock surrender. "I withdraw that last statement."

Finally, just as he and Vanessa had talked about, Michael called Chester Stewart to the stand. It was painful to witness the confusion on Chester's face as he stood up from his chair and looked around, at a loss for what to do next.

"They want you go up there," Fanny said, pointing at the witness stand.

Still the man didn't move or even acknowledge what had been said to him. In the end, Michael had to take Chester by the elbow and lead him step by step to the stand.

"Mr. Stewart, I need to ask you a couple of questions about the loan you took out with Mr. Branch," Michael said after the man had been sworn in. "Is that okay?"

Chester nodded, his eyes wandering nervously from Michael to where Fanny sat in her wheelchair.

"The loan you signed with Mr. Branch required monthly payments of twenty-five hundred dollars." Michael consulted the loan paperwork. "Two thousand five hundred twenty-four dollars and fifty-nine cents, to be exact. Is that correct?"

"Is that what your paper says?" Chester asked.

Michael nodded. "It does say that, yes."

"Then I guess that's right."

"It also says that you made the first payment on the day the loan was signed. Would you mind telling the court where you got the money to make that payment?"

Again, Chester's eyes darted to Fanny.

"Mr. Stewart? Can you please tell the court where you got the money to make the first installment on the loan?"

"Which was that?" Chester asked.

"The money to make the first payment of twenty-five hundred dollars on the loan you got from Mr. Branch. Where did the money come from? Did you write a check? Go into town and withdraw the money from a savings account?"

A look of confusion clouded Chester's face. "My son would know."

"Your son?"

"Yes, he takes care of all of that kind of stuff, Ronnie does."

Michael paused, unsure of how to continue. Then Fanny blurted out from her wheelchair, "You'll have to excuse him, judge. He gets confused sometimes. Our son Ronnie is dead. He was killed twenty years ago in a boating accident over at El Dorado."

"I see," Judge Stevens said. "Will both attorneys approach the bench?"

Michael let Sparks pass before him and then followed him up to the bench, where Stevens sat with his hand covering his microphone. "Will one of you tell me what in God's name is going on here?"

"This is just who Mr. Stewart is, Your Honor," Michael said. "His mental condition is one of the essential facts of this case."

"Mr. Sparks?"

"All due respect, Your Honor," Sparks said, "but if forgetfulness was an excuse for not repaying a loan, half of Ford and Hodgeman Counties would be off the hook, wouldn't they?"

Stevens glared at both of them, his eyes finally coming to rest on Michael. "I want this line of questioning wrapped up as soon as possible, you hear me? I won't have Mr. Stewart made into a spectacle in my courtroom."

"Yes, Your Honor."

"Back away. Both of you."

Chester's testimony continued the same as before. Michael would ask a question, Chester would get confused, Michael would rephrase the question, and Chester or Fanny would reply with some bizarre *non sequitur*, causing Judge Stevens to knead his forehead in despair. Finally, after establishing that the initial payment on the loan had drained the couple's life savings, Michael shrugged and said, "No further questions, Your Honor."

In spite of everything that had happened up to that point, Sparks insisted on trying to cross-examine Chester. However, when Chester began to refer to Byron Branch as "Ronnie," Sparks changed his mind, and Chester was allowed to return to his seat next to Fanny.

"Call your next witness, Wagner," Judge Stevens said.

"We rest, Your Honor."

"Well, thank goodness. Your turn, Sparks."

"The defense calls Leroy Wagner."

This is it, Michael thought. *This is where we either win this thing going away, or we lose in a cloud of competing greed.*

Even at this late date, after all the hours he and his father had spent together, bonding as never before over the gaudy details of Byron Branch's thieving ways, Michael couldn't be certain his father didn't want the Stewarts' land every bit as much as Branch had. That was just the way with ranchers, to always look over the fence at the next guy's land, wondering if and when he would lose his grip on it and be forced to sell, and if so, who would be lucky enough to snatch it up, and at what price? To acknowledge this bedrock reality was not to say that Leroy, like Branch, wanted to *steal* the Stewarts' land. That had never been his way. But if it happened that the Stewarts *did* have to sell some land to stay in their house, well, who better to help them than their good friend and neighbor, Bull Wagner?

Only, now that I'm involved, it won't be Dad alone who gets to decide, Michael thought. *So maybe the real question is not what Bull Wagner wants, what he's been waiting for so patiently all these years, but what do I want? How far down this particular road am I willing to travel?*

He watched as Leroy scooted to the end of the row and stood up with the aid of his solitary crutch. Annie's friend from Buffalo sprang up to help, but Leroy shooed him away. He would do it himself, by God. As the man hopped on his good leg with the aid of the single crutch, his other leg balanced before him in a position that suggested a punter about to kick a football down the field, Michael was visited by yet another thought: that this image before him, with its strange combination of sacrifice and nearly indomitable will, defined his father every bit as much as his rancher's desire to acquire and hold land.

"Please state your name for the record."

"Leroy Wagner."

"Do you swear to tell the truth, the whole truth, and nothing but the truth?"

"You're damn right, I do."

A wave of nervous laughter washed over the courtroom. "Mr. Wagner, I have to warn you," Judge Stevens began. Michael turned to look at where Annie sat beside Caroline, their eyes wide like his eyes, their mouths forming identical O shapes. *The stubborn sumbitch didn't hear a word I told him*, Michael thought.

After the judge finished chastising Leroy for his language, Melvin Sparks rose from his place beside Byron Branch and asked his first question. "Mr. Wagner, did you recently have occasion to visit Mr. Branch at his home?"

"Yes, I did," Leroy said, his black eyes looking straight at the lawyer, tracking him as he left his place behind the table and walked toward the witness stand.

"And while you were there, did you tell Mr. Branch that you were giving him a 'last chance'?"

"That's right."

"And what did you mean by that? Last chance to what?"

"To give back the land he stole. I mean, that's why we're here, right?"

Oh boy, Michael thought. *Here we go.*

Sparks offered a thin smile in reply, then turned to Judge Stevens. "Permission to treat this witness as hostile, Your Honor?"

"Go right ahead," Stevens said.

"Isn't it true, Mr. Wagner, that you went to Mr. Branch's house that day because you wanted to threaten and intimidate him?"

Leroy shook his head. "No, that's not right."

"And when that didn't work, you tried to run Mr. Branch over with your pickup, didn't you? In his own driveway, you tried to run him down."

Leroy laughed and shook his head. "What, you think I was trying to kill Branch?"

"Well? Were you?"

"Not even close. Because, believe me, if it had been my intention to *kill* him, that sumbitch would be dead right now."

Michael closed his eyes. It was just as he'd feared. Leroy was gonna bull his way through his testimony the same way he'd bulled his way through everything else in his life. Head down. Caution to the wind.

"I don't doubt that one bit," Sparks said. "You strike me as exactly that kind of person. The kind of person who'd—"

"Objection," Michael said. "Argumentative."

"Sustained," Judge Stevens said. "Ask your next question, Sparks."

Sparks threw his shoulders back, making himself tall. "Isn't it true, Mr. Wagner, that this whole suit was your idea? That you went to the Stewarts and talked them into bringing it? That, in fact, you're paying for it out of your own pocket?"

"I haven't paid anyone a dime," Leroy said.

Well, that was true as far as it went, Michael thought. The old man's habit of sitting on unpaid bills had saved him there. It was Michael, not his father, who'd paid Harold Krebs what he was owed; Michael who'd managed, with Russ Frederick's blessing, to convince the firm to write off the rest of the suit as pro bono work.

"But even if I was the one paying," Leroy continued, "that doesn't change the fact that Byron Branch *stole* that land right out from under the Stewarts. That's what matters here. That's what we've got to keep our eye on."

"So you say, Mr. Wagner," Melvin Sparks said. "But you know what I see when I look at this whole deal? I see a sore loser, Mr. Wagner. I see a man who lost out on his chance to get his hands on land he already thought of as his—"

"Objection!" Michael said, coming out of his chair.

"Withdrawn," Sparks said. "Your Honor, I'm through with Mr. Wagner."

Michael remained standing while Sparks returned to his seat. He needed to ask something to minimize the damage Leroy had done with his undisciplined testimony. But what remained to be asked? Nothing that he could think of, especially if he meant to stay true to the very first rule they taught you in law school, which was never to ask a question you don't already know the answer to. He turned and looked at Vanessa where she sat by his mother. She gave him a single, confident nod, as if to say, *Go for it. What have you got to lose?*

He turned back to his father. "Mr. Wagner, opposing counsel has implied that you involved yourself in this case because you stood to gain something for yourself. Is that true?"

"No."

"Okay, then. Why did you get involved?"

Leroy paused, his eyes sweeping across the room to take in Branch and Sparks where they sat behind their table, then Caroline and Annie and Vanessa where they sat behind the Stewarts, then the Stewarts themselves. "Because I made a promise, that's why."

"A promise to whom?"

He nodded across the courtroom. "To them. The Stewarts."

"Go on."

"It was twenty years ago this summer," Leroy continued. "I remember because it was right after their boy, Ronnie, drowned in El Dorado Lake, and just before our oldest boy, your brother, died of a brain tumor." He stopped, gathering himself. "Of course, I didn't know any of that was coming at the time. All I knew was that they were neighbors, and they were hurting. And so, when the funeral was over, I asked Chester if there was anything I could do to help, and he said to me, 'I need to get out from under these cows and rent the pasture.' And I told him, right then and there, I'd do it. I'd buy his cows and rent the pasture and do whatever else they needed me to do, for as long as they needed me to do it. I didn't know that in another couple of weeks it would be us, me and you and your mother and sister, sitting at Wade's funeral, feeling all that pain and confusion." He turned in his seat to look at Judge Stevens, then across the courtroom at Byron Branch. "If you haven't been through it, if you haven't lost a child like that, had one taken from you like that, there one second, then *boom*, gone forever the next, well, you've just got no idea, that's all, and there ain't a soul in the world who can explain it to you. I'll tell you this, though. A promise is a promise, and I aim to keep mine."

Michael allowed his father's words to settle over the courtroom like a blanket of snow after a long drought. When the sun came out, the snow would slowly melt into the ground, causing the grass to come up a little greener in the spring, after the snow had been long forgotten. "No more questions, Your Honor."

A little before noon, Judge Stevens retired to his chambers. Michael spoke quietly with Chester and Fanny Stewart, reassuring them that they'd have a verdict soon, then gave his mother and Annie a hug, and sat down next to Vanessa, putting his arm around her shoulders. "Well, that's it," he said. "I guess we'll know soon whether we won or lost."

Vanessa leaned in close, her hand on his. "Your dad, though. Holy cow."

He turned and looked at where Leroy sat listening to some question Sam was putting to him, then back at Vanessa. "Yeah. Holy cow is right."

At a quarter past twelve, earlier than Michael was expecting, the door behind the bench opened and Judge Stevens resumed his seat. Michael had to scramble to make it back to his place beside the Stewarts.

"On the questions of fraud and fiduciary responsibility, as well as the larger question of punitive damages, I'm finding in favor of Mr. Branch," Stevens said, looking straight at Michael. "You overstepped yourself there, son."

Michael looked down as Branch and Melvin Sparks began to pat each other on the back.

"I wouldn't celebrate just yet," Stevens said, turning to them. "Mr. Branch, I have to say that I'm fairly appalled by this whole situation, and especially the part you so clearly played in it from start to finish. But at the end of the day, the citizens of Ford

County aren't paying me to be appalled. They're paying me to decide cases based on clear legal principles, and here are mine. By your actions in this matter, Mr. Branch, you made a promise to the Stewarts that you later broke in the very terms of the loan you extended them. Because of that broken promise, I'm giving the Stewarts sixty days to refinance, get current on their payments, or put the land they attempted to buy—when it was abundantly clear they couldn't afford it—up for sale at public auction." Then *smack*!—the gavel fell. "That's it. We're adjourned."

Michael turned to Chester and Fanny Stewart, who looked at him with a mixture of incomprehension and fear.

"You got your house and your land back," he said. "Congratulations."

"But what was that about sixty days?" Fanny asked.

"Don't worry about that right now," Michael said. "The main thing is, the judge ordered a do-over on the loan, and we've got time to make it right. And this time, it *will* be done right. You've got my promise on that."

"Thank you," Fanny said. "You're a good man."

He shook Chester's calloused hand, then stood and made his way to the far side of the courtroom, where his father waited in that pose suggestive of a punter, albeit a left-footed one.

"You did good," Leroy said.

"You think so? I still can't believe Stevens let Branch off scot-free like that. I mean, didn't you think we proved he set out from the beginning to rob the Stewarts?"

"Well, sure," Leroy said. "But don't forget, Judge Stevens has to live here, too. Same as Branch. Same as me and the Stewarts."

"And that makes it okay?"

"Of course not. But tell me this. Did Byron Branch get what he wanted?"

"No, he didn't," Michael said, beginning to smile. "Honestly, I thought we were sunk after your little soliloquy about what would happen if you ever *did* mean to kill somebody. What the hell were you thinking?"

Leroy chuckled under his breath. "Just then? I *wasn't* thinking. I was on autopilot." He reached out and put a hand on Michael's shoulder. "But it all came out okay in the end, because I had *you* there to get me back on track. Am I right?"

"Hell, yes, you're right."

"Good," his father said. "Now come on. Let's get out of here and go have some lunch. I feel like I could eat all of Ford County and half of Hodgeman and still have room for dessert."

FIFTY

To celebrate, they went to Kate's, an old cowboy bar across the railroad tracks that Caroline claimed was the place where she and Leroy had met forty years before.

"We met at St. Mary's," Leroy corrected her.

"That's true," Caroline said, winking at Annie. "But it was here that I first began to understand the kind of trouble I'd gotten myself into."

"And what kind of trouble was that?" Vanessa asked.

"You saw for yourself when he climbed into that witness stand to testify," Caroline said. "Bull Wagner in a China cabinet. Look out, people!"

They all laughed, including Leroy. Annie couldn't remember the last time she'd seen her father laugh. But he was flying high now, clearly relieved by the verdict. She thought about what he'd said when he took the stand. Not the King Kong crap about running people over with his truck, but the part about seeing when people are hurting and reaching out to help them. For the second time that day, his words had surprised and moved her.

"I wish Jimmy could be here," Caroline said, wiping her eyes.

"We'll order him something and take it by the hospital on the way home," Leroy said.

"Yeah, but what?" Caroline asked. "You know he doesn't eat meat."

"We'll figure something out. Grilled cheese, maybe."

She picked up a menu. "Where are you seeing grilled cheese?"

"You just ask for it, and they make it special," Leroy said with an air of authority on all matters related to ordering food at Kate's.

"Oh, is that right?" Caroline asked.

"Just wait," Leroy said.

Sure enough, when the waitress came and they put in their orders of tacos and cheeseburgers and schooners of red beer, Caroline asked for a to-go order of grilled cheese and onion rings, and the waitress didn't even blink. "I'll tell the cook to wait until right before you're ready to leave to put that cheese sandwich on the grill."

"See?" Leroy said to Caroline, striking a playful tone. "What did I tell you?"

"Well, will wonders never cease," Caroline said back to him, employing the same playful tone.

Who were these aliens who'd taken possession of her parents' bodies? Annie wondered. Had the violence of their respective car crashes done something to their brain chemistry? This new rapport they had for each other was wonderful . . . but a little icky, too.

"I'm going to the bathroom," Annie announced, getting up from the booth. "When I return, I want you all back in character."

But they ignored her, the joke not even registering with them.

On her way to the ladies' room, whom did she spot sitting at the end of the bar but DW, her father's former hired man. She hurried by him and took her time in the bathroom, leaning over the sink to inspect every freckle and open pore in her face. When she emerged, DW's barstool stood abandoned, his mug of draft beer still two-thirds full. But a second later, she spotted his back hunched over the booth where her father sat, broken leg extending into the aisle.

She hung back to watch. Even without dialogue, the scene was easy to follow: Cowboy asks rancher how he's been holding up since his accident. Rancher says fine, asks cowboy if he's had any luck finding work. Cowboy shakes his head. Not a whole lot, no. Rancher says, well you got my number. A guy who's made up his mind to stay sober can always call that number. Cowboy tips his hat, says thank you, I'll keep that in mind. Then hightails it out of there before the rancher's daughter can return from offstage, upsetting all of these carefully brokered plans.

It was such a familiar story. The only tricky part involved the rancher's daughter. What to make of her role in it? How to include her complicated backstory and shifting motivations? Her feeling that Kansas in general and the Bar W in particular was simultaneously the only place in the world where her life made any sense *and* the place she'd been born to leave?

A clue had been offered the night before, during the long hours when she and Jeremiah drifted in and out of sleep on the couch in the basement of her parents' house. Something the lumber-jack poet had said: Embrace the ambivalence. Write about it. Bring its complex reality to life on the page for readers, as only someone in her position could. It wasn't an answer, exactly. But it was a start, and that's all she was asking for—at least for now.

She slipped back into the booth next to Jeremiah and rested her head on his brawny shoulder. It was the last week of July. In a few days, the annual Dodge City Days celebration would commence, the grandstands at the rodeo grounds filling every night, the streets of the town overrun by ropers, bull riders, barrel racers, and would-be rodeo queens. It was a shame Jeremiah couldn't stay and experience all of that. But he really did need to get going if he was gonna have a chance of making it all the way up to Idaho and then back down to Dodge and on to Buffalo, all before the start of the fall semester.

"Frankenporsche will have something to say about that," he'd bragged.

She thought of Buffalo, how beautiful the fall and early winters were, especially in the Amish country near Allegany State Park. She took a sip from her schooner of red beer. What would Miss Kitty think about spending a year or two out there? she found herself wondering.

THIRTY DAYS LATER

Jimmy walked out of the Ford County Jail and Sheriff's Office to find his brother Michael waiting outside in his red Dodge Ram.

"You ready?" Michael asked.

Jimmy smiled, climbing into the pickup's high cab and rolling his window all the way down so he could feel the sun on his face and the wind in his long brown hair.

They headed west on Comanche. "My phone?" Jimmy asked.

Michael glanced around the cab of the truck. "I must have left it at Mom and Dad's. I did plug it into the charger, though."

"What about my guitar? The black one, Martin 000-17?"

"It's there, too."

"In its gig bag?"

"Yes," Michael said. "In its gig bag."

Jimmy leaned back in the cushioned seat. Thirty days. Thank God they were over. The original plea deal, negotiated by Michael on his behalf while he was still in the hospital, had called for Jimmy to spend just three weekends in jail followed by a hundred hours of community service and a year on probation. But Jimmy was having none of that. "No probation," he'd said. "Just tell me what I gotta do to avoid all that, and I'll do it."

"Well, I guess you could do the full thirty days in jail," Michael said, "but you know—"

"Fine," Jimmy said, swinging his legs off the hospital bed. "Take me there right now. Let's get the clock a-rolling."

He'd spent his month in jail doing push-ups and sit-ups on the gray concrete floor of his cell while simultaneously completing his GED and listening in his mind to all the songs on his "Back to Cali" playlist.

"And the money?" he asked as Michael turned off Comanche.

"It's right here." Michael reached into the cubby at his elbow and brought out a thick bank envelope. "All in twenties, just like you asked."

Jimmy took the envelope and tucked it into a side pocket of his cargo pants. It was all the money he'd saved working at the Flying J, plus what Michael had been able to get for his trailer, minus all the fines and court fees.

"Thanks, Bro," Jimmy said. "I know it's a haul for you to get out here."

Michael shrugged. "Vanessa and the boys are coming out tomorrow. We're gonna stay at the homeplace, make a weekend of it."

"No shit?" Jimmy said.

"No shit."

"Well, good for you."

To celebrate his freedom, they gathered on the patio of his childhood home on Country Club Drive, he and Michael and Leroy and Caroline and Sister Maggie. (Annie and her friend Jeremiah had returned to Buffalo a week or so before.) While Michael flipped burgers on the grill and his parents and Sister Maggie sat drinking iced tea in the shade of the patio, Jimmy walked out to the spot along the back fence where he guessed his backpack of Girl Scout Cookies had landed when he'd tossed it over. The bag was gone, of course. He'd been expecting that.

He followed the fence to the back door of the garage, entered it, and stood a few minutes looking around. Nothing but

Caroline's new car, some lawn equipment, and a vintage CB750 with New York plates he'd never seen before, though it did not take him long to put two and two together. The New York plates were a dead giveaway.

He entered the house through the garage and began searching closets and drawers as well as under beds and desks and other furniture. When he'd finished with the ground floor, he descended the concrete stairs of the bomb shelter and searched from one end of the basement to the other, including the finished part with its bar and overstuffed couch and bookshelves loaded with books. Nothing. Not even a trace. Not even a whiff of a trace.

Back in the garage, he pushed the button on the overhead door and watched as the evening light came streaming in, a beam falling as if by magic on a red wagon he'd missed on his first pass and illuminating it. The wagon held a shovel, some dried potting soil, and a dead shrub with brown clover-like leaves. A picture sprang into his mind: his sister and mother in the front yard on the day he'd led Dodge City's finest on the high-speed chase of their lives. While in jail, he'd heard that Bassett Hound had been suspended over that one, but he wasn't thinking about that now. He was following an imaginary trail of dried leaves and potting soil out the open door of the garage and around the corner of the house to what Caroline liked to call her Mary Garden. And there was the Holy Gal herself, listing a little to one side. It couldn't be that easy, could it?

He checked to see that no one in the backyard was planning any sudden movements, then carried the shovel into the front yard and stood looking at where Mary's down-stretched arms pointed at the ground below.

"Well, well," he said aloud. "What do we have here?"

He laid Mary face down in the grass and picked up the shovel. In three quick scoops, he felt the tip of the shovel touch the nylon wrestling backpack. Two more quick scoops, and he set the shovel aside, reached into the hole, lifted the backpack out, and pulled back the top zipper. A wide smile spread across his face. “Cómo estás, ladies? You’ve got no idea how good it is to see you all again.”

He stashed the backpack behind Caroline’s mower, filled the hole with dirt from the wagon, and helped Mary back onto her wobbly throne. Then he rejoined his family on the patio amid a rising cacophony of cicada song—the so-called dog-day cicadas; he’d read an article about them in the Wichita paper while sitting on his ass in county jail—and scarfed down three soy burgers and two bowls of chocolate chip ice cream.

“Well, I guess you got no objections to dairy,” Leroy observed.

“Not yet,” Jimmy said, smiling broadly. “But give me time. I’ll get around to it.”

“I have no doubt you will,” his father said.

When Caroline rose to gather the dishes, he saw his chance. “No, no, I’ll take care of all that,” he said. “Really, sit yourself back down.”

“Are you sure?” his mother asked.

“Hell yeah, I’m sure.”

For added effect, he bent down and gave her a kiss on the cheek.

“Well, okay,” she said, laughing. “I guess we’re not through witnessing miracles, are we, Sister?”

“I guess not,” Sister Maggie said.

So he laid one on her cheek, too.

“What’s this?” she shrieked. “You crazy boy!”

“What about you?” he asked Leroy. “You want one, too?”

“Maybe later,” Leroy said, sipping his iced tea.

Jimmy carried the dirty dishes into the kitchen in one tall pile, loaded them into the dishwasher, and turned it on. He was sorry he’d missed Annie and her friend, but there was no helping that now. He unplugged his phone from its charger, stuck his earbuds in, retrieved his 000-17 Martin from the guest bedroom, and put his arms through the padded straps of its gig bag. Then he went into the garage and got the Girl Scout Cookies, divided them between the Honda's fiberglass saddlebags, and straddled the bike. The key, predictably, was right there in the ignition. He switched it on and thumbed through his "Back to Cali" playlist until he found "Coming into Los Angeles." After a short acoustic intro, Arlo Guthrie's high-stepping voice filled the earbuds.

He kicked the old bike to life, eased her out of the garage, and followed Country Club Drive to its base at Comanche, where he turned west, then south on Fourteenth, then west again on Wyatt Earp. He rolled past the Thunderbird Motel and the Dodge House, where Wyatt Earp turned into US 50, the Loneliest Road in America.

Nine miles west of town, he passed the ruts of the old Santa Fe Trail, their deep contours visible in the slanting light. He pulled the bike's throttle as far back as it would go, giving that air-cooled twin all the beans she could handle.

"Adiós, amigos!" he shouted to the wind.

She wasn't no '74 Bonneville, but he figured she'd do for now.

ACKNOWLEDGMENTS

It is often said that writing a novel, particularly a debut novel, is a lonely, solitary slog. Happily, that has not been the case for me. Throughout the twenty-plus years I've spent dreaming and producing drafts of this book, I've received what has felt like constant encouragement, support, and feedback from a large network of family, friends, and fellow writers. I would like to thank a few of these special people here, with apologies to anyone I may have forgotten.

Thanks, first and foremost, to Alyssa Chase, writer, artist, editor, and gardener extraordinaire. In addition to being my soulmate, you are my first and best reader. Thanks also to our children, Ria and Jake, to whom, along with my late parents, Bill and Patricia Rebein, this book is dedicated.

Thanks to the members of my bimonthly writers group, Anne Williams, Hannah Haas, and Adam Carter, who stuck with me through thousands of pages and three separate drafts beginning in the mid-2010s and extending right up to the moment I submitted the final version to my editor at Meadowlark Press in November 2023.

In addition to Alyssa and my writers group, I received important feedback from Mary Obropta, Benjamin Clay Jones, Bryan Furuness, Kyle Minor, Thomas Cotsonas, Will Allison, Sarah Layden, and Hozy Rossi, each of whom read the entire manuscript at one point or another. I owe each of you a tremendous debt of gratitude.

Finally, several members of the extended Rebein clan, including my late mother, Patricia Rebein, my brothers David Rebein and Paul Rebein, my sister-in-law Susan Rebein, and my nephew Adam Rebein, read drafts of the book or otherwise helped me to make the setting and the family dynamics as realistic as possible. Thanks also to my late father, Bill Rebein, and my brothers Alan Rebein, Tom Rebein, Joe Rebein, and Steve Rebein. Without your encouragement and helpful advice, this novel would not exist in its current form—and maybe not at all.

Thanks to my wonderful colleagues in the English department at IU Indianapolis (formerly known as IUPUI), especially my department chair Estela Ene, my former chair Thom Upton, my colleagues in creative writing Karen Kovacik, Terry Kirts, and Mitchell Douglas, my office neighbors Megan Musgrave, Ronda Henry, David Hoegberg, and Jennifer Thorington Springer, as well as the aforementioned Hannah, Kyle, and Sarah. You are the best.

Thanks also to Joe Croker, JJ Stenzoski, Jake Nichols, Joe Lane, and Shane Bangerter for small but key contributions to the novel's storyline.

Thanks to the Millay Colony for the Arts for a month-long retreat during which the plot and characters for the novel were initially set down in a series of composition notebooks, and to the Indiana University School of Liberal Arts for a sabbatical leave during which the first, freewheeling draft was tapped out on the Olivetti Lettera 32 manual typewriter I hauled back from England and Tunisia in the early 1990s, and for a second sabbatical during which the galleys were edited (thanks, Ben and Tracy) and the audiobook version of the novel was recorded with the expert help of Linda Mutchman.

Finally, thanks to my editor and publisher, Tracy Million Simmons, who believed in this book and its Dodge City setting at a time when few others did.

ABOUT THE AUTHOR

Robert Rebein grew up in and around Dodge City, Kansas, where his family has farmed and ranched since the late 1920s. A graduate of the University of Kansas, Exeter University in England, the State University of New York at Buffalo, and Washington University in St. Louis, Rebein teaches fiction and creative nonfiction writing at Indiana University Indianapolis.

www.robertrebein.com

10.29.2024

A Note on the Type

The text of this book is set in Goudy Old Style (aka Goudy), a font originally created by Frederic W. Goudy for American Type Founders in 1915. Goudy came to his type design career late in life —36 when he designed his first typeface, 46 when he became a type designer by profession— and created more than 100 typefaces. He was a well-known author and speaker on matters of typography.

The headers are set in Seaford, designed by Tobias Frere-Jones, Nina Stössinger, and Fred Shallcrass. The title and chapter heads are in Zuume Rough Bold, designed by Adam Ladd.